COSETTE

OR THE TIME OF ILLUSIONS

François Cérésa is an award-winning critic, journalist
and writer. *Cosette* is his tenth book.

COSETTE

OR THE TIME OF ILLUSIONS

FRANÇOIS CÉRÉSA

translated by Howard Curtis

MACMILLAN

First published 2003 by Macmillan
an imprint of Pan Macmillan Ltd
Pan Macmillan, 20 New Wharf Road, London N1 9RR
Basingstoke and Oxford
Associated companies throughout the world
www.panmacmillan.com

ISBN 0 333 90874 0 (HB)
0 333 90875 9 (TPB)

Copyright © Plon 2001
Translation copyright © Macmillan 2003

Originally published in French 2001 as
Cosette ou le temps des illusions by Plon, Paris

The right of François Cérésa to be identified as the
author of this work has been asserted by him in accordance
with the Copyright, Designs and Patents Act 1988.

1 3 5 7 9 8 6 4 2

A CIP catalogue record for this book is available from
the British Library.

Typeset by SetSystems Ltd, Saffron Walden, Essex
Printed and bound in Great Britain by
Mackays of Chatham plc, Chatham, Kent

To Louis Nucera

Part One

I

Since the events of 1832, life in Paris had become frighteningly constitutional and monarchical. Sundays and Mondays were for pleasure. In the afternoons an endless stream of carriages filled the Rue Saint-Honoré, circled the Place Vendôme and then formed a long line from the Bastille to the Madeleine and all the way to the Champs-Elysées. Society ladies called for their barouches and set off along the Boulevard des Italiens. As they passed the corner of the Rue du Helder, just beyond Devisme, the armourer's, they would admire the members of the future Jockey Club, who leaned over the balcony, smoking cigars and regarding the crowd with a phlegmatic disdain typical of yellow gloves. Yellow gloves was the common name for the dandies, the fashionable young men about town who were a race apart. Further on, in the windows of the Café de Paris, gentlemen would be blowing furiously into hunting horns, heralding the kill. Elegant women and grisettes alike had been given due warning. Derision had found its place in life.

A place in life was what Marius Pontmercy lacked. He had lost all sense of direction and no longer knew what to do to please his young wife, Cosette. Perhaps he was suffering from the malady he diagnosed in her.

It was September 1833. Jean Valjean had been dead for two months and Cosette had still not recovered from the shock. As if deliberately, fate had dealt her and Marius another blow. Marius's grandfather, Luc-Esprit Gillenormand, had died in his ninety-second year. With the death of Cousin Théodule in Algeria, it had all been too much for Marius. After the funeral, where he had met Frédéric Rivolier, an old friend from the barricades who was a medical student and journalist, he had realized that living with his aunt was impossible. It was making Cosette unhappy. Life in the Rue des Filles-du-Calvaire under the same roof as that bilious old hag was no longer bearable.

And then, all at once, seeing the high society around him, he thought that he, too, had a right to happiness and luxury. Against his expectations, he inherited two hundred thousand francs from his grandfather and, with the six hundred thousand francs left him by Jean Valjean, he was now quite wealthy.

An idea took root in his mind. He took a fiacre to the Invalides, then turned into the Rue de Babylone and walked as far as the Rue Plumet. His heart pounding, he stopped in front of a little two-storeyed house, which brought back wonderful memories. It was here that he had been reunited with Cosette when she was still living with Jean Valjean. Here they had exchanged vows of eternal love in the tiny garden and only the absence of a balcony had prevented Marius from playing Romeo. A sign on the gate announced that the house was up for sale or rent and that all enquiries should be addressed to Henri de la Roche-Dragon, who lived a little further along the street in the Montmorin mansion. He was a vain young man, with a mind as frivolous as his cravat.

'Do you want to rent or buy?'

'To buy,' Marius replied.

'In whose name?'

'My own – Baron Marius Pontmercy.'

This answer pleased the young nobleman. In the Saint-Germain district, one didn't sell to just anybody. 'Would you like to see the house?' he asked.

'If I may.'

Henri de la Roche-Dragon led Marius to the property. 'I'll leave you, Baron,' he said, opening the gate. 'I hope we will become friends.'

Marius shivered. The wide gate was still the same, with twisted pillars on either side, crowned by a pediment. Through the creepers twisting around the railings he could see the garden, overrun by brambles and weeds, and at the far end, gleaming like a shell at the bottom of the sea, the little pavilion surrounded by ivy and virgin vines. Nothing had changed. Like faithful warriors, two chestnut trees still stood guard, through which the hazy, dust-filled sunlight filtered. Here, in this ultra-royalist district alarmed by Louis-Philippe, in the midst of Legitimist plots and illegitimate debauchery, beauty had found a home. It was the New World in a mandarin's temple, an urban Eden touched by God's hand.

Marius had no wish to prolong his stay. He decided – he would buy the house in honour of Jean Valjean's memory and also to give Cosette somewhere in the present that would recall past happiness and carry her resolutely towards the future. The house would be theirs – a shelter from the dark.

So, without telling Cosette, Marius bought the house in the Rue Plumet and started to restore it. On Henri de la Roche-Dragon's advice, he entrusted the work to a reputable pair of contractors, Lespinasse and Sanglars, the former specializing in gardens, the latter in old stone. In just two weeks they brought order back to the garden without sacrificing any of its original charm. The little stone bench had been scrubbed and the trellises nailed back on the walls. Two statues representing Psyche and Cupid watched over the bench where once Marius and Cosette had declared their love. Marius had little time for allegories, but this mythological touch delighted him. The walls and the railings had also been repaired, as had everything that gave the garden its character. Mortar, steel wool, paint, sickles, shears and hoes had all been used to restore this enchanted spot, from which Charles Perrault himself would have drawn inspiration. In the house itself, Marius touched nothing. He left that for Cosette.

Once the work was finished, he took her to the Rue Plumet.

'Where are we going?'

'It's a surprise.'

Before they entered the fiacre, he blindfolded Cosette. She burst out laughing. His sudden attentiveness seemed very different from his usual volatile moods, his cold rages, his fits of remorse. The truth was that their relationship had deteriorated in the last two months.

The streets smelled of leather and lilacs and passers-by turned to look at the fiacre carrying Monsieur and Madame Pontmercy. Cosette looked so young and fresh, with her blonde plaits twisted into a bun, in her purple cape with its pink sleeves and her patent leather shoes. Unlike the ladies who went to Herbault or Mademoiselle Touche for their clothes, she made her outfits herself. Only once had she allowed Marius to take her to the Palais-Royal and buy her a navy-blue silk evening dress, with a low neckline and an unpleated lace bertha. She loved it and wore it whenever they went to the theatre.

For now, in her simple dress of tulle and taffeta, she was like a princess on her way to a banquet in the *Arabian Nights*. With the loose strings of her muslin bonnet making a halo around her face, she looked ravishing.

At last they arrived. Marius helped Cosette down from the fiacre and took off her blindfold. When she saw the gate and the garden, Cosette was speechless. 'But—'

'You have come home,' said Marius before she could finish, pushing her forward.

Hesitantly, Cosette opened the gate. The garden was fragrant with pepper and lavender. On tiptoe, like the ballerinas whose grace and lightness she admired at the Opéra and the Bain Chinois, Cosette walked towards the bench. Marius followed her.

'Is that you?' she asked, pointing to one of the statues.

'That's us,' he said.

Psyche's and Cupid's fingers were barely touching, like God's and Adam's in Michelangelo's *Creation of the World*.

'I'd like your hand to stay in mine for ever,' she said. 'This is our creation.'

Marius embraced her and placed a kiss on the nape of her neck, at the roots of her wild hair. She smelled of green tea and clean linen.

All of a sudden, Cosette fainted. Marius caught her before she could fall.

'What's the matter?' he asked.

'I don't know . . . I've been feeling nauseous, getting dizzy spells . . .'

'There's always something wrong with you,' he said testily.

Here he was, trying to please her, and she had to have a fainting fit. She was always so silly and simpering. Take the business with her name. For two months now, as if denying the name Cosette, she had been calling herself Euphrasie. True, this was the name on her birth certificate – Euphrasie Fauchelevent – but Marius thought it ridiculous. And now there was her reaction to the house. Pride and humility often being different sides of the same coin, he felt that he had put part of his soul into this house. Didn't Cosette realize that? Wasn't it a superb gift? Wasn't the setting magnificent?

But as in art, however beautiful the frame, it was the painting that mattered. And that was the problem.

Marius took Cosette's hand and led her towards the house. She followed him, wondering if she was really going to get her husband back, wondering, too, why he was so obstinate and so passionate about appearances. Did he think a house could fill the void caused by disenchantment?

The trouble was that Marius had acquired a taste for the world of money and letters and his one ambition was to become part of it.

In Marius's eyes, Cosette was the epitome of routine. She was a wife, he was a husband, and this all-too-evident fact was repugnant to him. Should he follow the example of many of his acquaintances and take a mistress? Should he live in mediocrity, on love and stagnant water, letting life take its course without doing anything to change it? Should he become just another weak-kneed idiot, full of complacency, ignorance and privilege, and happy to lick the boots of the government, which was nothing more than an enterprise backed by speculators for the benefit of the stupid?

Buying the house had reassured him. It was his way of evading the underlying causes of his doubts, of placing himself beyond criticism. But though his thoughts might calm him, his actions tended to contradict them. The paradox occasionally justified his unease at always putting off until tomorrow what could best be done today. Worst of all was that he had nothing with which to reproach Cosette. He would have found it so much easier to find a scapegoat, someone to blame for his fits of abstraction, a comforting answer to what he was finding so hard to explain to himself.

Yet there was no doubting his love for Cosette. She was still his passion, his little girl. He might think her a spoilt child, overprotected by Jean Valjean, but for her he had abandoned his legal career, for her he was trying his hand at dramatic criticism for *Le National*, putting his name to articles in a journal that attacked both *Le Journal des débats*, devoted to the July Monarchy, and *Le Revenant*, which had sold itself to the Legitimist cause. And he was beginning to make a name for himself. He had even met La Fayette at the house of Armand Carrel, the old liberal fighter, as well as meeting Thiers in person. He was anxious to present himself as different. There were too many obsequious people in this glittering society who were not worth the brushes they used to shine their shoes. So many things needed to be said. And Marius also had many things to say to Cosette, things that he did not say and, thanks to his exaggerated sense of propriety, would probably never say. Why didn't she realize?

But Cosette did not realize and so she suffered. Marius snubbed her mercilessly, exasperated by what he took to be pity, for people who suffer or who think they are suffering are often irritated by the compassion others show them. She would smile sadly, thinking how dependent melancholy is on enthusiasm. Perhaps Marius's enthusiasm for exacerbating his own melancholy was merely a sign of passing unease. But when would it pass?

Cosette could have left Marius. She was young and attractive. But when she heard people talk about separation, her whole being opposed it with a speed completely unexpected in someone so apparently slow in other respects. Cosette had been given a great gift – being in harmony with life, she would never agree to the division and confusion of feelings. The simple name for this gift is love of life. Her gaze was like a powerful light penetrating all human beings. From her past sufferings and weaknesses, which perhaps she had forgotten or simply buried, she had drawn the strength that God had hidden in them, as well as the strength her father had instilled in her.

She was well aware that Marius was escaping from her. While the sensitive young man in him daydreamed, the twenty-three-year-old bourgeois tried to raise his spirits by investing. Marius invested, speculated, hoarded money – excited, for example, when government bonds stood at seventy-five francs.

'You're the real bourgeois,' Cosette would remark mockingly.

He would fly into a rage. Feeling ashamed, he would cite examples of his own generosity. Had he ever forgotten to invite Frédéric Rivolier to eat at their house once a week? Or to go to the theatre with Cosette at least twice a week? Or to take her out to dinner, once to Le Véfour, and once to Les Trois-Frères-Provençaux?

Cosette did not deny it. In fact, she tried to reassure him. She encouraged him in his journalism. He owed a lot to Armand Carrel, who occasionally checked his theatrical reviews, and to Frédéric Rivolier, who had introduced him to Carrel.

'You're lucky,' she would tell him. 'Frédéric is a loyal friend.'

For most of October Cosette busied herself with the decoration and layout of the house. The atmosphere in the two bedrooms on the first floor was soon imbued with her grace and sensitivity, as were the two downstairs rooms. To help her, she had hired a reliable maidservant named Madeleine.

Marius could not conceal his admiration. He saw how carefully Cosette had worked, banishing opulence and ostentation, choosing curtains of dark red brocaded damask for their bedroom, and a delightfully simple canopied bed strewn with bouquets of lavender; placing her father's silver candlesticks on the mantelpiece in the drawing room; scouring the overmantels in the two bedrooms to reveal the warm honey colour of the beechwood, and changing the celadon green of her boudoir for sky blue. It was magnificent. The lavatory, as in Jean Valjean's day, was Japanese porcelain. Cosette had retrieved the Coromandel lacquer chest of drawers, and placed it reverently between the two windows in their room. The room was panelled at chest height. There was a round table with a Sainte-Anne marble top next to the chest; on it a ewer of Tournai porcelain, filled with sunflowers and immortelles arranged like a carousel wheel, added that touch of grace and gaiety with which women, with virtually nothing, can breathe life into the most insignificant things. Finally, four Aubusson tapestries, bought in the Rue du Temple, with multi-coloured flower bouquets and knots of ribbons on a cherry-red background, brought to both their bedroom and the drawing room a hint of red, which, according to popular belief, wards off evil.

When everything was completed, Cosette asked Marius what he thought.

'I couldn't have done better myself,' he replied, making himself, as usual, the touchstone. Nonetheless he congratulated her on the colours and shades. 'There is harmony in all these blues, just as there is in your eyes. When you are sad, they are sapphire, when you are happy, sky blue. Whatever the mood, they are always precious stones.'

Cosette blushed and lowered her eyes. When Marius paid her a compliment, it was always unusual. And at these times her doubts vanished. Did any man love his wife more?

After they had settled in, he could not resist the desire to add more to the house. On the one hand ardent, generous and dignified, on the other temperamental, cold and grandiloquent, he was the kind of young man for whom too much is never enough, as if in excess he could find absolution for his own shortcomings. And so he bought a mahogany wardrobe with double doors, some Louis XIII chairs, a rosewood chest of drawers, and a Louis XV wall clock shaped like a violin, which chimed every fifteen minutes.

'Was it really necessary?' asked Cosette, when all these things were delivered from Saint-Antoine.

'Everything is necessary for our happiness,' he replied, with a quiver in his voice that expressed discontent, even vexation. 'The superfluous is just as necessary as the essential, perhaps even more so.'

Cosette had a dread of the superfluous. But one's style of life, according to Marius, had to reflect one's wealth. In trying to conceal his confusion, he was always anxious to be seen to do the right thing.

Calculations like this were alien to Cosette. Her common sense made her suspicious of too much mental speculation. Her contact with ordinary people had left her well balanced, even though, thanks to her father, Jean Valjean, who was anything but ordinary, she had never wanted for anything.

'That's why you sometimes behave like a silly little girl,' Marius would say reproachfully. 'Yes, a silly little girl. What about pleasure? What about imagination?'

No doubt. But Cosette knew as little about the vice of possessiveness, which is called jealousy, as she did about the vice of jealousy, which is called envy. She had a simple heart and a generous soul. Unlike Marius, she had no desire to shine. Above all, it was left to her to assume what Marius would not – responsibility for the management of their daily affairs.

'Why shouldn't I enjoy myself?' she remarked one day after Marius had called her, yet again, a spoilt little bourgeoise.

'Fine, go ahead! Without me, you're lost!'

'You might be surprised,' she insinuated.

'With Frédéric? Is that what you're saying?'

Cosette had not replied. For her, abandoning everyday routine was not a solution. Nothing seemed to her more pernicious than to conceive of a world in the image of your own ambitions. She had realized this after reading books by Pascal, Benjamin Constant and Jean-Jacques Rousseau which Frédéric had lent her. She did not need to wait until she was old to understand that an embittered romantic of twenty will be a sated cynic at forty. That was why she feared the worst for Marius. And she was not wrong. For now that they were settled, what would happen next?

That night, the Théâtre Français was full. Marius and Cosette were there with Henri de la Roche-Dragon. On the bill was a revival of a comedy, *Les Trois Quartiers*, which had been first performed in 1827. The play still seemed up to date, being about a struggle which, while not yet that of the masses, was nonetheless extremely close to it. During the Restoration, as now under Louis-Philippe, the divisions between the nobility, the bourgeoisie and the people had been deep. The comedy did not have to look far for conflicts of pride and self-interest for its tableaux and sketches. In Marius's opinion, the play was artificial. He thought that it was not much of a plot to describe a colourless character in search of an advantageous marriage and move him from the Rue Saint-Denis, a popular neighbourhood, first to the Chaussée-d'Antin in the financial district, and then to the aristocratic Faubourg Saint-Germain, his pretensions growing with his wealth.

And the story would come to seem all the more premonitory in that the hero was constantly being led on by an idle dandy, an amusing parasite, whose tone changed according to whom he was addressing, a cynic who did not give a fig for the common people, the nobility, or the bourgeoisie.

The performance was marked by a number of incidents. During the first two acts catcalls aimed at the authors came thick and fast. And during the third act an individual in the front row began gesticulating forcefully.

'Who is that rude man?' Cosette asked Henri de la Roche-Dragon.

He leaned towards her. 'A charming agitator whom I'm proud to number among my friends, Baroness,' he replied in a whisper, with a smile both embarrassed and malicious. 'Say white, he'll answer black – say black, he'll answer white. He is contrary and nothing displeases him more than popular fashions, which are the mark of the mediocre.'

Marius had overheard Monsieur de la Roche-Dragon's praise. For some reason, which he could not explain, the description pleased him.

The spectators in the stalls finally lost their patience. 'Throw him out!' they cried.

'I demand fifty thousand francs for the authors!' replied Henri de la Roche-Dragon's agitator. This suggestion was greeted with laughter, hoots and whistles. The man repeated his proposal more insistently.

'But why?' cried the claque, imagining that this was some whim on the part of a fervent admirer, which might be turned to the play's advantage.

The agitator, who was accompanied by an affected and extravagantly dressed man, retorted, 'Because if Messieurs Picard and Mazères had fifty thousand francs, they wouldn't feel obliged to write any more terrible plays like this!'

As they left the theatre, Marius expressed a desire to meet this lively orator, who was gifted with a no less lively wit.

'Let's wait for him here,' Henri de la Roche-Dragon suggested, pointing to the arcades of the Palais-Royal. 'He should be here any moment now. If I know him, he'll be taking a fiacre to the Idalie.'

Leaning on Marius's arm, Cosette was wearing an evening dress with a plunging décolletage and, instead of a hat, a black velvet turban decorated with a drooping feather, which perfectly complemented her blue-sleeved cape. She looked magnificent.

As soon as the newcomer arrived, still accompanied by the extravagantly dressed man, his eyes lit up at the sight of Cosette. Usually, he was careful to ignore women, not allowing the slightest emotion to show on his face. He was content to pose and swagger, trying to make himself desired for that which was least desirable in him. But now, in the presence of this young woman who was not yet twenty and whose blonde hair smelled of lemon and green tea, he went so far as to kiss her hand.

'Marquis Amédée d'Iguerande,' he said proudly.

'Comte Louis de Vergne,' his companion said in his turn.

'Baron and Baroness Pontmercy!' declared Henri de la Roche-Dragon.

Marius and Amédée d'Iguerande exchanged a handshake, which in other circumstances would have seemed out of place. In the fashionable world a nod of the head usually sufficed. But the marquis's intervention during the performance definitely deserved a handshake.

'So you are friends of Monsieur de la Roche-Dragon?' asked the marquis absently, fanning himself with a glove.

'Yes, indeed,' replied Marius, who went on immediately to criticize the play.

The marquis pretended to be interested in what Marius was saying, but all the while he was watching Cosette out of the corner of his eye. He was clearly fascinated by her. Where had this ravishing young woman sprung from? He had never seen her before. Her big porcelain-blue eyes and the bold arch of her eyebrows must drive men mad. Baroness Pontmercy? It was the first time he had heard the name.

Cosette noticed that the marquis, doubtless for fear of spoiling his hair, had not had the courtesy to remove his hat. This pomaded swell, she thought, seemed very sure of himself – and quite arrogant – and quite ridiculous. It was enough to see the big knot of his cravat reflected in his shiny shoes. Clearly, his sole aim was to disconcert. He stood with his weight thrown slightly onto one leg, and there was something discouraging in his gaze. But above all – and this struck Cosette most forcefully – a disturbing impression of ruthlessness emanated from the tall, fair-haired young man.

His eyes met hers. 'To be discerning in one's elegance and elegant in one's discernment,' he said pretentiously, 'all one needs is a certain *je ne sais quoi.*'

This *je ne sais quoi* echoed seductively in Marius's ears. He was spellbound and agreed at once to everything Amédée said, seeing humour and greatness in his most insignificant remarks.

'Baron Pontmercy also possesses this *je ne sais quoi,*' said Henri de la Roche-Dragon. 'He has just bought a charming house in Saint-Germain.'

'Indeed?' The marquis peered intently at Marius. 'Perhaps you would do us the honour of accompanying us to one of the many little dance halls in this district?'

Without asking Cosette, Marius accepted eagerly. At last, this was his chance to enter high society. Henri de la Roche-Dragon, for his part, declined the invitation, explaining that he absolutely had to groom his horses the next morning. 'I have five horses in my stables, including a beautiful mare with red and white markings and a superb English stallion with white stockings. If you should buy a horse, dear Baron, I'd be delighted to stable it.'

And so Cosette, Marius, Amédée d'Iguerande and Louis de Vergne found themselves at the Idalie, an underground dance hall in the Passage de l'Opéra. This was a den of ill-repute, noted for rum, aggressive behaviour and loose morals, where late at night the delinquents of Belleville would come to dance the *chahut*, a popular dance of the day. It was a euphoric scene. Louis de Vergne did not dance. He was a short, frail, effeminate man, with balding hair and a chubby face that seemed prematurely aged. He was full of witty sayings and loved to gossip. He immediately regaled Cosette with stories of Mademoiselle Mars, who according to him had put on weight, and Lord Herbert, a very smug Englishman sitting two tables away, who was known as Dumb Face. When Cosette mentioned to him that Marius wrote for *Le National*, he spread his fingers in approval.

'Armand Carrel's paper? How wonderful. My friend Stendhal used to write for it before he was appointed consul in Civitavecchia.'

He seemed to exist only through the existence of others. While acknowledging the effusive greetings of a number of gaudily dressed men, he went on talking, about Victor Cousin, whose definition of man – 'a universe in miniature' – he agreed with, and about some of the socialites here present, like Alfred de Maussion, the Don Juan of foreign women, and Charles de Mornay, the mature ladies' Casanova.

'It's all so intoxicating, dear Baroness, don't you think so?'

'Absolutely . . .'

Gossip left Cosette indifferent. She heard Louis de Vergne without listening to him. Her eyes were fixed on Marius and the marquis, and on a creature with jet-black hair, who sprawled across Amédée's knees, occasionally grazing Marius's cheek as she burst into peals of laughter. The marquis was greedily stroking her décolletage. Aware of Cosette's disapproving gaze, he did it the more.

'Adultery?' he declared. 'I consider it necessary. Compromise? Salutary.

Charity? A fig leaf. Virtue? The worst of vices. Generosity? Mere selfishness. Gallantry? Stupidity disguised as ignorance. Nobility? It doesn't exist. The Republicans? They want to take the place of something that no longer exists. The people? They are being left to die, but beware the day when they awake. Our king? An unsavoury individual. And long live the nation!'

And he burst into uproarious laughter, banging his fist on the table and roughly pushing the bare-breasted creature off his knees.

'You see, Baron, there is nothing reasonable about reason,' he continued, looking in Marius's eyes to be sure of the effect he was producing. 'Do I offend you? Well, that's too bad. I, too, was once a disciple of Rousseau and Babeuf, full of indulgence and leniency, hashing over the great revolutionary ideas. And for what? I ask you. Man is nothing but a dog. You whistle to call him, you kick his backside, and he always returns to his own vomit. That's the truth. It's up to us to believe in nothing and take advantage of everything. The republic of pleasures, Baron!'

This litany, far from repelling Marius, reminded him of the time when he, too, had held everything in contempt – the bourgeoisie, the nobility, injustice, the institutions of power, all those men in black with their processions and jubilees who were helping themselves to France. Now it was over. He no longer cared. Listening to Amédée, he felt as though he had found a soulmate in a world of instant gratification, a role model who would finally show him how to live.

Cosette was getting impatient. Marius paid for everybody. Then, just as the music was reaching a deafening pitch, a young man in evening dress approached the marquis, his eyes shooting fire.

'Monsieur, contrary to what you seem to think, not everything should be allowed in life. You are an ill-mannered person. Not content with offending the authors of the play, you offended a young girl in the cast who is dear to my heart.'

Louis de Vergne leaned towards Marius. 'I think this young girl has been sharing the marquis's bed,' he whispered. 'In fact, it was she who invited us this evening.'

The young man slapped Amédée's face.

Drunk though he was, Amédée shot out of his seat, seething with rage and particularly upset at being slapped in front of Cosette. 'Monsieur, you will give me satisfaction,' he hissed between his teeth. 'Tomorrow morning at eight, at the Clichy gate.'

'I am at your disposal, Monsieur,' the young man replied. 'Monsieur—'

'Marquis Amédée d'Iguerande, formerly lieutenant in the Algerian army under the Comte de Bourmont. Not at your service, Monsieur.'

'Choose your weapons.'

'Swords.'

'Who are your seconds?'

Amédée turned to Marius and Louis de Vergne. 'Baron, may I count on you?'

'I am obliged to you, Marquis.'

Marius was infuriated by this impudent young man, and even more so when he revealed that he was a young Carlist named Théodore Bigarrat, an ardent follower of the Duchesse de Berry, and when he nodded with a mixture of self-importance and provocative disdain as the Marquis d'Iguerande cited his military past and named his seconds.

'As you wish. Until tomorrow, gentlemen.'

The evening did not last much longer. Urged by Cosette, Marius took his leave of his new friends, who, hardly troubled by the impending duel, continued their party.

'I hate that man,' said Cosette, once they were in the street.

'Well, I think he's remarkable,' Marius retorted.

Meanwhile, in the dance hall, the marquis turned to Louis de Vergne. 'This Marius fellow may be useful to us. We must introduce him to Clémence. As for the charming baroness, I fully expect to have her in my arms before very long.'

The following morning, Marius ignored Cosette's lectures and kept his appointment at the Clichy gate. Young Bigarrat was already there, with his two seconds and a doctor. Marius nodded to them. A moment later, Amédée d'Iguerande arrived, accompanied by Louis de Vergne and a stranger. He looked pale and morose.

'Let's get on with it,' he said, handing his frock coat and hat to the stranger, a sly-looking, hunchbacked man whom he introduced as his steward.

They studied the terrain. As the earth was damp and slippery, they chose a stretch of ground nearby, behind a factory and opposite the Ile Saint-Ouen.

The two adversaries took up their positions. After three or four passes, they both thrust at the same time. The marquis's sword penetrated young Bigarrat's groin.

His seconds stopped the fight. 'One man down!' they cried.

'Two!' jested Amédée, displaying the red streak on his forearm.

The doctor ran up to check the young Carlist's wound, which was quite serious. Meanwhile Marius handed his handkerchief to Amédée, who examined it suspiciously and gave it back to him. 'I thank you, my friend, but my blood will take only silk or cambric.'

The wounded man's seconds laid him on a cart and carried him to the factory. He was losing a lot of blood. It was obvious that because of the risk of haemorrhage they could not take him by carriage all the way back to Paris. He would have to be operated on right there in the factory. Some of the workers, who had already been at work for a good two hours, laid him on a mattress. They worked fourteen hours a day for a wage of two francs – another world.

'Everything one doesn't want to be,' said the marquis, casting a disdainful glance at the thin, ragged men. He turned to Marius. 'Go on, give the pompous fool your handkerchief. I'm sure his blood can take cotton.'

The young Carlist's seconds were angry. 'Monsieur, please! Our friend had never held a sword in his life!'

Amédée d'Iguerande gave a slight pout, at once regretful and fatalistic. 'I'm sorry to hear that, gentlemen. But I have other things to attend to!'

From that day on Amédée and Marius were inseparable. The die was cast. The pleasure-loving world of Paris was about to embrace them.

A month passed. The two new friends frequented the Café de Paris, Tortoni, Lord Seymour's fencing school, the horse market, and the first-class tailors on the Boulevard and the Palais-Royal. Amédée replenished Marius's wardrobe and taught him to fence. They were seen in all the fashionable places, dressed in black cashmere and embroidered velvet, talking from morning to night. Marius admired this heaven-sent friend with his broad, square head, and his large, disturbingly pale blue eyes under their clear lashes. Amédée, for his part, tolerated this anxious and emotional boy, who was so generous with his money, and whose passionate, dark eyes matched his wavy, raven-black hair. The baron and the marquis were a pair, one a dark god, the other a blond devil.

'And how is the baroness?' Amédée would sometimes ask.

'She's cultivating her garden,' Marius would reply.

'Euphrasie is a follower of Rousseau, then? That's positively fascinating.'

Amédée had an absurd verbal mannerism – he stuck the adverb

'positively' into his sentences even when his sense was negative, which was often the case.

'Euphrasie? You're joking, Marquis. My wife's real first name is Cosette. She also loves sewing.'

'So she's a homebody?'

'Alas, yes!'

'What a waste!'

And the two men burst out laughing. Emotion being the height of vulgarity, the one art they practised with skill was being disagreeable. The only things that counted were nonchalance and indifference. Enthusiasm, admiration, or any other feeling that might penetrate the icy shield they had built around themselves, were forbidden.

'One must refuse to be surprised,' Amédée would assert.

'And what about love?' Marius would ask him, intrigued by the hostility he openly displayed towards that emotion.

'Love is a thorny subject, Baron. The women one loves are statues; those one sleeps with are whores. I've come to the conclusion that it is better to undress whores than statues.'

Marius was impressed, as he was by Amédée's opinion of work, which echoed his own. Yet Marius had not abandoned his career at *Le National*, nor did he go out in the evenings.

'Afraid to offend the baroness?' Amédée would jest.

'A certain idea of marriage . . .' Marius would reply, in an uneasy attempt to justify himself.

At which the marquis would shake his head. 'Just like your Republican ideas? Well, nobody's perfect, old chap. The worst thing is not to be a Republican, a Legitimist or a Bonapartist, it's to have ideas.'

Marius and Amédée went every day to Lord Seymour's fencing school, in a mansion on the corner of the Rue Taitbout and the Boulevard, just beyond the Café de Paris. Three large rooms had been converted and were equipped with changing rooms and a perfectly trained staff. The entrance was decorated with two swans so wonderfully sculpted that they looked alive. These were framed by columns, from which hung curtains of pale blue satin lined with white, the old colours of the Bourbons.

'One day the tricolour may help you win a bout,' Amédée often said. Marius would curse because he never won. The two men were always accompanied by Amédée's steward, who dressed completely in black. His name was Louis-Désiré Burdin, and the marquis could find no better way to thank him for his devotion than to tell him that he was unattractive. The steward would stifle an embarrassed laugh. He idolized his master.

That day Marius and Amédée had one of their ritual bouts. It was the end of the year and the atmosphere was festive.

First, they saluted each other. To salute, Amédée suddenly drew back his shoulders and thrust his neck forward. Marius, as usual, tried clumsily to imitate him. Louis-Désiré counted the points.

'*En garde*, Marquis.'

'At your service, Baron.'

The swords merely touched, making a clinking sound. No thrust was made. As their hands moved with a flick of the wrist from *tierce* to *sixte*, the two men looked as if they were performing a puppet show. Suddenly Amédée made two rapid passes, touched Marius's outstretched arm, and thrust. Marius did not retreat. He simply held out his sword and the two men executed a *coup fourré*.

'Not bad,' said Amédée, nodding his head appreciatively. 'The lessons of Roussel and Bertrand have, it seems, borne fruit. You're making steady progress, old chap.'

Marius paled, slightly irritated at his friend's sarcasm.

'My dear Louis-Désiré,' the marquis said, touching the steward's hump with the blade of his foil, 'go and find a jug of punch for two brave warriors who, like Achilles and Hector, have not yet managed to kill each other.'

Louis-Désiré, whose waxy face resembled a death mask, immediately did as he was told.

A few moments later he returned with a silver ewer and two crystal glasses. The master of the house did things in style.

'Now,' said Amédée, raising his glass, 'let's drink a toast to Lord Seymour, our host, who had the fine idea of opening this fencing school to welcome his friends.'

Marius imitated him. With his foil under his arm and his forehead beaded with sweat, he swallowed his punch in one draught. It was a drink that was all the rage in the drawing rooms of the Opéra and the Palais-Royal.

Then the two men took up their positions again, wearing neither masks nor breastplates.

This time, the exchange was rough.

'I touched you!' exclaimed Marius, breaking away.

'I don't think so, old chap. It was I who touched you. What do you think, Louis-Désiré?'

The steward would not offer an opinion.

'Let's start again!' said Marius excitedly.

'If you wish,' said Amédée, 'but I'm too fast for you.'

Between the hammering of their heels on the parquet floor and the clashing of the blades, once again the exchange was passionate. Both men wanted to win. Then, all at once, Amédée stopped, made an exaggerated turn and lunged all the way, almost in slow motion as if to humiliate his adversary, so that the point of his foil ended up over Marius's heart. It was a thrust that was impossible to parry.

'You're dead,' he said, with no other expression on his face except that of a task accomplished.

He resumed his original position, handed his foil to Louis-Désiré and removed his gauntlet.

'You're still too strong for me,' admitted Marius, 'but one day I'll win.'

While the two men were dressing, Amédée turned to Marius. 'By the way, would you like to celebrate this sad New Year with us tonight?' he asked. 'There's a boring reception at the Ney mansion, but then we'll be doing the rounds of the dance halls and taverns. Louis-Désiré has seen to everything.'

Marius seemed embarrassed. What would he do about Cosette? Finally he made up his mind. 'I accept gladly.'

'We'll meet at the Ney mansion at eight-thirty,' said Amédée. A calculating look came into his eyes. 'Will you be bringing your charming wife?'

Marius stiffened. 'I fear not,' he replied. 'Cosette doesn't like to enjoy herself.'

Amédée concealed his pique with a flippant gesture. But he was patient. With the plan he was constructing, he would soon see the beautiful Baroness Pontmercy, for whom he had feelings he had never before experienced.

At three o'clock, still troubled by Amédée's invitation, Marius left the Café de Paris, a temple of fashion haunted by every boulevardier, where he had just drunk an infusion of wine and lemon known as a bishop. After Amédée and his steward had left, he had seen Arago, Dumas, Roqueplan and Musset deep in conversation. Even the Romantics, ever alert to fashion, were becoming Republicans.

Once on the Boulevard, all bright and gleaming with its new pavements, its bollards and its avenue of tall trees, Marius strode on determinedly. The cool winter air smelled of orange and sweet almond. Cane in hand and opera hat tipped to one side, he passed the Café Anglais, the Café Riche and Tortoni, on whose three legendary steps were gathered powdered young men wearing blood-red clothes, all talking about the evening ahead, which they would spend at the Mabille and Valentino balls. Marius looked longingly at the tables around the ice-cream counter. If only someone would recognize him! His clothes must be part of the problem. What he needed was a horse and spurs, and the zephyr-blue suit that was all the rage among the boulevardiers. He would have to remedy the lack as soon as possible. He gripped his cane tightly and continued on his way. He had not yet found his place in this world, which was opening its arms to him. He no longer knew who he was or where he was going. Bitterness hung like a chain around his neck. He felt angry with himself. He was a disappointed man.

Disappointed with what? With everything. It was obvious and it obsessed him. His jaw clenched, his head low, he thought about his father-in-law's death as he walked. He had the feeling that he was in free fall. Though he might not have liked to admit it, the young Republican with noble ideals had changed. He still bore the scars of the events he had taken part in and they continued to torment him. The deaths of Enjolras, Grantaire, Eponine and Gavroche, Javert's suicide, the deaths of Jean Valjean and his own grandfather, were all just beneath the surface. The list was overwhelming. Now, by denying all authority and every rule – except rebellion against the inevitable – he was making himself the be all and end all. When he used words like religion, humanity, God, the infinite, he was talking about his own heart, and his heart was in chaos. That was why meeting Amédée had been so fortuitous. He had found a model – a man who had been through everything and wanted nothing, a detached and libertarian aristocrat, an accomplice.

Marius left the Boulevard and walked towards the Opéra. When you have time to kill, you walk. Or else you kill yourself. Without thinking you kill yourself. But Marius was thinking – much too much – and his thoughts were unpleasant. As he was wandering, he knew that he would avoid the districts of Saint-Antoine and Saint-Denis – especially by day. He would avoid his own memories. The Café Musain and the barricades of June 1832. The ghosts of his friends killed in combat or mown down by the troops. Poverty. The grim workshops, the murky factories, the illegal businesses, the wage slaves. When you pay poverty a visit, it looks strangely at you. It doesn't point an accusing finger, there's no need. The smell takes hold of you because it's always through smells that things arrive, birth as well as death. Afterwards, long afterwards, you still have the smell in your heart. It won't go away. And this was what had happened to Marius. The stench of poverty – and of guilt – stayed with him.

He walked faster. He was thinking too much. But a walker who does not think is not a true walker. The walker watches, examines, contemplates, thinks, meditates. He observes the steps he takes. He loves the shapes of the cobblestones, the clip-clop of the horses' hooves, the laughter of the working girls, the clouds playing hide-and-seek with the sun, all the stories that cling to the house gables, the street singers, the blind musicians, the water carriers and the cardboard-box merchants, the flower sellers and the brass polishers, the criers and the ragmen, the Jesuits and the umbrella carriers. The walker loves his solitude, his abundant and contradictory thoughts, the whirl of inexhaustible images.

But walking cannot erase everything. Like the Romantics he despised, Marius felt isolated, misunderstood, a stranger among his fellows, persecuted and cursed. Of course, there was politics. There were his past commitments. But France now – with Soult as prime minister – was the France of treason and profit. Soult had betrayed both the emperor and Louis XVIII, and persecuted his former comrades, the retired soldiers.

Marius felt nauseous. His father, Colonel Pontmercy, a hero of Waterloo, had died because of men like Soult. Not to mention the others, all the treacherous marshals – go-getters and opportunists to a man, shameless predators.

Marius swung his cane and struck the parapet of the Pont de la Concorde. What had become of the eagle of Austerlitz and Wagram? With Thiers at the Ministry of the Interior and Guizot at Education, France was a country of mediocrities and speculators!

He caught his breath, exhausted by the resentment building up within him.

On the other side of the river he saw the quays of the Left Bank. He decided to go back to the Tuileries and cross the Pont-Neuf to the Latin Quarter. The Left Bank, Saint-Germain ... He smiled and shook his head. His one satisfaction in all this muddle of disappointment was that he had moved from the Rue des Filles-du-Calvaire to the Rue Plumet.

He passed the Tuileries, where Louis-Philippe strutted like a bourgeois, while infantry officers in purple trousers strolled along the Seine, and came to the Pont-Neuf and Henri IV's equestrian statue. To the crowds of workers in smocks and caps who were heading towards the Cité, the statue seemed to be little more than an object of ridicule. Few people cared for gallantry now, all they wanted was beer in their bellies.

Marius crossed the bridge and turned into the Rue Dauphine, where the first street lamps had been experimented with. Today, thanks to Prefect Rambuteau, gas lighting was widespread in the capital. The installation of a proper sewer network was also due to him, as were fire hydrants, paved streets, raised pavements and urinals.

Before reaching the Rue de l'Ancienne-Comédie, Marius cast a cautious glance at an old house with a courtyard and wrought-iron balconies, where, according to Frédéric Rivolier, agitators from the Society for the Rights of Man were plotting against the government.

Marius gave a slight, equivocal smile. All this agitation left him cold. The failed insurrection of June 1832 and the deaths of his friends had cured him of any political commitment and wounded his soul. What was the point of fighting for Republicans or Legitimists when the bourgeoisie, pandered to by Monsieur Guizot and his like, always came out on top?

After walking up the Rue de l'Ancienne-Comédie, he decided to have an iced coffee at La Taverne on the Place de l'Ecole-de-Médecine. His indecision exasperated him. He had no idea what he wanted to do. Everything and nothing. And of the two he preferred nothing.

At the Odéon crossroads he noticed a fiacre heading in the direction of the Place de l'Odéon. His blood froze. In the fiacre, he thought he recognized Cosette and, beside her, Frédéric Rivolier – his friend Frédéric.

For a moment he stood there, stunned, then he rubbed his eyes and started to run. Too late. By the time he reached the Rue de Condé the fiacre had vanished.

Surprise gave way to anger. Was it true? Was Cosette deceiving him with Frédéric?

Sitting on the terrace at La Taverne, he fumed. Then he turned his anger on himself. Wasn't he a dandy? A detached being, despising everything? He ordered a coffee and congratulated himself on accepting Amédée's invitation. He turned his eyes towards the university. Students were singing, advocating permanent revolution, promising the bourgeoisie days of violent demonstrations and riots.

Marius glared at them. Like them, Frédéric was a medical student. Marius's mood darkened again. To think that he had been feeding this traitor, this drunkard, this half-baked revolutionary! But what of Cosette? Tears welled in his eyes. How could she? Just wait till he got his hands on her! Then she'd see!

He rebuked himself again. Instead of brooding, he should be thinking about Amédée and a future of pleasure. He wanted to discover all the things he had never seen before. He had been trying to find a direction in life. Well, now he had found a number of new directions! Nothing is more pleasant for souls haunted by dark ideas than the contemplation of their own faults. Had he been feeling remorseful about Cosette? Well, he wouldn't any more! He, too, would enjoy wild nights, pavements thronged with people of every type and description, shouting with joy and blowing into trumpets, and carriages of every sort carrying their cargo of hectic revellers. He would have strumpets and depraved women galore! He would run to the Variétés, the Franconi circus, the Vaudeville, the Idalie, the Ambigu, the Olympique circus, the dance halls of the Porte Saint-Martin, the Boulevard du Temple and the Rue Saint-Lazare with his friends Amédée, Louis de Vergne and Henri de la Roche-Dragon! A hellish and intoxicating life, even more intoxicating than hellish. And he would spend all his money like a true dandy – with a light heart and heavy eyes. And no regrets.

He had finished his coffee, paid and was just standing up, when he saw Frédéric. His eyes glazed over and he began to tremble. To make matters worse, Frédéric had spotted him and was coming towards him.

'Marius, what are you doing here?'

'As you can see – waiting for you . . .' His hands shook as if he had a fever.

Frédéric took a chair and sat down next to him. 'I'm in luck,' he declared with a forced smile. 'I've been dying to see you.'

'What about?'

'About your wife.'

Marius felt as if a dagger had been plunged into his heart. But, thinking of Amédée, he assumed an ironic tone. 'So you were just passing?'

'In a way, yes.'

'And in another way?'

Frédéric leaned his elbows on the table and ordered a carafe of wine with lemonade. Distressed, he looked at Marius. 'What's happening to you, Marius?'

Marius looked Frédéric up and down. He was wearing a blue coat buttoned high, a white waistcoat and a red cravat. If his clothing was rather gaudy, it was belied by his resolute attitude. A polemical journalist for *La Tribune* as well as a student doctor, Frédéric seemed older than his years. He was twenty-six and carried his head high. He was the son of a Republican, and a Republican himself, whom Marius had met during the events of June 1832 and who had managed to escape the barricade in the Rue de la Chanvrerie when the troops had laid siege to it. He had curly red hair, a broad, open forehead, and eyes filled with dignity. His sensitive smile revealed teeth made white, by the colour of his chestnut-brown moustache. Until now he had been an extremely scrupulous friend. Just a little too fond of his drink, Cosette always said with a smile. Whenever he was invited to dine in the Rue Plumet, he would bring a bottle of Chambertin.

'The emperor's favourite drink!' he would proclaim, losing no opportunity also to proclaim his loyalty to revolutionary ideas.

Was it to make Marius feel guilty, to win him over to his ideas, or simply to get him out of his lethargy? Whatever it was, Frédéric had noted that Marius was not the same, that he seemed bitter and distraught. They had met again in the simplest way imaginable, at the funeral of Marius's grandfather. Frédéric, who hated the royalist newspaper *La Quotidienne* but read it regularly, had seen the name Gillenormand among the death announcements. He had remembered that behind that name was that of an ardent young man who supported liberal ideas – Marius Pontmercy. Today, filled with enthusiasm for Auguste Blanqui, who had taken the workers' side during the revolt of the Lyons silk workers and talked of the defence of the proletariat, Frédéric was a member of the Society for the Rights of Man. He attended all their meetings and wrote incendiary articles against the monarchy, bringing down the wrath of both the government and the Legitimists on his head. Virtually worshipping the Montagnard leaders of the Convention, he demanded universal suffrage, the right of assembly and genuine reforms to help the working classes, who were bearing the brunt of the economic depression.

'What's happening to you?' he asked again, seeing Marius lost in thought.

'Nothing. Or rather, yes, something is happening to me, something that should happen to any sensible individual. I want to live, to take advantage of what I've never taken advantage of before, I want to become a master of derision in a world in which all of you, exploiters and exploited, the bourgeoisie and the workers, the nobles and the commoners, are merely the servants of illusion. I want to be sceptical, ironic and insolent. I want to make my life a work of art. I want to flaunt my uniqueness with a pride that abhors bourgeois triviality. I want to say a strong no to everything that smugly says yes. I want to eat, drink and dress like a dandy, when everyone else aspires merely to dress themselves, feed themselves and quench their thirst in a mediocre way.'

Frédéric emptied his glass greedily, poured himself another and contemplated his friend with apprehension. 'Quite a manifesto,' he said. 'But you're wrong, Marius.'

'And what of you and your kind, the pure – aren't you wrong? Everything that is pure is deceptive, and everything that is deceptive is destructive, for in the name of purity you eliminate anyone who can't live up to that purity. That makes you unique.'

Frédéric spread his hands in a gesture of impotence. 'Unique? What makes *you* unique? All you're doing is copying those men in high society who, through their contempt, show their ignorance of the people's sufferings.' He drank a second glass and placed his hands flat on the table. 'In any case, I wasn't talking about politics. I was talking about your life. You have purity at home, her name is Cosette.'

'What of it?'

'You are unsettling her with your sudden changes of mood and making her unhappy by your absences.'

Marius stretched his neck in disdain. What business of Frédéric's was this nonsense? 'You seem to know a lot of things,' he said.

'I know nothing, I merely guess. I wouldn't be so tactless as to interfere in your private life, even though I do claim to be a loyal friend, but Cosette is wasting away. I can see it in her complexion, in her eyes. She is too strong-willed to complain. She simply suffers.'

Was it the doctor or the lover who was talking? Marius almost lost his temper. How could Cosette be attracted to this pompous sermonizer? 'All women suffer,' he said, imitating Amédée. 'They suffer because they lack originality, imagination and, above all, independence.'

'Your independence is very like indifference.'

'Was it Cosette who told you that just now?' asked Marius triumphantly. 'Don't lie, I saw the two of you in a fiacre!'

Frédéric's face showed that the blow had struck home. Yes, he had been with Cosette, but not for the reasons that Marius was insinuating. 'Your Amédée d'Iguerande is having an unfortunate influence on you,' he said, finishing the wine and lemonade. 'You've become quite vile.'

This time, Marius flew into a rage. 'Vile? You dare say that? You spend all your time drinking and spouting woolly ideas with fake revolutionaries, you see Cosette behind my back, and you dare to call me vile?' He cleared his throat. 'I'll have you know that in life one chooses one's friends. And I have chosen Amédée d'Iguerande!'

'He's a bad friend,' replied Frédéric. 'And what's more, he's not quite the gentleman he seems.'

'What are you trying to insinuate?'

'What I'm insinuating is that he's paying court to your wife and that you, blinded by your idiotic admiration for him, haven't even noticed.'

'That's too much! Take care, Frédéric!'

And he left La Taverne without a backward glance, leaving Frédéric stunned and anxious.

Marius was walking quickly. At the memory of Amédée's question – 'Will you be bringing your charming wife?' – he stiffened. What were these stories Frédéric had told him about Amédée? But were they really stories? He found the thought disagreeable. Two feelings were stirring in him – a sudden aversion to Frédéric and an equally sudden confusion about Amédée.

When he opened the gate in the Rue Plumet, Cosette had her back to him. She was pruning rose bushes on the trellis of the winter garden, the garden she had created from scratch with only Madeleine to help her.

Marius thought she looked beautiful. A woman is never more attractive to her husband, he told himself, than when she has something to hide. He advanced quietly, plucked a rose and planted it in Cosette's hair. She turned in surprise, her face pale. She was holding a pair of shears.

'Oh, it's you.'

She opened her arms and covered Marius with kisses. But he pushed her away, uncertain whether, seductive as they were, they might not be inspired by remorse.

'This evening I'm meeting the Marquis d'Iguerande in a grand mansion in the district,' he said through clenched teeth. 'So I won't be here for supper. Anyway, I think they should abolish these stupid end-of-year celebrations.'

'Which ones?'

'Christmas and this damned day that drops us from one year into the next.'

'I had been hoping we could spend this evening together, just the two of us,' Cosette whispered, putting down the shears.

'This evening is vital to my career,' Marius lied. 'The two of us can spend another evening together.'

Cosette looked at him for a long time. 'Another evening, I may not be here.'

2

That afternoon a violent wind swept through the alleys of Saint-Denis. The pale light from the street lamps was reflected in pools of blood, which filled the spaces between the uneven cobblestones. A man wearing a hat made out of catskin was walking along, his back bent. He looked about sixty, with a vulture's neck, a hollowed and furrowed brow, a nose as sharp as a beak, a grey moustache and a badly cut beard, which followed the line of his jaw. He passed a flock of sheep and pinched his nostrils. Here animals were slaughtered in the street. Their throats were cut and their blood streamed into the gutters. All around stood carts heaped with bodily remains. The worst thing was the smell. Throughout the day the killing went on, and the blood flowed and stuck to your feet as you walked.

'Good God,' grumbled the man in the catskin hat, 'to think that the emperor built five abattoirs in Paris and we're still being poisoned!'

The Catman had gained respect for the ferocity with which he worked, and for the scrupulous persistence with which he practised deceit. Friendly to the rich, uncompromising to the poor, he used any means of extortion to make a profit, counting on his boldness and hypocrisy to commit his crimes with impunity.

'Well, well,' he muttered, spotting a group of cats fighting over an old slice of bacon rind. 'There they are, my darlings.'

To succeed, he had taken up a foul trade, which he still practised. When night came he would attract cats with animal lungs, drug them with valerian, then kill them by inserting a stiletto into the backs of their necks. He had started on his own, but now he had a whole gang of helpers. He would sell the flesh for ten sous to the owners of cheap restaurants and the skins for fifteen sous to tanners. In less than six months he had made a tidy sum. And, as business was prospering, he had bought the ground floor of a building in the Rue Aubry-le-Boucher, not far from the church of Saint-Merri, as a workshop for carding wool. Here the Catman employed young boys aged from seven to fifteen. Most were orphans he had picked up near the Pont-au-Change, whom he had promised better days. Some of them had been supplied to him by an accomplice.

'They can be turned into first-class cut-throats,' he would say to the Catman. 'First they learn to work, to obey, to go without. Then they learn to lie, to steal, to kill.'

The boldest of the children chased cats with snares and lures, gutting them right there in the street and skinning them back in the workshop. The weaker ones remained at the loom. To each his speciality.

The Catman was walking up the Rue Saint-Denis. He took a wicked pleasure in stopping from time to time to observe poverty at close quarters. With his thick, black, fur-collared coat and his catskin hat, he inspired fear. A few months earlier, when he had first settled in the district, he had often been seen in the company of a dangerous dandy named Lacenaire. They had been planning a counterfeiting swindle when Lacenaire had been arrested for stealing silver cutlery from a restaurant. For this crime he had already served several months at Bicêtre and was now imprisoned in La Force.

Before he was sentenced to thirteen months, Lacenaire had recommended to the Catman a friend of his, a Jack-of-all-trades named Alexandre Tixier. Tixier, who went by the nickname of Jesus, was not out of place in the Catman's academy – a coterie of murderers, pimps, thieves and ex-convicts.

The Catman turned down the narrow gully of the Rue Greneta. On impulse, he went into a few buildings, and then a small abandoned courtyard, where poor children often played. As soon as he entered, he was mobbed by a pack of sickly, misshapen children with pale and sallow faces, all of them filthy and foul-smelling, begging him for alms.

'Get off me, scum! Get off or I'll skin you alive!'

Terrified, the children bolted back to their lairs – piles of rubble, or lean-tos, or inside the flues of disused chimneys, with potato stalks and straw to sleep on.

'And make sure I don't catch you at it again!' the old man shouted, smiling wickedly and brandishing his cane. 'Except if you want to eat and sleep in a proper bed!' He assumed a more winning tone. 'With me, my little ones, there's no more poverty. You know the address, don't you? See you soon, little ones!'

To the average person, poverty and degradation seemed all the more cruel because of the scandalous contrast they offered to the extravagance of a small, brilliant and idle society that frittered away its wealth on elegant clothes, glittering parties and gargantuan meals. It was enough to make anyone rebel. But the Catman was not the average person. The sight of these children dying of hunger delighted him – poverty put a smile on his face. It was his livelihood.

Glancing quickly behind him, the Catman pushed open a big door flanked by two copper key-plates. A covered passage led to a wash house, where he kept rabbits.

'Just in case – you never know,' the Catman would say. 'I distrust informers like the plague. If the cops come here, I'll show them my rabbits. No one's going to accuse me of deceiving them about the merchandise.'

The building consisted of a ground floor occupied by a wine shop, the wash house with the rabbits and a large shed, and three upper floors. If you carried straight on, you came to a little courtyard lacking air and light, and heaped with refuse. The Catman occupied two rooms on the third floor with a view of the courtyard, and the shed on the ground floor. A real prison.

He took out a bunch of keys, opened the shed door and let out a contented sigh. The sight of his shameful success brought balm to his soul. The walls were made from thin, worm-eaten strips of wood; a big barred skylight occupied the roof slope, and candles threw a murky light onto grease-stained workbenches. The floor was completely hidden under rotten straw, filthy rags, gnawed bones, grease, tufts of wool, skins streaked with blood and crates filled with cats' heads. Although the intestines were kept outside, the smell was indescribable – a mixture of urine, body odour and excrement. To the left of the skylight was an oblong wooden mezzanine, which could be reached by a stepladder and where it was impossible to stand upright. Fixed to the bare wall of the mezzanine was a partition with a porthole shaped like a bull's eye in the centre, through which the children would slip to reach their sleeping space.

'Working hard?' said the Catman to no one in particular.

Nobody looked up. There were about ten boys working, supervised by an old man in a rocking chair. He was a cripple who could neither move, talk, nor hear. But he could see and his work consisted of just that – seeing. Or rather, informing. He was called the Pointer. The only movements he ever made were to raise his hand and point an accusing fore-finger at one of the children.

And indeed, just as the Catman walked in, the Pointer raised his wrinkled hand and pointed his hooked forefinger, with its long black nail, at a little boy dozing over his work.

At that moment a horrible rasping voice rang out. 'That little runt again! Just wait till I get my hands on him!'

A big red-headed man emerged from the shadows. Square, squat and as hairy as a bear, he had a flat face, a pug nose, pig's eyes, short legs and a prominent belly. He was the foreman, known as the Mullet, after the red fish. Before becoming a wool carder, he had been a scrap-metal merchant, and his apoplectic cheeks were covered in red blotches. When he lost his temper his features turned an even more vivid red. His mouth was a thin line in his slack face, so thin that it seemed to disappear into the funnel of his powerful neck. Always unshaven, he was an ugly character.

Without even greeting the Catman, he rushed at the little wool carder. As the boy had not shown much skill at catching cats, the Catman had placed him in the workshop. He was just seven. Carding and scraping without a break, the child worked from four in the morning to ten at night for less than two francs a day. He tried his best, but sleep would overcome him and he would doze off at his job. Whenever that happened, the Pointer would raise his forefinger and the Mullet would intervene to hit him across the nose with the back of his hand. The child had no blood left.

'Monsieur Mullet, please forgive me,' he would say. 'I'm so sleepy . . .'

The capital was full of little wretches like him. Their fate was unenvi-able. In Paris alone there were as many as ninety infanticides a year. In the working-class areas one child out of two died and those who did not die at birth were abandoned or forced into living by theft. It was not until 1841 that the law forbade the employment of children under the age of eight and night work for those under thirteen.

The Mullet stood in front of the little wool carder. 'So, you little good-for-nothing, still asleep standing up? You should thank the Pointer, he's going to save you from a decrease in wages!' As slaps were not enough, he also used a thick rope to beat malingerers. 'Take that!'

The blow was so violent that the boy collapsed.

'Hey, go easy, Mullet!' came the Catman's voice. 'That's my livelihood you're damaging!'

'You should get rid of this one,' said the redhead.

The old man gestured vaguely with his hand. 'We'll talk about it later, Mullet. That's not what I'm here for right now.'

But the redhead would not give up. 'There's not only this damned Raphaël, there's also that one over there – Horse Face. He's insolent and a troublemaker to boot. It's time to take action!'

'I'm the one who decides when to take action, Mullet,' declared the Catman, adjusting his bonnet. 'Horse Face is a good skinner. As for Raphaël, he'll learn to card.'

While he was saying this, Horse Face had abandoned his work to come to Raphaël's aid. He helped him to his feet, then stood looking defiantly at the Mullet and the Catman.

Horse Face was a thin, dark-skinned lad of fourteen, with a huge jaw and eyes that gleamed like hot coals, who possessed a savage moral energy and incredible physical strength. His hands were like pincers. When he caught a cat, he would break its neck instantaneously and quickly skin it like a fish. Over his grey worker's smock, he wore a brown catskin waistcoat.

He put his arm around Raphaël's shoulders. 'How are you feeling, kid?'

The little boy was snivelling. His face was starting to look puffy.

'If you want to wallop me, go ahead,' said Horse Face, addressing the Mullet. 'But I warn you, the Catman won't like it. And from there to tipping the two of you in the Seine, you and your old man, isn't a big step.'

The Mullet stifled an oath. Talk like that about his father, the Pointer, put him in a terrible rage. He tightened his hand on the rope, lifted it and whirled it in the air to hit Horse Face. The youth retreated, lowering his head. He knew he was not strong enough to be a match for the redhead.

'Leave him alone or you'll have me to answer to!' roared a voice from the entrance.

It was a proud-looking, brown-skinned young man. Everyone had recognized Jesus. But the Mullet was beside himself. 'Oh, so here he is!' he cried, whirling his rope. 'Come here and I'll pull you to pieces, you heathen!'

All the boys stopped working. The Pointer no longer knew where to point. The athletic young man who had burst into the workshop was holding a bludgeon. He was wearing a blue smock and had an otter-skin hat on his head. He had a brown, velvety complexion, black hair parted above one temple and a strawberry mark under his left eye. He wore a ring on his finger, a gold ring of a snake with emerald eyes. He glanced round the room, where, besides the skins, the workbenches and the wool, there were also an oven, a tub, some chipped cups and a ewer. He took a few steps forward. A candle flame cast a sliver of trembling light onto his face. His lower lip twitched.

'Come on, then, let's have it!' said the Mullet, to provoke him.

Thinking the moment favourable for an attack, he rushed forward. The children were holding their breath, while the Catman watched with a threatening glint in his eye, which gave his weasel face an expression of perverse pain.

The Mullet stopped right in front of the young man and looked at him defiantly. 'Oh, I'm so scared of little Jesus!' he sneered.

Then, groaning as he did so, he struck Jesus with the rope. The young man abruptly stepped back and struck the Mullet's arm with his bludgeon. The Mullet let out a roar that terrified the gathering.

'Make him bleed!' cried Horse Face.

Jesus took the Mullet by the neck and pushed him roughly against the only window in the room. He had dropped his bludgeon, and in its place was a knife with a horn handle and a sharp, shiny blade. 'You threaten me again and I'll cut your face so bad your own father won't recognize you.'

'I love the friendly, open atmosphere here, my children,' said the Catman, finally breaking his silence. 'You see, Mullet, Jesus is a sensitive soul. The slightest squabble and he's ready to beat you up. Lacenaire was right. Jesus can be very useful to us.'

The Mullet looked at the Catman shiftily. 'He broke my arm, Catman . . .'

A snigger greeted this plaintive observation. 'You had more than you needed, Mullet! If you've got two left arms, you can let one go. Isn't that right, Jesus?'

Jesus nodded silently and put the knife away in his smock. It was Lacenaire who had given him the nickname Jesus. Before going to prison, Lacenaire, who had been a blackmailer, had befriended this dark young man, who prized the poetry of François Villon and the books of Rabelais. The blackmailer's job was to exploit the fear that some bourgeois had of seeing their unnatural passions exposed. To do this, he trained young men, who set up the victims so he could pose as a police officer and catch the sinners *in flagrante delicto*. The name commonly given to such a young man was 'Jesus'. It was a dirty profession that was practised dirtily, but in which considerable sums of money often changed hands.

Composing his face into a painfully afflicted expression, the Catman waved his cane in front of him, as if to signify that the game was over. 'Mullet, listen to me. I need five or six girls for tonight.'

The redhead rubbed his arm. 'Beautiful?' he asked.

'Definitely. Half-past ten at the Clan Destin.'

'You'll have them.'

'What about me?' asked Jesus.

'You're going to help me keep an eye on high society. We're going to celebrate 1834 in style!'

The Clan Destin was a little further up the Rue Aubry-le-Boucher, a dark and dilapidated street which during the uprising of 5–6 June 1832 had seen the erection of a huge barricade. The dregs of Paris all assembled at the Clan Destin. The police hardly dared venture there. As a bed cost only three sous, the place attracted housebreakers, cutpurses, confidence tricksters, cat burglars, cut-throats and every other imaginable kind of villain.

In short, the Clan Destin was a thieves' den. It was a place to eat and drink and dance the *chahut*, that hideous, noisy and chaotic free-for-all so beloved of pimps and whores, in which the master of ceremonies, known as the ogre, bustled at the speed of a meteor, constantly rewriting the palimpsest of debauchery with excesses that would have shocked Sardana-palus. It was not so very different from Denoyer's or Franconi's, though more sordid.

The Clan Destin occupied the ground floor of a building which fifty years earlier had housed the Saint-Fiacre brotherhood of gardeners. Times had changed. The seeds sown there now were quite different.

A lantern hung above the front door. The Catman entered and took a deep breath of the tainted air. The big room was lit by a Quinquet oil lamp, and its ceiling supported by greyish beams. 'So, Gammy Leg, is the stew ready?' he called to a fat woman, who was busy with her plate-warmers.

'You bet, Catman! Rabbit just the way you like it!'

Shaken by a nervous laugh more like a yelp, the fat woman moved a big spatula, on which a cat's head steamed. She had a hoarse voice, imposing red arms and a bearded chin. A big black cat lay curled at her feet.

'You love me, don't you, Demon? You're the only one.'

The Catman advanced towards the kitchen. 'I hope you're not going to poison them for me?'

Gammy Leg gave him a dirty look. Constant work at the oven and too much red wine had given her a fiery complexion. She wore a brown bonnet and a shawl crossed over her chest. She put down her spatula, left her cooking and took a few steps towards the Catman, who was open to all offers. She was called Gammy Leg because of her exaggerated limp.

'Poison them?' she echoed, wiping her hands on her greenish-yellow woollen dress, the bottom of which gave a glimpse of her feet, covered with warts and blackened by constantly treading on hard floors impregnated with charcoal. 'Poison them? On New Year's Eve? Now, would I do such a thing? Have you seen how I prepare my dishes, you old skinflint?'

The Catman looked around the low room, the space reduced at one end by a buffet fixed to the wall with strong iron clamps. There were ten tables, five on the left, five on the right, with pewter jugs and a big bunch of dried flowers on the buffet. In the kitchen extension, next to a smoke-blackened counter, was a wooden staircase, at the foot of which an armful of straw had been thrown as a makeshift carpet to provide access to the sleeping quarters. The invitation was clear.

'Excellent,' said the Catman appreciatively. 'We're going to fleece all those yellow gloves.' He gave an insidious half-smile. 'What about the Kitten?'

Gammy Leg placed her hands on her hips. 'Her? She's lazier than a grass snake, the whore. She'll turn up late as usual.'

With that she returned to her ovens. The Kitten was, to all intents and purposes, the other wife of Gammy Leg's husband. The ménage à trois amused everyone – except Gammy Leg, who was furious about the menial tasks to which she was relegated.

In the shadows, six men were drinking in silence. While watching them and talking to Gammy Leg, the Catman seemed to be thinking. These six weren't villains, he told himself. They were workers. You could tell by their caps and dirty smocks, and the way they were looking at each other like china dogs. They sat slumped on their chairs, not saying a word, overcome with exhaustion, alternately smoking their pipes and drinking. Their gestures were heavy and stiff. What had they been doing all day?

Cutting copper? Spraying cotton? Smoothing bronze? Thinning iron? Planing wood? Forging steel? Blowing glass? Plaiting harnesses and braids? Or had they been hatching some fleeting plot, one of those rebellions all too easily kept alive by misfortune, poverty, brandy and dry bread? Weren't ideas of insurrection festering in all these minds, these hearts beating in houses filled only with famine, in filthy taverns and soulless streets that seemed to lead nowhere? Everywhere there was a murmuring, a thousand muffled cries of woe. The need for material betterment, common to all workers, had always been a weary habit, if not a resigned slavery, but now it had become a throbbing pain without hope of change or relief. Decay was written on every face. It was a situation that could not last.

The Catman tapped the floor with the tip of his cane, not in a gesture of sympathy, but in irritation. When were these ragged men going to leave?

Suddenly a voice distracted him. 'So he's here, is he?'

The man who had spoken and who had just entered the restaurant was Gammy Leg's husband. He was known as Perfect Love, which was the name of an adulterated drink. Tall and well built, with curly hair like a troubadour's, huge eyebrows and short side whiskers, he was dressed in a coat whose colour was made indeterminate by layer upon layer of grime and mud. He had once been a carpenter in Saint-Antoine, famous for his spiral staircases.

'Flights are my speciality,' he would often say.

He still kept a little workshop in the Place d'Aligre in the artisans' district. To make oak sing under the plane was his one distraction from the hardships of a complicated existence. Now he followed two professions, as both innkeeper and seducer, preferring the latter, for he would forget all about the management of his business when lust darkened his mind.

For a long time now, his energy had been devoted solely to loving the Kitten.

It was common knowledge that this beauty of just twenty had coaxed Perfect Love with a clever mixture of fluttering eyelids and voluptuous gestures. But she was also rumoured to have ambitions, grand ambitions. She was determined to control the purse strings, and saw herself replacing Gammy Leg in running the business. In addition, the boldness of her gestures was combined with a fiery character. One October evening she had even given Gammy Leg a good thrashing during a quarrel whose nature was not hard to guess. Captivated by the animal impetuosity of this

Fury, eyes charged with sensual electricity, Perfect Love had stayed in his corner, dumbfounded and breathless, looking on.

At first glance, nothing seemed to predispose the Kitten to such outbursts. She had a wild beauty, it was true, but she was small and angelic looking. Under her jet-black hair she had a prominent forehead, a short straight nose whose nostrils dilated at the slightest emotion, and an impertinent mouth hiding perfect white teeth. Her arms were slim, her waistline neat, her breasts lavish. Her only fault – and it was a major one which marred this otherwise idyllic portrait – was that she was very cross-eyed. Her eyes, though a beautiful deep black, rolled in all directions like ebony marbles. Quite simply, you never knew where they were pointing.

'Precisely,' Gammy Leg would observe. 'The reason you don't know is because the bitch never dares look you straight in the face. She's a real tart.'

Despite this, the Kitten, who answered to the sweet name of Clotilde Lepetit, never failed to inflame men. Even her clothes were the epitome of shamelessness. Almost every day, she dressed in a loose red skirt that displayed her muscular but slender thighs. On top she wore men's jackets like those of English cavalry officers, white, black or red, never buttoned, over shirts of white lace, opened to the navel, which showed off her plump throat and prominent breasts.

'My little quail here will serve,' Perfect Love declared, taking her by the hand.

At that moment, as the six workers were standing up to leave, a man dressed in black entered the restaurant. The Catman immediately went over to him and the two shook hands.

'I've been waiting for you,' said the Catman. 'There are details to be arranged.'

The man in black looked like a police inspector. 'Spare me your whining,' he replied, without taking off his top hat. 'Your friends will be paid in due course. They've already had something on account, haven't they?'

'Indeed, my friend. But they'd like to be reassured, because—'

'Because what?' the other cut in. 'Never forget you owe me everything, Tardier. Your new papers, your position, all the rest.'

'I don't forget, my friend,' said the Catman, whose real name was Tardier. 'Would you care for a drink?' he asked, pointing at the counter with the tip of his cane.

'No time. I just wanted to make sure that everything was ready and that Jesus will be here tonight.'

'He'll be here, my friend, he'll be here.'

'In that case, we have nothing more to say to each other.'

The party at the de Roure mansion, the former home of Marshal Ney in the Rue de Lille, looked set to be an extremely lavish affair, Marius was in no doubt about that. The New Year had to be celebrated fittingly. The house still bore the imprint of the Comte d'Orsay, who had lived there for some years. Since his financial ruin he had lived in Seymour Place in foggy London, trailing his nostalgia around St James's Square in a dragon-shaped sleigh, pulled at breakneck speed by a coffee-coloured horse covered with a tiger skin. Unlike that stiff and stupid marionette Brummell – a wax doll according to Alfred de Vigny – Alfred d'Orsay had turned out to be a perfect gentleman. He had been at once brilliant, friendly, lively, witty, seductive and warm.

The de Roure mansion had something to astonish all its guests, so brilliant was the gathering, so sumptuous the decor. Access from the street was through a portico facing an avenue of cypresses, lit by flaming torches, and gardens that ended in a terrace overlooking the quay. Many of the guests were strolling along the paths between the trees, padding out their conversations with derisive and cynical comments and a generous sprinkling of English. The current owner of the property, the Marquis de Lilliers, was not there. He had let his mansion to a wheeler-dealer who went by the portmanteau title of the Chevalier Aurélien Malartic Dupartel, and who had made his fortune supplying materiel to the army, first in Spain then in Algeria.

But the Chevalier Dupartel himself, a lithe, sleek and placid but indolent character, had honoured his guests with his presence. A corpulent man with a face like one of the Bourbons, framed by ebony side whiskers and a carefully curled beard, he was one of those who in the old style was called a pedant, and in popular language an ass.

'Basically, he's a miser and a cuckold,' said Amédée to Marius. 'It's not for nothing that he has Guizot's ear. But there it is, one has to compensate. The stupid fellow is able to limit the loathing he inspires because of the vulgarity of his wealth and the fear he arouses. Between ourselves, I recommend his wife.'

Marius laughed and glanced at the short woman with lively eyes whom Amédée had indicated. She was waving her arms like a semaphore signaller. With her high voice and low waistline, she seemed to possess every frivolous attribute.

'I shall leave you, my friend,' said Amédée. 'I'm sure the observation of these rare insects will enchant the dedicated entomologist in you.'

Marius followed Amédée's advice. He busied himself observing these people, who were stifled by the need to do nothing and the luck of being well born. And this New Year's Eve confirmed what he had already predicted – namely, that different worlds were no longer avoiding each other as they once had.

Even two years earlier the societies of Saint-Germain and Saint-Honoré, in other words the old nobility and the nobility of Empire, had already been mixing easily, but both recoiled from the idea of frequenting the third, that of the Chaussée-d'Antin, whose wealth derived from business.

Now this gulf no longer existed. High society and high finance visited the same places. There was not a single millionaire whose daughter could not marry a prince if she wanted to. Ostracism was a thing of the past. Duchesses and marquises had at their disposal the same clothes, the same manners and the same mannerisms as the women of the boulevards. Men, aristocratic or not, no longer amused themselves at the expense of the bourgeois sovereign, who went everywhere on foot, his wife on his arm and his umbrella in his hand. Or if they did, it was on the quiet, rather as they were doing this evening with the Chevalier Dupartel. It was the done thing to copy the English and exaggerate everything you wore, from the knot of your cravat to the laces on your shoes. Brummell had inspired imitators. People dressed in embroidered linen, multi-coloured satin, gold chains, tousled curls and shaved eyebrows. They looked like boiled apples emerging from a fruit dish. It goes without saying that it was almost impossible to distinguish the false from the genuine in such people. Who was a marquis, who a commoner? That was the question. This party allowed them to exchange their impressions on such subjects as grooms, the English bootmaker Gay, tilburys, clubs, sport, the Indian Tea Warehouse and English boxing. Like all fashions, Anglomania was currently the most ridiculous thing in the world.

Not far from Eugène Sue, who was recounting his experiences as an assistant surgeon on board a Royal Navy ship, Amédée d'Iguerande stood sipping his flute of champagne. Beside him, Comtesse Marie d'Agoult was watching him passionately. In his black suit with its buttons of precious stones, his white cravat and black velvet cap with a twist of silver, the marquis was competing with Eugène Sue, who wore a tight-fitting suit of the kind sported by racegoers. His neck was buried in a white and crimson cravat so ample there was enough material in it to make a nightshirt. But the handsome Eugène also had broad shoulders, splendid blue eyes and admirable side whiskers.

'I only served for six months,' observed Amédée. 'I was allergic to a military career. What can I do? I just don't know how to obey.'

Eugène Sue shook his head maliciously. 'My dear Marquis, the army kills and makes one sad. Just ask Vigny. But what would one do without it?'

'Like the Comte de Bourmont at Waterloo – run away.'

This remark, delivered in a thin, piping voice, provoked general laughter. Its author was Louis de Vergne, who was flanked by Henri de la Roche-Dragon and another friend named Robert d'Androisy.

A tireless talker who never lost himself in the maze of his own boasting, Eugène Sue gave Louis de Vergne a dig with his elbow, which was not in the best of taste and told the company how he would appear on the Champs-Elysées in his four-seat phaeton, which was the height of fashion. Then he began to hold forth about his horses, his equestrian skills being second to none, and expressed surprise that nobody was wearing spurs this evening.

Amédée d'Iguerande lowered his eyes wearily. It exasperated him to see his own faults reflected in someone else, even a friend. He left the group and went into the adjoining room, where the waltz and the *galop* were being danced and couples were executing *chassés*. In passing, the marquis took another flute of champagne. You had to take advantage, after all. In general, at balls in Saint-Germain, it was not deemed necessary to go to great expense. But this evening, the hostess, Eléonore Dupartel, whom Amédée had had the weakness to seduce a year earlier and the strength to reject six months later, had done everything in style. Champagne flowed, the buffet staggered beneath the weight of ice creams, pâtés and cakes, and the Mortimer silver and Sèvres porcelain circulated happily from hand to hand.

Amédée d'Iguerande, straight as a rake, checked that his Brummell trousers were correctly buttoned over his instep, and gave a satisfied little pout. He was getting impatient. His steward had informed him that everything was ready at the Clan Destin and he looked around for his friend Marius. Amédée always needed a generous benefactor to whom money was no object, and for the moment Baron Pontmercy fitted the bill. All that was necessary was to corrupt him a little, give him a taste for inviting flesh, and introduce him to the pleasures of romantic orgies. Talking of which, had Clémence gone on the offensive yet?

Amédée stood on tiptoe and looked around the crowd. No Clémence. His lips curled in irritation. She was indispensable to his plan. While she was looking after Marius, he would deal with Marius's wife. He was not indifferent to little Cosette, who wanted to be called Euphrasie, and had even written her a letter. A very respectful one, of course, but a letter nonetheless. By befriending the husband, he hoped to win the favours of the wife. It was the way he had always operated – his cynicism knew no bounds.

He looked at his watch, noting it was the hour that he normally arrived at parties to produce the maximum effect. The quadrilles would last till morning. But that kind of sensation was not for now. Tonight, there was another sensation in view.

Not far from the front steps, he hailed Louis de Vergne, who was talking to a charmingly dressed Englishwoman.

'Have you seen our friend the baron?'

'Not since I arrived,' de Vergne replied, flicking dust from his friend's shoulder. He looked embarrassed. 'By the way, I didn't tell you, but Eugène is determined to go with us. He's never seen a thieves' den.'

Amédée thought for a moment. 'That idiot Sue? Well, so be it. Your bungling has struck again, my dear Louis. And I suppose Monsieur Sue will be accompanied by Marie d'Agoult, that idiotic Romantic who seems to think she can attract Rossini and Chateaubriand to her house. Six inches of snow on twenty feet of lava, as they say of her.'

'One can't hide a thing from you, dear friend. The high priestess of soirées at the Mailly Nesle mansion will indeed be coming, even if she is increasingly attracted by Monsieur Liszt.'

'I can just see the serenades. That means there'll be fifteen of us. Well, so much the better. The more idiots, the merrier – as the foolish say. We must keep our dear Marius amused.'

He tapped his friend's cheek affectionately and asked him to take care of Eugène Sue and the Comtesse d'Agoult. 'The baron will go in my tilbury with Clémence and this young Englishwoman you've introduced me to.'

'But I thought—'

'Naturally, she'll accept,' Amédée continued. 'I count on your discretion. Come on. Hurry up, the two of you!'

Outside, between paths lit by flaming torches, among clumps of ornamental box trees, young people were chasing each other and shouting noisily. Not far away, the torchlight illuminated a young man, a true young man, something rather rare in Paris in these times of exaggerated dandyism, a man who wore with pride that passionate and daring coat that goes by the name of youth. He was walking slowly, his hands behind his back.

Marius was anxious. He was angry with himself for having treated Cosette so badly. But something told him not to regret in any way what he had done, or rather, not to humble himself by telling her his regrets, which usually has more effect in the eyes of the beloved. He had too much pride and too much self-respect for that. And he was all the more anxious as his life with Cosette, which was now very distant since they slept separately, left him in a state of permanent irritation. Irritation at her reserve, although she was always smiling and loyal; irritation at his own guilt; and irritation at hurting himself as much as he hurt her. By way of self-justification, he thought of lying to Cosette and to himself, with the aim of avoiding drama and of heightening reality to make it wilder and more beautiful. Haunted by death, which in a young man of twenty-three is nothing but a sly way of tricking life, he thought that everything would end in the infinite. He had explained this to Cosette.

'The infinite?' was her reply. 'What infinite? That which means abandoning me?' She had given him an object. 'It's a rock crystal. A sort of talisman. Apparently you can see every kind of light in it. But there's only one that interests me – you. Be careful that it doesn't go out.'

He had taken the crystal without replying and slammed the door as he left.

Too many confused thoughts were attacking him. He searched in the pocket of his frock coat, took out the crystal and studied it with care. Was it really magic? Suddenly he asked himself what he was doing here. Where was he going? Would he one day be repaid for the absence of joy in his present life? Did you have to be either a joyful pessimist, as Amédée advocated, or an embittered optimist like all the puppets here tonight?

'I've treated Cosette as the lowest of the low,' he said to himself.

He passed his thumb over the crystal and put it back in his pocket. His lips were trembling. What if he went back to the Rue Plumet and took

Cosette in his arms, apologized profusely and told her how much he loved her?

He lowered his head, turned resolutely on his heels and, as he did so, came face to face with a young woman dressed in black, who emerged from the shadows like a temptress.

'Excuse me,' he said, as he brushed against her.

'You seem melancholy, Monsieur,' she said, standing her ground and tilting her head to one side. 'I've watched you for a good part of the evening. You haven't drunk any champagne, you haven't danced, and now you're wandering like a lost soul. Would it be indiscreet to ask what is worrying you?'

Marius said nothing. The woman fascinated him. His eyes flared suddenly, giving his face a cruel beauty that frightened her.

'I'm sorry, Monsieur, I'll leave you.'

Marius reached out his hand. 'No, please don't . . .'

As he said this, he was surprised to feel, beneath his unhappiness, a breath of desire.

A bewitching smile filled the young woman's face. The flickering flame lit up her dark green eyes behind her lashes, and her brilliant orange lips.

'You're beautiful,' said Marius breathlessly.

She laughed silently. 'You scared me a little, Monsieur Pontmercy.'

'You know my name?'

'Amédée has told me about you. I'm Clémence de Lavely.'

Marius bowed slightly. Around them the dense foliage shimmered in the light. The young woman's eyes widened and Marius read in their emerald brightness a mixture of surprise and amusement.

'It's particularly mild tonight,' she said. 'Mild and gentle. I love gentleness in life, as in feelings. What about you?'

'Above all in feelings,' said Marius.

She nodded silently.

Marius took her hand and kissed it, as if to say that his friends' friends were his friends, too.

'I find you rather forward, Monsieur Pontmercy.'

Taking back with one hand what she was giving with the other, she threw him a deep, languorous look, filled with candour and the passion that troubles men.

'I think we may be spending some of this evening together,' she said, with a smile that softened her narrow chin and gave her face a calculated sweetness, in spite of the hard, straight line of her nose, the selfish arc of her lips and the heaviness of her jaw. 'Shall we walk a little?'

She placed her hand on Marius's hand, instantly took it away again, and pirouetted away from him. She laughed again and then they walked towards the house, side by side.

Marius tried to walk slowly, to inhale Clémence's perfume, which he guessed was a subtle mixture of lily and honeysuckle.

'I think our friend Amédée has a surprise in store for us,' she said. After a moment, she placed her hand lightly on his forearm. 'Look, there he is, coming to meet us.'

Ahead of them the marquis stopped and folded his arms, waiting for the couple to come level with him. 'So this is what the two of you get up to when my back is turned?' he asked provocatively.

Marius stammered an excuse – they had met by chance, it had been dark . . .

Clémence giggled. 'It was the darkness which brought us together,' she said. 'And perhaps the darkness will separate us.'

Amédée put a fist on his hip and raised his other hand, wagging a finger. 'You're a liar, Baron! And here was I looking for you for the past hour to introduce you to people of quality.'

Marius frowned, breaking the delicate line of his eyebrows. 'I don't know what to say, Marquis. I hadn't really understood, I—'

'Come on, Marius, I was joking!' Amédée interrupted. 'How impressionable the boy is! Clémence, I'm counting on you to take him under your wing and teach him a thing or two. As for myself, I give up. I've been trying for two months and I've failed lamentably.'

'You know you can count on me,' replied Clémence with a complicit smile.

They made their way to the front steps of the house to collect their cloaks. But when Clémence and Marius headed for the drawing room, Amédée stopped them with a brief gesture. 'No, not that way, my friends. Let us dispense with these tedious courtesies. My tilbury is impatient and my little finger tells me that a charming young Englishwoman is waiting for me inside it. What's more, Eugène and Robert have challenged me to a race. The first to get to Saint-Denis!'

'Aren't we going to say goodbye to our hostess?' asked Marius in surprise, his hat and cane in his hand.

'What a darling he is,' said Clémence, placing her head on his shoulder.

Amédée raised his eyes to heaven. 'I tell you, Clémence, he's incorrigible. Say goodbye to whom, my dear Baron? That pomaded idiot and her contemptible husband? A true gentleman should just run away.'

Marius did as he was told. He followed Clémence and Amédée as they crossed the garden to Amédée's tilbury, where a young redhead languished, half hidden by a quilted bonnet. Amédée did not even bother to say anything to her. He simply pinched her cheek, took up his riding crop and winked conspiratorially at Marius. Then he lashed the horse's rump and the vehicle set off.

The race was lost by Amédée, who, being the good sport that he was, had pointed out the best route to his rivals. He arrived third, after Eugène Sue with Robert d'Androisy, and Louis de Vergne and Henri de la Roche-Dragon. They did not wait for the marquis to arrive to take over the tavern.

Meanwhile, just as the marquis's tilbury was slowing down, a piercing cry was heard. Amédée and Marius jumped down from the carriage at the same time. They found two boys lying on the pavement, one of them an adolescent with a huge horse-like jaw, the other a ragged, barefoot child. Of the two, the child seemed the more injured.

'It hurts,' he complained, lying curled up, rubbing his leg. 'It hurts and I'm cold . . .'

A biting wind was blowing through the dark warren of· alleyways between the Rue Saint-Denis and the Rue Saint-Martin. The carriage had merely brushed against the two wretches, but it had been enough to knock them backwards onto the pavement.

Marius leaned over the boy. His little round face was covered in dirt and scabs, but his hair was the colour of fine gold. Marius spread the tails of his cloak and knelt down. 'Let me have a look.'

The youth with the horse's jaw had already got to his feet. 'Leave him alone!' he protested vehemently. 'We can manage without you! You rich people are all the same!'

'What do you mean?' asked Amédée.

'I know you and your dirty ways! All you want to do is humiliate us!'

'Good gracious!' said Amédée. 'I've never seen anything more aggressive than this awful brat. Unless I'm much mistaken, he's the very devil.' He turned to Clémence and the young Englishwoman. 'Did you hear, ladies? This is what we call the common people.'

Meanwhile Marius was examining the fair-haired little boy. His only wound was a grazed knee, but he was still in shock and he was shivering with cold.

'You're shaking, my child.'

Marius took off his cloak with a swift movement, so swift that the child protected his face as if he were about to be hit.

'No, no, don't be afraid,' Marius stammered, taken aback by the child's distress. 'What's your name?'

Timidly, the child lowered his arms and sat up. 'Raphaël, Monsieur.'

'Raphaël? That's a nice name. Here, take this coat. I'm giving it to you. Take this, too, and buy yourself some shoes.' He slipped five sous into the boy's hand and covered him with his cloak.

'You never cease to astonish me, Baron,' said Amédée d'Iguerande. 'These scum are not worth the ground we walk on. Still, that's your problem. When you've finished, join us at the Clan Destin. It's a little way down on the right, in the Rue Aubry-le-Boucher.'

The mention of this address struck Marius like a thunderbolt. Still kneeling, he almost lost his balance and fell on Raphaël. Two years earlier a child had died not far from here in the Rue de la Chanvrerie, a child named Gavroche. And now this boy lying on the cobblestones, in practically the same place, seemed like the brother of all the poor children Marius had met then.

'I'll join you later,' he managed to say, amid bursts of laughter and the sound of footsteps on cobblestones.

He finally turned his head and followed the shadows that danced in the dark ravine of the alley. Then, abruptly, he stood up. The youth with the horse's jaw was watching him silently. Little Raphaël looked up into the face of this proud and generous young man, a face that reminded him of Jesus's. This young man had just given him money and his cloak. He would never forget him. It was the first time anyone had lavished so much kindness and attention on him. And like the child he dreamed of being, whom nobody had ever considered him to be, he held out his ice-cold hands to the young man. Marius took the child in his arms, lifted him off the ground and clasped him to his chest. Then he put him down and searched his pockets again.

'Here, Raphaël, take these two francs as well and buy a shirt and trousers.'

Raphaël stuffed the money in his pocket and went to shelter by his companion. 'Did you see, Horse Face? The man who looks like Jesus gave me more sous.'

'Jesus?' said Marius. 'I'm flattered.'

Horse Face gave a half-smile. He had put on his cap and seemed to be challenging Marius with his eyes. 'So you're off to the Clan Destin, Monsieur?'

'Indeed, my boy.'

'Are you a friend of the Mullet's?'

'I don't have the honour of knowing him.'

'So much the better. Or, if you're lying, so much the worse. Because, if you want to know, the Mullet is the biggest bastard ever to walk the earth.' Horse Face turned and wrapped both himself and little Raphaël in Marius's cloak. Taking the child by the hand, he turned again. 'Well, thank you, Monsieur,' he said.

Marius waved his cane in a final farewell, turned and, with his cane over his shoulder, walked to the crossroads. There, at the beginning of the Rue Aubry-le-Boucher, he noticed that rain had started to fall, a fine, clinging rain. He thought about little Raphaël and wondered how anyone could let a child that age roam the streets at such a late hour. He passed a carriage entrance, where a lopsided sign announced that there was a cotton factory on the other side of the courtyard. A group of women and children were coming out. None of them paid him any attention. Thin, dirty and emaciated, the women walked barefoot on the muddy cobblestones. Having no umbrellas, they put their aprons or their underskirts upside down on their heads. Empty baskets swung from their arms. The children, no less dirty, no less haggard, followed them, running in circles. Better protected than the women – their clothes had been made waterproof by the grease that had fallen on them while they worked – they brandished the pieces of bread they had saved all through the working day, which had only just finished.

'It gets softer in the rain!' they cried. 'After fifteen hours' slogging, it's bloody good!'

Marius stopped. He thought again of his friend Frédéric Rivolier and his noble ideas. His face, wet from the rain, remained impassive, betraying not the slightest hint of rebellion or indignation. It was as if the horror inside him had turned to stone. He brushed his thoughts away, telling himself, absurdly, that feelings of guilt are merely a response to circumstance.

'How horrible to open one's eyes,' he murmured.

He opened the door of the Clan Destin and was greeted by squeals of laughter. They echoed in his ears like a distillation of all the evils of his time. So much the better. To obliterate what he had seen, he would make a conscious and deliberate effort to copy this unthinking good humour. He would no longer fool himself with the thought that he had another dimension. Debauchery opened its arms to him.

All evening Marius drank and drank, to the point of self-disgust. When the strokes of midnight rang out from the church of Saint-Merri, he took off his frock coat and joined the dancers, who were yelling and stamping their feet. The tavern was full to bursting. Marius embraced Clémence impulsively, Henri de la Roche-Dragon and Robert d'Androisy grabbed two of the loose women provided by the Mullet, Eugène Sue kissed Marie d'Agoult's hand, and Amédée clasped the young Englishwoman to his chest, while Louis de Vergne watched Amédée and applauded half-heartedly. And then there were the others – Amédée's court, lesser nobility, twins in harlequin costumes with three whores in their arms, young men from the outskirts, prophetesses with Gorgons' heads, strangers behaving like villains. Most were disguised as workers and swore like troopers, for to a worker an oath is what a sigh is to the idle man. It was good and it was free. People even kissed each other full on the mouth. Shabby clothes and bad breath were no deterrent. Naturally, the rabbit stew had been served cold and the red wine tepid, but it hardly mattered. In the smoke-blackened interior, where the nightmarish creatures revelled, sounds and voices crescendoed together, creating an atmosphere made all the more diabolic by the presence of a strange dark-haired vestal with a painted mouth, dressed only in a red tunic, who was showing off her belly and buttocks to all and sundry.

'Quite a backside, Kitten!' cried a group of revellers who had nothing to do with the marquis's gang.

Leaning on the counter, Perfect Love was rolling his eyes in fury.

In front of the counter there was a band, consisting of three murderous-looking individuals and a dwarf with a face like a gargoyle, playing the flute, the violin, the viola and the clarinet, and a paralytic young woman who accompanied them on the bass, clinging to her chair and sometimes hugging her instrument obscenely. They were barely audible above the din. Gammy Leg was being helped to serve by two strumpets with bare breasts, who aroused the parties at the tables by rolling their hips like whores. To make the audience laugh, they would blow into their breasts and rub them with the edges of their hands.

At the back of the room, near the sideboard and the staircase, three men were watching the scene with interest – the Catman, Jesus, who was playing with his knife, and the Mullet, who had his arm in a sling. The Catman had not taken his eyes off Marius. When the young man arrived, he had almost reared up in his chair.

'What's the matter?' Jesus had asked, holding the chair down.

'Nothing, son, nothing at all. I thought I saw an old acquaintance . . . An old acquaintance who still has the charm of youth,' he had added sardonically as if to himself, once he had calmed down. 'Now I understand.'

'You understand what?' the Mullet had asked.

'It would take too long to explain, my friend. But just look at all these yellow gloves – they've eaten cat and not one of them suspected. Look at them leaping about!'

And he had smiled knowingly at the man in black, who was sitting in the shadows near the counter, pretending to be appalled by the goings-on in this alcove, which smelled of stables, fried food and human sweat, but who still responded to his accomplice's glances.

A few moments later, when Jesus and the Mullet were absent briefly, the man in black had seized the opportunity to approach the Catman.

'So, did you see?' he had whispered in his ear.

'I saw.'

'Pleased to see him again?'

'Very.'

And the man in black had returned to his seat.

The Catman had been thinking. The resemblance between Marius and Jesus was striking – the same imposing presence, the same hard expression in the eyes, tempered by sadness. Not every feature matched, of course. It was a question of the general bearing.

The Catman wondered what the man in black had in mind.

'Where did you meet that fellow who never shows his face?' asked the Mullet.

'It's a long story. Let's just say he put me back on my feet when I was in Saint-Malo.'

The Mullet was surprised. The Catman didn't usually refer to his past. 'Saint-Malo?'

'A man like me – I could have had a future in the Americas. Just as I was about to leave, I was the victim of a mean trick.'

'You?' The Mullet guffawed. 'You could sell laced boots to a legless cripple!'

'You don't know me, Mullet. I am an innocent astray in a world of pimps and godless rogues. I used to be a soldier. A sergeant decorated at Waterloo, I'll have you know. I even owned a tavern.'

'You're going to make me cry, Catman,' said the Mullet with a nervous laugh. 'But none of that tells me how you come to be in cahoots with the stranger in black.'

'You're too curious, Mullet. Maybe you'd like to take my place, eh? That may yet happen, who knows? But in the meantime, what you've got to realize is that you don't have what it takes. Oh, I'm not talking about strength, you have strength enough, you even use it on helpless children. What you lack is brains. My friend, now, he has them. He's the same calibre as me. And when I met him for the first time in a tavern in Saint-Malo, we understood each other straight away. He lent me money in exchange for various little services. With the two of us, it's always been a case of "You scratch my back, I'll scratch yours." It's a question of balance, Mullet. Not like you. You're one of the impenetrables. You're always unbalanced.'

He paused for a moment.

'You see,' he continued, with a confident air, 'the little marquis and his friends are very fond of their pleasures. All pleasures. That's what the rich are like. When you're weak, you need strong sensations, to make you think that at last you exist. But you, Mullet, you're weak and poor. So you need a boss like me to exist. A boss who can offer the wealthy strong sensations. There's the proof.'

The Catman waved his hand at the ill-assorted company, who were drinking and dancing in the expectation of other, more feverish, less lawful pleasures.

'One more word of advice, Mullet,' he said, in a curt tone that was quite unusual for him. 'Little Raphaël, the boy you've taken a dislike to, was entrusted to me by my friend, who asked me to make him into a first-class cut-throat. So if he should die at his work, like little Louis three months ago, it would not be viewed well. Our pleasant business would collapse. And my friend would make you pay dearly for it. An accident can happen so quickly . . . Do we understand each other?'

The Mullet lowered his eyes in submission.

Meanwhile Marius had sat down again. Eugène Sue was writing in a notebook. Marie d'Agoult, seated by his side, looked longingly at him.

'He's writing,' she said to Marius confidentially. 'He records everything. And you, Monsieur, do you write?'

'I don't have that fault, Madame. I am so perverse that I have a much more ingenious way to conceal my vices.'

Marie d'Agoult stiffened. Eugène Sue stopped writing and looked up at Marius, who returned his glance. Eugène went back to his writing.

Not unpleased with the effect he had made, Marius turned to Clémence and, posing somewhat, showed her a tormented expression, while his eyes wandered to the back of the room. 'I like you,' he said, hiccuping.

'I like you, too,' she whispered and kissed him. The kiss seemed to last for ever. Despite his conscience, Marius felt desire rising within him.

'You're beautiful, Clémence, you're charming . . .'

The words fell out of his mouth in confusion. Clémence responded to Marius's enthusiasm by caressing his body with a practised hand. In this unreal atmosphere, where there was everything to play for, she said the first thing that came into her head.

'I want you, Marius. Will you take care of me? Will you spoil me?'

Near the counter, between the tables, loud shouts echoed, while the musicians played on interminably. People were drinking straight out of the bottles, spraying each other with white wine, embracing with lecherous moans. The dwarf whirled his flute as he offered his hideous manhood to the paralytic girl, who at once kissed him. The louts watching applauded, and two of them even began fondling each other, inflamed as much by the sight of the dwarf as by Robert d'Androisy, who was foraging under a hussy's skirts with an expression on his face like St Sebastian's as arrows pierced his flesh.

Sitting next to Clémence, Marius was becoming aroused by all he saw around him. He was losing his innocence. What horror, he said to himself. But what madness, too.

All at once he leapt to his feet. 'Food fit for the gods!' he exclaimed, raising his arms to heaven.

At that moment, he could distinguish little among these damned souls writhing in torment. The ceiling was rising and falling. He thought he saw Amédée rushing down the staircase with the young Englishwoman, the dwarf falling on top of the paralytic girl, cut-throats fighting in a corner, a dethroned queen reaching out her arms to him, pathetic clowns clinging to the curves of the waitresses.

'I have to pay,' he shouted.

'Good idea!' Amédée replied from a distance.

Marius picked up his frock coat and swayed towards the counter, where he came across Perfect Love. 'Good evening, my good man,' he declared. 'Tell me how much I owe you.'

Perfect Love passed a greedy tongue over his lips. 'If I've added up correctly, Monsieur, three hundred francs.'

Marius took out a thousand-franc note and handed it to the innkeeper. 'Keep the change,' he said, tottering dangerously.

Gammy Leg, who had been waiting for this moment, spirited the note from her husband's hands. 'For those who graft!' she exclaimed.

On the other side, the Catman had not moved. He knew perfectly well that they were talking about money at the counter. But he was patient. Division of the spoils would come later. After all, it was he who had advised Gammy Leg to take the note. 'But easy does it,' he had warned her. 'With the Kitten around, your man's no longer in his right mind.'

In Marius, he had found a fine sucker to fleece. And perhaps also a score to settle.

'I want that little darling,' said Marius, pointing at the Kitten, without suspecting what was brewing on the other side of the room.

He lunged at the Kitten, who was moving excitedly around him. He took her in his arms and whirled her around.

'Oh, dear, I'm afraid we're in for trouble,' said Amédée, standing with his back to the counter and watching Perfect Love's face turn crimson.

The innkeeper rushed at the couple and separated them violently. Gammy Leg, in her corner, was stroking her cat and smiling. She had already recovered the thousand francs; maybe now she would recover her man. Two birds with one stone.

'Contrary to what you might think, Monsieur,' thundered Perfect Love, 'not everything here is for the taking!'

'I have an idea,' said Amédée, placing himself between Marius and the innkeeper. 'Perhaps this should be settled with a fight.'

'You're right,' said Perfect Love, rolling up his sleeves. 'We working people don't go in for duels. That's for the rich.'

The Kitten, delighted with what she had provoked, moved towards the Catman's table.

Perfect Love gripped Marius in his powerful arms. Marius did not even struggle. His legs flailed the air in an ungainly dance.

'Our friend still needs lessons in French and English boxing,' Amédée said to his steward. 'I will have to intervene to get him out of this. Isn't that the best way to get me noticed by his charming wife?'

Louis-Désiré nodded respectfully. 'Indeed, Monsieur. Baroness Pontmercy has a soft spot for you.'

'Do you think so?'

'I don't think, I'm sure. It's not easy to deceive a man who has lived, Monsieur. If I may be allowed to say so, Baroness Pontmercy must be bored with a man like her husband. And a woman bored is a woman conquered.'

Amédée d'Iguerande took off his frock coat imperiously. But at the same time he had the feeling that his legs were about to give way and he was sure that his steward could hear his heart pounding. Why had a man of his standing fallen for that little Cosette?

'You know you often fall in love with your friends' wives,' Louis de Vergne would say. 'With me, you won't have the opportunity.'

Amédée looked at Marius, who was offering no resistance and whose eyes had glazed over.

'That's enough, innkeeper!' cried Amédée, with a voice like a tribune in the National Guard. 'Can't you see you're suffocating the man who's paid you? Let him go!'

Jesus, who had also been about to intervene, stopped in his tracks. He glanced at the Catman for help, then went back to his seat.

Perfect Love finally loosened his grip and released Marius. Clémence and Gammy Leg seized him under the arms and took him to the counter.

'If you want to take me on, I'm your man,' shouted Amédée, clearing a space around himself.

Perfect Love looked at him in surprise. 'All right, then. Come on! Knock me out!'

This time people jostled openly to get a ringside view. Eugène Sue was in the front row, a handsome pirate ready to attack, along with his patroness, Louis de Vergne, Henri de la Roche-Dragon, Robert d'Androisy and the young Englishwoman, who were all curious to see how an aristocrat fought with something other than a sword.

As he had done with Marius, Perfect Love tried to wrap his arms around his adversary to immobilize him and throw him to the ground. But Amédée swerved to avoid the innkeeper, who found nothing but air, then kicked him in the small of the back. Perfect Love staggered under the blow. As quick as lightning, Amédée repeated the kick, before hurling himself on the innkeeper, grabbing him by the throat and throwing him against the counter.

Perfect Love stumbled, weakened by the iron grip that had seized his throat. But he soon recovered his strength. 'I'll have you, damn you!' Furiously, he threw himself at Amédée, whose appearance gave no inkling of his agility.

Amédée moved aside and again avoided Perfect Love's charge. As he did, he stretched out his leg and his adversary fell headlong into the tables. He stood up with the help of some onlookers and attacked again, roaring like a wild animal.

This time Amédée used his fists, just as he did in Lord Seymour's school, where boxing gloves lay side by side with oak cigar boxes perfumed with bay and vanilla. A straight jab to the solar plexus, then another on the temple, followed by a hook to the chin. The innkeeper froze, his fists flailing in the air. A black veil was obscuring his sight. He swayed on the spot, then collapsed heavily.

'Long live the marquis! He's even better than the Lord of the Ruffians!'

There was wild shouting and applause. Amédée wiped his face, raised his arms to acknowledge his friends, and retrieved his frock coat.

'Why are you hiding?' he asked his steward, who was lurking in the shadows

'Out of humility, Monsieur.'

Amédée retied his cravat. 'The things you make me do, my good Louis-Désiré! Next time, find us a more peaceful address.'

'I was sure you would like this one, Monsieur.'

'Oh, I do. In fact, on reflection, I shall certainly be back. But we have to humour our dear baron. How is he, by the way?'

Marius, supported by Clémence and Gammy Leg, was babbling incoherently, his eyes rolled upwards and his mouth dribbling. In his torpor, he vaguely understood that Amédée had got him out of a tight corner. 'I . . . I am much obliged to you,' he stammered.

The marquis assumed an expression of painful modesty. 'Let's take him home, my dear,' he said to Clémence.

'Why not take him to my apartment?' suggested Clémence brightly. 'The baron's condition requires close attention.'

'I expected no less of you.' He put his hat on, wrapped himself in his cloak and walked to the exit.

The cool air sobered Marius. In Amédée's tilbury, he searched in his pocket and could not find Cosette's crystal.

'Have you lost this?' asked Clémence, brandishing the stone. 'If you want it back, you'll have to look for it here!' she cried, sticking out her chest and slipping the crystal into her bodice.

Marius had neither the will nor the energy to resist her. Once they were at her apartment in the Rue Transnonnain, he followed her meekly like a child. Clémence pulled him into her bedroom and sat him down on a love seat.

'I love stones, too,' she said, taking off her cloak and hat. 'I want you to shower me with gifts, my little baron.'

As she spoke, she undressed before him, lasciviously undulating her pelvis, until she was completely naked except for her shoes.

'Here, have your stone back,' she said, putting the crystal in Marius's hand. 'But in exchange I want kisses and lots of gifts!'

The flickering candle flame cast shadows and moving lights on her body. Marius admired the beauty of her high, pear-shaped breasts, her firm and slender thighs, her rounded hips. He undressed slowly. By the time he was naked except for his shirt, Clémence's hunger for him was so great that she ripped it from his body with her bare hands.

'You're mine, Marius Pontmercy,' she whispered, as she led him to the bed. 'Mine alone.'

3

In the weeks that followed, Marius continued to visit all the fashionable venues as well as all the disreputable places in the capital. He maintained that his moral decline was the one thing in his life at which he had succeeded brilliantly and he wasn't wrong.

'The mind takes pride in its own ruin,' Louis de Vergne had said to him one evening.

Marius had smiled, finding Louis de Vergne sententious.

On the morning of New Year's Day, Marius had returned from Clémence de Lavely's apartment to find the table still laid in the dining room of the house in the Rue Plumet. In Marius's place setting, wedged between a champagne flute and a wine glass, was a little card signed *Cosette*. On it, in black ink, were the words: *Happy New Year, light of my life*. Marius had not had the heart to find Cosette. He had gone to his room and sobbed in silence. His light was more like darkness and Louis de Vergne's pronouncement was not so wide of the mark.

On Amédée's advice, Marius took up boxing and improved his fencing. His outward appearance belied his inner reality. Clémence accompanied him everywhere, as beautiful as a painting by Clouet, constantly flashing him tender smiles, which revealed a strictly premeditated passion. He had already given her a pearl necklace, a cashmere cape and a felt hat with a low brim and silk trimmings. She had everything she could ask for.

'I love you so much,' she would say to Marius, considering that she had every right, since she had every need.

Inspiring more desire than she chose to satisfy, Clémence prided herself on always telling the truth, but all she meant by that was that she rarely told pointless lies. She loved only what was showy. All the rest was simulation.

When Marius confessed to her that he was merely newly rich, she replied that only the word 'rich' mattered. She would smile, not very sincerely, for experience had taught her that all men were disagreeable when they were satisfied. And for him the memory of the happiness he had felt on meeting Clémence was more precious than any happiness he might feel in being with her now, for he found the present impossible to grasp and only felt comfortable in the past.

'How could we possibly be in love?' he asked her one evening in the Café de Paris. 'We're too happy.'

He was not wrong. He did not listen to her and she only rarely understood him. That aside, they got on perfectly.

One morning, at the horse market between the Rue Duméril and the Boulevard de l'Hôpital, Marius bought a chestnut horse with a snow-white flash on the forehead, its head held high, its forelimbs hot-tempered. He dreamed of imitating the men of fashion he had seen at Auteuil, the Rond de Mortemart, or the Champ-de-Mars. He had become so frivolous that his rare moments of seriousness disconcerted Clémence.

'I don't want you to lie to me any more,' she said to him.

Marius looked alarmed. 'But I don't lie to you, my dear. It's simply that I'm sincere in many different and paradoxical ways. What do you call that?'

'Duplicity, Marius. I want you to love me truly.'

'I do love you.'

'I don't think so. You're too impetuous.'

'That may be because life is nothing but a succession of brief moments that drag on and on. All I'm doing is speeding up the process.'

Clémence grew animated. 'That's why I am reproaching you. You seem to think of me as a poor little thing who must immediately surrender to your every whim. Whatever happened to the sincerity and the delicacy you displayed when we first spoke?'

Marius was just then paying the horse merchant – four hundred francs, including the English-style harness. He gave Clémence a sidelong smile. 'I suppose you are referring to the first night we spent together, on New Year's Eve?'

Clémence gave him a withering look. 'You are making yourself almost as disagreeable as your friend Amédée, Baron. But you lack his style.'

Marius slapped his forehead, like a man who has just remembered something important. 'I'll try to do better next time,' he replied.

If he was not insensitive to Clémence's charms, Clémence felt no love for him, only a sort of maternal affection that she could hardly explain to herself. Falsely passionate, falsely gay, she was of an age that allowed her to lend rather than give fully of herself.

'You're a child,' was her final comment. 'To have character, it's not enough to copy from one's friends. Trust a woman who has reached her thirties.'

Marius's day was divided between the time he spent with Clémence, who incited him to seek distractions from his bitterness, and the time he spent at Lord Seymour's fencing school. His clothes were impeccable. His muscular legs, with their slender ankles, were tightly clad in black trousers, and his elegant feet were covered with openwork silk stockings and polished low-fronted shoes without heels. The ends of his white quilted waistcoat showed beneath his black tail coat. His neck was enfolded in a cravat of black satin, and his naturally wavy hair was topped with an opera hat. It was quite evident that these trousers, buttoned above the ankle and as close-fitting as a knitted vest, this coat with its elegant cut and gracefully falling tails, and this quilted English waistcoat with carved gold buttons came from the shop of a renowned tailor on the Boulevard de Gand. This was true chic.

He felt even more chic parading on horseback on the Boulevard, proud of his chestnut, his spurs, his red velvet caparison and his cane with its curved tip, which he held against his thigh like a cavalryman's carbine. Anglomania was all the rage and was driving out the cultivated French style of horsemanship, the horses with their buttoned bridles, all the skills of the old school. To adopt this English manner, or rather its parody, Marius would sit with his body bent double, and his legs far forward in the saddle and wide apart. He looked ridiculous. To add the finishing touch to the picture, he would read the stud-farm newspaper, *Le Journal des haras*, and would meet Amédée, Louis de Vergne, Eugène Sue and other lovers of the turf for steeplechases and private tournaments. They would bet crazy sums – from two hundred to five hundred francs – all from Marius's pocket.

A society already existed to improve horse breeding in France, and now, in its wake, the Jockey Club had just been founded. Lord Seymour and Eugène Sue were already members. Towards the end of January Marius toyed with the idea of joining. The subscription was a mere four hundred francs for the first year, three hundred the following years.

'Derisory sums,' judged Marius who, as time passed, juggled with money without a care for the future. 'Don't you think so, dear friend?'

'Absolutely,' Eugène Sue assured him, declaring that the atmosphere of the club was very merry and that its members indulged in all sorts of eccentricities and practical jokes.

It all sounded great fun, and Marius was getting impatient. One day, at the Café de Paris, Eugène Sue informed him that Alfred de Musset, despite the backing of Prince Belgiojoso and the Count of Alton-Shee, had been refused membership of the club.

'It's positively hilarious,' declared Eugène, aping Amédée, delighted at the misfortunes of the sickly little Romantic, who had been knocking around with the awful George Sand, and whom he considered a mere flunky of Romanticism. 'Romieu and myself are the only men of letters to have been accepted into the Jockey Club,' he added.

Marius's face dropped, for he, too, considered himself a man of letters. 'Meaning what?'

'Simply, my dear Marius, that you'll never become a member.'

Marius took offence at this, surprised that money couldn't buy everything. He swore to himself to go even further in excess. He would not give a fig for respect, which in any case was merely a qualified form of praise.

'I quite agree with you,' approved Amédée, who had also been refused entry to the Jockey Club. 'We'll demolish those nonentities. We'll be so devil-may-care, it'll be a slap in the face to all of them.'

To do this, Amédée and his friends made the most of what they had. They were seen everywhere – at the Bal des Variétés, where silly old women and fishwives queued at the ticket offices, at the theatres on the Left Bank, where they watched grim spectacles that Marius took a wicked pleasure in savaging in the pages of *Le National*. One evening at the Odéon Amédée caused a scandal by introducing a young woman dressed only in a boa and gloves. Marius did not greatly appreciate this dubious joke, for the young woman was none other than Clémence.

'Did you like my costume?' she asked him later in her apartment, her eyes full of insolence tinged with pride.

'Absolutely,' replied Marius, making an effort not to lose his temper. 'At least it allowed me to see your legs. They're so slender, you could take a foot bath in a twin-barrelled rifle. Is it your age or simply a miracle diet?'

That evening Marius got back to the Rue Plumet very early, leaving his horse in the stable of his illustrious neighbour, Henri de la Roche-Dragon. The art of being disagreeable suited him perfectly.

*

Marius had abandoned both Cosette and politics. He carefully avoided his friend Frédéric, though sometimes in the corridors of *Le National* he passed Armand Carrel, for whom he predicted, not without insufferable grandiloquence, a fine future within the Republican party. Armand Carrel, a true libertarian, shrugged his shoulders. There was no doubt, he thought, that the young man had changed a lot.

The beginning of February saw Marius and his friends visiting other places, even though they invariably finished the evening at the Idalie or one of the dance halls in the Opéra district. They would put in a brief appearance at the Maine gate, an area full of open-air taverns, not to mention the fashionable Bal Tonnelier, which was famed for its restaurant, which could seat two hundred, a garden and an orchestra that played lively quadrilles, and then end up in the little theatres on the Boulevard de Belleville.

Louis de Vergne, Robert d'Androisy, Henri de la Roche-Dragon and Marius followed faithfully wherever Amédée led. Amédée was like a heaven-sent master of ceremonies.

'Amédée has everything I like,' Marius confided in Louis de Vergne one evening at the Café Riche. 'A passion for freedom that enchants me, a freedom of behaviour that I subscribe to, and an insolence of expression that delights me.'

'Take care, Marius,' replied Louis, anxious to temper the other's enthusiasm. 'I know Amédée well. He's a man of whim. To be so misanthropic at his age means that he has loved people too much in the past, however little he loves them now.'

'Do I detect a hint of jealousy, Louis?'

Louis did not flinch at the question, however offensive he might have thought it. 'My dear Marius, love exists only among adolescents and the idle – the former because they have nothing to lose, the latter because they have nothing left to gain. But I'm quite unable to tell you where our friend Amédée stands.'

'Do you love him?'

'That is one of my failings. The most amusing part of it is that he can count on me in a way that I can't count on him.'

'That is amusing,' said Marius appreciatively. 'But I think that bitterness is leading you astray, Louis.'

That very evening, Amédée invited his friends to the Idalie, the underground dance hall in the Opéra district which was notorious as the haunt of pimps, prostitutes and dealers in forgeries. The fact that Amédée invited every last one of his friends and acquaintances, even the villains, could mean only one thing – for once, he was going to pay.

Eugène Sue was one of the guests. He was accompanied by a brown-skinned young woman with black hair held back as tightly as a whip, the shape of her face and the brightness of her eyes betraying her Oriental origins.

'Her name is Rebecca, like a character in a novel by Walter Scott,' Eugène Sue told Amédéc as soon as he saw him. 'And she doesn't speak a word of our beautiful language.'

The marquis ordered punch. 'In that case,' he said, ironically, 'you'll be able to dispense with all those boring preliminaries, my dear fellow, and she won't be tempted to sue.'

Eugène nodded, perceptive enough to have noticed the pun, but man of the world enough not to pick up the gauntlet and to enjoy an insult that for once did not come from him. 'I see you're on brilliant form, dear Marquis. But look, here's Monsieur de la Battut. I'm sure he'll appreciate the extent of your mockery.'

There was little likelihood that the man who had just entered the dance hall, followed by a mass of fashionable young men, could ever pass unnoticed.

'Hello, men!' he exclaimed hoarsely. 'And too bad if I'm wrong!'

He was a tall, robust fellow with a coarse manner and a gaudy style of dress. His hat was tilted exaggeratedly over one ear, revealing a tuft of russet hair. He pulled up a table next to that of Amédée and his friends, greeted Eugène Sue and sat down noisily. While Amédée studied him from head to foot with a mocking air, the man buttonholed Eugène Sue and, using his voice to full dramatic effect, talked loudly about the forth-coming Mardi Gras celebrations.

Marius leaned discreetly towards Louis de Vergne. 'Who is that queer customer?'

Louis de Vergne put his hand in front of his mouth. 'He's the carnival king, the prince of criminal relations, the god of the people and the cut-throats.'

'But what's his name?'

'Why, Charles de la Battut. The poor man's Lord Seymour. The Lord of the Ruffians.'

Marius examined this spectacle more closely. With his thumbs hooked inside his multi-coloured waistcoat, the man was holding forth about Thiers and Guizot as if they were old acquaintances of his, and predicting imminent revolution. From time to time he would smooth his red moustache between his thumb and his forefinger, or else lightly touch his pink cravat, with its pin as big as a bottle stopper, or his short frock coat with its large check pattern or his sky-blue trousers with their black velvet stripes. He looked like a puppet, an impression accentuated by the twitch which occasionally furrowed his face.

'Who wants to arm-wrestle me?' he asked in a powerful voice, having exhausted the subject of politics.

Eugène Sue, with a wink at his Oriental friend, pounded on the table with his fist. 'I accept the challenge!'

'So do I!' added Amédée.

There were cries, cheers, applause. The din was staggering. The motley crowd bore little resemblance to the delighted but starchy crowd that squeezed into the other dance halls of the Opéra district. These were the real people.

'Every would-be villain in Paris,' said Louis de Vergne to Marius, 'swears blind he's met Monsieur de la Battut more than a thousand times in every tavern in town and imagines he applauded him one carnival evening. The problem is that he gets confused with Lord Seymour.'

Marius once again looked at La Battut, who had taken off his frock coat but had kept his hat on his head and a cigar in his mouth. Now he downed his glass of punch in one gulp and bit the glass until it shattered.

'Bare arms!' he cried to Eugène Sue.

He subjected another glass to the same fate and with the back of his hand made two jagged heaps on the table. The first heap he spread to the left of Eugène Sue's right arm and the other to the left of his own right arm. 'Ready?'

'Ready,' replied Eugène Sue, while Rebecca looked on darkly.

When the two protagonists took up position, a murmur of anticipation grew from the people gathered around. Eugène Sue was panting like a pair of bellows. He pushed, he forced – but in vain.

The spectators' breathing grew faster. It was like a drum roll. La Battut was sitting bolt upright, his body completely still, his left hand flat on the table. All at once, he let out a roar like that of a wild animal, and slammed Eugène Sue's forearm down onto the heap of broken glass. Eugène let out a cry of pain, leapt back and in a daze contemplated the red streaks on his forearm.

'Bravo! Bravo!' cried the onlookers, who had ceased panting.

A good loser despite his disappointment, Eugène Sue congratulated La Battut and held out his arm to Rebecca, who hastily bandaged it with a large transparent veil.

La Battut was as red as a beetroot. Amédée sat down opposite the ruddy-faced bull and took up his position. The panting resumed. Although his resistance was greater, the marquis finally gave way under the pressure. There were more bravos and yells. La Battut saluted his troops, rolled his shoulders and ordered a drink. But he was rubbing his biceps, as if they were numb.

'I want to try, too,' offered Marius.

His friends exchanged knowing looks, as if to say: The poor baron has already been thrashed by the innkeeper of the Clan Destin and now he's asking for more.

The two men sat down. Before placing his arm on the table, Marius smiled at his adversary, all the while observing him. It had not escaped his notice that La Battut was weakening. The man had a squat, somewhat arched body, a back that threatened to break the bars of the chair, massive shoulders, a strangler's hands and the face of an unfrocked priest. He was breathing heavily and beads of sweat had formed on his brow. Marius had noted that La Battut sat bolt upright – too upright – at the moment of greatest effort, a position bound to cause cramp. He had also observed that La Battut never began the hostilities first, which allowed him both to test and to tire his adversary. Marius would therefore attack. He had strong arms, bold movements and formidable muscle tone.

The matter was settled in the twinkling of an eye, so to speak. La Battut had not expected such a lightning thrust. He felt a burning pain in his shoulder and let go at once. No sound emerged from his mouth as his forearm was gashed by the shards of glass. A hushed silence filled the room.

La Battut examined his arm, collected a little blood on the tip of his forefinger and licked it with a savage rapture. 'I definitely prefer rum!' he declared, an outrageous statement that was greeted with gales of laughter. He waited to make sure that Marius's friends were busy with their own affairs, having fun and gossiping, then gave his victorious adversary a look in which admiration was tinged with a kind of distrust. 'So,' he asked him in the middle of the hubbub, 'Horatius has vanquished Curiatius?'

'I beg your pardon?'

'Only joking. But allow me to say, my friend, that you're not one of them.' He turned to the others. 'Gentlemen, I suggest we go gambling at the Palais-Royal! Fortune awaits us there!'

And so the members of this valiant troop swept into the eight gaming rooms of the Galerie Valois, above the Café Borel, where it was possible to lose 1,500,000 francs in a single evening. Intoxicated by this speed, Marius ran from one room to another, in each of which there were no less than six roulette tables. He won two hundred francs at *biribi* and La Battut the same sum at *trente et quarante*.

Then, afraid that the night would end too soon, Amédée, La Battut and the others went on to the Café des Aveugles, a strange place if ever there was one, where men who looked like provincial pharmacists indulged in feverish fondling before an orchestra of five blind musicians.

At about two in the morning La Battut stood up, straight as a die, and announced that he was leaving. At the same time, and not without a certain elegance, he invited his friends to meet him again a week later for the descent of the Courtille.

'You'll be my guests for Mardi Gras!' he said to the assembly. 'And guests of the Lord of the Ruffians are allowed to enter his coach! I'm counting on you!'

He turned once more to Marius and lowered his voice. 'I insist, you are not one of them, Monsieur. It's a pleasure to have made your acquaintance. Until we meet again at the carnival.'

Marius felt decidedly uncomfortable as he watched La Battut walk away. What on earth had he meant? Why, when he spoke, had he made a face that distorted his lower lip? Did the fellow think he was some kind of prophet?

He crossed and uncrossed his legs, feeling a twisted pleasure in his own irritation. For some time now, despite all his attempts to evade the problem, he had been continually asking himself the same questions, at once relieved and furious to see his instinct atrophied by so much mental speculation. But the questions would not go away. So is this what so excites people? he would ask himself. To taste forbidden pleasures in contact with the lowest, vilest creatures on this earth? To copy their rites, their customs, their habits? To take delight in stooping to their level? To imitate their language, eat out of the same troughs, get drunk with them, and gain a fleeting impression of belonging to their world and learning something useful from such a noxious and corrupt education?

'What are you thinking about?' Amédée asked him. 'Why so peevish? Are you missing Clémence's love?'

Marius's nostrils quivered, as if something astonishing were about to emerge from his mouth. 'I believe in passion more than in love,' he declared. 'But even more in friendship than in passion.'

Amédée made a satisfied little pout. His hand lingered on Marius's. 'And what about Clémence, you devil? Don't you know she loves you?'

In his private attempts to adapt to circumstances and live a comfortable life, it seemed to him that the solidity of the relationship between Marius and Clémence guaranteed his lifestyle, and he had no desire to see this guarantee disappear.

'Cosette also loves me,' protested Marius, as if defending himself.

Amédée clapped his hands with an air of dismay. 'One doesn't prevent the other, my dear friend! And if that's all, leave it to me – I'll console your charming wife and reassure her about the depths of your feelings.'

He spoke reluctantly, his body thrown back, his reserve composed of both modesty and dissimulation. Marius did not dare meet his friend's eye. He was thinking again of what Frédéric Rivolier had told him.

January 1834 had been icy cold. During those long winter weeks, when the days were more like nights, Cosette had busied herself as best she could. She saw little of Marius, and when she did, she tried to hide her anxiety in affectionate solicitude. She never upset him, never nagged him and was only critical to protect him from himself. Whenever he brushed her aside with that air he had of putting himself knowingly in the wrong, she tried to believe that it was merely a passing aberration. If she chose not to play the part of victim, it was because she refused to let her heartache overwhelm her. Strangely, in discovering Marius's weaknesses, she discovered her own. The most miserable part of her childhood came back to her occasionally in fragments, revealing how thoughtless her adolescence had been. But that was her father's fault. He had wanted to protect her – protect her, above all, from the vanity of men, from their cruelty, their inconstancy, their selfishness and jealousy, their mediocrity.

Having been so protected, Cosette had remained credulous. With a husband like Marius, any other woman would have taken a lover. But she was not like other women. She would seize on anything, however small, to distract herself from what she was afraid to acknowledge as resentment. This beautiful young woman, who was only twenty, saw her dreams gradually falling to pieces, but she still held fast in the eye of the storm. Her memories were urging her not to surrender – memories of a wonderful father, the most honourable of men, whom she had, to her shame, neglected for a time, and memories of a husband who was equally wonderful, a proud and haughty Daphnis, perhaps a little too proud, too haughty, but whom she continued to idolize and idealize. All that was worth fighting for. She might be a frail young woman, but she had energy and determination, and she felt that luck was on her side. She had, too, some inestimable assets left her by her father – honesty, integrity, rectitude.

On the principle that there is always someone more disadvantaged than oneself, Cosette found refuge in religion and good works. Every day she attended vespers at Saint-Sulpice. The parish priest, Father Rillet, was an excellent man who had saved many lives during the cholera epidemic of 1832. It was said that he had gone up and down the banks of the Seine with a handcart, helping those who were trying to commit suicide. Even the prefect of police, Monsieur Gisquet, held him in the highest esteem.

'An exceptional being,' he would tell his colleagues. 'I am always available to him at any hour of the day or night.'

This exceptional man fascinated Cosette. Sometimes she would tell him that all she wanted was to withdraw from the world to a convent. Whenever she weakened like this, he would comfort her.

One day in the confessional she spoke to a man she thought was Father Rillet. 'Father,' she said, 'it is I, Cosette Pontmercy. I would like to ask your advice, but I must—'

She did not finish her sentence. A voice answered that was both harsh and filled with emotion and she realized that she had been talking to the wrong person.

She left the confessional and saw on the church flagstones a dark and massive, almost menacing, shadow. The broad-brimmed hat, the frock coat's flaps and the enormous cane seemed disproportionate. She looked up to see a man with an austere face standing before her. She nearly accused him of being an impostor.

'Who are you, Monsieur?'

The man said nothing because at that moment Father Rillet came striding towards them. In his easygoing way, the priest introduced him to Cosette.

'Monsieur Verjat was simply picking up the chasuble that was lying there. You know how scatterbrained I am, whereas Monsieur Verjat is extremely methodical.'

Cosette shook hands with the man, who had a grey beard and wore a brown frock coat.

'Monsieur Verjat is a great help to me,' Father Rillet continued. 'He takes classes in the penal code for our young students and even deals with the administration of the parish. As God's my witness, I can't do without him.'

Later, in the sacristy, Father Rillet told Cosette that Verjat had known great misfortune and so had chosen to live henceforth according to reasoned instinct.

'Before that, on my advice he went to Paray-le-Monial, a village in the Brionnais in Burgundy, where he lived as an anchorite. Contemplation brought him closer to the paths of the Lord and familiarized him with the customs of the Benedictines. Sometimes, to tease him – though I never succeed – I tell him he was a spy, as a priest is and so he could be a priest as a spy is.'

Cosette was surprised. 'Monsieur Verjat is not a man of the Church, then?'

'No, but he could be. He used to occupy an important position in the administration of justice. Let's just say that he was converted like St Paul on the road to Damascus. Having spent much of his life watching and waiting, he now wants nothing more than to meditate and commune with his thoughts. His vision of things may sometimes be excessive, but it's impossible to ignore. Frankly, the man's humility never ceases to amaze me. I've often urged him to write his memoirs, but he's always refused. It's as if he no longer wanted to share anything with the living. To the best of my knowledge, he has neither wife nor child, nor friends. Even his name is assumed. But he's a good man.'

Cosette thought of her father. As she left the church, by one of those coincidences destiny has in store she came across Monsieur Verjat again. They talked of Burgundy, the Song of Songs, people who change their lives. Monsieur Verjat, who was often cold and abrupt with people, proved talkative and quite friendly. Cosette and he walked a little between the church and the seminary of Saint-Sulpice. Passing a stall, Verjat bought an orange and a stick of barley sugar for Cosette, whose big, porcelain-blue eyes he found quite disturbing.

It was late afternoon when they parted. They promised to meet again the following day.

'Baroness, I have a confession to make,' said Verjat just before leaving, with that grave air that so impressed those to whom he spoke, turning his deep, dark eyes on her. 'I was quite startled when I heard your name in the church. It reminded me of a past I thought was dead and buried. The name Pontmercy is not unknown to me.'

'Where do you know it from?'

'Soon I shall tell you.'

But in the following days Monsieur Verjat offered no further revelations. Cosette and he would walk in the Luxembourg Gardens and she would talk about her father. Verjat's gaze grew more intense on hearing this or that detail. He rarely answered Cosette's questions and would lower his head with obvious resignation whenever they passed other people. Near the exit of the Théâtre de l'Odéon, towards the Rue de Vaugirard, he would regularly buy two oranges from a street trader, peel them with precise and meticulous gestures, using a horn-handled pocket knife and removing the peel in a single zigzag movement, and give one to Cosette. Once, when Cosette alluded to men with a sense of duty, he cut his thumb and almost lost his temper.

'There is nothing worse than people who claim to be inspired by integrity, conviction, or a sense of duty. The quest for absolute purity is dangerous, Baroness. People who seek it go about their fanatical mission sincerely and with Machiavellian candour, and in doing so are responsible for the worst excesses. Think of Saint-Just, Torquemada, Fouquier-Tinville.'

'But what about loyalty?' objected Cosette.

Verjat laughed as he finished peeling the orange. 'There is no loyalty for people like that, Baroness. They would kill their own fathers and mothers if they thought it would help their ideas to triumph. Let me tell you a story. You know the church of Saint-Sulpice? Well, it was in that wedding cake that Camille and Lucile Desmoulins were married, with their friend Maximilien Robespierre as a witness. A few years later, in 1794, friend Robespierre sent Camille to the scaffold, because he thought that the nation was paramount and that Camille, who in his eyes was too indulgent and too close to Danton, was no longer faithful to his ideals. There's the loyalty of such people.' Terribly pale, he handed the orange to Cosette. 'Some people steal a loaf of bread and are sentenced to thirty years' hard labour, while others rob thirty million Frenchmen and are sentenced to every honour. I know whereof I speak.'

Impressed by his tone, which was like the Commendatore's in *Don*

Giovanni, Cosette ate her orange quarters in silence. Fear and astonishment crossed her lovely face.

Stopping abruptly, she turned to Monsieur Verjat. 'Why do you refer to experiences that you have had but that you never explain? Could it be that you're deceiving your present with your past, Monsieur Verjat?'

Verjat crossed his hands behind his back. 'The good dream of what the bad do, Baroness. That's the way it is. We all lead double lives. It's a privilege for the artist and a curse for the ordinary man. One has to get used to it.'

Cosette persisted. 'Why do you so seldom give direct answers to questions, Monsieur Verjat?'

Verjat uncrossed his hands and took Cosette gently by the arm. Without confronting her eyes and her disarming smile, he walked her to the exit from the garden.

'What do you want to know?' he asked calmly. 'It's a terrible thing to know too much. In life, our words are improvisations and our actions careless mistakes that end up by becoming habits. Fate being the distraction of the gods, I distract myself by evading questions that I never asked myself in the past. We are in the hands of the improbable, are we not, my dear Cosette?'

It was the first time Verjat had called Cosette by her Christian name. She was pleased, and vowed not to trouble him any more with questions which he answered evasively. 'It's funny,' she remarked nonetheless, 'you always know whereof you speak, and I never do.'

Out of the corner of his eye, Verjat had seen her pearly teeth gleaming between her rosy lips. He liked Cosette's tenacity. She had finally made him smile.

Cosette's conversations with Monsieur Verjat gave her renewed energy. She placed tokens of her love around the house, which were designed to make Marius stop and think. They might be flowers arranged in the shape of hearts, two nightdresses hanging on a peg with the sleeves tied together so that they seemed to be embracing, or that little note she had placed between the glasses on New Year's Eve. There was also the rock crystal. The other day she had taken it from Marius's pocket, wrapped it in silk and put it back in its place. Between the stone and the silk, she had slipped a little note: *Part of my heart is contained in this crystal, Marius. Keep it by you. Crystal has magic properties.*

Marius had said nothing, but Cosette knew that he kept the crystal in the pocket of his trousers or his waistcoat. Even though his silence frightened her, she still believed their love was eternal.

Frédéric Rivolier, who visited Cosette twice a week, usually late in the morning, advised her not to appear too moderate.

'It's better to react, Cosette. Moderation isn't the sign of a vigorous human nature. With moderation, which is close to patience, you gradually slip into monotony, you allow life to do things to you and you don't do anything to life.'

This remark cut her to the quick. 'You needn't worry about me, Frédéric. You know me, I'm not always so moderate, and when I am it's not for long.'

Cosette's relationship with Frédéric was untainted by any amorous ambiguity. She appreciated his frankness, his vitality, and even his somewhat too epicurean gusto, though she would sometimes rebuke him in the kindest possible way for his two excesses – drinking and revolutionary zeal. She would call him a rascal and a Jacobin, which made him roar with laughter.

One day towards the end of autumn, he had suggested the idea of creating a winter garden. Cosette thought the idea excellent and with the help of an old gardener and Madeleine, her maid, she set to work.

'I want to prove to Marius that I'm not as thick-headed and as inactive as he thinks,' she told Frédéric. 'Once he even said I was a silly little thing.'

'You're nothing like that, Cosette. He's relegated you to that role.'

Cosette had looked at him severely. 'Don't be unfair to Marius, Frédéric, he's your friend. He may not be completely wrong. He takes me for a spoilt little bourgeois girl without imagination because that's the side of me he's seen most often. I don't suppose I surprise him any more. The day that I begged him not to call me Cosette any more, but Euphrasie – my true first name – he laughed at me wickedly and called me a pretentious lump.'

Frédéric lifted his eyes to heaven. 'For once, I agree with him. Cosette is a very pretty name. I don't know why you want to change it. Euphrasie sounds like a flirt and a schemer.' He assumed a more serious tone. 'Marius idealizes you so much that he no longer knows how to talk to you simply. Do you know what you should do? You should make him jealous.'

Turned slightly away from him, one hand on her hip and the other in her hair, Cosette smiled impishly. 'I've thought of it.'

He burst out laughing.

'Enough joking,' continued Cosette. 'Men are so naive and vain. Who knows, one day I may show you the letter the Marquis d'Iguerande sent me. Can you imagine? On the evening I saw him for the first time, he thought I was smiling at him intentionally. What a conceited man!'

'Oh, don't talk to me about him!' growled Frédéric. 'To think that Marius has fallen into the clutches of that ridiculous, self-infatuated puppet!'

Cosette turned and pointed to the clematis-covered arbour at the bottom of the garden. 'The Marquis d'Iguerande reminds me of that clematis. He's an arrant hypocrite who's taking advantage of Marius's friendship.'

Frédéric stamped his foot. 'The Marquis d'Iguerande? Sometimes I wonder where he got that title! Believe me, if ever the opportunity presents itself, I'll put that yellow glove in his place as he deserves!'

One morning, Frédéric arrived at the Rue Plumet carrying a potted rhododendron. He stood at the entrance to the winter garden, admiring it. It was built in the form of an arch, dense and verdant, with glass walls and a trellis fence composed of green squares and diamonds. Cosette was proud of it. Who, seeing this splendid achievement, could still claim that Baroness Pontmercy was a silly little girl incapable of lifting her hands to do anything?

On the outside of the garden, ivy and rambling roses wound through the trellises. Inside, the greenhouse was divided in two by a fence of bamboo and lemon trees provided by Frédéric, as well as by a row of camellias dotted with white and purple flowers. A wicker wing chair stood beneath a glossy fig tree.

Frédéric greeted Cosette and Madeleine from a distance, then entered the greenhouse. Seeing Cosette, with her apron and fingers dirty with earth, he folded his arm behind him with a stunned air. 'My dear, you will soon have labourer's hands,' he joked.

'Is that for me?' asked Cosette, seeing the rhododendron.

'For your garden.'

Cosette threw her arms around Frédéric's neck and kissed him on both cheeks.

'Please save your strength,' he cried, pretending to protect himself. 'Who are you trying to outshine?' He assumed a more serious tone. 'May I remind you that we still have one more appointment. You hadn't forgotten?'

Cosette was already starting to replant the rhododendron in a large pot. 'No, Frédéric, I hadn't forgotten. But, as you see, I'm content to follow the precepts of Monsieur Voltaire. I am cultivating my garden. It's you who recommended that I read him.'

'Yes, indeed, but even so . . . It's been two months,' he went on in a low voice. You ought to be reassured by now.'

'About not having cholera or not being pregnant?'

Cosette had asked the question in an innocuous tone. But her worries had been real enough when the first symptoms had appeared – fever, cramps, nausea, vomiting. Frédéric had immediately reassured her. Cholera was fatal in twelve to thirty-six hours.

'In 1832, there were twenty thousand deaths in Paris, and more than a hundred thousand in the whole of France—'

'You have a strange way of reassuring me!' Cosette had found the strength to joke.

But if it was not cholera, it must be a child. As she was feeling exhausted, Frédéric had quickly taken her to a doctor he knew of, near the Odéon theatre. That was the day that Marius had spotted them together in a fiacre.

'And he started imagining I don't know what,' said Frédéric.

'I haven't told him anything,' Cosette said, 'but I've been feeling nauseous again.'

Frédéric turned on his heels, aping the courtiers of the Tuileries. 'It may no longer be for the same reasons.'

'What do you mean?' asked Cosette.

He took a step forward, and stroked a glossy leaf on the lemon tree. 'I've made an appointment for next week with Dr Taburin in the Rue Taitbout, Cosette,' he finally replied. 'He's an eminent scientist, who is attentive and scrupulous. We can count on his discretion.' He looked at his watch, and slapped his thigh. 'I must leave you.'

'Already?'

'I have a meeting in the Rue Dauphine.'

'More plots?'

'They aren't plots, Cosette. The future of France is at stake. All this inequality can't last.'

'I suppose not, but do take care, my friend.'

Frédéric kissed the hand Cosette held out to him, and lifted his hat to Madeleine, who was busy tending the begonias with yellow calyxes.

'Long live the Republic!' he cried cheekily.

Cosette put on her leather gloves. As Frédéric disappeared behind the railings, she shook her head tenderly. 'I'm worried about him,' she said to Madeleine. 'He's so unyielding, so generous with himself and his ideas.'

Madeleine placed her secateurs on the ground and wiped her hands on her check apron. 'Oh, Monsieur Rivolier can take care of himself, Madame. Like all young men of his age, he needs to get worked up about a cause. But since the July Revolution, we've seen how little comes from all of that. Nothing will happen.'

'May God hear you, Madeleine. There are so many alarming rumours. And so much violence. That left-wing deputy, Dulong, I think his name was – well, he fought a duel with General Bugeaud and was killed by a shot in the head.'

Madeleine shrugged. 'Well, I think that Bugeaud is cashing in on all sides. Like the others. Bonapartist yesterday, royalist today. And tomorrow? Politics are a bad thing, Madame. A dish fried in rancid fat for the use of the dishonest, begging your pardon. If only people would mind their own business, everything would be fine.'

That said it all, and there was nothing to add.

Cosette's days were well organized. Madeleine and she spent a good part of the morning planting, watering, weeding, digging, hoeing, taking cuttings, and placing stakes. She came and went along the paths, armed with watering cans and shears, shod in thonged clogs, tending the tropical trees planted on slopes of heather, and the flowers that bloomed in the borders. The garden was a riot of colour, with tulips, narcissi, Christmas roses, amaryllis, mimosa, hyacinths and even cyclamen.

At the beginning, Marius had been scornful. 'Apart from petty arguments, women are incapable of constructing anything at all,' he mocked.

He seemed to regard his wife's occupations with commiseration, as if he were the final arbiter of everything that was done in the house.

When the work was finished, he was quite surprised. One day he had even left a palm tree in a red clay pot at the entrance to the greenhouse, though without saying a word.

Cosette reproached him about this. 'Don't you have anything to say?' she asked.

'People talk too much,' he replied in an ironic tone. 'They should only communicate in writing.'

So Cosette communicated with Marius in writing. But he did not reply. What more could she do? 'I'll finally get tired of it. And then . . .'

*

As Cosette was getting ready, the bell rang at the gate.

'Who could that be?' asked Madeleine, putting her dibble and weeding hoe away on a wooden shelf.

'I'll go, Madeleine,' said Cosette, asking her to go and brush her coat, as it was time for her visit to the Rue du Bac, where she performed good works with the Daughters of Charity.

Cosette put a shawl around her shoulders and walked to the garden gate, where she was surprised to see the Marquis d'Iguerande, tying the reins of his chestnut to the railings.

'What good wind brings you?' asked Cosette immediately, without losing her composure. 'Aren't you with my husband?'

'Your husband is becoming unbeatable at fencing, Madame. He's improving every day and seems also to be developing a taste for boxing. He's going to become a strapping fellow.'

Cosette had still not opened the gate. She moved closer to the railings, where Amédée seemed to be waiting for her. He was stroking the brow of his horse, which was shaking its head and making its bit jingle. He smiled affectedly, replaced his opera hat gracefully, arranged his hair and, with his tasselled cane under his arm, thrust his head between two railings and stared impudently at the young woman.

'Just imagine, I was passing and I said to myself: "My dear Amédée, it would be completely improper not to say hello to your best friend's wife." I hope I'm not disturbing you?'

Silently, but as if to explain what she was doing, Cosette held out her still gloved hands.

'And would it be possible to see those charming hands without those awful work gloves?' asked Amédée, well aware of his own daring.

Cosette removed one glove and passed her hand, still smelling of leather, through the bars. The marquis found its sudden whiteness and nakedness quite disturbing. He wiped it with a perfumed silk handkerchief, kissed it with as much respect as he had shown boorishness in wiping it and took another handkerchief, a cambric one this time, to wipe his forehead.

'Was my hand dirty?' asked Cosette.

The marquis stretched his neck in embarrassment. 'Please excuse me, but this horse is so lively that he occasionally causes me unbearable cold sweats. It's positively maddening.' He stood on tiptoe and turned his head from side to side, trying to catch a glimpse of the winter garden through the branches. 'So this is the work that Marius has told me so much about,' he said. 'It's positively superb. May I come closer to admire it?'

'As you wish, Marquis.'

Cosette let Amédée in and led him to the winter garden. As soon as they had entered, she took off her shawl and sat down in the wicker armchair.

'Admire away,' she said. 'Perhaps in future you might be prepared to admit that women can achieve things as well as any man.'

Amédée appeared to be outraged. 'Oh, but I've never claimed the contrary,' he defended himself, pretending to be in ecstasy over the plants, which meant no more to him than a lettuce in a vegetable garden. 'Your husband takes everything I say too literally. And if you consider my influence over him to be harmful, then just one word from you and I swear I will never see him again.'

Cosette stretched her arm along the back of the chair. 'Come, Monsieur, no big words or useless oaths. I forbid myself to intervene in any way in my husband's life, even if I do think he wastes too much time on people and places that are unworthy of him. I know Marius. Eventually he'll come to realize the emptiness of some activities. In that sense, I should rather thank you.'

Amédée tensed slightly. He looked around cautiously and drew closer to Cosette. The temperature in the greenhouse was warm and humid, making it necessary to dress lightly. Cosette was wearing a beautiful crimson skirt dotted with a black pattern, and a white shirt with a musketeer collar.

'To garden, one does not follow fashion,' she observed ironically.

This outfit, casual to say the least, seemed to fascinate Amédée. He stopped two paces from the chair and looked down at Cosette. Half lying, with one leg crossed over the other and one arm along the back of the chair, she was playing absent-mindedly with a necklace of grey pearls. Under the opulent crown of her golden hair, she looked supremely beautiful.

Amédée contemplated Cosette in silent wonder. He admired her mouth and her shy smile, which stamped her face with nostalgia. At twenty, she had the feeling she was a hundred. But the perfect oval of her face, the sheen of her hair, the bold blossoming of her bosom, seemed ageless.

What most seemed to hypnotize Amédée was that the second button of her shirt was undone, giving a tantalizing glimpse of the curve of one breast. And what a breast! Amédée had never seen one so perfect or so charming. He had always looked down on the pedants who loved to show off their ideas and their culture, the ecstasies into which mediocre people loved to go, but now he thought immediately of a bather by Ingres, and even of Delacroix's painting of Liberty leading the people. He watched in fascination as a bead of sweat rolled over one breast like a dewdrop. Though its raspberry tip was hidden from his eyes, the breast attracted him irresistibly.

'Madame,' he said, in a cracked voice, 'I wish I had the talent of Alfred de Musset to tell you how much you light this place with your beauty.'

A slight blush coloured Cosette's cheeks, and she raised her arm and quickly did up the button that had escaped her vigilance. Of course, it was flattering to her to know that she was desirable. For a brief moment she felt a twinge of doubt about herself and Marius and all that she had built. After all, since her husband no longer paid her any attention, why shouldn't she yield to Amédée's attentions, just as a game, as Frédéric had advised her? It would have been perfectly fair. Hadn't this world which she rubbed shoulders with taught her that a man began by loving love and ended up loving a woman, while the opposite was the case for a woman? But she could never deceive Marius. The idea of playing such a dangerous game repelled her. Neglected by Marius, courted by Amédée, she had the feeling that the former was not aware of what the latter was plotting. It was true that Marius was often out and made a thousand excuses to devote himself to what he claimed to be vitally important activities, but he always came back. That was why Cosette still only had eyes for him. She could never feel anything for Amédée, who was convinced of his own charms, underhand enough to betray his friends and tireless in pursuit of his aims.

'Yes, Madame,' continued Amédée. 'Call it boldness if you will, but I should have liked to write a poem dedicated to you.'

Cosette folded her arms, put her knees together and sat up straight. 'You mean . . . something similar to your letter?'

Standing there awkwardly on his long legs, which for once did not make him look like a fencer, and blushing with embarrassment, the marquis averted his gaze from Cosette and lifted his cane to contemplate the knob. 'It was madness, Madame, I should never have written it. Must I throw myself at your feet and implore your forgiveness?'

Cosette gave a shrill laugh. 'And make yourself even more ridiculous, Monsieur? Don't you think your reputation as a seducer would suffer?'

Amédée turned his eyes away and tapped his cane on the ground in pique. Cosette was nothing but a little madam who gave herself the airs of a great lady. Why, then, could he never find the right riposte to her cutting remarks? It was not usually so difficult to assert the pride and independence of his character. He would sprawl on round-backed ottomans, click his spurs in the faces of his wondering female admirers, and humble them with his ironic retorts. But not here. Here, he felt like a little boy who had been reprimanded and made to stand in the corner.

'You're right,' he said, with false good humour. 'That letter was ridiculous. In fact, the whole thing was ridiculous.'

He folded his arms and turned away.

Cosette had been thinking about the writing of the letter, its downstrokes and upstrokes which revealed a peacock nature she could never accept. She stood up and gave him a smile with a hint of benevolence. 'I must leave you, my friend.'

The humiliating show of emotion in her tone irritated the marquis even more. He took a few steps around the greenhouse, brushing against a thick plant with the end of his cane, parting the petals of a camellia with a jerky gesture. And he thought again of his letter, which he knew by heart.

Madame,

Will I one day have the signal joy of seeing your features again other than in my memories? Not wishing to be accused of being overly familiar in my dealings with you, yes, I confess it humbly, I nourish the impertinent hope that I shall see you again, be it only for a single moment. Perhaps you will be irritated with me for ever for this seraphic whim, for I consider you an angel astray in our earthly sphere, but I have no other excuse to offer than that of madness. As I wrote a few lines earlier, my letter will no doubt seem to you much too insolent because it is too sincere, and much too egotistical for not taking your own sincerity into account. The women one meets nowadays are often fickle and capricious, whose weapons are fearsome but whose sentiments are derisory. I belong to that world, it is true, but will you deign to throw a few sous of charity and indulgence into the suppliant hat of a poor devil overwhelmed by your beauty?

Your devoted friend and servant,
Amédée d'Iguerande

Frankly, the letter was perfect, there was nothing to take away or add. Amédée had no doubts about it. He stopped next to the door and waited for Cosette. He let her go out before him and bowed. 'The angels in heaven do not always have wings, but those in hell are often spiteful and cold,' he declared in a high-pitched voice.

Cosette made a vague gesture. 'Look at these clematis, Marquis. I was looking at them earlier with a friend, and we thought of you.'

Amédée's face lit up. 'Of me?'

'We remarked that they were very lively and that they clung everywhere.'

Amédée smothered an oath. This was too much. And, anyway, who was this friend she was talking about? 'The red-headed man I saw this afternoon, who looks like a groom?'

Cosette, who was walking towards the house, stopped and turned to face him. 'Marius's friend, Marquis. A true friend.'

'A friend you're seeing behind Marius's back?'

'Don't be vulgar, Marquis. Your finest quality ought to be clemency. A boundless clemency towards life and your fellow creatures.'

Amédée almost replied that he knew a woman called Clémence, of whose existence this little birdbrain would be very sad to learn, and that the same Clémence was enjoying some happy moments with her wretched husband. But he restrained himself. No sound came from his mouth. Cosette exasperated him. Now he saw her as she really was – by turns playful and sad, chaste and passionate, modest and provocative. A silly little goose, yet quite skilful at deflecting his shots. Only she had lit in his heart, dry and narrow as it was, an inextinguishable flame. For that reason, and that reason alone, he swore to himself that she would one day be his. He did not know how. But he would have her.

'Farewell, Marquis!' Cosette said to him, with a little offhand gesture.

Without replying, Amédée waved his cane in her direction. All right, then, farewell, my angel, he thought, but believe me, we'll meet again sooner than you think.

And he walked with an alert step to the gate, got into the saddle, and set off back to the Right Bank.

Cosette got ready for her daily excursion to the Rue du Bac and Saint-Sulpice. Before she left, she asked Madeleine to buy a loaf of bread and prepare dinner, consommé and fattened chicken and rice, and to lay the table.

'For two, Madame?'

'For two, Madeleine.'

Even when Marius did not dine at home, as was very often the case, Cosette had a place set for him – as if to ward off ill fortune.

She had got into the habit of dressing simply. Sometimes she would go by way of the Quai d'Orsay, past the house which had been d'Artagnan's, and sometimes she would take a melancholy stroll through the Luxembourg Gardens.

As she walked, for she always made the journey on foot, she thought not of that pathetic dandy Amédée d'Iguerande, but of Frédéric Rivolier. As she sometimes read *Le National*, on which Marius worked, she was up to date with the political situation. She had read that the Society for the Rights of Man had made contact with a number of workers' brotherhoods and associations that had not hitherto been involved in politics. The president of the Society, Godefroy Cavaignac, pulled no punches in his attacks on the government. In a manifesto he had had circulated throughout Paris, he declared that he wanted to spread Republican ideas among the working class and to recruit soldiers for the revolutionary battle from its ranks. He predicted demonstrations, riots and strikes. Cosette had read an extract from this manifesto which made her shudder. It claimed that France's population of 32,000,000 consisted of 500,000 sybarites, 1,000,000 happy slaves and 30,500,000 serfs. The manifesto also stated that although a monarchy could redistribute happiness and suffering, only a republic could dry up the source of the suffering and give each individual his share of joy and gladness. But why, wondered Cosette, would Frédéric get involved in this world of disturbances and violence, in which the names of Louis Blanc, Barbès, Blanqui and Fourier were increasingly being held up as examples?

Cosette's first stop was the Châtillon mansion. She delivered some clothes to the nuns of the Daughters of Charity, before continuing on her way to Saint-Sulpice.

There she never missed the opportunity to see Monsieur Verjat after vespers and ask him about the disastrous events that were looming. He was such a good man, such a sensible man. With his deep respect for other people, he reminded her in a way of her father.

'But who are these fanatics who start strikes, who've created a working-class press and who are campaigning for a reduction in working hours or an increase in wages?' she had asked him one day.

Monsieur Verjat had answered in his own fashion. 'They are people who've never contemplated the danger of their own extinction, Baroness. But I have. I am a man risen from the dead who can no longer live and yet who lives, a dead man who aspires to nothing more than to meditate on his life and who still lives his death.'

It often amused Monsieur Verjat to juggle eruditely with what he called the unchanging hardships of existence, and in such a dazzling but incomprehensible manner that it would leave Cosette baffled. That day, however, he had gone on to clarify his thoughts.

'In short, the agitators of whom you speak, Baroness, and with whom I often had dealings in the past, are people who earn their living in the old trades. I can put your mind at rest, they have nothing to do with the brigands who used to darken my horizon. They are good people, the mainspring of our beautiful France – carpenters, tailors, printers, locksmiths. The others, the heavy infantry of the factories, are too exhausted by their work. In Paris, many silversmiths, mechanics, bakers, glovemakers, weavers and building workers also belong to societies with Republican tendencies. But the people who really run things are the journalists, the men of letters and certain liberal-thinking politicians. They leave the dirty work to the down-and-outs. It was ever thus. Vulnerability is a dreadful thing, Madame Pontmercy. And I should know.'

Monsieur Verjat, who was aged somewhere between fifty and fifty-five, was above average height and quite well built. His everlasting brown frock coat and his broad-brimmed black felt hat pulled down low over his eyes made him easily recognizable. As a cane, he used a pilgrim's staff. Whenever he passed, he left in his wake a particular smell of oranges and old prayer books. Some of the theology students at the Saint-Sulpice seminary, to whom he gave classes in civil law and spirituality – a strange mixture that covered both St Augustine's soliloquies and the chapters of the Napoleonic Code – had nicknamed him the last of the just. He knew it, though he took no pride in it. He was a chaste and solitary man.

Physically, Monsieur Verjat was forbidding. Whenever he was lost in thought, which was often, his features were particularly sombre. His grey hair was parted in the middle and perfectly smoothed down over his temples. He had a long beard, which softened his stern and stoical expression, a slightly bent back, and huge hands with broad, flat fingers. He was one of those men who are respected all the more because of the coldness of their attitude and the fear they inspire. Monsieur Verjat was not a man to spin a yarn. For him, everything had to have a meaning and a significance, especially the blatant absurdity of man's passage on earth.

*

After vespers Cosette arrived a little late for her usual rendezvous.

Verjat, who was always very punctual, was getting impatient. With his hat tilted to one side and his cane in his hand, he was munching an orange as one might an apple. He always ate gluttonously, never stopping to take breath, never taking the time to savour what he was chewing. He was burning with impatience to tell Cosette things he had never told anybody else. Since meeting Jean Valjean's daughter, he had started to think that perhaps happiness existed after all, even if it always went hand in glove with sorrow.

When he saw Cosette enter the church square with a spring in her step, he straightened his hat and stood admiring her shoulders, over which her beautiful fair hair hung loose. She apologized for her lateness and they walked off together in the direction of the Luxembourg Gardens.

Cosette told him at once how worried she was about events looming on the horizon, which seemed to her to presage nothing but disaster. Verjat, as usual, replied by evading the issue, though he did point out that it was not fitting to talk about oneself or to dwell at length on an idea, and that all improvements, in politics as elsewhere, stemmed from pain.

'We are responsible for what is refused us and what is conceded to us,' he added somewhat mysteriously.

Cosette next turned to the subject of those fashionable young men known as dandies, who, by means of provocation and impertinence, demonstrated their rebellion and freedom in an area far from politics.

'I know one who is exerting a deplorable influence on my husband,' she said confidentially.

Verjat blinked. It was the first time Cosette had spoken of Marius. As they walked, he gripped his cane between his thumb and forefinger and held it out in front of him, so that it seemed to hover, weightless. 'Oh, such people are not dangerous, Cosette. Their superficiality impresses nobody but themselves.'

'Yes, they are dangerous, Monsieur Verjat. Under the pretext of indifference, they destroy everything they touch. Marius was a proud and generous boy, full of ideals and Republican fervour. And, to use your language, I know whereof I speak. He was even seriously wounded during the riots of June 1832. He only survived thanks to my father's courage: he saved him by carrying him on his shoulders through the maze of the Paris sewers. These events ought to have given him exceptional strength of character. Instead of which, he's become indecisive and mistrustful. He's destroying himself by destroying what we've been trying to build together.'

Verjat, who was still playing with his cane, felt his knees tremble. 'And what of your father?' he managed to say.

'He died after we were married. Marius and I are orphans, Monsieur Verjat. That's why I shudder to think that my husband is drawing his inspiration from someone like the man I mentioned and not from someone like my father.'

In his confusion, Verjat tripped against a step and had to use his cane to stop himself from falling.

'Are you all right, Monsieur Verjat?'

'It's nothing, Cosette. You know, the desire that certain people have to be disagreeable always ends by turning against them.'

'Why do you say that?'

'Because whatever happens to us is only temporary. One must learn to be mistaken in order to learn to be suspicious.'

Cosette made a face, like that of an indignant little girl. 'It's clear you don't know the Marquis d'Iguerande, Monsieur Verjat. Marius is even neglecting his work on *Le National* because of him.'

Verjat stopped dead and put his head in his hands. 'Iguerande. Well, well, how strange. I know a place called Iguerande in Burgundy, not far from Paray-le-Monial, a little village on the Loire.' He resumed his walk, with Cosette hanging on his arm. 'To return to your husband – you mustn't worry. I'm sure he's an intelligent and well-balanced young man, who sets great store by his habits. Creatures of habit need the unexpected to confirm them in their habits. He'll come back.'

Cosette gave a little sigh and pressed her hand to her heart as if to restrain its beating. 'May God hear you, Monsieur Verjat. If only Marius would take my father as a model. He was a just and good man.'

Verjat stopped again, turned to face Cosette, and placed his large hands on her shoulders. 'I know, Cosette. I have a friend who knew your father well.'

After his daily fencing and boxing sessions, and in the absence of Amédée, who was busy paying his impromptu visit to Cosette, Marius had set off for Clémence de Lavely's house in the Rue Transnonnain. He sat astride his chestnut. He had placed his mount's head, arranged the stirrup leathers at walking pace, and adjusted the reins at a jog. He took great pride in his newly acquired knowledge of horses. Earlier he had told Eugène Sue, not without compunction, that he liked them light and nicely turned out with a perfectly curved neck, and supple in the shoulders and the haunches. He believed himself to be part of the very select world of horsemen. He saw himself as fierce, dignified, intemperate and solitary, and loved horses for their strength and their spirit, the way they bolted in anger or reared up in terror on their hind legs. He crossed Paris in a silence punctuated by the pounding of the hooves and the clickety-clack of the curb chain on the bit. Now that he had a horse, a position and a mistress, what more could he ask?

Clémence, as so often, was waiting for him stark naked. He embraced her, making his spurs jingle exaggeratedly on the floor. She laughed, threw her head back and drew him into the bedroom. Unable to control himself, he threw her down on the bed.

'When you take me in your arms,' she whispered, 'I lose my head completely.'

And under Marius's skilful caresses she began to rave as if transported, delighted with the desire she read in her lover's eyes, but calculating enough to avoid losing her head completely.

Later, lying on the bed, Clémence stretched, and feigned the offended modesty of women who have just offered themselves. She veiled herself with the air of a madonna who is getting ready to ask for something.

'Darling, I saw a wonderful ring today. It was all in gold, with a little diamond encircled in coral.'

'Where?'

'At a jeweller's in the Rue Saint-Denis.'

'It's yours.'

Clémence cast aside her veil and embraced Marius. 'How I love you, my little baron.'

Marius kissed Clémence's brow, got up, dressed and announced that he was going straight to the jeweller's. When he saw the triumphant expression on his mistress's face, he felt afraid. He had been fooled right from the start. True, Clémence had some formidable weapons in her armoury. Her big green eyes, brilliant and languorous beneath dark eyebrows, were capable of feigning sensual delight, and her heart-shaped mouth, pink and moist, could utter the most impassioned declarations of love without her frozen heart ever beating. Marius had realized that her natural charm – but was it really so natural? – went hand in hand with her greed. They were like the two halves of an hourglass, one emptying as the other filled.

Marius left his horse in the stable of an inn in the Rue Beaubourg and set off with a heavy step in the direction of the Rue Saint-Denis. Once again he was angry with himself. He thought of Cosette and felt terrible pangs of guilt. Clémence would never have that ring.

He passed the jeweller's shop and saw the ring in its silk-lined box, but did not stop. A sudden fancy had come into his head. He would go to see little Raphaël again.

In the street, the sight of so many gaunt, deathlike faces, gnawed by poverty, revolted and attracted Marius at the same time. Tradesmen yelled, children howled, fishwives traded insults. A few cut-throats sauntered along dragging their legs, either bareheaded or wearing broad fur caps, sporting gaudy waistcoats or velvet jackets with cerise collars. They half smiled when they saw policemen patrolling with their huge cocked hats.

As it was dark and cold, Marius was walking heavily, wrapped in his overcoat, his hat down low over his eyes. From everywhere unknown sounds came to him, strange cries, words whose meanings escaped him.

He walked faster, past poor wretches, most of them one-eyed, crippled or hideously deformed, their bodies riddled with vermin, who sat or lay on the muddy pavements chewing on pieces of bone or vegetable scraps. Others were luckier and had a right to the harlequin, which was a mixture of meat, fish and other ingredients thrown together out of the leftovers from taverns or bourgeois houses. From time to time, a quarrel would erupt with lightning violence, then just as quickly subside, and the wretches would return to their unspeakable meal, sucking or licking the food from their makeshift bowls with slobbering mouths, huddling together, glancing sidelong at one another, undeterred even by the kicks aimed at them by passing street urchins – on the contrary, it delighted them to excite hatred and derision.

It was like a huge cauldron, a dense, putrid miasma rising into the air, an inferno of sly-looking turncoats and skinflints dying of hatred and poverty, fallen angels covered in lice and threadworms, all of them misshapen and sniggering, prisoners of life's dirty inconsistency. Saint-Germain, the Opéra, the Chaussée d'Antin – how far away all that seemed! This was poverty as Marius had known it in 1832 in Coufeyrac's house in the Rue de la Verrerie. He was rediscovering it now and the shock overcame him. He felt as though he were bathing in filth. He was staring poverty in the face – there it was, a gross creature, hot and feverish with that extreme, incurable unhappiness that is known as despair.

Near the Rue de la Verrerie, more or less on the same spot where

Horse Face and little Raphaël had been knocked down by Amédée's tilbury, he bumped into a beggar who was holding out his hand.

'Charity, Monsieur.'

Marius stopped, searched in his pockets, and took out his purse. As he was about to give the tramp two sous, a furious gust of wind arose, causing a dilapidated chimney to collapse on its side, break into a thousand pieces and come crashing down into the street. Marius leapt backwards so swiftly that he dropped his purse and his hat. He found himself against a wall, his arms outstretched, his coat open and torn. Nobody had been hit by the chimney. The beggar had taken advantage of the situation to pick up the purse and run off as fast as his legs would carry him.

'Stop, thief!' cried Marius, as soon as he recovered his spirits.

His cry was in vain. There was panic in the street. The shadows had turned purple. The hurricane seemed to redouble in intensity. Alerted by the cries, people were pressing around the remains of the chimney, lifting their eyes to the roofs, placing their hands over their hats, pointing to other chimneys that were also threatening to come down. Others were running from all directions – porters, linen maids, artisans, people in rags – some fifty people at least. Among them were two men who had just emerged from the Rue Aubry-le-Boucher, a big red-headed man who looked both stupid and cruel, and an old man in a fur hat. They stood a little apart from the crowd.

'Good God,' said the old man to his companion. 'Look, it's him. Fate itself has sent him our way.'

'How's that, Catman?'

'Is Jesus in the workshop?'

'For sure.'

'Do you recognize that idiot?'

The Mullet looked at Marius, then turned to the Catman's hideous face. 'Well, no.'

'No matter,' said the Catman, his dark eyes burning. 'As you can see, he's had a shock. Offer to show him round the workshop, to give him a chance to recover.'

'There must be better places for that,' said the Mullet, in surprise.

'Don't argue,' replied the Catman. 'Take him to the workshop and on the way mention there's a terrible fellow who runs it and mistreats the children.'

'Is that me?'

'No, you idiot – Jesus. It has to be Jesus, don't you see? Overdo it a bit, tell him about the rope, show him the dormitory on the mezzanine. Jesus, of course, mustn't know anything. I'd like those two to go out in the street and have a fight. Do you see what I'm getting at?'

'Oh, I see, Catman, that's a good idea. We have to keep Jesus in check.'

'Keep him in check? No,' said the Catman. 'All I want is a good row with lots of witnesses, including you. And no question of clearing off, eh?'

'You can count on me, Catman. I knew you still had confidence in me.'

So the Mullet went up to Marius, picked up his hat, handed it to him pleasantly and made the proposal suggested by the Catman. Trustingly, the young man followed him.

It was pouring with rain. On the way the Mullet told Marius what the Catman had instructed him to say. By the time they reached the door of the workshop, Marius was, of course, seething with rage against the owner of the premises and ready to do battle forthwith.

'It's totally iniquitous,' he said, while the Mullet was fighting with his bunch of keys.

'That's right, you said it, it's really iniquitous,' replied the Mullet, without understanding.

In the driving rain, a sinister figure had followed the two men along the street. As soon as he saw them enter the workshop, he went and huddled in the corner of a carriage entrance. From there he hailed a little boy, the son of the porter next door, and asked him to go and fetch Sergeant Carignol.

'Why the rozzers?'

'Just get a move on. There's going to be a fight. Look, here's a sou.'

The boy pocketed the coin and ran off.

Marius retched as he entered the workshop. The smell was indescribable. Casting his eye around the room, he saw the children at their work, the mezzanine with its obscene hole that gave access to the sleeping quarters, the crates full of refuse, pieces of bone, coils of wool.

He noticed an old man on a chair, his chin almost touching his knees, shivering under a tartan cover which gave a glimpse of his scabby and atrophied calves. He appeared to be dozing, but was watching everything with a fierce eye. When he recognized the Mullet, he pointed his fore-finger at a child who had fallen asleep at his work.

'That's the Pointer,' said the Mullet to Marius, pretending not to have seen the sign his father had given him. 'A dirty old informer.' He picked up a pitcher from the windowsill and smiled complacently. 'Good rain water, Monsieur.' He took a dirty bowl, filled it with water and offered it to Marius. 'Here.'

Marius drank the fresh water in long gulps and gave the bowl back to the Mullet. His eye had wandered to a woman who was working over a little range and a filthy cooking pot. She wore a shapeless dress and a frayed old jersey.

'Don't pay any attention to her. That's Mother Fouillet, who cooks for our little workers. She's deaf and dumb.'

All at once, a cry rang out. 'Monsieur! Monsieur!'

Marius turned his head and saw a little boy with fair hair sitting at his work. He felt his heart beating very loudly. It was Raphaël.

'The gentleman from the other night!' the boy cried to a companion. 'The one who gave me his coat!'

His companion was an older boy with an enormous jaw. He had got to his feet and stood with his weight on one leg and a mocking expression on his face.

'Back to work!' the Mullet found himself bellowing. It was not easy for him to forsake his usual role.

Marius went up to Raphaël. He lifted the child's chin and contemplated his unhealthily livid little face with surprise and indignation. His abundant fair hair made a terrible contrast with his sickly complexion. His eyes were lacklustre, and his pale lips were like a slit in his bony face.

'This child is cold,' said Marius, turning again to the Mullet.

In accordance with the Catman's orders, the redhead had crept out of the workshop, and in his place stood a young man with dark eyes, watching Marius with folded arms. The children were immediately struck by the resemblance between the two men, a resemblance that was more to do with their bearing than their actual features.

The two men stared at each other like two adversaries about to fight.

'Are you Jesus?' barked Marius.

'So they say.'

'Your name does not suit you, Monsieur.'

Jesus uncrossed his arms and looked rebellious. 'We don't choose our names.'

Marius shot him a murderous look. 'You ought to change yours.'

'And you should change your tone. And first of all you'll do me the pleasure of clearing off as quickly as possible. You don't belong here.'

Jesus had not received any orders from the Catman. It must be admitted that he felt as if he had been caught off his guard, for he had no particular antipathy towards this young man, whom he had recognized as the one who had fought with Perfect Love at the Clan Destin. The question was, what was he doing here? And where had that idiot, the Mullet, vanished to?

'Come on, just leave, Monsieur,' he repeated in a more honeyed tone.

Marius's expression was as defiant as ever. 'Monsieur, you are a monster.'

And he swooped down on him, his fist raised to hit him in the face. As quick as lightning, Jesus parried the blow and twisted Marius's arm.

'No, Jesus, he was kind to me!' cried Raphaël.

'I hate to say it, but it's true!' said Horse Face, going one better.

Jesus did not loosen his hold. 'We'll see about that,' he growled. Still twisting Marius's arm, he pushed him unceremoniously into the corridor, and flung him violently through the front door. 'Go on, out of here! And never set foot in this house again!'

Marius slid on the cobbles, narrowly avoiding a fall. Behind Jesus he could see the children pressing together, their expressions both mocking and regretful – especially little Raphaël, who was on the verge of tears.

Bareheaded in the rain, Marius looked around for his hat, which had rolled on the cobbles. As he was shouting loudly, some onlookers came running.

'I'll kill you! You'll answer to me for your unspeakable attitude! With pistols or swords! You'll soon find out who Baron Marius Pontmercy is!'

People were leaning out of the windows, others huddled under umbrellas. Remarkably, the whole angry outburst had been witnessed by a police sergeant. His name was Carignol, and he had never distinguished himself by his courage or his decisiveness. In fact, he was a complete idiot, who, in exchange for a few bribes, was more than happy to turn a blind eye to the Catman's business transactions. In sending for him, the old man had known exactly what he was doing.

'Move along now,' was all this ineffectual representative of order could say. 'There's nothing to see.'

Nobody was listening to him because in fact there was something to see. They were waiting for the confrontation and had even noted the names.

'All right, come on, I'm waiting for you,' Jesus finally retorted, and immediately regretted making a spectacle of himself. 'You lot, back inside!' he yelled at the children.

A few steps further on, under the carriage entrance, the Catman was lapping it all up. Everything was falling into place. It was even better than he had expected. The Mullet, standing beside him, seemed disappointed that the two men had not come to blows.

Marius put his hat back on his head. 'We'll meet again!' he shouted. 'I'll kill you, you blackguard of a Jesus!'

4

By day the Clan Destin was scarcely more inviting than by night. The next-door buildings set the tone. The few windows that punctuated their walls were without panes, and their frames were riddled with woodworm. The street lamps swaying in the wind looked like gallows. Dark alleyways led to small airless courtyards where no light penetrated – and these grim courtyards to even grimmer staircases, on which it was necessary to grip the guard rail firmly in order not to slip on the steps. In spite of the cold, ragged and barefoot children played in the refuse and chased each other into the middle of Rue Aubry-le-Boucher, where a damp, icy wind carrying the stench of rotten wood and excreta soon made them turn tail and run away. Indeed, the temperature that February of 1834 was not conducive to play. It was close to freezing, by virtue of which the Clan Destin offered a refuge, if such a sordid and pitiful place could be described as that. Inside, despite the kitchen stove blazing like a forge, it was damp. And the floor of beaten earth, impregnated with mud and straw, did not help matters.

'We just let them freeze!' Gammy Leg never tired of repeating, as she busied herself in the kitchen, a bonnet pulled down over her ears and a patched old shawl on her back.

At that hour there were only two customers. Gammy Leg put some tripe on the fire, filled her footwarmer with hot ashes and slid it under her clogs. She had good reason to be in a foul mood. A few minutes earlier the Kitten had passed through, smartly dressed and perfumed, her cross-eyes drifting in all directions, and had given Gammy Leg a lecture, exhorting her to take better care of the restaurant and even pay more attention to the way she dressed.

Apoplectic with rage at the little madam's effrontery, Gammy Leg had sought refuge in the kitchen, where she had taken her big, black, yellow-eyed cat in her arms.

'At least you, my Demon, never try to annoy me.'

She adored the cat and the two of them were inseparable. It was the only creature that still showed her any affection.

The Kitten had left again without so much as a by-your-leave, and with a disdainful glance at the two customers, who had not even looked up. Still with their hats on and wrapped in their coats, they sat downing a sweet liqueur known as a consolation because it consoled the drinker's entrails for the aggressions of the usual gut-rot on sale here.

'Wine is for victims,' declared the Catman, wiping the table with the back of his hand.

'So's vitriol,' sighed the man in black.

The Catman's cowardly off-white face took on an expression at once solemn and agitated. 'Vitriol? Who for?'

'Can't you guess?'

'No, I can't guess. And I'd rather not.'

'Just think for a moment,' the other went on. 'Don't you find the Kitten a nuisance?'

'The Kitten? That's risky.'

'There's no risk. Since you dealt so brilliantly with fomenting a quarrel between our friend Baron Pontmercy and that little thug Jesus, I'm going to help you take over the Clan Destin. We just have to play our cards right. I knew a doctor when I was in the army. We've kept in contact. He sold his soul to Lucifer and now runs a brothel. He'll let me have a phial of sulphuric acid – no questions asked. I give it to you and you give it to Gammy Leg.' He paused, his black eyes endowing his face with an air of jubilation and cruel eagerness. 'First, you have to skin her cat,' he explained, in a whisper. 'Tell Gammy Leg it was the Kitten who did it. When you suggest the vitriol, she'll leap at the opportunity.'

'What about Perfect Love?'

The man in black shook his head. 'When he sees what's happened to his little fairy,' he said conspiratorially, 'he'll go mad with grief. And then I don't rate Gammy Leg's chances.'

'Ingenious,' said the Catman appreciatively, putting on his green spectacles, which had the advantage of letting him see while hiding him from the gaze of others. 'And what about the baron?'

'He's a nice boy,' said the man in black suavely. 'He has great human qualities and a generosity about which there can be no doubt.' He always spoke this way about matters of the heart, as if determined to become known for what he himself was not. 'Monsieur Marius loves honours.

But I can imagine him in Jesus's shoes. Or vice versa, it doesn't really matter.'

'What do you mean, it doesn't really matter? And does the marquis know about all this?'

'That great booby doesn't need to know everything. He has his eye on the baron's wife and I think the charming Cosette might not be averse to the idea.'

He finished his drink and stood up. The two accomplices went out together. The man in black put up his umbrella, but did not offer to share it with the Catman.

'By the way,' he said peremptorily as they approached the Rue Saint-Martin, 'when all this is over, you'll be able to use your real name again!'

The old man looked left and right and then lowered his head in a servile manner. 'You mean Thénard?' he caterwauled, bending exaggeratedly, his face exposed to the rain.

'When I met you in Saint-Malo, you were calling yourself Thénard. But I'm not talking about that name. I was thinking of the other one, the real one – Thénardier.'

'It's a little early—'

'It's always too early, my friend. If it's too early for you to reveal your real name, then it's also too early for you to take too close an interest in my affairs.' He offered the Catman a corner of his umbrella, then immediately withdrew it. 'There are those who know how to take cover and those who don't, Tardier. I think we understand each other.'

Cosette was anxious. Her first failure haunted her. Would the diagnosis finally be positive? Just before the visit to the doctor recommended by Frédéric Rivolier, whom she was due to meet in the Rue Taitbout, she went to Saint-Sulpice to speak to Monsieur Verjat, whom she had not seen for several days. Father Rillet had made himself her go-between.

Cosette was wearing an emerald-green crepe dress decorated with red and white camellias, an ill-matched mantlet, a grey silk moiré hat and a white veil. To anyone seeing her for the first time, her beauty lay less in the regularity of her features than in the inexpressible charm of her countenance. Monsieur Verjat was struck by it every time they met. When she arrived in front of the church, his heart began to pound.

'I have a bone to pick with you, Monsieur Verjat,' said Cosette immediately, without lifting her veil.

Verjat blinked and turned slightly pink. Usually so stern and unruffled, he melted before Cosette. He raised his wide-brimmed hat in greeting and put it back on his head without a word. Then, searching in his frock coat, he took out a little package and handed it to her. 'It's nothing, just a sweetmeat I brought back from Paray-le-Monial.'

'Were you there?' she said in surprise, unwrapping the tissue paper to reveal a golden brioche scattered with pink sugared almonds. She lowered her nose to smell it. 'You shouldn't have, Monsieur Verjat!' she said, in ecstasy. 'What a delicious smell of butter and sugar!'

'It's a speciality of the Brionnais region,' said Verjat, assuming a severe air. 'To make it even better, warm it in the oven for five minutes.'

As he spoke, he was watching her face tenderly. He could find no fault in it.

Cosette tasted the brioche and offered a piece to Verjat, who refused it with an abrupt wave of the hand.

'What were you doing in Paray-le-Monial?'

Verjat paused. 'I need to go there regularly,' he replied, in a somewhat different voice. 'It's a place that changed my life, Cosette. And I know whereof I speak.'

She could not help smiling. 'Again! You're quite the man of mystery, Monsieur Verjat. Why do you always say that?'

Verjat took her by the arm and led her in the direction of the Luxembourg Gardens by way of the Rue de Tournon, where he pointed out the seller of oranges and barley sugar. Indignation had replaced his usual anxiety. He bought an orange and began to peel it as he walked. Not until they had reached the Luxembourg Palace, where the Chamber of Peers sat, did he answer her question.

'If I say that I know whereof I speak, it may be because I conceal my immorality under an appearance of austerity and piety.'

Cosette shrugged, giggling. 'I don't think so, Monsieur Verjat. You lie as easily as you breathe.'

'You're mistaken, Cosette. I don't lie as easily as I breathe, I lie in order to breathe.'

'Well, you can say whatever you like, but I don't believe you. I think you're a good man, just like my father, fair, impartial and magnanimous, but for some strange reason you love to belittle yourself and make yourself out to be more wicked than you are. Besides,' she went on without pausing, 'the last time we met, you told me that one of your friends used to know him well. Do you want to talk about it?'

'It was so long ago, Cosette. At that time, I was not what I am now.

I always looked for an ulterior motive behind the most honest sentiments. Now I try to make the most of the time that is left to me. I say this because the society of which I was an active member demanded zealous servants. It deprived them of the very notion of pleasure, and in its place gave them frantic appetites and idiotic distractions, which led to the most futile acts.'

'How bitter you are!'

'I'm simply trying to explain to you that a man has the right to be mistaken and to have a second chance.'

Verjat's leaden features barely concealed his emotion. He swallowed his orange quarters without even chewing them, then moved away from Cosette and leaned on the balustrade. The weather was grey and rainy. Cosette joined him. They were on the side of the Observatory facing the ornamental lake. Both looked in silence at the garden spread before them.

'Winter is always sad,' murmured Verjat with a smile that he tried to keep free of irony.

He wore his hat tilted to one side, and the ends of his grey cravat hung over the collar of his frock coat. He seemed to take a morbid delight in plunging again and again into the furnace of his remorse, even though it might consume him. His half-closed and swollen eyelids loomed large in his pallid, cadaverous face.

'I used to have an ideal,' he said in a hollow voice, staring at the shimmering reflections on the surface of the lake. 'It was to be above reproach. That was the case with your father. I am going to tell you the circumstances in which I met him. It was during the turbulent events of June 1832. In a way, it could be said that he saved my life. I should have been killed on the barricade in the Rue de la Chanvrerie.'

Cosette clasped her hands to her chest, impatient to know more. 'And how did he save your life?'

'By tearing me from the grip of the young insurgents who had decided to have me shot.'

Cosette recoiled indignantly. 'Have you shot? Good heavens, why?'

'They took me for a spy.'

'And were you?'

'In a way, yes.'

Cosette seemed to be searching in her memory. She raised her veil. 'Your story reminds me of a policeman whose name I forget and whom my father, according to Marius, saved by letting him run away instead of executing him.'

'One does not execute a man thus,' said Verjat, looking intensely at Cosette. 'I used to respect authority and hate rebellion,' he went on. 'To people like your husband and his friends, I was the devil incarnate, always turning up in the most unexpected places, but that was to overestimate my importance somewhat. To be perfectly honest, I was a mere functionary, a servant of the state, sacrificing everything to duty. I led an austere and serious life. My timetable was regulated like a musical score. In twenty years of service, I never had any doubts about myself or the mission I had to accomplish. Until the day your father gave me back my freedom. Then the devil found himself back in hell – though in truth, this devil had never known heaven. I had so few pleasures. I read, I drank two glasses of burgundy a day, I allowed myself a few pinches of snuff. You see, not enough to make a fuss about.'

Cosette lowered her veil again and moved away from the balustrade. She drew back her shoulders slightly. 'And then?' she asked.

Verjat straightened up too, and once again looked at Cosette sombrely. Nothing could have been more proud than her face and manner at that moment.

A sort of self-resentment made Verjat look grimly determined. He had decided that he no longer needed to conceal his face. Contact with Father Rillet, the monks of Paray-le-Monial and now with Cosette had given him a love of independence and free will. It was unpleasant to relive the past, but if he had to . . .

'I saw your father again at one of the exits from the Paris sewers,' he went on. 'He was carrying a young man on his shoulders, a young man with whom I'd exchanged a few words on the barricades in the Rue de la Chanvrerie. It was your husband, Cosette. Later, I don't know when exactly, for everything is a little confused in my mind, our paths crossed again. Paris was in a state of war, or very nearly. You could be shot for the slightest thing, and there was a cholera epidemic raging. Be that as it may, I found myself on the banks of the Seine. I think I must have blacked out. I fell in the water. Some witnesses stated that I sank to the bottom, others maintained that I struggled like the very devil. I don't remember a thing. Only Father Rillet's face bending over me. That saintly man had been passing with his handcart. He had a young boy with him who helped him to load the dead. The father had fished me out of the river. When he saw that I was still alive, he stripped my wet clothes off me and changed them for those of a dead man. I may have stammered a few words, said that I wanted to lose the man he'd saved from drowning. Father Rillet did not ask me any questions. He threw the dead man in the water, with my clothes and my papers, then made the sign of the cross and administered the last rites as the body sank into the black waters of the river.'

'So you're a miraculous survivor?' asked Cosette gravely.

'I prefer to call myself a man risen from the dead,' corrected Verjat. 'Let's just say that I see things differently now. When we first spoke, I told you how much I mistrusted the proponents of purity. For almost two years now I've had the chance to reflect, to meditate, to question everything I believed in. I've come to the conclusion that faith exerts a form of terror over men, a terror all the more appalling because the pure are its agents. And I was one of the pure, Cosette. I took pride in obedience.'

Verjat's tone was less firm than usual. His harsh voice, which admitted no objection and brooked no opposition, seemed to crack gradually as he unravelled his tangled web of memories. His face was taut with an expression at once hard and nostalgic, and his eyes appeared faded and colourless, their energy touched by sadness. To spare Cosette, he had embellished his account of his encounter with Jean Valjean. Cosette must never know that her father had been an escaped convict. Or that the man she was talking to now had once been his fiercest enemy. A sort of devil, as he himself admitted. A scrupulous agent of the law, who had spent twenty years of his life determined to track Jean Valjean down, to pursue him relentlessly, to ruin his life, to tarnish his memory, to separate him from his nearest and dearest, to hound him into a corner. And what had all that determination been for?

Even today, Verjat could not answer that question. Sometimes, when he looked at himself in a mirror, his face filled him with horror. A face that had shown no pity when Cosette's mother, Fantine, had died. A face as hard as marble. Although there had been some changes, he still had the same sombre eyes, the same self-righteously pinched mouth, the same pug nose with deep nostrils. He found himself hideous. Before, he had never even thought about it. He had been the sword of law and justice. Tall and gaunt, with his turned-down hat and his big cane, he had been an austere demon, tenacious and omnipotent, engaged in a quest for absolute good. It would have been an exaggeration to say that he had found redemption, for nothing was more foreign to him than conventional notions of salvation and immortality. Meditation had simply helped him to distance himself from what he had been. He had become human. Perhaps it was true that the past always catches up with you. If so, it was a kind of determinism that suited Verjat. Perhaps, under Cosette's influence, he was secretly, but genuinely, planning to mend his ways and confront, once and for all, the man he had once been and whom he no longer wanted to be. So yes – he had lied to Cosette and he would lie again. He took full responsibility for his lies. What would have been the point of telling her that the body of a drowned man had been found under a washerwomen's boat between the Pont-au-Change and the Pont-Neuf in June 1832? Or that the body, which was not his, wore his clothes and carried his papers, those of Javert, who had been an inspector of the Paris Sûreté? Why would he have shown her an issue of *Le Moniteur* dated 15 June 1832 reporting his drowning? Javert was dead. True, the ex-policeman had not made much of an effort to conceal his name – Verjat was an absurdly transparent anagram. But who, two years later, would bother to make the connection between a Javert who had been declared dead and a Verjat who was very much alive?

Verjat had often evoked this preposterous idea, finding a solution in irony. He himself was irony personified. Yesterday a policeman, today nothing at all.

'Shall we walk a little?' he suggested to Cosette, suddenly lively, as if relieved of his intolerable confusion.

Cosette made a gesture of panic. 'What time is it, Monsieur Verjat?'

He took a turnip watch from his pocket. 'Four o'clock.'

'I must leave you. I have an important appointment with a doctor.'

'You frighten me.'

Cosette drew her mantlet round her shoulders and looked mysterious. 'A strange sickness, Monsieur Verjat. And I know whereof I speak!'

She laughed and waved goodbye as she hurried off towards the Rue de Tournon.

At first disconcerted, then shaking his head with a pinched smile, Verjat watched her run down the steps at the end of the terrace.

'When will you come and see me again?' he called to her.

'Very soon, Monsieur Verjat!'

'If anything should happen to you, Cosette,' he called again, standing, hands on hips, as if talking to a young tearaway, 'you can count on my help!'

And if you can count on me, nothing is impossible, he added to himself somewhat grumpily. Hadn't Javert been one of the best sleuths in the French police force?

*

97

By the time Cosette and Frédéric Rivolier emerged from the doctor's consulting room, the Rue Taitbout was swarming with people. Everyone was getting ready for the Mardi Gras celebrations. Despite the biting cold, a number of under-dressed harlequins and columbines were parading up and down the street, playing cornets and tambourines and shouting at the yellow gloves and the bourgeois women in their hooded landaus. Holding on to Frédéric's arm, Cosette looked at the spectacle. Frédéric hailed a fiacre.

'Rue Plumet,' he commanded the cabman. 'You can drop me in the Place de l'Odéon.'

They climbed into the fiacre and set off. Unknown to them, a man on horseback had been watching from the other side of the street. Boiling with rage, he repressed the desire to intervene immediately and slap Cosette's companion in the face. He had just come out of his fencing lesson. Before that, he had been with Amédée, Louis de Vergne and Eugène Sue at the Café de Paris, where they had feasted on rock partridge, whose flavour recalled the peppered scent of scrubland, and pheasant garnished with truffles served on toast spread with a purée of woodcocks and surrounded by Seville oranges coated with *sauce Périgueux*.

Marius followed the fiacre at a distance. In the carriage, Cosette was telling Frédéric the doctor's diagnosis.

'That's wonderful,' declared Frédéric, with that infectious warmth that was so typical of him. 'You see, you were wrong to worry. I'm sure Marius will be delighted by the news.'

'I'd like to believe you, Frédéric. But is this the right moment? Marius seems more distracted than ever. Something is worrying him, and I don't know what it is. He scarcely talks to me. We sometimes pass each other in the house like strangers. Monsieur Verjat and you are my only support.'

'I will speak to him.'

'Don't upset him, Frédéric.'

'I shan't upset him, Cosette. I promise. But he must know.'

'Know what, Frédéric?' asked Cosette, suddenly terrified.

He turned to her with a look of undisguised tenderness, took her hand and kissed it gently. Marius saw everything.

'Know that he has the most delightful wife in the world,' said Frédéric.

The fiacre stopped and Frédéric got out. He waved goodbye and Cosette leaned over the door to return his wave. The fiacre moved off.

Frédéric began walking in the direction of the Rue Dauphine, where Blanqui and Barbès, infuriated by the retaliatory measures of Prefect of

Police Gisquet, were supposed to be holding a meeting. Gisquet was waging a relentless struggle against the Society for the Rights of Man, infiltrating every branch with his spies. A law had been passed in January 1834 requiring town criers to be licensed – the licences would be revoked if they fell foul of the authorities. They were almost all members of the Society for the Rights of Man. In Lyons, sporadic strikes by silk workers had broken out, led by friendly society members, to fight against pay reduction in the tailoring trades. The government's reaction had been to arrest six of the leaders, who were due to be tried on 9 April. Wages had been cut for all workers, except typographers, printers, carpenters and stonecutters. The talk was of twelve- to fifteen-hour days, but in fact eighteen was more typical. A quarter of the population of Paris lived in poverty. Of these, fifty per cent were concentrated in the eighth, ninth and twelfth *arrondissements*. The situation could not last. Thiers at the Ministry of the Interior, Barthe in Justice, Broglie in Foreign Affairs and Guizot in Public Education were the lackeys of the profiteers and speculators. Marshal Soult, prime minister and hero of Austerlitz, was the lackey of Louis-Philippe.

Frédéric felt a particular antipathy towards Adolphe Thiers. In his opinion, the little opportunist was getting off lightly. The founder of *Le National* had soon found that life as an opposition journalist held no further attractions for him and had lost no time in seizing control of the affairs of state. Politicians were all the same – dedicated humanists before gaining power, eloquent but treacherous when they had it. Thiers's greed derived both from his ambition, which was justified by his intelligence, and from his impatience to possess, to enjoy and to command, often found in those who, starting with nothing, have been the architects of their own fortunes.

'Look at the three hundred thousand francs he got as a dowry when he married Mademoiselle Doisne!' Armand Marrast, editor-in-chief of *La Tribune*, had reminded Frédéric. 'Look how he stuffs himself with chicken Marengo at the Véfour with Sainte-Beuve and Lamartine! What does he know about the people's hunger?'

Frédéric had remembered the lesson. Thiers was not a serious Republican, but a short-sighted and reactionary Marseillais. He was not a man of the left. His party was nobody's party but his own. Beneath his Jacobin exterior beat the heart of a tyrant, as was evident from his unfortunate tendency to characterize all opinions other than his own as absurd, insane and foolish.

Frédéric made no bones about sharing this opinion. He was one of those who were nostalgic for the Terror. Of course, it is easy to be nostalgic for something you haven't known. It is the privilege of those pampered by life, the fanaticism of spoilt children.

All the time that Marius was watching Frédéric, images of duels were crowding into his mind. When he drew close to his friend, he leapt from his horse and barred his way.

'What a pleasant surprise!' cried Frédéric, though in fact he felt more anxiety than pleasure.

Marius's horse neighed loudly, and Marius nervously struck at his boots with his riding crop. 'A pleasant surprise?' he asked, in a voice that sounded false. 'Do you really think so?'

'I seldom have the opportunity to see you. You've become such a busy and hard-working gentleman.'

Marius laughed sardonically. 'I accept the title of gentleman. And a gentleman's weapon being the sword, I shall therefore expect you at Vincennes tomorrow morning to find out if you are a rascal or a seducer. And here's a good reason for you to pick up the gauntlet!'

Marius tried to whip Frédéric in the face, but Frédéric seized his wrist in a firm grip. 'You're mad, my poor Marius,' he said, looking him straight in the eye. Then he let him go. 'Be on your way and leave me alone. I shan't fight you.'

'You won't get away so easily!' roared Marius, stepping to one side to stop Frédéric from passing.

'I repeat – I shan't fight you.'

'Are you a coward, then?'

'If that's what you want to think.'

'I despise you, Frédéric. What were you doing with Cosette? Don't deny it. I've been following you since you left the Rue Taitbout.'

Frédéric grew pale. He started to speak, but the words died on his lips. His pallor increased and he looked around him in surprise, as if he was waking from a nightmare.

'Not so pleased with yourself now, are you?' cried Marius, triumphantly. 'Are you feeling the faintest twinge of remorse?'

'You're my friend,' Frédéric whispered finally. 'How could you imagine for one second that I could betray you?'

'I don't imagine, I saw.'

'You saw nothing. You thought you saw something, but it was what you wanted to see. You've been spending too much time with your new friends. It doesn't agree with you.'

'I shall spend time with whoever I choose!'

'Well, you'd do better to spend a little more time with Cosette. You have no right to break her heart. One day she may leave you.'

Marius leaned against his horse in an attitude of nonchalant cynicism, with his shoulders up, his head tilted to one side and his weight thrown onto one leg. 'I have no right to break her heart, you say?' he said somewhat less angrily. 'And I suppose you have the right to pick up the pieces of that broken heart and put them back together as you see fit?'

'You're despicable, Marius. If you weren't my friend, I'd make you swallow your words this minute.'

'Oh, really! Finally a little recklessness! Only I'm the injured one, Frédéric, and you must answer my challenge. I'm not a drunken ruffian like you, and I don't fight like one. But I don't suppose a scoundrel of your kind knows anything about the art of fighting.'

Hardly were the hurtful words out of Marius's mouth than Frédéric seized him by the throat. 'Do you want to know the rules of *my* art?' Watched by a number of amazed onlookers, to whom he paid no attention, he pulled Marius away from the horse and drew him into a carriage entrance. 'Let me tell you this, my poor Marius – you're no longer yourself. As for your model, that pompous fool Amédée d'Iguerande, he has a knack of confusing nobility with chaos, elegance with dissension, and style with blasphemy. He's enticed you with his preposterous stories and you've fallen into the trap like a greenhorn, to the point where you've repudiated your wife and your true friends. It's appalling.' He let go of Marius, who was shaking with rage and shame and seemed to be on the verge of tears. 'Never provoke me again, Marius. If you have something to ask, ask your wife. If I were you, I'd arrange to spend Mardi Gras evening in her company, and I'd dismiss that band of yellow gloves who claim to be your friends.'

Marius dusted himself off and lifted his head proudly. 'I'm not taking lessons from you. I am already engaged for the Mardi Gras evening. I shall make the descent of the Courtille with the Lord of the Ruffians and, whether you like it or not, I shall finish the evening with my friends at the Clan Destin in the Rue Aubry-le-Boucher. Now it's my turn to warn you. If I see you with Cosette again, I'll kill you.'

He walked back to his horse, took the reins and leapt into the saddle.

'Goodbye,' murmured Frédéric. He lowered his head despondently, crossed the road, and plunged into the surrounding greyness with an uncertain step. He was determined to find Amédée d'Iguerande. It was something that could not wait.

Amédée was pacing up and down his room under Clémence de Lavely's sardonic gaze. Ostentatious as the Marquis d'Iguerande's apartment might seem at first sight, closer inspection cast doubt on the level of material comfort he claimed to enjoy. The building was not in Saint-Germain, but in Saint-Antoine, a working-class district – which, as Amédée himself acknowledged, was a severe lapse of taste. The fact remained that this was where he lived, in a little house at the end of a courtyard, next to an eyesore with a sloping roof which was Louis-Désiré's home.

The marquis had little space to indulge his delusions of grandeur. The ground floor consisted of a small grey drawing room that led into a dining room, which was separated from the kitchen by a staircase of blended and polished oak dating back to Louis XIII with yellow and red ochre wall tiles. Little light penetrated to the ground floor.

On the first floor there was a bedroom full of mirrors and gilt, a bathroom and a small library, which contained a fine Erard piano, an authentic Boulle console table and two Louis XV armchairs upholstered in Gobelins tapestry. The curtains and other trimmings were cabbage-green damask and at forty sous a metre nothing to boast about.

Amédée d'Iguerande was pacing up and down his room in his shirt-sleeves. He stopped abruptly and turned to face the bed, on which Clémence lay sprawled.

'I want you and our friend to be reconciled,' he said testily. 'If you let him slip out of your hands, then he slips out of my hands too.'

Clémence folded her arms. Before answering, she looked at the man who had once been her lover and who, it would seem, still sporadically fulfilled that function. There was no tenderness in her gaze. Amédée's borrowed manners displayed that peculiar vigour, that sense of certainty and self-importance which domination conferred. But there was the rub – poor Amédée no longer dominated anything and Clémence despised him all the more.

'*You* want?' she said at last acerbically. 'And what about *me*? Why does nobody ever ask me what *I* want? What can I do, if your little baron hasn't shown himself for days? When he left me, he said he was going to buy me a ring, and I've seen neither him nor the ring since. Is that any way to treat a lady?'

Amédée looked her up and down with a mixture of self-importance and hostile irritation. 'A lady?' he scoffed. 'You flatter yourself.'

Clémence stood up, furious. 'Now we see your true colours, Marquis! I may not be a lady, but you're no man!'

A resounding slap in the face sent her back onto the bed.

'All right, then,' said Amédée through gritted teeth, rubbing his hand. 'If my friend the baron is so much better in bed than I ever was, what are you waiting for? Go and throw yourself into his arms!' He paused. 'Come, let's stop quarrelling, Clémence,' he went on, in a more accommodating tone. 'Haven't we become the best of friends? Haven't we a common past? A common aim?'

Clémence grew pale. 'What past are you talking about?' she asked, and her voice was cold. 'Shall I remind you? Oh, I know, I wasn't a good enough match for you. You would never have compromised yourself by asking for my hand in marriage. But not content with seducing me, you knocked me up, Marquis. Yes, I know, such street language shocks you, except when it's in your own mouth. Since you fell in love with that stupid little goose the Baroness Pontmercy, you've become as shy as a virgin. You've never spared anybody, but we all have to spare you. And that child you spirited away from me, what happened to him? He must be eight by now . . .'

Amédée was tying a crushed-strawberry silk cravat around his neck. When he heard this, his gestures became confused and his complexion deathly pale. 'I've already told you a hundred times – you lost consciousness and the child was stillborn. Louis-Désiré took care of everything.'

'Yes, it's always Louis-Désiré who takes care of everything for you, isn't it?' said Clémence with cold irony, picking up her things and starting to dress. 'Louis-Désiré, that's the only name on your lips! How very convenient! If anything goes wrong, blame Louis-Désiré Burdin! Dump it all on his shoulders!'

Amédée was putting on an embroidered waistcoat and an overquilted grey frock coat. 'Cruel words to use about a hunchback, my dear Clémence,' he said, quite pleased with himself.

'*You* are the cruel one, Amédée. I loved you and I still love you. You destroyed me and you know it. So don't talk to me about our common past. I carry that past like a burden, and you throw it in my face whenever it suits you.'

'You're exaggerating, Clémence. I love you, too. You may have reached a certain age, but you're still charming and desirable. You must take advantage of that, my darling. And, I would add, take advantage of it positively.'

Clémence bit her lip, but no tears flowed. A haughty young woman, she was too elegant to let her humiliation show. She felt a tenacious resentment towards life which in the end was merely an extension of her disdain for men, and for Amédée and Marius in particular. Even though she had no personal fortune, she swore to herself that they would soon be smiling on the other sides of their faces.

Once she was ready, Amédée saw her to the door. 'Can I count on you for Mardi Gras evening?'

'As usual, alas.'

'You're an angel, Clémence. I'll love you as long as I live.'

No sooner had she left than Amédée's steward made his appearance. The master turned to his servant conspiratorially.

'Were you eavesdropping?'

The hunchback bowed deferentially. 'I would never do such a thing, Monsieur.'

The marquis burst out laughing and clapped his hands. 'Madame de Lavely will calm down soon enough. Without us, she's nothing. Do you remember? She had a deaf lover in those days, and she could never get used to the idea that her new lover – yours truly – could hear. Positively comic, isn't it, my dear Louis-Désiré?'

The steward smiled in agreement. 'You whispered something about it to me, Marquis. Madame de Lavely has always been destined for a career as Messalina. If you have the wisdom of Claudius, nothing can happen to you.'

'And what of you, my dear Louis-Désiré?' asked Amédée anxiously. 'Are you reserving the role of Narcissus for yourself?'

'I dared not say so, Monsieur.'

'Don't you know that Narcissus, after all his scheming, was finally put to death?' Amédée smiled when he saw his steward's face drop. 'By the way, talking of Madame de Lavely, why have you never shown me the child I had with her?'

'He died,' replied the steward, in a tone that tried to be both sincere and full of pathos. 'Are you implying I'd have had the audacity to kill a child?'

'Certainly not – though it is quite a fashionable sport nowadays. But women are like that. If they don't see things with their own eyes, they don't believe them. They lack imagination. They're idealists when we court them and then, when they think we belong to them, they become materialists. We're exactly the opposite. In fact, their whole being exudes frivolity, just as frivolity explains their being. It's downright disconcerting. Take that little Cosette. Can you imagine? She's resisting me.'

'Be patient, Marquis. She'll make a fine match.'

Amédée gave a twisted grin. 'What do you mean? Cosette isn't free. She's Baron Pontmercy's wife.'

'I meant that she's a good match for the game you're playing,' the steward corrected him with an avuncular expression. 'To seduce the wife of one's friend is a distraction that can be quite entertaining. Especially when one has one's eyes on the husband's fortune. Besides, you know as well as I do, Marquis, that he who pays still has obligations, and he who is paid still has rights.'

'Come, come, my dear Louis-Désiré, don't count your chickens before they're hatched. Do I have to remind you that I love Madame Pontmercy as I've never loved before?' He took up his hat, coat and cane. 'By the way, is everything ready for this evening?'

'Everything, Marquis.'

On Mardi Gras evening Marius told Cosette that he would not be spending the evening with her. She glared at him. That afternoon she had told Verjat that she was expecting a baby.

'In September,' she had said.

During her last visit to the doctor with Frédéric Rivolier, Cosette had learned, to her immense relief, that she was one month pregnant. Since the cholera alarm and her previous failure, she had been fearing the worst.

Verjat, clearly delighted, had wished her every happiness – thinking perhaps as he did so of the time when he had heaped misfortune on Cosette's mother. He had sown so much terror and grief around him. Having once had the strength to hate, he must now have the strength to love. He enjoyed reading Rousseau and Diderot, two writers with opposing views from whom he drew both the comforting thought that the general good and individual happiness could coincide and the depressing thought that reality and the constraints of society must constantly clash. He made an effort not to be unhappy, while always thinking the opposite.

Marius, lacking Verjat's wisdom, took cover in cynicism. Cosette, though, was less resigned. 'So is all we've been through nothing but simulation and duplicity?' she asked him, with a melancholy look. 'You must tell me, Marius. And if you want me to leave you or to find another man, you must say that, too.'

Marius was struck dumb. Until now Cosette's apparent passivity had exasperated him. He had taken her sense of propriety for indifference. But now his little girl was rebelling and it made him pause. He gripped the rock crystal in his pocket and thought confusedly of the happy moments they had shared, but also of the sight of her and Frédéric sharing a fiacre.

'I promised Amédée I'd be with him,' he said shakily.

'And what of me?' retorted Cosette. 'What do you promise me?'

He did not know what to say. Cosette had become a mystery to him, and to solve this mystery would require too great an effort on his part. 'In the future, many things are going to change,' he finally said, folding a letter destined for Amédée.

Cosette walked with him to the garden gate. Although she was on the verge of tears, she was strong enough to restrain herself and not offer him her weakness as a sacrifice.

'Why are you so stubborn, Marius?'

'That's just the way I am.'

'So am I. So it's the last time I'll tell you this – be careful.'

Marius lowered his head like a child being punished, and put his hat on. He had made no mention of Frédéric, had uttered no reproach. He had retreated into that painful silence he called stubbornness, but which was merely the pathetic consequence of his inability to talk, to snap his fingers at his pride, at his so-called self-esteem. There are people who miss the opportunity to feel simple joy for fear of revealing their true feelings or stooping to what they consider to be weakness. In making others suffer, they suffer themselves.

In the Opéra district, towards the south side of the Boulevard des Capucines, Marius mingled with all those insignificant buffoons to whom nothing mattered any longer except being casual and light-hearted. Amédée was voluble, Louis de Vergne sententious. Eugène Sue and Robert d'Androisy were parading in a multi-coloured cabriolet, in which a huge coachman was ensconced on a seat with a broad silk-fringed cover.

The Lord of the Ruffians, dressed like the marquis of the chain gang, had invited Marius and Amédée into his coach, a magnificent vehicle pulled by a team of six black horses, which aroused the admiration of the thousands of onlookers massed on the pavements and at windows along the route. Everybody applauded Charles de la Battut, the organizer of this brilliant carnival, who stood in his coach, preceded by his grooms and followed by hundreds of tilburys and landaus filled with his friends in extravagant fancy dress.

Marius and Amédée had not put on fancy dress. One sombre, the other radiant, they waved magnanimously to the grisettes in ballet shoes who were throwing them flowers and sugared almonds.

'To the Courtille!' bellowed the Lord of the Ruffians. 'To Belleville! Let the festivities commence!'

'What's going to happen now?' Marius asked Amédée.

'The same thing that happened in 1832 and 1833, my dear fellow.'

'Which is what?'

'All of fashionable Paris is getting ready to go up to Belleville with the people of the outskirts. Do you see all these carriages?'

Behind the Lord of the Ruffians' coach stretched an uninterrupted file of fiacres, cabriolets, wagons, open carriages and four-wheeled barouches. The people in them, dressed as marquises, Turks, Mohicans, clowns, lansquenets, Roman emperors or Comtesses du Barry, were screaming abuse and throwing eggs at the frenzied crowd, who were drinking and dancing the cancan.

'Flour and eggs?' Marius said in surprise, with a touch of indignation in his voice.

'And why not, my dear fellow?'

'I'm thinking of all those who are dying of hunger . . .'

Amédée made a casual gesture. 'I can only agree with what you are saying. But if you and I weren't here, do you think it would make a jot of difference to the world? Insolent wealth is merely a response to insulting poverty. We are but pawns in a fantastic game that demands masters on one side and slaves on the other. If we have to choose, isn't it better to be on the side of the masters and of insolence?'

Marius turned and threw a murderous look at the two powdered footmen standing at the back of the coach, as if he held them responsible for his indignation. He resumed his position, grumbling.

All at once, the coach swerved slightly, and La Battut was thrown to the side.

'So, Lord Seymour, can't you stay on your feet any more?' cried an elegantly dressed man brandishing a bottle.

La Battut's only response was to jump out of the coach and give the dancer a punch that sent him flying backwards to collide with a woman selling eau de Cologne.

'He won't confuse me with Lord Seymour again!' he said to Amédée, as he got back into the coach.

The procession headed for Belleville and the Faubourg du Temple. The old village of Belleville was on a plateau, flanked on the north by the Butte de Chaumont and the Butte de Beauregard. The lower part of Belleville's main street, known also as the Haute-Courtille, consisted almost entirely of open-air taverns.

Marius no longer knew where to look. So this was the beautiful carnival encouraged by the regime of Louis-Philippe, was it?

'To see Paris without the Courtille is like seeing Rome without the Pope!' cried Amédée. 'Look at all those taverns! We've arrived. There's the Grand-Saint-Martin – they won't let you in there unless you buy a litre of wine per person.'

Marius saw a huge tavern, where a fat manageress with a ruddy face and a moustache sat enthroned behind a counter open to the street, which was piled high with all sorts of dishes – fricassées of game in wine and fish in sauce, loins of veal, huge steaming legs of mutton seasoned with garlic, salads and beans. A crowd of swaying shepherdesses and villainous-looking harlequins was yelling obscene refrains. Everywhere people were knocking against each other, dancing, jostling. Wine flowed in all the restaurants – the Boeuf-Rouge and the Coq-Hardi, the Epée-de-Bois and the Galant-Jardinier, the Carotte-Filandreuse and the Papa-Dénoyez.

Amédée, standing in the coach, spied a brazen young woman with bare thighs. 'Hey, you!' he called. 'I'll have you! Join me at Le Sauvage!' Le Sauvage was the fashionable restaurant in Belleville for yellow gloves and society women.

At that moment there came a terrible crash of broken glass, and a miller emptied his sack of flour over La Battut's coach. Instead of laughing and taking the incident lightly, Marius lost his temper and insulted the miller.

'Come on, we're supposed to be enjoying ourselves,' said Amédée to calm him.

Marius wiped his frock coat with the back of his hand. 'You may be enjoying yourself, Amédée,' he replied furiously, 'but I'm not. When you learn that your wife is deceiving you, you don't feel much like enjoying yourself.'

Amédée felt himself blush with confusion. Luckily, his face was covered in flour.

'And what's more, with someone I considered my best friend,' Marius continued.

'But . . . what do you mean?' stammered Amédée.

'A journalist like me, a fierce Republican who drinks full to bursting and dreams of quenching his thirst with the blood of the bourgeoisie.'

'By Jove! Is that so?' said Amédée, breathing a deep sigh of relief. He thought immediately of the man he had seen coming out of the house in the Rue Plumet, the man of whom Cosette had talked evasively. Uncontrollable rage soon replaced his embarrassment. He, too, wiped the traces of flour from his face and clothes. Perhaps, even at that crucial moment, he was polishing one of his eternal sarcastic remarks, for his mouth had tensed to mock poor Marius for his inability to keep an eye on his own wife. What he longed to tell him above all was that if a man loses a woman, it is because he is not capable of keeping her. But he restrained himself. He was thinking of the future. Clémence was in the vicinity, waiting to make a dazzling and triumphant entrance, accompanied by his faithful Louis-Désiré. He had foreseen everything. 'My dear fellow,' he said in his most neutral tone, 'why do you do things for which you reproach yourself later? Train yourself to be cold and indifferent, accept your contradictions. If we have to be dependent on one thing, Baron, let it be our superior egotism.'

Marius turned to Amédée, took his hand, and shook it effusively. 'You're right, Amédée. You're always right. And that's why I'm going to give you this letter. In fact, I was planning to give it to you anyway.'

He took a folded sheet of paper out of his frock coat and handed it to Amédée, who blushed deeply, thinking of the letter he had sent Cosette. Then Amédée read it. It was very short. In the event that any harm should come to Marius, he, Amédée, was charged with taking care of Cosette and managing her inheritance. All duly signed and dated.

'You're mad,' was Amédée's immediate embarrassed response. 'What makes you think any harm is likely to come to you?'

Marius looked Amédée straight in the eye. 'Are you my friend?'

'Don't you know that by now?'

'Then don't refuse me this. I should be most horribly disappointed if you did. It's very important to me that you keep this letter. As you can see, it's signed by my notary, Maître Barrot. Promise to do for me what I would do for you.'

'I promise, Marius.'

Just as he was about to put the letter away in his waistcoat, Amédée had one of those sudden uncharacteristic scruples of his. 'I agree to everything, Marius, but I'd like you to add a caveat to the letter.'

'What?'

'That it's valid for a period of two years, and that when those two years are up it's null and void.'

Marius made a gesture at once detached and resigned. 'Your request proves to me what a noble soul you have, Amédée. If that's what you really want, give me the letter.'

Marius complied with the request, and handed the corrected page back to Amédée. Surprised by his own generous impulse and barely able to explain it even to himself, Amédée tucked the paper away in his frock coat. 'I'm indebted to you, Baron. I owe you the happiness you deserve. As you'll see, I have a surprise for you.'

He stood up and waved to the occupants of one of the cabriolets that was just then parking. Louis de Vergne answered the wave, and then himself waved to the occupants of another tilbury that stood some distance away.

It was the signal for which Louis-Désiré had been waiting. With the icy deference that made him seem more a master than a servant – indeed, he often had both the tone and the manners of a master – he helped Clémence de Lavely out of the carriage. She was wearing a very long black hooded cloak that covered her down to her ankles, and her face was hidden by a black mask trimmed with lace.

'Take this,' said Louis-Désiré to Clémence. 'You may find it useful.'

Clémence examined the little flask. 'Another devilish trick of yours?'

'It's no trick, Madame de Lavely. I'm simply making use of the prodigality of nature. Between you and me, it's a perfectly innocuous mixture.' He drew closer to the young woman. 'An elixir that can give your beloved all the energy with which your devastating beauty deserves to be honoured,' he explained, with a mixture of hypocritical solemnity and revolt against the role he had imposed on himself.

'Devastating?' murmured Clémence, in an altered voice. 'Like the way you intervened seven years ago to spirit my child away?'

Louis-Désiré took offence. 'Madame, the child was dead! I was merely doing my duty.'

'Your duty? You call that a duty? To remove a child from his mother's eyes, no matter if he was dead?'

'I have no regrets about it, Madame, even now,' the steward continued solemnly. 'I thought I was doing the right thing in sparing you needless torments. And my master will not contradict me on that.' They were about to walk to La Battut's coach, but Louis-Désiré stopped Clémence and handed her another flask. 'Let me also give you this. It contains a powerful narcotic. Whoever takes a massive dose of the stimulant I gave you will find himself literally in a state of madness. Every remedy needs its antidote, doesn't it? I think it will bring you luck.'

'Oh yes?' said Clémence, feigning surprise, and with a rapid gesture she placed her hand on the steward's hump. 'And wouldn't this give me even more luck?'

Louis-Désiré could not help giving a start. 'Indeed, Madame,' he said between clenched teeth, then winked. 'But don't abuse it. Luck is like a bird flying behind a blind man's back. You have to know when to seize it as it passes, otherwise it turns against you.'

'Is that a threat?'

'I wouldn't dream of it, Madame.'

And they made their way to La Battut's coach, where Marius and Amédée were waiting for them.

It cannot be said that Marius was especially delighted with Amédée's surprise. But he was in such a state of abandon that he made no protest when Clémence, adjusting her mask, climbed into the coach, as Amédée climbed out and walked off with his steward.

Amédée lost no time in informing Louis-Désiré of the insane mission which Marius had entrusted to him. The hunchback responded with a smirk of triumph. They reached Le Sauvage, where La Battut had already preceded them, flanked by his court and by a multitude of *marquises* whose breasts burst from their bodices just as in the good old days of the Directory.

Inside the coach, Clémence snuggled into Marius's arms. 'You don't love me any more, you naughty boy.'

Marius denied the accusation. 'I was busy, I've had problems . . .'

'And my ring?'

'It wasn't beautiful enough for you.'

Clémence planted her lips on his and kissed him passionately. 'I love you so, my Marius. You're so different from the others. If we lived together, I'd make you the happiest of men. You'd be my little boy.'

Marius caressed Clémence under her cloak, took her by the chin and moved her face back from his. He noted that everything about her was exquisite, except her mind. Her conviction that she could make him happy seemed to him an insult to his intelligence. He was not unaware that, under the cover of a sweet countenance, she had a coldness of heart which her scheming and feigned bursts of enthusiasm could not always conceal. But he understood that she was unhappy, and it seemed to him that her unhappiness might go some way towards explaining her insincerity. He knew almost nothing about her past, and nothing at all of the ties that had bound her and still bound her to Amédée. Would that have changed anything? It was far from certain. When women are shared, troubles finish – but when feelings are shared, troubles start. Yet Marius did not love Clémence and Clémence did not love Marius.

'What are you thinking about?' asked Clémence. Her big eyes with their long lashes were diabolically beautiful.

'About you,' lied Marius.

Clémence lifted her black cloak and bent her head with a virginal air. 'Look how I dressed for you.'

Beneath her cape, she was naked but for a pair of grey stockings held up by ribboned garters that set off her alabaster thighs and the abundant fleece of her pubic hair. Marius felt passion rise in him, all the more so in that Clémence, lifting her cape even higher, now uncovered part of her bosom. The young man looked around and kissed Clémence's neck with renewed desire.

'Aren't we going to be seen?' asked Clémence, suddenly anxious at the favour she had just granted.

Nobody was paying attention to the coach, still less to what was happening inside. Everyone was drinking and feasting. Clémence drew Marius to her while her dimpled hands probed feverishly beneath the delicate fabric of his shirt. He gave in to her caresses, transported by the touch of her voluptuous body, his desire all the greater for the unusual situation in which they found themselves. Then everything else ceased to exist.

Amédée and his companions gave La Battut's troops the slip after midnight and continued the festivities at the Clan Destin, in an ambience that was hardly more intimate, because the place was full. The man in black was already there – he might have arrived with Amédée and his friends. At an opportune moment, he disappeared into the kitchen, where the Catman was waiting for him.

'There are too many people here, Tardier. I really can't trust you, can I? Look, here's what you need to bring the Kitten down a peg or two.'

The Kitten was parading up and down the room on the arm of Perfect Love, who, like the good sort that he was, had not even recognized the young man he had almost suffocated a few weeks earlier. When Marius reminded him of the episode, Perfect Love held out his hand. 'No hard feelings?'

'No hard feelings, even if you did try to strangle me.'

Jesus, of course, had not been invited to the festivities. He was on guard at the workshop. The man in black was surprised. He cast a disdainful glance at his accomplice. Tardier never did exactly what was expected of him. To tell the truth, the man in black did not like the old sycophant, whose every word was soft and conspiratorial, whose one thought, one passion in life, was plotting, betraying and selling his fellow men down the river. In punishment, he did not tell him about the letter that Marius had given the marquis. In future, he would keep him informed only of what was strictly necessary.

'Jesus?' caterwauled the Catman. 'We've got the Mullet and his cut-throats, just in case.'

The other raised his eyes to heaven. 'I don't trust that Mullet of yours. I don't want him to see me. What's been happening with him and little Raphaël?'

The Catman seemed preoccupied. 'He beat him black and blue again. If I hadn't intervened, Jesus would have done the Mullet in.'

The man in black glared at him. 'If the Mullet carries on like this, he's going to be in trouble. I've already told you, I want Raphaël made into a cut-throat, and a good one. I may need him one day.'

As he left the kitchen, he passed Gammy Leg, who was again cursing the Kitten. 'Don't worry,' he said to her in a conciliatory tone. 'Everything will come out right in the end. In fact, I believe the Catman has a suggestion for you.'

He continued on his way and sat down in the shadows.

Now everybody was dancing the *chahut*. Clémence, almost as drunk as Marius, occasionally lifted her black cloak to show him her velvet thighs. A little earlier, they had climbed the stepladder to the first floor, where couples were making love, and Clémence had offered herself to him. He felt ashamed. Beside him, Amédée was with the little grisette he had picked up in the Courtille, kissing her full on the mouth and fondling her.

She must have been fifteen or sixteen, her flesh glowing provocatively with rude health.

Marius turned to Clémence. 'She's so young . . .' he murmured, with a shocked air.

'You're never too young to be soiled,' retorted Clémence, with bitterness in her voice.

In the room downstairs the Kitten was dancing between the tables, and watching everything with a proprietary eye. This fine society, she kept telling herself, was not so very different from her own. She vowed to turn the Clan Destin into the meeting place for fashionable Paris.

Huddled in the darkness that suited him so well, the man in black observed her. A smile widened his narrow mouth. That slut would be the first on the list.

Suddenly three masked men burst in. The one who appeared to be their leader charged straight at Amédée, who was busy with his grisette and did not see the blow coming. He was snatched from his chair by an iron grip. His attacker, who wore a turquoise velvet mask, was tall and well built, with curly red hair. He pulled Amédée up and threw him violently back onto the table where he had been sitting. The half-naked grisette shot out of her chair and ran to the counter, squealing like a mouse caught in a trap. Tardier, his face framed in the doorway, looked reprovingly at the Mullet and the two swaggering characters with him, and they stood up amid the din – the band was still playing – and hurried towards the intruders. The other man's companions drew pistols and pointed them at the cut-throats' chests.

'One more step and you'll be celebrating Mardi Gras in the other world,' said the tall redhead with a menacing air. Then he turned to Amédée, who was reeling, stunned and uncomprehending. 'So here's the slimy cock of the walk who defiles everything he touches! How ugly and ridiculous he is!' Without any warning, he took two steps forward and slapped Amédée hard across the face. The marquis did not even have time to dodge the blow. 'I hope you'll do me the honour of crossing swords with me, you filthy scoundrel!' said the stranger in a resonant voice.

When he heard that voice Marius broke through the circle that had formed around Amédée and the intruders. He was as pale as death.

'I don't fight with a mask,' retorted Amédée, pulling on the lapels of his frock coat.

The man took off his velvet mask and threw it at the Mullet and his henchmen. 'Are you satisfied?'

'I'm the offended party,' said Amédée, noticing Marius's stunned expression. 'I therefore choose pistols.'

'You're right, Marquis. Pistols are better suited to a blackguard like you.'

Amédée exchanged a brief look with Marius. He, too, had recognized the man. It was the fellow he had seen coming out of the house in the Rue Plumet, Baroness Pontmercy's supposed seducer.

'You've insulted me and struck me, Monsieur,' said Amédée, with suppressed anger. 'You will answer for it at Vincennes tomorrow morning.'

Frédéric Rivolier did not bat an eyelid. 'Who are your seconds?' he asked.

Amédée indicated Louis de Vergne, Robert d'Androisy and – Marius.

'No, not me . . .'

Amédée glared at his friend.

'In that case,' said Frédéric, 'would Baron Marius Pontmercy agree to be my second, together with these two gentlemen?'

Marius turned his head in search of support, but the only face he could see was Tardier's troubling and gleeful countenance, looming out of the shadows like a ghost, and he did not even recognize him. 'I need to think,' he said, trying to make his voice sound stronger than he felt. 'Monsieur Rivolier and the marquis are both friends of mine, and I—'

'You can't choose, is that it?' Amédée interrupted. 'You disappoint me, Monsieur.'

'He has already disappointed me,' said Frédéric, turning back to Amédée. 'Until tomorrow, then, Monsieur. Vincennes at eight o'clock.'

The three men went out backwards and their departure provoked a slight uproar among the revellers. Nobody was pressing around Marius. Even Clémence responded with polite silence when he reached out his hand to her. Amédée turned his back on him and slipped out quickly in the company of Louis de Vergne.

'You ought to walk home,' said the Kitten to Marius with a giggle. 'There's nothing like fresh air to buck up your ideas!'

Marius put on his top hat and left the Clan Destin. Tardier watched him go. 'It's so wonderful, all the things that happen here!' he murmured, rubbing his hands.

5

Marius did not sleep a wink that night. He rose early in the morning, opened the shutters of his bedroom, stretched and looked out. The rising sun cast long, thin orange rays on the panes of the winter garden. He inhaled the sweet scent of the blooming narcissi and turned back into his room to look at his watch. In less than two hours it was quite possible that one of his friends would die – and still he had not chosen. At about three or four in the morning – he was no longer sure of the exact time – he had almost gone to Cosette's bedroom. But how could he break the news to her? How could he confess to her that he had to choose between two friends, one of whom might be about to kill the other? And to think that he had been stupid enough to tell Frédéric where he was going to be that evening, and had even given him the address of the Clan Destin!

He put on a white shirt, a shiny waistcoat and his sky-blue frock coat. He looked again at his watch. His jaw tensed. He put on his Sikorski boots, knotted his navy-blue cravat, quickly brushed his hair and tiptoed downstairs. Once in the kitchen, he swallowed a glass of milk and forced himself to eat a piece of bacon with a slice of bread. He was not usually such an early riser. Although he had been trying hard not to make a noise, he woke Cosette.

'What are you doing up so early?'

Her voice startled him.

'As you can see – having breakfast . . .'

'You seem strange, Marius.'

'What on earth are you talking about?'

'You look as if you're hiding something.'

He stared at her. Her face, usually a little pale, was this morning tinged with the most vivid colours. With her loose hair, her embroidered and topstitched cotton nightdress with the sky-blue silk ribbon, and her olive-green cashmere shawl, she looked beautiful. Her big eyes seemed to see right through the man seated before her, the man who each day was a greater disappointment to her.

'I have to go to the paper, then to the Bois de Vincennes,' muttered Marius. 'Our friend Frédéric has a duel on his hands. I'm his second.'

Cosette slumped, overcome by the news. 'A duel?'

'He had some fairly sharp words with a certain gentleman and the gentleman asked him for redress. It's fairly common.'

'Fairly common, you say?'

Cosette sat down next to Marius, placed her elbows on the table, and buried her head in her hands. Marius made a slight movement, as if he were about to take her in his arms and tell her how much he shared her distress. But Cosette's abrupt dejection, instead of moving him to pity, simply made his jealousy and hostility towards Frédéric all the stronger.

'You're getting into quite a state over our friend. You must really love him.'

Cosette looked up, her jaw clenched. 'You don't seem to set great store by your friend,' she said, breathless with emotion as she wiped her tears feverishly. 'I wonder what's happening to you.'

'What's happening is that I don't like betrayals.'

'Who's the betrayer here?'

Marius glanced at his watch again and stood up hurriedly, doubtless feeling a certain shame at accusing Cosette of his own fault. 'I have to go. Affairs of honour can't wait.'

Cosette made no gesture to keep him. 'You always have to go,' she said in a neutral voice, wrapping her shawl about her. 'But it's strange how you imagine things about me that aren't true and I'm not allowed to imagine things about you that are true. It's a terrible thing to say, but I don't believe you any more.'

At once troubled, distraught, hurt and irritated, and not knowing which of these feelings was uppermost, Marius said nothing, but took up his gloves, his cane and his hat.

Cosette, however, was unrelenting. 'One more thing before you leave. I know who's going to fight Frédéric. I can see it in your eyes. A gentleman, you said? One day perhaps, though I know it would be a cruel blow for you, I shall enlighten you about the person you call a gentleman. Monsieur d'Iguerande deserves neither the name nor the honour.'

'I forbid you to insult my friend!' retorted Marius, opening the door. 'You've guessed right, of course. Yes, Amédée is going to fight Frédéric.

And in case you have any doubts, let me tell you that I'm sick with worry at the thought of what's going to happen. But what can I do? It was Frédéric who challenged Amédée and not the other way round. Do you have a solution? And you don't know the worst of it. Both of them have asked me to be their second. What would you do in my place? Would you go? Or would you wriggle out of it?' He crossed the threshold and pulled his hat down furiously. 'Yes, I know,' he went on, in a tone that was both aggressive and sardonic, 'in my place, you would choose Frédéric. Being as close as you are to that gentleman, who boasts of being my friend, you can only support his just cause.'

Cosette shook her head sadly. It was at an hour like this that she had fallen in love with Marius, spontaneously, unthinkingly. It had been self-evident and inevitable. Her love had blossomed as if by magic, in a reckless, impetuous, inspired impulse that had seemed to spring from her and her alone. Now she realized that it was an impulse that depended on, and drew sustenance from, a similar impulse from Marius. Seeing him as he was now, so cold, so indifferent, and so pitiful, the fear seized her that she would henceforth be incapable of loving him.

'For the first time I find you ugly, Marius.'

Marius ran through the garden to the gate, walked to La Roche-Dragon's stable and saddled his horse. He was not accustomed to that tone from Cosette. Despair was stinging his temples.

Duels were always the same. No matter if the weather was fine or gloomy, the sky lost its colour. The men wore black, the surroundings were like the darkness of death. Grey was the colour of apprehension.

And yet it was a fine morning in Vincennes. A beautiful day not to die.

The two adversaries had already arrived. Marius dismounted, glanced at the carriages parked near two huge chestnut trees, and headed straight for Amédée and his seconds. Frédéric stood waiting, bareheaded and in shirtsleeves. It was clear that his friend had chosen.

'Monsieur,' said Marius to Amédée, 'I'm here to second you.'

'I'm delighted,' said the marquis, with a quiet sense of triumph.

Marius bowed his head and avoided meeting Frédéric's eyes. Frédéric, caressing the pistol, which had been presented to him in a mahogany case, did not seem surprised by his friend's choice. Louis de Vergne and Robert d'Androisy were present. The former was finding it difficult to conceal his emotion, the latter wore a mawkish and self-satisfied smile. He was a tall, stooped man with large, transparent blue eyes, a face like St Sebastian riddled with arrows, and thinning hair, which he combed forward and tried to keep out of draughts and sudden gusts of wind. He carefully avoided letting anyone guess his thoughts, and never replied to direct questions except with commonplace remarks. Using his apparent frankness as a shield, which succeeded in deceiving his peers, he liked to present himself as a jovial fellow and a rebel, which deceived nobody. Cowardly and timorous, Robert d'Androisy was the very image of the polite society in which he moved, a society whose only commitment was to its own self-interest. He had the bearing of a courageous knight and the mind of a thief. When he spared other people, it was the better to spare himself. He was a false rebel and a true lackey.

Marius hated this insipid aristocrat with his Jesuitical manners and his evasive rhetoric. The sight of his smile immediately made him regret that he had chosen Amédée's camp. 'Why are you smiling like that?' he asked, with a touch of aggression in his voice.

Being a night bird, Robert d'Androisy did not greatly care for daylight. Still less did he care for direct attacks. His smile froze at once. 'Your hostility grieves me, dear Baron. I'm not delighted at anything, believe me. I always tell the truth.'

Marius laughed. 'If you love the truth so much, Monsieur, why do you try to conceal your baldness under that rug of dirty hair? I advise you to avoid smiling in that way again.'

'Come, Baron,' said Louis de Vergne in a low voice, 'what are you trying to prove? That you are the kind of person with whom it is impossible to associate?'

'Precisely,' said Marius, stubbornly. 'And I don't like Monsieur d'Androisy's smile.'

'Who's fighting, Marius?' Amédée cut in. 'You or I? Come, now – a little dignity, please. Can't you see that our opponents are laughing at us?'

Without further ado, he took off his hat and his frock coat, which he entrusted to the inevitable Louis-Désiré. A pistol was presented to him, and he reached out his hand to take it. His trembling lips, his pallor, his distraught expression – all announced the terrible emotion of that supreme moment.

Finally Marius calmed down, and the seconds, as was the custom, conferred. The usual advice was given, and the two adversaries were placed thirty paces apart one from the other. It had been agreed by both sides that Robert d'Androisy would clap his hands three times, and that the third clap would be the signal for Amédée and Frédéric to fire.

The two adversaries stood half turned, with pistols raised, studying each other. Hatred could be read in Amédée's eyes, an amused detachment in Frédéric's. It was as if Frédéric, and not Amédée, was now the dandy. Whatever the case, at the third clap Amédée and Frédéric fired. Frédéric's bullet went wide of the mark, while Amédée's lodged itself in Frédéric's chest. Frédéric dropped his weapon, swivelled and fell to his knees.

Amédée took his pistol by the barrel and threw it to Louis-Désiré. Then, the only expression on his face that of a duty fulfilled, he moved away nonchalantly, took his things from Louis de Vergne and walked towards his carriage. In passing, he brushed against Marius. 'There's an obstacle out of your way, my friend,' he declared in an expressionless voice. 'Though, knowing you, I'm sure you will try to help the man who betrayed you. So I'll leave you to it. By the way, I agree with you – I don't like Monsieur d'Androisy's smile.' He put on his coat and hat and placed his hand on Marius's shoulder. 'You're a difficult man to fathom, Baron,' he said softly. 'Frankly, I wonder what possessed me to become besotted with you. And this time I'm sincere. All this is positively unfortunate. However, if you're in the mood, I'll be at the fencing school this afternoon.'

And he went back to his carriage.

Louis de Vergne, close on Amédée's heels, gave Marius a regretful look. Robert d'Androisy put the pistols back in their case and followed. As he passed Marius, his head lowered, Marius caught him by the arm, causing him to sway. 'You smiled again, Monsieur.'

D'Androisy took fright. 'You're mad, Marius. Stop this nonsense . . .'

Marius let him go. 'We'll meet again,' he said under his breath.

Then, at last yielding to his true nature, he rushed to Frédéric. His friends had laid him on his back.

'The wound is very serious,' said one of them, a young medical student like Frédéric. 'The lung has been perforated.'

Marius knelt and took his friend's head in his arms. Frédéric opened one eye and signalled to his friends to leave the two of them alone. Blood was trickling from the corner of his mouth. 'At least you can second me in my death,' he said to Marius, making an effort to smile.

'Don't talk nonsense, Frédéric. We'll take care of you, you'll pull through . . . Don't talk . . .'

Frédéric smiled wryly. 'I know, that's what they always say in situations like this . . .' Life was ebbing from him with every heartbeat. Blood gushed from his chest wound, staining his shirt. 'Marius,' he went on, gripping his friend's arm, 'I want you to know this – I haven't betrayed you . . .' It was becoming more and more difficult for him to breathe, but he resisted Marius's efforts to stop him speaking. 'Cosette was suffering from a strange sickness ... Her symptoms were similar to those of cholera ... I took her to see a friend of mine, a doctor ... Happily, what she thought was something bad turned out to be something good ... There it is, my friend ...'

Marius was overcome with emotion. How could he have been so wrong? 'I'm a wretch, Frédéric,' he said, his voice cracking. 'Forgive me ...'

'I forgive you, my friend ...'

A terrible hiccup interrupted the wounded man and he spat blood. Marius held him a little tighter. 'Do something!' he called to the two others. 'Fetch a doctor!'

Frédéric tensed for a brief moment, then his head fell to one side. And so he gave up his life, without anger towards his friend or fate, his heart at peace and his spirit light.

His two companions took hold of him, leaving Marius speechless and unhappy, once more in the grip of cruel and unrelenting doubts. They carried Frédéric to the carriage. One of them turned back to address Marius. 'In the event of his death, Frédéric asked us to proceed with the burial as quickly as possible. He didn't want any ceremony. The funeral will be at the Bagneux cemetery at two o'clock tomorrow. Will you be there?'

'I'll be there,' replied Marius.

Marius galloped to the gates of Paris. From there, he set off towards Ménilmontant. When he reached the Père-Lachaise cemetery, he got off his horse and entrusted it to a stable lad. He stood before the entrance for a good moment. The advantage with cemeteries, he tried to tell himself, is that you can look sad without really being sad. But he was sad. And his sadness was giving him the strength to overcome obstacles. Perhaps, by a supreme effort, he could rise above idle thoughts and vulgar weaknesses. He was twenty-four, the age of every folly, and he promised himself he would waste no more time revelling in ills he invented for himself. If giving direction to one's life had any meaning, then he undertook to give it one, and a true one. He would devote himself to Cosette, little Raphaël and his profession. He had had enough of nocturnal wanderings, enough of constant betrayals, enough of these ridiculous puppets who tried so hard to surprise everybody and surprised nobody. He had had enough of vague impulses and the company of shameful and irresponsible scoundrels. He would keep his distance, and merely observe from afar the excesses to which some men could be led by their low passions. Marius the immoralist was going to mend his ways and find a morality. Too many dead men had littered his path in the past year. And he had also had enough of blaming society or circumstances. Before changing society, Marius first had to change himself. He had to recognize that through his past errors he had indirectly provoked Frédéric's death. Frédéric was a martyr – the word was not too strong.

On entering the cemetery, he had the impression he was in the country. All around him stood elms, yews, oaks, chestnuts, acacias, sycamores, a forest of ancient trees and young shrubs, dense and overpowering, drawing their sap from the sap of the dead. He walked slowly, his cane held high like a drum major, unaware that a shadow was following him cautiously, hiding behind the tombs and mausoleums.

Marius walked, thoughtful and downcast, along the green, uneven paths of Père-Lachaise. He had spent his entire life squandering his passions, his gifts and his good intentions. He was now certain that in order to respect yourself you had first to respect others, even though you needed some imagination to make life more exciting.

A strange place, this cemetery, he thought as he passed close by the tombs, deciphering old inscriptions, marvelling at a name or a statue. He moved forward, sometimes hitting out at the air with his cane. The shadow still followed. Marius considered with amusement the monument erected to Héloïse and Abelard's memory. How pretentious it was! He thought he was going to burst out laughing. Instead, sobs gushed from his chest. He immediately struck his chest with his cane. 'You're not going to start again!' he reproached himself out loud.

He moved away from the monument, his head low and his hands behind his back, brooding on his bitterness. He climbed a small flight of steps to the Chemin du Dragon, where he found a name carved in letters of fire on a gravestone – Ney, Marshal of France. Marius stood for a while, staring at the last resting place of the hero who had lived in the Roure mansion, which was now the home of that vulgar upstart the Chevalier Dupartel. He let out a sigh and, letting his eyes sweep across this cemetery built on a hill like a gigantic arch, he uttered the name of the Bravest of the Brave. A name and a life that did not lack style – unlike Thiers, Guizot or even that miser Soult, who dreamed of bringing war to the streets of Paris.

He continued on his way, passing the vaults of Gobert, Lefevre and Murat. More illustrious names sounding the charge in a society that cared for nothing now but the last post. Were there any fine or loyal acts left to perform?

With a tender thought for his colonel father, who deserved to rest beside these heroes with their tricolour souls, it struck Marius that he had paid too much for other people – both literally and figuratively. He lumped together Clémence, Amédée and his friends. What about the letter he had given Amédée? Another mistake on his part, the kind of absurd whim so typical of his character. He was alive. Why should any harm befall him? But he would not cut every tie. Definitely not. He would continue to go to Lord Seymour's fencing school. One day he would even challenge Amédée and teach him a lesson. In the meantime, one thing was certain. As soon as possible he would break with Clémence.

All at once, he caught sight of an old wall and his heart began to pound. On it two warblers sang at the tops of their voices, while at its foot, near a yew tree pruned into the shape of a pyramid, half-hidden by couch grass and moss, stood a stone already blackened by the air and made green by the rain. Only the first words of the inscription were visible: *He sleeps . . .*

Here slept Jean Valjean, the man to whom Marius owed his life, Cosette's adoptive father, whose past she knew nothing of, and whose memory the cunning Thénardier, in coming to see Marius, had tried to tarnish. But the secret was safe. Cosette knew nothing of the penal colony, nor of the determined and fiendish Inspector Javert, who had committed suicide on 7 June 1832. Nobody must ever know. Ignorance was sometimes a blessing.

Marius meditated on the insignificant grave that sheltered the remains of a being who had been anything but insignificant. A just man among the just. A hero. Individuals of that calibre no longer existed. Marius measured how far he was from being that man's equal and how privileged he was in this world of the oppressed and the disadvantaged. If heaven existed, if there was a place reserved for the just somewhere, for men of good will, the unfortunate, the excluded, the outcast, the rejected, the little people, the generous of spirit and the pure of soul, then there was no doubt that Jean Valjean must be enjoying himself there in complete freedom.

Marius found himself addressing a wish to the God who demanded so much and who was so rarely seen. 'If I have to be like somebody, I'd like it to be Jean Valjean.' He held out his right hand. 'I swear, Jean Valjean, to honour your memory, to protect Cosette, to love her tenderly and to devote myself to living upright in this world, where too many people spend their time prostrating themselves before the laws of the ignominious and despicable.'

He took off his hat and bowed respectfully before Jean Valjean's grave. Then, as he took two steps back, he bumped into someone. He turned. His heart raced. The shadow that had followed him through the cemetery was Cosette.

'You?'

She looked straight into Marius's eyes. She, too, had been unable to resist the desire to come and meditate at her father's grave, and had been getting out of a fiacre when she'd seen him ride up to the cemetery gates. Surely this coincidence must be a sign of destiny? Clearly, all was not lost.

They stood speechless for a long while, embarrassed. Marius was thinking of all that wasted time. And of that day when, two years earlier, near the barricade in the Rue de la Chanvrerie, he had thought so hard about Cosette. It was impossible to live without her. How could he have been so wrong? Now he knew the truth, beyond any doubt. Cosette was the only woman for him, the light of his life.

He took a step towards her. 'Frédéric is dead,' he said. 'They're burying him at Bagneux tomorrow.'

Cosette nodded sadly. She had already guessed as much, seeing Marius's sombre expression as she followed him along the paths of Père-Lachaise. It had taken Frédéric's sacrifice to bring them back together. She held out her hands. 'My own true love,' she whispered.

Marius threw himself into her arms and held her tightly against him. Intertwined and magnificent, they let their tears run in a silence that seemed to last for ever. Happiness had found its refuge again.

The following day *La Quotidienne* reported that there had been a fatal outcome to a duel between a Republican and a Carlist, which was only partly true, and that the liberals were going to use this unfortunate incident to inflame public opinion once more, which was only partly false. *Le Journal des débats* devoted a mere paragraph to Frédéric's death, unlike *Le National* and *La Tribune*, which commented on the incident in vengeful terms. *La Caricature*, a particularly trenchant satirical newspaper in which an artist named Daumier displayed his talents, talked of the disgust inspired by the House of Orléans and called for an uprising. As usual,

everything was taking a political turn. Louis-Philippe was targeted person-
ally. Louis Blanc, for his part, lambasted the law passed in January that
required town criers to be authorized – an authorization that could be
revoked – even though he acknowledged that the criers were the 'heralds
of riot, the itinerant forerunners of insurrection'. There were reports that
workers were on the verge of rising in Lyons, Saint-Etienne and Marseilles, and that Mazzini was ready to invade Piedmont with a revolutionary army. That was the last straw. But the law on the criers was merely
the opening skirmish.

'I fear the worst, my dear fellow,' Armand Carrel had said to Marius
after Frédéric's funeral. 'The government is bound to intensify its offensive
against the revolutionary party. Throughout the history of monarchy, it's
only ever been misfortune that has made princes interesting. We're going
to get our money's worth.'

He was not far wrong. In the days that followed a new law was
introduced, banning associations of fewer than twenty people. The Society
for the Rights of Man, which had been circumventing the law, was its
main target.

The Republican party also came under fire, especially those Jacobins
who took their inspiration from 1793. It amounted to public humiliation.
But more was to follow. The time for half-measures was over. The deputy
Etienne Cabet, author of an impassioned *History of the Revolution of 1830*,
was sentenced to two years' imprisonment and a fine of four thousand
francs for violently denouncing the king in his newspaper, *Le Populaire*.

Towards the end of March the situation grew even more bitter. The
Republicans Guinard and Cavaignac published an open letter, in which
they referred to 'two men as justly and universally despised as Messieurs
Guizot and d'Argout', and called them 'loathsome', while Carrel, in *Le
National*, published an article entitled 'How to Make a Nation Disgusted
with Order'. To add insult to injury, the verdict on the members of the
Lyons friendly society who had been arrested in March was expected on 9
April and was sure to cause a public outcry.

Meanwhile Marius devoted himself relentlessly to his work. He read,
wrote for *Le National* and went out a great deal. One afternoon he went
to buy the ring Clémence had demanded – he had an idea at the back of
his mind.

Cosette often went with him to the theatre. One evening they saw a
performance of *Angèle* at the Comédie-Française. As they were coming
out, they ran into the author, Alexandre Dumas, accompanied by Raspail

and Arago, and with Marie Dorval, the play's blonde heroine, parading on his arm. To Cosette's great surprise, Dumas greeted Marius and urged him not to be too severe with his 'Angèle', punctuating his remark with a musketeer's laugh, before he drew Marie Dorval into a fiacre.

Cosette seemed impressed. 'Do you know Alexandre Dumas?'

'Oh, let's just say he knows me!' replied Marius nonchalantly.

The following evening, 9 April, Marius took Cosette to dinner at a great Parisian restaurant. 'To celebrate our wedding anniversary, even if I'm a month and three weeks late,' he explained, somewhat embarrassed. 'Wasn't it 16 February 1833?'

His first thought had been to take her to Véry in the Galerie du Beaujolais, where the portly Balzac, taking a respite from his four litres of coffee a day, would gorge himself on Ostend oysters, duck with turnips, Normandy sole and roast partridge. But finally he opted for the Café Hardy, because he had a craving for luxury and meat.

'So you hadn't forgotten the date of our wedding?' said Cosette in surprise, at once moved and troubled.

'You know how hopeless I am with dates. But not with things that dazzle me.'

Cosette was certainly dazzled by the restaurant, where you could enjoy kidneys and andouillettes with truffles and you could choose your meat from a buffet, where the head waiter would stab it with a fork and grill it in a white marble fireplace. Marius let Cosette choose the wine.

'A Saint-Amour,' said Cosette, without even a pause for thought.

'A pity there's no Saint-Valentin,' observed Marius with a smile.

Cosette looked him directly in the eye. 'Are you referring to the day of that name? It's passed, Marius. But I hope every day will be St Valentine's Day.'

'Then here is something to seal that perpetual present.'

Marius took the rock crystal from his pocket and showed it to Cosette. She felt a burning sensation, as if warm liquid had suffused her veins. Then, when she closed her eyes, he seized her hand and slipped something on her ring finger. She opened her eyes and stared at the ring.

'Is this for me?' she asked.

'Who else would it be for?'

He gazed in wonder at his wife's golden hair and her shining eyes. He had not told her often enough how beautiful she was, or that her beauty was the reflection of her soul. Of course, it would take more than words to change him, and he vowed to be a little less proud and a little more relaxed – and, above all, to stop wallowing in despair.

Cosette had eyes only for him. In his sky-blue frock coat from Staub's, she thought he looked magnificent. For once, he had abandoned his usual reserve, and was unafraid to make expansive gestures, while those around them scarcely dared to move. For Cosette, he was the only person alive among all these narrow people.

At the end of the evening they went to the Café Turc in the Boulevard du Temple, where summerhouses, arbours and avenues dotted the gardens. Anxious that Cosette should share the joys he had known with his friends, though in different places, Marius danced hair-raising quadrilles with her. During the pauses, as the dancers executed a series of figures, he would surreptitiously steal a kiss. She would throw her head back and pretend to protest, and her thin voice would crack at the end of each sentence.

Later still, they went on to the Variétés for onion soup. Here a cheerful group passed close to them and a tall, fair-haired, affected man, with two rosy-cheeked grisettes hanging on his tails, stopped by their table.

'Dear Baron,' said Amédée d'Iguerande triumphantly, clicking his heels. 'My friends and I have been complaining that we no longer see you. Are you angry?'

He flashed Cosette a charming smile. It was still his firm belief that she had granted to another what she had refused him.

Marius stammered some excuses, uneasy at the sight of Clémence standing between Louis de Vergne and Robert d'Androisy.

'We had a funeral,' replied Cosette.

Amédée, throwing back his shoulders exaggeratedly, threw her a tearful look. 'Good lord! I do sympathize with your grief, Madame. It's so sad to lose a friend in the prime of life.'

'I think you knew him, Marquis,' said Marius.

'Really? Do you mean that scoundrel I had the honour to kill in a duel? I'm truly sorry. But a duel is a duel, Baron. It's not just an exercise. I think every man learns that at his own expense.'

Marius would have leapt out of his chair if Cosette had not restrained him.

'Still as impulsive as ever?' laughed Amédée. 'I am at your disposal whenever you wish. In the fencing school, of course. It would be positively disastrous for friends to fight, wouldn't it? When I have a friend, I don't betray him,' he added gravely.

Marius had to make a superhuman effort not to stand up and hit him for insulting the memory of his departed friend.

Amused, Clémence stepped closer and took Amédée's arm provocatively. She noticed the ring that Cosette was wearing, and stared at it, her mouth twisted in a bitter smile. 'So, Monsieur, you neglect the people who are foolish enough to have some feelings for you? That's bad. You may have to pay for it one day. Perhaps with a ring.' She gave a forced smile, and offered her lips to Amédée, as if begging for a kiss, then pirouetted away at the last moment. Both Marius and Cosette felt embarrassed by her games, though not perhaps for the same reasons.

'Well, we must leave you!' said Amédée. 'We can't keep pleasure waiting!'

Louis de Vergne gave Marius a friendly wave, Robert d'Androisy ignored him, and the two grisettes passed without a glance in his direction.

'I'm never going to see those people again,' said Marius, with a sigh of relief.

'I'd like to believe you, Marius,' said Cosette, her eyes suddenly so deep-set that they seemed to disappear beneath her large forehead. 'But why did that woman mention a ring? And why did she keep looking at the one you gave me?'

He blushed slightly. 'All tarts love rings. Yours is so beautiful, it can but inspire envy.'

Outside, in the Passage des Panoramas, Amédée d'Iguerande tried to shrug off Marius's attitude. But the fact was he was hurt. However unwillingly, he had begun to realize how attached he was to him. 'The fool!' he said. 'He thinks it's all over.'

'Haven't you got all you wanted?' said Clémence, playing devil's advocate for Marius despite her own resentment. 'Why not leave him in peace?'

Amédée put his arms around the shoulders of his former mistress. 'I've obtained nothing, my dear. You must keep him busy while I busy myself with his wife.'

Clémence freed herself from Amédée's embrace. 'Do you love her so much?'

'To be honest, I wonder that myself. But I must have her.'

'You're truly vile.'

'Absolutely. Vile, but persistent. The two may seem contradictory, but they sometimes combine quite productively.'

*

It was on the evening of 10 April that news of the uprising in Lyons first reached Paris. There was enormous excitement in the revolutionary societies. People were talking of following the example of their brothers in Lyons. There were gatherings in the Rue Jean-Jacques-Rousseau and the Rue Saint-Martin. The slowness and prolonged uncertainty of the news from Lyons merely increased the government's anxiety. For a time there was even talk, among the ministers, of dividing power – Guizot in Lyons with the Duc d'Orléans, Thiers in Paris with the king – but nothing came of it. The army sorted out the opposition. It had emerged that there were more revolutionaries than workers among the insurgents in Lyons. The struggle was more political than social and their demands were not about rates and wages, but about the Republic. Louis Blanc was going all over Paris with his henchmen, spreading the word that three hundred were dead. One hundred, countered the government. Through its spokesmen, it asserted that most of those involved in the fighting were outside agitators, some from abroad. Exaggeration was the order of the day. According to the official version, even some Legitimists had joined the movement in the hope that they could turn it to their advantage.

Marshal Lobau, a count of the Empire who had been made a marshal by the July Monarchy, was strutting at the head of an army of forty thousand men and a well-organized National Guard. Like a dictator in waiting, Thiers lost no time in taking advantage of the situation. As a public-safety measure, he banned *La Tribune* and ordered the police to round up some hundred and fifty leaders of the Rights of Man. At the same time, *Le Moniteur* warned anyone insane enough to want to riot that considerable forces were standing by. Any uprising would be swiftly and decisively quashed. Nobody was going to be caught unawares. Everyone's cards were on the table.

Marius, too, laid his cards on the table. During a pause at the fencing school he told Amédée of his intention to break with Clémence. 'I imagine she's strong enough to get over it and forget me as she must have forgotten so many others.'

Amédée removed his mask and put down his foil. 'She'll be crushed.'

'There's no going back on my decision. I don't love Clémence.'

'Thank goodness for that, my dear fellow!' exclaimed Amédée, slapping his thigh. 'Where would we be if we loved the women we seduce? It's not a question of loving at all, but of making oneself loved. There's a subtle difference. I kill myself telling you these things and you simply move abruptly from one indecision to another.'

'I'll go to see Clémence tomorrow night and tell her my decision,' said Marius, lifting his head stubbornly. 'I'm sorry.'

Playing with his foil and barely concealing his exasperation, Amédée whistled between his teeth. 'You may be. You're just like your friend Frédéric Rivolier. One step forward, one step back – you never know what you want. Tomorrow's the thirteenth. A risky day.' He made sure his plastron was in place, and simulated an attack on Marius, which the latter parried with the back of his hand. 'Are we still friends, Baron?'

'Of course, Marquis.'

The man in black and the Catman met, as they often did, in a shop near the church of Saint-Eustache in the Rue du Jour, which belonged to a dyer who was often a middleman in the catmeat trade. The two men emerged and walked a little way together.

'This time they're at our mercy,' whispered the man in black. 'Isn't that so, Thénardier?'

The Catman stretched his vulture-like neck, with a disapproving but cautious look in his eyes. 'Don't call me that. You know how much I cherish being incognito.'

'We need to act fast and hit hard,' continued the man in black, pretending not to have heard him. 'That idiot Marius will be in the Rue Transnonnain tomorrow evening. And tomorrow will be a fine day for an uprising. That'll give us a chance to introduce a nice diversion.'

'You mean the poison?' the Catman sniggered. He bowed to an imaginary crowd, and the depth of his bow increased the unusual curvature of his back. 'At night all cats are grey,' he added, sniggering once again.

The man in black stopped him with a gesture of the hand. 'Talking of cats, have you got someone to deal with Gammy Leg?'

'I'll get on to it right away, my friend.'

'And what about Jesus?'

'That's for tomorrow. That imbecile the Mullet will be more than happy to take care of it himself.'

'Make sure that Jesus is outside the house in the Rue Transnonnain very early in the morning.'

'In the state we agreed?'

'Of course.'

'And the money?'

'Everything comes to those who wait.'

*

Following his conversation with the man in black, the Catman returned to the workshop, where he found the Mullet once again setting about Raphaël. The child had rolled onto the floor.

'That's enough!' bellowed the Catman. 'Jesus tells me Horse Face and Raphaël worked well last night. So we're saving on the labour force! Understood, Mullet?'

The redhead returned to his foreman's desk without a protest, keeping his thoughts to himself: Enjoy it while you can, old man. Once I've taken your place, you'll be eating out of my hand.

The Catman glanced at the Pointer, who sat slumped in his armchair, fierce-eyed as ever, with mucus dangling from his nose and his hands buried under the cover spread over his knees. We'll have to get rid of that one soon, he thought. He's a nuisance, polluting the workshop and informing on all and sundry. He moved towards Raphaël and held out his cane. 'Here, my child, stand up.' But at the last moment he pulled away his cane and the child almost fell over. A convulsive giggle shook the Catman from head to foot.

'Come here, you,' he called to Horse Face. The youth with the big jaw stood up nonchalantly and waddled over to the Catman, who pulled him outside and began to speak to him as if he were talking to an adult. 'The Mullet's strict with you, isn't he? He really gives you a hard time. But don't worry, we'll have him. If you ever have any problems with him, I want you to see me. We'll come to an arrangement. You tell me whenever he helps himself to the takings, and in return I'll entrust a few confidential errands to you. Do you have any idea of the sacrifices I make for you all? That I kill myself for all these inferiors who are eating the clothes off my back? They cost me a lot. But I know you're a good lad. And I like to reward good lads.' Horse Face was hoping for a small coin or two, but he knew how mean the Catman was. 'Well, I'm going to do you a good turn. Do you want to get your revenge on the Mullet? At no cost to yourself?'

Horse Face grumbled under his breath. As far as money went, it was clear he didn't have a prayer. 'What do I have to do?' he asked, with a natural insolence that made people want to slap him.

'Do you know the Clan Destin?'

'Never set foot in it.'

'Well, now's your chance, my boy. It's like this, you see. The Mullet loves nobody and nobody loves him. But he's always hanging around the Clan Destin. And do you know why?' Horse Face shook his head. 'Because there's someone there he loves and who loves him in return. Do you give up? I'll tell you – it's a cat. Yes, a cat. And the worst kind of cat – the kind that does nothing but eat and sleep all day long. A real pest. But not hard to do in, if you follow me.'

Horse Face stared wide-eyed. He'd had it up to here with cats. What was one more or less? He couldn't give a damn. 'Put him in the sack?'

'Not this one, my boy. This one's not for cooking. We need something more aesthetic for him. Hang him up and cut him open from the top, guts in the air.'

'That's easily done,' said Horse Face laconically. 'But I don't know why you're telling me this, Catman, seeing as you're so thick with the Mullet.'

'Thick with him? Not really. I suspect he's having money problems. He's getting greedy. The ones I'm thick with are the obedient ones. That's all. By the way, do you have what you need?'

'In my pocket, Catman.' Horse Face rummaged in his pocket and took out a big knife whose blade folded into the handle. 'Sharp as an axe,' he said, opening the blade.

The Catman cast an expert look at the edge of the knife. His eyes sparkled. 'Well?'

'All right, Catman! But what bothers me a bit is that I won't be there to see the Mullet's face.'

'Don't worry, I'll tell you all about it.'

When she found her cat lying half-skinned and crucified on the counter of the Clan Destin, Gammy Leg dropped the two buckets she was carrying, spilling the water over the floor, and fell to her knees. She let out a heart-rending cry that could be heard around the block. Great coughs tore her throat, followed by spasmodic sobs.

'My Demon . . . My Demon . . .'

There were no customers at this time of day. Gammy Leg stood up finally, her head in her hands, and stayed like that for a long moment, facing the counter, her feet in the water. Who could have done it? She lowered her hands and limped to the kitchen. Not a soul about. She took a knife and set about unnailing the poor beast. Once that was done, she placed her cat's corpse in one of the buckets. Her shoes were soaked and her toes were frozen. She kicked off her slippers furiously so that they hit the wall. Then, mechanically, she returned to the kitchen to get a floorcloth. She was shaking with misery. She knelt very gently, like someone at the end of her tether, unable to bear life any longer, and began to wipe up the grime. The blood was beating in her temples. She lost her balance and collapsed on her side. Her big callused hands gripped the counter. She had known poverty, resignation, the whole of sordid humanity flaunting itself in this squalid dive, and she had resisted, she had held out – but now, for the first time in her life, she had lost the desire to struggle. She begged death to take her. Who could have done this? she kept repeating. And the more she asked herself the question, the more other questions came into her mind. Everything was getting mixed up and inverted. So she forced herself to scrub harder in order not to think.

'So, Gammy Leg,' came a mocking voice, 'still giving you the dirty jobs, are they?'

The old woman turned and looked imploringly at the Catman. 'They killed him ... They killed my Demon ... They gutted him and then crucified him ...' She pointed at the wooden counter with a limp, trembling hand.

'They killed your cat?' he repeated, feigning sympathy. He went to Gammy Leg and helped her to her feet. 'If that's all, I'll buy you another. After all, I know a thing or two about cats.'

'That's kind of you, Catman ... But it was my Demon I loved ... No other cat can take his place ...'

The Catman touched Gammy Leg's hands. 'Hey, you're going to catch cold!' he exclaimed, pretending to be alarmed. 'Come with me to the stove.'

She laid her head on his shoulder and staggered with him to the kitchen. Good God, he thought, how heavy she is! He sat her down on a stool and went to look for a bottle.

'Here, have a drop of brandy.'

Gammy Leg snatched the bottle from his hands and drank a quarter of it in next to no time.

'Hey, steady on, Gammy Leg, you'll get drunk!' said the Catman.

'There was nobody ...' replied Gammy Leg. 'You understand, nobody ... I can't see who could have done that ... He was so calm, my Demon ... such a good animal ...'

The Catman put three pieces of wood in the stove, took another stool and sat down facing her. 'Well, it certainly wasn't the Holy Ghost who did it!' he declared with a detached air, moving his weasel face forward. All at once, he tapped his forehead. 'Now I come to think of it, I was passing earlier with one of the kids from the workshop, and I saw the Kitten come in here. But I suppose you must have seen her – she's not exactly the discreet kind.'

Gammy Leg had been clutching the bottle in her hand, looking at it grimly. Now she put it down. 'The Kitten? That ugly cow came here?'

'That's what I'm telling you.' He glanced at his watch. 'About twenty minutes ago.'

'That's when I went to fetch the water,' said Gammy Leg, her voice growing stronger.

The Catman assumed the innocent air of a newborn child. 'You mean—?'

'I don't mean anything, Catman – I know! That cheap whore killed my cat.'

'Well, I never!' said the old man. 'Attacking a poor innocent animal like that! I have to admit I'm astonished. You have my support, Gammy Leg. I'll tell Perfect Love.'

Gammy Leg leapt to her feet, picked up the bottle and took another gulp. 'Useless,' she said through gritted teeth. 'Leave Perfect Love to his carpentry. I'll deal with the Kitten this time.'

The Catman stood up in his turn and placed his hand on her shoulder. 'Listen, I like you, Gammy Leg. The Kitten's a bitch. She gave you a good thrashing the last time and I wouldn't want that to happen again. The only reason this place is well kept is because of you. People don't say it enough, but you're the queen of the kitchen. And I don't say something like that if I don't mean it.'

Gammy Leg lowered her eyes slightly. Now that she had a culprit – and what a culprit! – ideas of vengeance were running through her mind. 'I'll kill the bitch,' she growled.

As she moved towards the restaurant, the Catman caught her by the elbow. 'Here, to improve your chances, let me make my own modest contribution.' And he held out a flask filled with an opaque liquid, advising her to handle it carefully.

'What's this?' asked Gammy Leg.

'The elixir of vengeance, my dear. Vitriol. One good squirt in the face and that's the end of it.'

Gammy Leg took the flask. 'Thank you, Catman . . .'

The Kitten was on her way back to the Clan Destin. That morning, before leaving, she had extorted a few francs from Perfect Love. Chicken feed, of course, but it had meant she could go shopping for haberdashery and soft furnishings in the Rue Saint-Denis and the Rue du Petit-Lion, and buy curtains, cords, braids and ribbons – in short, it was enough to change the look of the Clan Destin. The second stage, she told herself, would be to refurbish the floor and the walls. The idea thrilled her. She could easily imagine a tiled and glazed red floor. They could see about the furniture, the stairs and the kitchen later. But everybody had to pull their weight – especially Gammy Leg. Her place is in the kitchen, thought the Kitten. The less we see of her, the better.

She went in through the door of the Clan Destin, blissfully unaware of what awaited her.

'Is there anybody here?' she asked, putting her packages down on the first table she found.

The restaurant seemed empty. A smile crossed her lips at the thought that it would soon change, and change completely. She had already thought of a new name.

At that moment, Gammy Leg put her head round the door of the kitchen.

'Oh, you're here, are you?' said the Kitten.

'Why, isn't it allowed?'

'It shouldn't be. If we want to improve things around here, you really ought to do something about the way you look.'

Gammy Leg emerged from the kitchen, a bucket in her hand. The brandy had given her strength. There was a wild glint in her eyes. 'The way I look's my business, like it or lump it,' she retorted, taking up a position in front of the counter.

The Kitten shook her head as if abandoning the contest. 'Look, Gammy Leg, if you want to spit your venom at me, you've chosen the wrong moment – I'm in a really good mood! As you can see, I've bought a few things to give this tavern an appearance worthy of the name of tavern.'

Gammy Leg put a hand on her hip and swept the air in front of her with the other. 'A tavern where you could come and go as you please? Like this afternoon, for example?'

'I come here when the fancy takes me. In case you don't understand, this is my home.'

'Oh, this is your home, is it?' Gammy Leg burst into a laugh so terrible that the Kitten felt a sort of shiver. 'And is this what you do at home?' she asked, and threw the contents of her bucket at the young woman.

At the sight of the bloody and half-skinned cat, the Kitten recoiled in terror. Then she lifted her chin, took off her smart hat, which made her look almost ladylike, and said something that she should not have said. 'Well, what are you waiting for? Why not make your cat into a stew?'

The old woman threw herself on her like a Fury. The Kitten stepped back and tried to trip her up, but missed, leaving Gammy Leg facing her, hands at shoulder level ready to scratch.

'Do you want me to flatten you like last time?' the Kitten cried.

Gammy Leg looked down and felt for the flask in the pocket of her blouse. This momentary inattention allowed the Kitten to seize her by her hair, catch her arm and bite it furiously. The blood gushed from under her teeth. Then she leapt backwards, out of reach of her adversary. 'Ugh! You really stink, old woman!'

Gammy Leg had not let out a single cry. She charged straight ahead, head down, like a ram.

The Kitten caught a head butt on the end of her chin. She lost her balance and took Gammy Leg down with her. There followed a furious set-to, with muffled groans and dull thuds.

The heavier of the two finally gained the upper hand. After rolling on her side, Gammy Leg lifted a foot, brought it down on the Kitten, and succeeded in sitting astride her, gripping her thighs and pelvis between her legs. The Kitten waved her arms, occasionally scratching Gammy Leg's flabby and bloated face. But the older woman held out. Despite the avalanche of blows, she slipped her hand into her pocket, took out the flask, popped out the stopper with her thumbnail and, after jabbing the Kitten in the eye with her elbow, poured the contents over her face.

There was a spluttering, like the sound of water being thrown into burning oil, followed by a terrible scream. Gammy Leg moved quickly out of the way, letting out an infernal burst of laughter. She stood up, breathless, her bonnet askew. When she saw the Kitten lying face down on the floor, her body taut and arched, in the grip of terrible convulsions, she dropped the flask. She could not believe her eyes. She walked around the tortured body trying to see the face, the foaming mouth, pointing at it in fierce jubilation.

'Let's see your pretty little face now!'

When the Kitten turned her head with a groan of agony, Gammy Leg grew faint. It was no longer a face but a viscous crater, which looked like a dish of kidneys topped with cheese.

'Shouldn't have killed my Demon...' muttered Gammy Leg. 'Shouldn't have...'

Horrified by the repulsive effects of the vitriol the Catman had given her, she retreated to the counter, moving from foot to foot, unable to control her panic. What was she going to do? The Kitten was still moaning, could not stop moaning. Gammy Leg thought of Perfect Love. If he found out about this, he'd kill her. The thought of ending it once and for all crossed her mind. Finish off the Kitten with a knife, to stop her from moaning and alerting the neighbours. Only, she was frozen rigid, unable to move a muscle. And the neighbours were already gathering at the door of the Clan Destin, among them someone who had witnessed almost the whole scene – the Catman, of course, who stood barring the way into the tavern. He had already told the Mullet to go and fetch Perfect Love.

'A family quarrel,' he was saying to the crowd in a honeyed voice. 'Better not get involved – you never know what might happen.'

A voice rose among the onlookers. 'Call the rozzers! Somebody's being murdered in there!'

'Oh, yes!' the Catman retorted. 'Call the rozzers, and they'll run us all in!' He had to calm things down. The only person who needed to be fetched was Sergeant Carignol, the policeman he had safely in his pocket – but not yet. 'I've already sent for the husband,' he said conclusively, as if letting the crowd into a deep secret. 'He'll show up soon. Things will be clearer then.'

The dregs of the district had congregated around him. Pickpockets, tricksters, small-time voyeurs and big-time pimps, procurers, wretches who thought others more wretched than themselves, as well as the usual incorrigible gossips, like cesspool emptiers, women porters, ragmen and vagabonds of all sorts – the kind of people who never tire of the spectacle of other people's misfortune. They were pushing, jostling, baying for blood.

'All right, I'm going in,' said the Catman at last. 'The rest of you wait here.'

He lifted the latch, went in and closed the door carefully behind him. What he saw warmed his heart. He advanced towards Gammy Leg, still prostrate near the counter. 'What are you doing there, old girl?' he asked calmly. 'You're mad, what's got into you?'

Gammy Leg was staring, her head thrust into the fleshy part of her shoulders, her arms hanging. 'Shouldn't have, shouldn't have,' she was repeating.

'Of course you shouldn't have!' cried the Catman, with concentrated rage. 'Do you have any idea what you've done?' he asked. 'What's Perfect

Love going to say, eh?' With the end of his foot, he turned the Kitten's head slightly. The Kitten, who had almost fainted, moaned again. 'Bloody hell! You really sorted her out!'

All at once, his attention was attracted by a clamour from outside. The door opened with a crash and Perfect Love appeared on the threshold, followed by the Mullet. 'Where is she?' he shouted.

Never one to be caught napping, the Catman turned to Gammy Leg. 'You almost killed our poor Kitten!' he cried reproachfully. 'She's disfigured for life! Don't you realize what a terrible thing you've done?'

Out of the corner of his eye he was watching Perfect Love, who, already warned by the Mullet, was brandishing a vengeful fist at his wife. The expression of bold good humour that often covered his broad face had given way to a Dantesque fury. Even if he had wanted to – which clearly he did not – the Catman could have done nothing to calm his anger. So when he saw Perfect Love rush at the old woman, he made no attempt to prevent him. 'No! No!' he cried so that the people outside would hear him. 'Don't do it, Perfect Love!' Simultaneously, he made a peremptory gesture to the Mullet. 'Look, they're fighting! Run and fetch Sergeant Carignol! Go, quickly!'

Having seen his beloved's face with horror, Perfect Love had placed his hands like a necklace around Gammy Leg's throat and was squeezing with all his might. Agreeing to her punishment, perhaps intent on expiation, the old woman did not even try to struggle. Her flaccid skin was turning scarlet beneath her bulging eyes. She might even have been grateful to her husband for shortening her sufferings and releasing her from a life of misery and degradation. Gammy Leg had reached the end of her existence. Now that her cat had gone, she no longer even hoped to join him. She imagined she could see a field of flowers. So pretty, she thought, a field of flowers in springtime. It was the last thing Gammy Leg saw.

'So much for you, you old bitch,' said Perfect Love, gasping for breath.

When the Catman saw Gammy Leg's eyes glaze over and her arms drop and Perfect Love lower her to the floor, he turned his head to the door. 'Murderer! Murderer!' he cried.

A muffled stamping could be heard outside the entrance to the tavern, a confused noise that announced the arrival of the law. Rifle butts hammered on the wooden door. A police captain, recognizable by his sash, entered the Clan Destin, followed by Sergeant Carignol. The two gendarmes who were with them immediately seized Perfect Love.

'Can you tell me what happened here?' the captain asked the Catman.

'Captain,' replied the Catman respectfully, 'on a sudden impulse, this man has strangled his wife. He goes by the nickname of Perfect Love, an innkeeper by trade. I can vouch for his honour and probity.'

'A sudden impulse, you say? And who's the woman on the floor?' The captain, grave and severe like all captains, walked over to the Kitten. 'Sergeant,' he said to Carignol, 'put the cuffs on this Perfect Love.' He crouched to examine the Kitten's condition, and his face fell. 'We have to move this poor woman as soon as possible. What's her name?'

'Clotilde Lepetit.'

'Vitriol?'

'You're a perceptive man, Captain. But this man saw more than I did. Isn't that so, Mullet?'

The redhead appeared nonplussed at first, but at his employer's prompting he nodded. He explained confusedly that Gammy Leg had thrown vitriol in the face of the young woman on the floor and that he had run to fetch the police.

'He's lying!' cried Perfect Love. 'It wasn't the rozzers he called first, it was me!'

'Nobody asked you,' the captain cut in. He turned to Carignol. 'Has the van arrived?'

'I think so, Captain. We'll put the accused inside.'

'I was the one, Captain, who asked the Mullet to tell the murderer – I mean Perfect Love,' said the Catman. 'When I got here and saw what was happening, I tried to intervene – all the witnesses can vouch for that – but I could do nothing. You've seen how the man is built – and just look at me. So I asked the Mullet to bring Sergeant Carignol, with whom I'm on excellent terms. Unfortunately, as you can see, it was too late.'

'Hmm,' said the captain, 'a confusing story. Still, what I need is witnesses, and I have them. It'll be up to the courts to settle the matter. And trust me, in these times of riots and rebellions, with all these so-called revolutionaries putting up barricades, the law won't be merciful, crime of passion or not. In the meantime, take the accused to jail and see to that woman double quick!'

Outside, a prison van had arrived, full of armed men – gendarmes and men from the Sûreté, as well as a squad of infantrymen. There were reports of a mob a hundred strong in the Rue Saint-Denis.

As the gendarmes were taking Perfect Love away, the captain turned back to the Catman. 'You seem like an honest man to me. Your evidence will help me to throw light on this affair and send the murderer off to do hard labour as fast as possible. People caught red-handed are dealt with quickly.'

The Catman took off his hat and saluted the captain. 'Don't be too hasty, Captain. This Perfect Love is an excellent man. That young woman there turned his head.'

'I'm not being hasty, Monsieur. I am merely the impartial agent of poetic justice. What's your name?'

The Catman bowed low. 'Tardier, Captain,' he replied humbly. 'I am a modest tradesman who raises rabbits to supply the local restaurants. And this gentleman here, known as the Mullet, is called Tricot.'

'Very good, Monsieur Tardier. I'm counting on you and Monsieur Tricot to hold yourselves available. I have a victim and a suspect, that's something already.'

In his deposition, Tardier, while pretending to speak in Perfect Love's defence, set out to get him even deeper into trouble. He was a man who stopped at nothing. The prospect of harming someone else and appropriating his goods put him in a state almost comparable to the pleasures of lust.

Tardier, who had been born sixty years earlier, was a categorical refutation of Jean-Jacques Rousseau's theories. He had been born bad and had done nothing but cultivate his bent. He ate nothing, drank little, hardly slept. Apart from doing harm and getting rich, nothing interested him. He had had a home, and had renounced it. Wife, children, relatives, friends – in short, everything that made up the ordinary life of a normal individual – had disappeared from his existence. He lived only for himself and for the residue of passion that still seethed within him like lava. Once, he had robbed corpses on the battlefield of Waterloo. Now, ever lurking, ever watchful from beneath greenish and worn-looking eyelids, he robbed the living. And this was just the beginning.

After making his statement, he ran to the workshop to find the Mullet and put the finishing touches to the next phase of his plan. In passing, he gave little Raphaël a sly glance. He was convinced that his accomplice, the man in black, was hiding something about the child's origin and destiny. Once he had fathomed this mystery, there would be no holding him back.

'Here, this is for you,' he said to Horse Face, giving him two sous. 'You did well, son. But keep it under your hat, eh? What would people say if they knew it was you that had gutted Gammy Leg's cat?'

Horse Face was struck dumb by this revelation. He would never again trust the old shark.

A little later the Catman joined the man in black in the dyer's shop in the Rue du Jour. He told him what had happened in the Clan Destin and assured him that everything was ready.

'It'll all be settled tomorrow,' said the man in black.

While Tardier and the man in black were finalizing the details of their plan, little Raphaël was thinking about the past. Would he ever see again the kind gentleman who had given him his coat and had almost come to blows with Jesus?

'You must be joking!' Horse Face whispered to him. 'Your elegant friend has vanished into thin air since Jesus cut him down to size. As for the coat, the Mullet's grabbed it for himself. He always manages to screw us, the bastard. And the Catman's not much better. He made a fool of me over a cat. You have to get used to it, kid, this dump is our life. And if we don't get out of here, it'll be our death too.'

This dump was the only refuge for Raphaël and his little companions in misfortune. A hovel that was both prison and home, with a single barred window and a thick bolted door. They were all in the same boat. Getting up at six in the morning, bacon soup with not much bacon, almost always cold, a crust of bread for the day, a little glass of brandy in the afternoon, work until ten at night, more bacon soup, this time full of scraps found in the vicinity and thrown into the pot by Mother Fouillet, a vile stew that swelled your stomach and gave you ulcers. Then bed at eleven. The ones who hunted cats had a special dispensation – they did not start work again until ten in the morning.

'One of these days, we'll get out,' said Horse Face.

'Where will we go?' asked Raphaël.

'That's the problem, kid. We don't have anywhere to go.'

For the moment the workshop was their only home. Here, at least, they were safe. The children slept on straw mats, and kept themselves warm on winter nights. There were ten of them. Naturally, they would have liked to enjoy themselves a little, to play like other kids their age, but they were so tired, so exhausted with work, that they couldn't find the energy. The fear and the cold had made them ill. They coughed, spat, scratched, and relieved themselves where they could, often in the closed courtyard, sometimes on the mezzanine or their straw mats. It was squalid. They all wore torn scarves knotted around their necks. And, as they went barefoot, bronchitis and head colds were all too common. At the beginning of the summer, one of them had died of exhaustion, whether as a result of malnutrition or the Mullet's mistreatment nobody knew. He had simply died, the little boy with thick brown hair, scrofulous, flea-ridden and full of infections, whose nickname was Little Louis. The Mullet had taken a handcart and tipped him into the Seine on a moonless night. Poor Little Louis. He had given Raphaël a piece of wood carved in the shape of a doll and Raphaël had made some clothes for it out of a few pieces of wool. He called the poor doll Lentil because he had stuck on two lentils as eyes. Lentil never left Raphaël. At night, he would fall asleep holding it. After the Mullet had taken away Little Louis's body, Horse Face, much to the Pointer's displeasure, had made a fire in a cast-iron cooking pot. All the children had gathered around this improvised hearth. Raphaël, who did not remember much, could remember throwing a pinch of salt into the fire.

'To stop the devil taking Little Louis's soul,' Horse Face had explained.

'Why would he go with the devil?' Raphaël had asked. 'He was nice, Little Louis was.'

The other children had agreed.

'Exactly,' said Horse Face, spitting in the fire to extinguish it. 'The devil prefers the nice ones. They're easier to catch. Especially if they're poor.'

'And what about God?'

'God only cares about the rich. That's why heaven's so bright.'

'I'd like to go to heaven,' Raphaël had concluded.

Children sometimes have crazes. Since Raphaël had started going out more often, strange ideas had been going through his head. He had seen fruit and vegetable sellers, water sellers, coconut sellers, all those street pedlars whom Prefect Gisquet considered dangerous parasites. He dreamed of oranges and barley sugar.

'What I'd really like to do is sell things in the street.'

'One day we will,' Horse Face promised him. 'We'll get out of here.'

'To do what?'

'Well, to do what you just said, of course!'

At about eleven, after work, when they climbed the ladder and went through the bull's eye into the foul dormitory and were hidden behind the partition, Horse Face and Raphaël would sometimes still find the energy to talk about these scavengers who lived on the street.

'What I like is that work like that isn't governed by any regulations,' Horse Face would say with a superior air. 'We'll be free, kid.'

'Do you think so?'

'I'm telling you!'

'And will the Mullet give me my coat back?'

'The one your elegant friend palmed off on you? Don't count on it. When the other bastard pinched it from you, he didn't intend to give it back.'

'The Mullet's a bad man.'

'You said it. His dad and him both. We'll bump them off.'

Raphaël would disappear beneath the cover and hug Lentil.

'Only you see,' Horse Face would add in a whisper, 'to pull it off, tomorrow, in a month or in a year, we first have to endure.'

'What does that mean, endure?'

'That's means we mustn't die, kid.'

And they would fall asleep in a heap.

Cosette was worried.

'They say there are barricades at the Porte Saint-Denis, in Les Halles, the Place de la Bastille and Saint-Jacques,' she told Marius. 'And shots have already been fired. Can't you put off your appointment?'

'I'm not going anywhere near those places,' lied Marius. 'Anyway, I have your crystal in my pocket as a lucky charm.' He put on his coat and picked up his riding crop. 'My trusty steed will get me through, I promise!' he said in a cheerful tone.

Cosette huddled in his arms. 'It would be stupid to lose each other just when we've found each other again.'

This remark made Marius thoughtful. He kissed Cosette's lips. 'There's only you,' he said in a voice muffled by emotion.

'If you're lying, you'll lose me for ever.'

'I'm not lying. I simply want to be at peace with myself.'

He kissed his wife once more and opened the door which led into the garden and the Rue Plumet. He took a few steps and stopped. It was late afternoon, the sunlight was pale, and there was a cool breeze. The colours in the garden were beautiful. The winter garden resembled a Moorish dome, its picture windows reflecting crescents of light. Marius touched his Sikorski boots with the tip of his riding crop and turned back to Cosette. Standing in the doorway like a Flora by Titian, her weight on one leg, Cosette looked like a queen descended from her palace to reign over the roses and the lilacs.

'I love you,' he said.

She placed both hands on her belly. The desire to tell Marius the good news was burning her lips. 'Marius?'

'Yes?'

'No, nothing . . .'

Marius waved his hat in the air as a last farewell and headed resolutely for the gate. As he walked along the street, he had a vague presentiment of danger. After saddling his horse in La Roche-Dragon's stable, he thought of Frédéric's death and the days of 1832. Once he was in the saddle, his sombre thoughts evaporated immediately and he set off at a jog trot.

Riding through Saint-Germain and the Latin Quarter, Marius was struck by the festive atmosphere everywhere. Elegant men and women were talking about the return of Musset, whose stay in Venice with George Sand had been a fiasco. Malicious gossips, like Mérimée, claimed that the lady of Nohant was no more gifted at making love than she was at writing French. At the crossroads, farces were being enacted. Young men praised the use of opium under the eyes of fat bourgeois who were getting drunk on absinthe. People walked in the streets as if nothing was happening, or loitered in the doorways of taverns and cafés laughing loudly. A few forlorn students ran through the streets crying, 'Long live the Republic!' Near the Rue des Boucheries Saint-Germain, which would later become the Boulevard Saint-Germain, Marius saw a man in a monk's robe waving a pilgrim's staff.

'Long live Fourier! Long live freedom!'

He crossed the Pont-Neuf to the Right Bank. Here the atmosphere was quite different. All the shops were closed, there was nobody at the windows and a deathly silence lay over everything. There were soldiers and barricades, and Marius had to turn back three times to make detours. In the Rue aux Ours and the Rue Geoffroy-l'Angevin, rioters behind their barricades raised their rifles when they saw him.

'A spy! Take aim, comrades!'

Without a sound, Marius spurred his horse and plunged into the dark maze of alleys in the Saint-Denis district. In the Rue Saint-Martin, seeing the sign of the Fer-Rouge, he decided to walk and to leave his horse in the inn's stable.

'For the night, Monsieur?' asked an ostler with brutish manners.

'I think it's better, my good man,' Marius assented. 'I'll be back tomorrow during the day. Here.'

He gave the stable lad some money and went on his way.

In the Rue Aubry-le-Boucher, there was another barricade. The rioters were smoking and swearing to whoever would listen that they would have the hides of Thiers and Bugeaud. Marius saw the sign of the Clan Destin. This time nobody aimed at him as he approached. In fact, the atmosphere here was quite good-natured.

'What are you doing, friend?' asked one of the insurgents, who was wearing a red scarf and brandishing two pistols.

'I'm on my way to the Rue Transnonnain.'

'Be careful then. Some of our comrades have put up a barricade there and their trigger fingers are a bit itchy. Since they found out that Bugeaud is on his way at the head of several thousand soldiers, they're shooting everything that moves.'

'Bugeaud?' said Marius in surprise. 'The hero of the Napoleonic wars?'

The other brandished his pistols even more. 'Your hero is no longer a hero for us, friend. He's a lackey of the government, and only fit to guard the Duchesse de Berry. He'll get what's coming to him. On your way now, bourgeois! And live with the times!'

The tone was less cordial. Marius was no longer a friend, but a bourgeois. He took his leave and wished the man good luck.

'Long live Robespierre!' he replied aggressively.

Marius made himself scarce without a backward glance. The rebel had advised him to live with the times, while calling on the name of Robespierre. It was comical. Marius thought again of Armand Carrel, who had spoken to him bitterly of the fanatics who claimed inspiration from the Terror. He thought, too, of little Gavroche, who had died in front of a barricade in June 1832, and of Raphaël – what had become of him?

History was clearly repeating itself. When Marius reached the Rue Beaubourg, he discovered another barricade. And there was yet another in the Rue Transnonnain. Luckily it was still possible to gain access to Number 14, where Clémence lived. One day, he vowed, I'll go and find little Raphaël – and that Jesus had better behave himself. Having said it, he felt he had to do it. Why not tomorrow?

Pleased to have made the decision, Marius climbed the steps two by two. When he reached Clémence's apartment, he pulled the bell. Clémence opened the door.

'What a pleasant surprise,' she said ironically, though she did not seem in the least surprised. 'Please come in. You know the way, don't you?'

Marius did not like her tone. 'I won't be long, Madame.'

'Come, Baron, with all these people swarming about the area you're not going to tell me you braved the barricades just to insult me and leave as soon as you arrived? Give me your hat and coat.' Marius obeyed and Clémence winked ostentatiously. Her attitude seemed to him to bode well. 'Come and sit down, my friend. You'll have a drop of port, won't you?'

'If you insist.'

Marius took a seat on the ottoman, where a half-naked Clémence had so often posed provocatively. He did not miss it, though he had to admit that Clémence, in a daringly low-cut red velvet dress trimmed with ribbons, had never looked more desirable. He noticed an eyelash on her cheek and asked her to make a wish. 'If you guess where the lash is, the wish will come true.'

Clémence poured the port into a Murano glass. A little earlier she had put some of the narcotic Louis-Désiré had given her on Shrove Tuesday into the same glass. Amédée's steward had, in fact, called to see her early that afternoon on his own initiative, without informing his master. When Clémence told him that she wanted to avenge herself on Marius by keeping him with her all night, he had advised her to use the drug sparingly. 'It would knock out a horse, Madame. I don't think you'd like to make an attempt on the baron's life, would you?'

'Of course not, Monsieur! I'll keep to the dose, you can be sure of that.'

'There's one problem,' said Louis-Désiré. 'It's such a powerful narcotic that he may still be asleep in the morning.'

'What do you suggest?'

'So it doesn't cause you any trouble, especially with these demonstrations, which are likely to get worse, I will send some of my men to take care of the baron. They'll help him, carry him away – get him back on his feet, in fact.'

'That sounds like a good idea. Are the effects immediate?'

'You have to wait just an hour, Madame. After that, it works like a charm. And if the baron should open his eyes again, don't hesitate to give him another small glassful.'

Clémence had learned her lesson well. But to be on the safe side she had doubled the dose. She felt perfectly calm as she handed the glass to Marius, even humming a tune as she did so. 'A lash?' she said. She felt her right cheek with her forefinger, removed the lash, stared at it for a long moment and blew it gently. 'I've made my wish,' she said, sitting down in an armchair facing Marius.

Her serenity troubled him somewhat. He put the glass to his lips, drank the contents in one gulp, and put it down on the pedestal table next to the ottoman. 'What I have to say to you can be summed up in one sentence, Clémence. Our relationship is over, as of today. I think it's best for both of us.'

The look Clémence gave him was one of such calm and withering contempt that Marius was disconcerted. He had thought she would burst into tears, grovel at his feet, or else try to entice him as only she knew how. Not a bit of it. She straightened up and put down her glass too. 'I think it's best for *me*,' she hissed. 'You promised me a ring, then gave it to your wife. You're a small man, Marius. I don't blame you for being like other men, cowardly and evasive, my God, no. I only blame you for being what you are – stupid, indecisive and conformist. You don't come up to Amédée's ankle. You want to be his friend, but you're nothing but his plaything. And, above all else, you're boring.'

Without making the slightest movement, without letting his anger show, Marius frowned and looked Clémence straight in the eye. 'You don't know what love is, Clémence. You've never known what it's like to suffer in secret, unable to control an emotion that beautifies life and lets one hope to feel something other than just derision. You're dry, rigid and dry. You're nearly thirty and you're already old.' He knew that he had touched her on a sensitive spot. 'What's more, you love life so little that you'll never give it.'

Clémence grew quite pale. She thought of the child she'd had with Amédée, the child who had been taken away from her, and the consequences of the labour, which had made her sterile. She crossed her right leg over her left knee, took her foot in her hand, then abandoned it, seized the cushion from the armchair, and threw it at Marius's face.

'Oh!' exclaimed Marius catching it in both hands.

He put the cushion up as a shield, ready for an onslaught of blows and insults. But when he moved his head to look at Clémence, she was bent double in her armchair, her head between her knees, shaken by wrenching sobs. He put down the cushion, rose quickly and went and sat down at the feet of the woman he had hurt.

'I'm sorry,' he said, placing a hand on her long brown hair. 'You're beautiful, you'll find a man who'll be able to make you happy, you know I talk a lot of rubbish . . .'

Clémence raised her head. Her tears were not feigned. A terrible despair distorted her features. 'No, you're not talking rubbish, Marius. I really am dry, cold and selfish. But I have my reasons. Seven years ago, I had a child. I never even saw him. I lost consciousness and they took him away from me. Later they told me he was stillborn. And now I'm alone, Marius. I'm nothing but an easy woman men pick up and throw away as they wish.'

Marius was deeply moved by these revelations. At the same time, his head felt heavy. 'You weren't married?' he asked.

'That was my misfortune.'

'And the father?'

'His name was Amédée d'Iguerande.'

'Amédée? But . . . why didn't you continue living together?'

'Because he can't give a woman what she has a right to demand. He collects conquests to make everyone believe he's a great seducer. He's nothing but an impostor.'

'No, he's a monster, that's what he is!' cried Marius, taking Clémence's face between his hands.

'He loves nobody, Marius. He uses everybody. He's using you just as he's used me and his friends. The only thing that interests him is your fortune.'

'I have no fortune.'

'And your wife.'

'What?'

Marius released Clémence and tried to stand – but in vain. His head and his limbs felt numb and heavy. 'I have to lie down . . .'

Clémence helped him crawl as far as the ottoman. He could no longer even get to his feet.

'What's happening to me?' he said, moving his head from side to side.

Everything was getting blurred. He was dizzy. He lay down on the bare floor. Clémence, sitting cross-legged, took a cushion and slid it under his head. She stroked his face. Cries and sporadic shooting could be heard from outside. Clémence was undisturbed by them.

'Sleep, my little boy,' she whispered. 'Sleep.'

Part Two

I

As Marius was arriving at Clémence's apartment, the Mullet was getting ready to leave the workshop, accompanied by Jesus. He double-locked the door and placed his hand on Jesus's shoulder.

'Where are you taking me?' Jesus asked, suspicious of the brute's sudden friendliness, and reluctant to go with him. 'What's this all about?'

'A lucrative business, my friend. A banker's draft. It's already drawn – you'll get your share. But first, we have to take care of the bank messenger.'

'Why me?'

'Because those were the Catman's orders,' explained the Mullet.

Jesus muttered under his breath. At Tardier's request, he had already spent much of the day at the Clan Destin, arranging the room and cleaning the kitchen. His face was so black from the work, it looked as if it had been dipped in walnut stain. 'This lucrative business, as you call it, is usually Pierre-François's reserve.'

'Lacenaire?' replied the Mullet, more impatient than ever. 'He's still inside, as far as I know. You're not going to spend your time waiting for him, are you?'

'Where is this place, anyway?'

'Not far from here. A little apartment in the Passage du Maire, near the Rue Transnonnain.'

Dragging his feet, and looking contemptuously at the Catman's rabbit hutches as they passed, Jesus followed the Mullet along the corridor to the exit.

On the other side of the door, Horse Face had heard everything. This sudden complicity between the two men portended no good. He quickly returned to work under the predatory eye of the Pointer.

Enjoy it while you can, you old sneak, he whispered, smiling venomously and brandishing a large wool comb. Your days are numbered.

Meanwhile, Jesus and the Mullet were walking in the direction of the Rue Transnonnain, hugging the walls to avoid the rioters and the barricades.

'Not a rozzer in sight,' remarked Jesus.

'Don't worry, when the time comes, it won't be the police who'll show up, it'll be the army.'

'There was a barricade in the Rue Aubry-le-Boucher when I came out of the Clan Destin. I thought I was done for. The idiots wanted to sign me up. When I refused, I really thought they were going to tear my head off.'

'Maybe you should have signed up,' said the Mullet.

'Why do you say that?'

'No reason . . .'

Jesus did not like the Mullet's insinuating tone. He clutched the knife in his pocket for reassurance. Further on, a group of fanatics were running towards a barricade, waving their weapons and crying, 'Down with the ministers!' At that moment shots rang out, and the Mullet and Jesus flattened themselves against a wall.

'Bloody hell!' roared the Mullet. 'I hope all these rebels get what's coming to them! They're ruining our trade!'

Not far from the Rue Beaubourg they took shelter in a carriage entrance, from where they watched a detachment of cavalry pass by, slashing the air with their sabres and spurring their horses until the blood ran, as if trying to impress the runaways they were pursuing. Nobody had been hit. The rioters had entrenched themselves behind a barricade and the horsemen stopped fifty paces away.

'Stop right there, Colonel!' shouted a voice that seemed to come from underground.

The officer to whom this demand was addressed bent low over his horse's neck to see who had spoken. Several shots rang out. The horse reared as if lifted by an invisible hand, fell and rolled on the cobbles. Several of the cavalrymen ran to help their colonel, who had lost his shako. He got his horse back on its feet, all the while throwing terrified, wide-eyed glances to right and left. He ordered one of his men to give him a carbine. Taking cover behind his horse's rump, he raised the rifle to his shoulder, aimed at the barricade and fired. An agitator collapsed on a heap of rubble.

'That's how we shoot in the army!' cried the colonel. 'Take a leaf out of my book, scum!'

'To the death! To the death!' responded the insurgents, opening fire.

The Mullet raised his eyes to heaven. 'They're shooting like pigs. The idiots are going to get themselves butchered. I've heard the soldiers of the thirty-fifth are on their way with Bugeaud at their head.' Observing that the cavalrymen had retreated and the coast seemed clear, he nudged Jesus with his elbow. 'Come on, we're nearly there.'

They ran across the Rue Transnonnain and into the entrance of a little building that the Mullet had pointed out. They had not been shot at once.

'Come in, it's in here,' said the Mullet, holding a door open for Jesus to pass.

Jesus, pale-faced, his hand already in his pocket, turned to the Mullet. 'I don't think this bank messenger of yours is going to show up, with all this disturbance. What is this – a trap?'

The Mullet was faster than Jesus. He had slipped his hand inside his smock and was now pointing a pistol at the young man's stomach. 'I don't advise you to take out your knife, little joker. Now turn round and go up to the second floor. One false move and there'll be blood on the stairs!'

When they reached the second floor, the two men stopped, Jesus in front and the Mullet behind. 'Knock three times on the door,' said the Mullet. More rifle shots came from outside and Jesus stopped to listen. 'Get a move on!' barked the Mullet, pressing the barrel of his pistol against the small of Jesus's back.

Jesus decided that the best thing to do was to obey. He thought that his last hour had come. The door opened and he went in carefully, ready to pounce. Two men were facing him. He recognized Pegasus, a burglar who knocked about with the Catman, and Twenty-Two, an albino who had done eight years' hard labour in Brest. The door closed again, revealing a third man, known as Gut Twister, a notorious pimp who marked his girls with a branding iron. Three high-class villains as well as the Mullet and his pistol – this wasn't going to be a fair fight. What made it worse was that the three cut-throats were armed with bludgeons.

'All right, then, you villains!' Jesus exclaimed, drawing his knife. 'It won't be said that Jesus had his throat cut without a struggle!'

The albino rushed to attack with his bludgeon. But Jesus tripped him up deftly, and with a backhand stroke to the back of his neck knocked him unconscious.

'One down!' he cried.

The Mullet, blocking the door, was wondering whether to use his pistol. But the orders were clear – no gunshot wounds.

'Make him dance!' he ordered the two others.

It was a savage fight. Jesus, finally convinced that he had a chance, was determined to make sure that his two adversaries, well built as they were, were made aware of his skill with a knife. Pegasus was cut in the leg, Gut Twister in the eye.

'Kill! Kill!' they egged each other on, ducking and weaving with all their might.

The blows they rained on their brave opponent finally overcame his resistance. Jesus fell to one knee, but managed to retreat to a corner of the room. The more furious of his attackers, Gut Twister, charged at him, squealing like a pig having its throat cut. Jesus, without really parrying the blow, sank on his side at that moment so that Gut Twister, caught off balance, was impaled on the shining blade. He collapsed without a word, the knife planted in his belly.

Only the Mullet and Pegasus were left. Terrified by Jesus's incredible energy, they hesitated to advance. Seeing his crony's wounded leg, the Mullet picked up Gut Twister's bludgeon and twirled it slowly. 'He's lost his knife,' he laughed triumphantly. 'We'll pin him down, one on each side.'

And there, in the darkness of the empty garret, a horrible scene was played out. The uninterrupted noise of blows struck unremittingly on a human body could be heard, punctuated by sinister cracks. Moans and convulsive bursts of laughter accompanied each blow. Then there was silence.

Jesus had somehow summoned enough strength to crawl to the door, but the Mullet and Pegasus had followed him and had taken turns beating him. Now they stood catching their breath.

'We have to finish him off,' murmured the Mullet, panting. 'He's still breathing.'

'Looks like Jesus doesn't want to die on the cross,' growled Pegasus, with a terrible smile. A big brown patch stained the fleshy part of his thigh.

Suddenly the door opened and the Catman appeared, his hat pulled down low over his eyes. He felt a hand gripping his calf. 'Well, well,' he said to Jesus, whose face was nothing more than a bloody pulp. 'Still not dead, my boy?' He turned to the Mullet. 'Give me that, useless.'

He seized the bludgeon, raised it above his head, and brought it down on Jesus's face.

There was a sound of bone shattering. Jesus let go of Tardier's calf with a jolt, gave a death rattle and breathed his last.

'That's the way it should be done,' observed the Catman, throwing the bludgeon into the room. 'What happened to the other two?'

'Gut Twister's dead,' replied the Mullet.

'A hearty fellow,' said the Catman appreciatively. 'What about the other one?'

'Knocked out.'

'Get him back on his feet, and go and bury Gut Twister in the cellar. We're lucky the building's empty.' He turned to the door. 'Tomorrow at dawn. Be there on time. You know what you have to do. And please, Mullet, make yourself a little more presentable.'

And then he was gone.

Clémence had slept much of the night in the same position, cradling Marius in her arms as a mother cradles her child. The folly of her action had not even crossed her mind. For now, she had a little boy all to herself.

At about six o'clock the next morning, she was woken abruptly by shouts and gunshots. She stood up and ran to the window. A desolate spectacle presented itself to her gaze. The barricade had been dismantled, and the rebels stood with their hands in the air surrounded by soldiers. The rifle shots of the previous evening had come from the Saint-Merri district, where a handful of insurgents had opened fire on the escort accompanying Thiers and General Bugeaud on a night reconnaissance of the area. A captain had been killed by a bullet fired from a basement window, and an official of the Council of State had also fallen.

Once more, the fighting had been confined to the Saint-Merri district, the scene of bloodshed in 1832. Interrupted during the night, it had started again early on the morning of the 14th.

There are still various versions of what happened next. Some say that a group of soldiers were carrying away a wounded lieutenant when they were attacked by a number of men, who emerged from a house and finished off the lieutenant. That did not happen. Others say that there was a shot from a house in the Rue Transnonnain, fired by a young man named Bréfort, who had been locked in his room by his father to stop him taking part in the disturbances. That did not happen either.

It is true that a shot was fired at the soldiers and the lieutenant was killed. But nobody had come running out of any house – and poor Bréfort did not even have a rifle. The reality is more sombre. The vile Mullet, seeing that things were calming down, had climbed onto the roof of 12 Rue Transnonnain from the roof of Number 14. He knew that for his plan to succeed it was vital that there should be total confusion all around, otherwise he would be spotted. He had already had enormous difficulty transporting the body of Jesus to Number 14. His accomplices, terrified by the scale of the riot, were still on the ground floor, huddled together in the corridor on the other side of the banisters, by a gloomy little courtyard, trying as best they could to conceal their burden and praying for everything to be over as quickly as possible.

The Mullet had climbed to the top floor of the building, from where he had been able to see the soldiers, the people at their windows and the wounded being extricated from the rubble. In the next-door building, although the occupants were hiding indoors, they could not resist the morbid desire to watch the events in the street. The Mullet crawled on all fours to the roof of Number 12 by passing from one dormer window to another. Once on his perch, half hidden by a chimney, he kicked a loose tile. It slid down the roof and crashed to the ground. Onlookers and soldiers moved away from the wounded lieutenant and looked up, but all they could see was a shadow. At that moment the Mullet chose the lieutenant as his target. He cocked his pistol, leaned against the chimney and fired. Below, the lieutenant on his makeshift stretcher arched violently and gave a death rattle. For a moment, there was a stunned silence. Then the signal was given for the killing to start.

'The shot came from that building!' screamed a soldier, mad with rage, pointing to a man at the window.

An officer on horseback tried to intervene, but in vain. The door of Number 12 was smashed down and some fifty soldiers, drunk with revenge, swept into the building.

Seeing the turn of events, Clémence closed the window and threw herself back in panic. She stared at Marius, who was still curled up asleep. Clémence plunged her head in her hands and began to sob. What if the soldiers came to her house? From here, she could already hear screams from the neighbouring building as the occupants were put to the sword or had their throats cut in their own homes. She fell to her knees and prayed to God to spare her. Then she moved, still on her knees, to Marius and shook him with all her might. In vain. He did not even open one eye. What if he was dead? What if the dose had been too strong? She did not think of taking Marius's pulse or placing her ear against his heart. Instead, she put his coat, gloves and hat on him. Then with a push of her back, she got to her feet and ran to the door. On the verge of madness, it occurred to her that Amédée's steward had trapped her, and that the soldiers were going to arrive at any moment, accuse her of killing Marius, and take her away and shoot her.

At the sound of footsteps on the stairs, she froze in terror. She slid down the door and curled up, her knees to her chin, terrified. I won't budge from here, even if I have to die, too, she told herself. And she buried her head in her hands and knees again.

Meanwhile, the Mullet had retraced his steps, going back via the two dormer windows to the top floor of Number 14. When he heard the distressed cries of Number 12's occupants and the vengeful curses and enraged shouts of the soldiers, he had run down the stairs two at a time. It was his steps that Clémence had heard. Once more, he made sure that nobody had been foolish enough to storm the building. He carefully opened the carriage entrance, letting a ray of light filter in. The street was dense with soldiers. People were hurling abuse on all sides.

'Stop!' some officers on horseback were screaming. 'Fall back! Bugler, sound the retreat!'

'They've killed everyone,' a bourgeois was moaning.

The Mullet closed the door again and ran to find Pegasus and Twenty-Two. When he saw Jesus's corpse, the blank face without a mouth and a nose, the hair clotted with blood and fragments of brain, he gave it an angry kick. 'So, this is what you've come to, is it?'

He told the albino to come with him and Pegasus to stay where he was. He stuck on a false moustache, adjusted the handkerchief he had knotted around his neck, and put on a top hat. 'How do I look?' he asked doubtfully.

'Like a real toff,' Twenty-Two assured him.

The Mullet and the albino quickly climbed the stairs. Arriving outside Clémence's apartment, they assumed a sober air and knocked at the door.

On the other side Clémence felt her heart turn over. 'Yes?' she said weakly.

'Madame de Lavely?'

'This is she.'

'We've come to fetch the young man who's with you.'

Relieved, Clémence stood up and opened the door. She did not even have the presence of mind to ask the strangers who had sent them. 'Quick, he's through there,' she said, indicating the drawing room.

The albino loaded Marius over his shoulder and left without a word. The Mullet doffed his hat to Clémence and asked her if she had the flask. She found it and gave it to him without a word. 'Don't forget this,' she said, handing him Marius's cane. 'Now, go quickly,' she added in an imploring tone.

'No sooner said than done, Madame.'

The Mullet closed the door behind him and hurried to rejoin his accomplices. Once downstairs, he asked Twenty-Two, who had already laid Marius down next to Jesus, what time it was.

'Seven.'

'It's all quiet now. Let's get on with switching their clothes. And hurry up about it, for God's sake!'

Outside, the soldiers had lined up in double column. Firemen, gendarmes and priests had made their appearance. A fair number of onlookers had started to gather. It was said that all the occupants of Number 12 had been massacred. It was also said that it was all over, that among the troops and the National Guard there were eleven dead and fourteen wounded, and among the insurgents fourteen dead and a dozen wounded.

By the time Mullet and his companions left Clémence's building, taking care to go in opposite directions, they had put Marius's clothes on Jesus and vice versa. It had all been done in great haste. The Mullet, for all his aspirations to become a criminal mastermind, was a mere factotum, whose aggressiveness made up for his lack of brains and whose only motivations were resentment and greed. His sole obsession in the affair had been to draw a strawberry mark in ink under Marius's eye and smear his face with charcoal – the illusion had to be perfect. Pegasus had been given the task of swapping the trousers, the shirts and the jackets and of putting Marius's gloves on Jesus's hands. Twenty-Two had soaked one of the bludgeons in Jesus's blood and placed it between Marius's arms. Finally, the Mullet had poured the rest of the narcotic down the young man's throat.

Everything had conspired to make the deception perfect. But for one thing – in his hurry to disguise Marius, the Mullet had forgotten Jesus's gold ring, an emerald-eyed snake.

Two hours later the Rue Transnonnain was still congested. News was spreading fast. The government had apparently already announced to both chambers its victories in Lyons and Paris. It was said that all the peers and deputies were going to the Tuileries to convey their congratulations to the king. Draconian measures were about to be taken. The ministers intended to present two bills the next day, designed to prevent the recurrence of similar disturbances. In one, they would request extra funds to put the army on a footing that would ensure internal order. In the other, they would lay down severe penalties for those found in possession of weapons of war. As for the Republicans, they were no longer to be seen on the streets, especially on that gloomy morning of 14 April. They walked with heads hung low, knowing themselves to be both hated and despised – hated for having caused so much fear and despised for having failed so miserably. The secret societies would very soon be disbanded and their leaders thrown into prison. As for *La Tribune*, where Frédéric Rivolier had worked, it would not be long before its publication was suspended. The government had to hit hard and quickly to take advantage of the general rejection of revolutionary ideas.

That morning, in a dark corner on the ground floor of 14 Rue Transnonnain, the building's porter, who lived on the far side of the little courtyard and had not seen fit to show himself when the shooting started, discovered two lifeless bodies. He did not have to go far to raise the alarm.

'Two more dead?' grumbled a police sergeant, with a frown. 'So what? We've got all the dead bodies we need next door!'

When the gendarmes brought out the bodies and placed them on a cart, it was noticed that one of the two victims was still breathing.

'A dead man breathing?' said the same sergeant in surprise, smoothing his moustaches. 'If he's breathing, that means he's not dead!'

To this subtle observer of human weakness, there was no doubt that the two were revolutionaries who had been shot as they had tried to take refuge in the building. One had died from his wounds, the other had miraculously survived.

'He's not moving,' noted a gendarme, after examining Marius. 'He seems to be in a daze.'

Onlookers were pressing around the cart and the gendarmes. Some distance away, a man wearing a strange little hat, like those brought back from Morocco by Delacroix, was sketching something on a sheet of paper, resting it on his portfolio. He had a lively eye, a thin neck and a goatee beard.

'It's that little dauber, Daumier,' commented a young dandy who looked like a Carlist. 'He's already done six months for mocking the king.'

Some inhabitants of Number 14 were leaning out of their windows, staring at the soldiers and their officers, who remained silent. They already knew that the barricades in the Rue Beaubourg, the Rue aux Ours, the Rue Aubry-le-Boucher, the Rue Geoffroy-l'Angevin and the Rue Trans-nonnain had fallen. Among them, on the second floor, a young woman was staring wild-eyed at the cart. At the sight of the inert corpse in Marius's clothes, its face covered with a white cloth, she thought she would lose her head. Distraught, she was unable to make the slightest gesture.

Below, in the street, a corpulent red-haired man stood in the crowd, watching the scene. He was wearing a worker's smock and a cap, having carefully disposed of the clothes and moustache he had worn in Clémence's presence. He forced his way through the assembled bourgeois, artisans, traders, prowlers and doormen, and approached the sergeant and the cart. 'Sergeant, I know that man,' he said hesitantly.

From above, Clémence had seen him, but had not recognized him as the man who had come to fetch Marius. What had happened? She did not want to think about it. The very thought of being bothered and questioned set her nerves on edge.

The sergeant looked the Mullet up and down. 'And who might you be?'

'A poor wool carder, Sergeant. A wool carder who couldn't even get home last night, seeing as how I live in the Rue Aubry-le-Boucher, and as you probably know, those bandits put up a barricade there.'

'Very well,' said the sergeant. 'And you say you know these men?'

'The one who's unconscious worked with me. A queer customer, believe me. All he thought about was drinking and running after tarts. Anyway, look, he's still got a bludgeon covered with blood in his hands. Mightn't it be the blood of this unfortunate?' The Mullet pointed at the faceless corpse. 'But that's not the most important thing. You see, like quite a few people, I employ children in my workshop. Well, this Jesus, because that's his name, or rather his nickname, because his real name's Alexandre Tixier, used to treat them bad. One day, a young man was visiting the workshop — although I'm no saint, I like to have strangers visit my little business to show them how pleasant I try to make the working conditions of these poor children — anyway, Jesus was pitching into a little employee and the young man took the kid's part. They even went out in the street to have a fight. There are witnesses, believe me.' The sergeant was clearly getting impatient, so the Mullet decided to get to the point. 'Well, the young man in question, Sergeant, was none other than this gentleman in the cart, who seems to me quite dead.'

'But how can you recognize him?'

'By his clothes, Sergeant. He's a very nice-looking young man. I can even tell you his name.'

'Oh yes? How's that?'

'The day he and Jesus had their fight, he shouted his name. You know, as a challenge, the way these young lads do when they want to fight. He's called Marius Pontmercy.'

'He's telling the truth,' came a voice.

The sergeant and the Mullet looked round. Sergeant Carignol was standing there, flanked by two other policemen, his arms folded, his blue eyes full of the infuriating self-importance that never left him. The Catman had asked him to be present at the scene.

The other sergeant opened his eyes wide. 'And how do you know?'

'I was there when that rogue Jesus and this young man almost came to blows.'

'And you did nothing?'

'There was nothing to be done because nothing happened.' The other sergeant scratched his head. 'The young man's name is Marius Pontmercy,' insisted Carignol. 'Ask your men to search him.'

The sergeant turned to them and gave them the order to search the dead man.

'There are papers here in the name of Marius Pontmercy,' said a gendarme. 'In fact, Baron Pontmercy. It's written on a visiting card.'

The sergeant touched his cocked hat lightly. 'Bloody hell! This business is getting complicated,' he said, almost regretfully.

Three squads of police armed with rifles and truncheons now arrived at the terraced house. In front of the house, which was already notorious as the site of the massacre, some men in black were talking. Two of them came towards the gendarmes, canes in front of them, hats on their heads. A captain and an inspector.

'They tell me something shady's happened here,' said the captain.

'That's right,' said the two sergeants.

And these two jewels of the police force revealed the facts.

The captain and the inspector then tried to question Marius, but in vain. Still deep in the artificial sleep provoked by the powerful narcotic, of which the Mullet had poured almost the entire flaskful into his mouth, Marius didn't respond either to slaps or prods.

'We shan't get anything out of him,' said the inspector.

'And what's the fellow's name?' the captain asked the Mullet.

'Jesus, Monsieur. Otherwise known as Alexandre Tixier. Between ourselves, I think he's a bit simple-minded.'

'That's obvious.' Carignol assumed an appropriate expression.

'Well, there's nothing like hard labour for the simple-minded!' exclaimed the captain good-humouredly. He turned to his subordinates. 'Do what's necessary to inform this unfortunate Monsieur Pontmercy's family.'

'Will there be a trial?' asked the Mullet.

The captain hugged his cane to him. 'A trial? With the events that have just taken place, only the politicals will get proper trials. This good-for-nothing will be dealt with quickly. If it was up to me . . .' He caught his breath and refrained from saying what he had on his mind. 'I suppose this Tixier will keep his head. The simple-minded have a right to favourable treatment – don't ask me why. Like me, you saw the bludgeon and the horribly mutilated face of this Monsieur Pontmercy. This Jesus ought to have his head chopped off without delay.'

'I quite agree with you,' said Carignol, closing his eyes heavily.

The Mullet was angry with himself for telling them that the supposed Jesus was simple-minded. 'Will I have to testify?' he asked plaintively.

The captain had wedged the knob of his cane under his chin. 'Of course, my good man. This Jesus fellow will have to appear in court, though I doubt that in these times of political disturbances they'll look too closely into the case of our Monsieur Tixier. In other words, they won't prevaricate overmuch.'

The Mullet turned. Some distance away stood a man wearing a catskin hat, with a half-smile on his face. The Mullet went straight to him.

'Well?' asked the Catman.

'They're carting him off to jail and he'll stand trial soon. According to the captain, it's an open and shut case.'

The old man rubbed his hands. 'The guillotine?'

'Doesn't look like it.'

'Hard labour?'

From the Mullet's joyful expression, he understood that the sentence would, indeed, be hard labour. That would teach a lesson to that conceited little swine who had thrown him out on his ear a few months earlier, and all because he, Tardier, Thénard or Thénardier, being the inveterate philanthropist that he was, had come to inform him that Jean Valjean was a murderer and an escaped convict.

'He wanted to be smart, did he? Well, let him get a taste of hard labour. And, since he's so frail, maybe he'll never come out.' He looked round at the comings and goings of the police and ordered the Mullet to return to the workshop. 'I don't like my little ones to be on their own for too long,' he explained in a whining voice. 'Especially as Horse Face must have been out hunting all night.'

A few minutes later a familiar voice made him jump. 'So, Thénardier, savouring the spectacle?'

'Enormously,' said the old man, and he gave a laugh like the sound of a cat wheezing. 'But, for God's sake, don't call me that.'

The man in black lifted his hat with the tip of his forefinger and stood on tiptoe. When he stood like that, his hunched back was noticeable. And for once his face was uncovered. He was none other than Louis-Désiré Burdin, Amédée d'Iguerande's steward.

'My dear Burdin, I think we've done it,' said the Catman.

And the two men laughed as one and shook hands.

They did not see the young draughtsman, who had sketched several portraits of them, bringing them wonderfully to life with his pencil, nor the fifteen-year-old boy with the enormous jaw who had been peering over the draughtsman's shoulders, following every stroke.

'What are you gawping at?' the draughtsman asked him.

'Your drawings. They're really lifelike.'

Out of the corner of his eye, Horse Face had seen the Mullet slip away. He had no idea what was going on. Why wasn't the man on the cart, who was just now being taken away by the police, wearing his ring – if he was supposed to be Jesus?

'If it interests you, my name is Daumier,' said the young draughtsman proudly. 'You can see my work in *La Caricature*.'

'Thanks,' replied Horse Face. 'I'll remember that.'

And he ran off, in a hurry to reach the workshop before the Mullet.

Marius was found not to be responsible for his actions. He had been examined by a court-appointed doctor, a pasty individual with hair plastered to his forehead, whose foul breath smelled of entrails and alcohol. Hurriedly sounding his chest and finding nothing suspect, he had declared that the young man had not been conscious of his actions at the time of the crime. That much was obvious just from looking at him, as he lay there prostrate and absent, in the grip of some terrifying and painful inner struggle.

This botched job saved Marius's head. It was concluded not only that he was subject to sudden convulsive attacks with loss of consciousness, followed by a state of prostration and deep despondency, but also that he was not in full possession of his mental faculties. As he was not, therefore, found to be truly insane, he escaped the asylum and the trial was quickly dispatched.

The captain responsible for Marius's arrest was called to the stand. Drawing on the facts he had unearthed during his brief investigation – namely, the allegations of a wool carder who had apparently employed the defendant and a somewhat self-satisfied police sergeant – he corroborated the doctor's point of view. There was no point in making things more complicated than they were – he had other fish to fry.

'Your honour,' he declared in his most earnest manner, 'it is common knowledge that the accused, Alexandre Tixier, known as Jesus, is simple-minded. But a simple-minded person who bludgeons a man to death – I remind you that the blows to the victim's face testify to the incredible savagery of the killing – and whose links with the shadiest circles are beyond doubt, this simple-minded man, insane though he may be, ought to be kept apart from society.'

The Mullet, as the principal witness, gave his testimony under his real name, Auguste Tricot. 'These two men had a fight once before, your honour. There were insults and threats on both sides. The people who saw this row will confirm it. It was as if Jesus had lost his mind. I'm not surprised at what happened.'

Sergeant Carignol confirmed this version of events, which was not challenged by any other witness, for the good reason that there was none. The only one who might have been called, Clémence de Lavely, was conspicuous by her absence and her name was never even mentioned.

In the dock, Marius, whose name was now Alexandre Tixier, looked deathly pale. Two policemen had to support him. The family or friends of the victim, who were absent from the hearing, had not been part of the prosecution. It was a parody of a trial. Everyone was in a hurry. The grave and severe face of the public prosecutor seemed to make no impact on Marius, even though it was well known that such men, who were impervious to the emotions of humanity, struck terror into the hearts of most defendants. But Marius kept nodding gently or lowering his eyelids without being aware of where he was, or why he was there. The policemen supporting him sometimes had to manhandle him to stop him dozing off in the middle of the hearing.

The jurors felt a certain compassion towards this handsome young man, who from time to time let out an uncomprehending groan. The public prosecutor demanded an exemplary sentence – hard labour for life. This eloquent but precise man, whose goatee beard bobbed up and down as he spoke, had a reputation for implacability, but in this case he was not excessively vehement. He was simply doing his job as a prosecutor. Like the doctor, the judges and the court-appointed defence lawyer, he seemed to have little interest in the trial or its outcome. Everyone was thinking about the great trials to come, those of the Republican vermin who had once more almost put the country to fire and the sword.

Naturally, the members of the jury were not unaware of the situation. Most juries, hand-picked and little inclined to indulgence as far as rebellion and equality went, were content to approve the closing speeches of these Torquemadas in red robes. But this particular jury seemed reluctant to uphold the prosecutor's casual severity.

When the fateful moment came, they retired to deliberate. They were not out for long.

An usher appeared in the doorway of the jury room. 'The court, gentlemen!' he cried in a squeal.

The judges took their seats in silence and the jurors sat down on their benches. It was all done briskly.

'Guards,' said the presiding judge, 'bring in the accused.'

The eyes of the public turned to the door through which Marius was to enter. The door opened and he appeared, pale, unsteady on his feet, his eyes rolled upwards, still supported by the two policemen. He was made to sit down near his lawyer, a balding young man, emotional and laborious, whose dull face had become briefly animated during his faltering and unintelligible closing speech.

The presiding judge asked in a dry tone for the indictment to be read out. It was short but damning. The attention of the public was still on Marius, who was looking around him with wild eyes, tilting his head now towards the first policeman, now towards the second.

When the reading was over, the presiding judge asked Marius for his Christian name and surname. Marius, of course, was quite incapable of rising and stringing together the shortest sentence, so his lawyer did it for him.

In the name of the king, and in an appropriately resonant voice, the judge pronounced sentence. 'Alexandre Tixier, the court sentences you to twenty years' hard labour.'

No uproar greeted the verdict. After all, Alexandre Tixier had benefited from the jury's clemency. Given the gravity of his crime, there was nothing to quarrel with. As he would need to be imprisoned for a time because of his deranged state, he would be immediately taken to Bicêtre, where he would stay until he was put in irons and sent to Toulon as part of a chain gang.

'Gentlemen, the court will rise,' said the presiding judge, gathering his files, not unhappy to have finally got this chore out of the way.

Everyone had lost interest in the fate of Alexandre Tixier. He was not the only one in his situation. There had been another trial the day before, of an innkeeper and former carpenter, who had strangled his wife in a fit of jealousy. A prosecution witness by the name of Tardier had been merciless. The defendant, driven mad with indignation, had struggled so violently that he had been expelled, and the court cleared. He, too, had received twenty years. It was all the fault of the political situation. That, at any rate, was what Perfect Love had told himself when he heard his sentence pronounced.

Amédée's first reaction, when Louis-Désiré informed him of Marius's death, was one of disbelief. 'Marius dead? Are you sure? Attacked by a madman coming out of Clémence's building?'

The steward adopted an appropriate expression. 'I regret I must confirm the terrible news, Monsieur. I knew nothing about it until today.' In fact, he had waited until the trial was over to tell his master about Baron Pontmercy's death. 'I've invented nothing, Monsieur. Look here, it's in the newspaper – the same paper in which the baron exercised the remarkable but sometimes thankless activity of dramatic critic.'

Amédée snatched Le National from his steward's hands. There, indeed, was an obituary of Marius, written by Armand Carrel. 'I can't believe it,' he said in a changed voice, suddenly very pale. 'And what about Clémence? What happened? It's impossible!'

'Sadly, Monsieur, it's the truth.'

'Leave me!' retorted Amédée.

In the grip of a terrible depression, he did not see the look, both indulgent and exasperated, that Louis-Désiré Burdin threw him. I did all this for him, thought the steward, and now look how he treats me. He withdrew without a word and returned to his room.

Apart from the marquis's reaction, which was not the one the steward had expected, everything had gone perfectly. Burdin was satisfied. That morning he had met Tardier at the dyer's shop in the Rue du Jour. It was the first time they had seen each other since the bloody episode in the Rue Transnonnain and they did not say much to one another. The happy outcome of a feverishly hatched plot often makes those who have profited from it feel dizzy. Relief gives way to dejection. And, though he is not like other men, a criminal may feel, just like other men, the consequences of his actions. An inexpressible languor takes hold of him and leaves him dazed from having passed the point of no return.

Burdin had finally broken the silence. 'I think we should avoid each other for a while.'

'Just as long as it takes me to take over the Clan Destin,' Tardier had replied. It was clear he still had his wits about him. True, he had become thoughtful, but only because he hadn't believed that everything would work out quite so well. A strangled chuckle escaped him, as if he was trying to contain a fit of the giggles. 'We did it, Burdin!'

The steward had nodded cautiously. Unlike Tardier, who aimed low to aim straight, he aimed high. Tardier was an executant, he was a strategist. He never got involved in a scheme without making sure he grasped how it worked. His will drove him on. His will made it possible to conquer one passion with another – cowardice with greed, treachery with ambition. Being content with little meant nothing to this cautious but vain man. In the letter which made Amédée Marius's sole legatee, he had seen an opportunity to make his master and himself rich. The document was locked in the safe of Amédée's notary. It would take time and patience, but Amédée would eventually purchase the house in the Rue Plumet, marry Cosette and sell the shabby house which he currently owned. Then would come the question of making it all yield a profit. That was where he, Louis-Désiré Burdin, would come in. He knew only too well how negligent his master could be when he felt guilty, which was why he needed a real steward. Well, who better than himself to fill the role? He had raised Amédée from an early age – he had furthered his studies, paid for a private tutor, interceded with a staff officer who owed him money so that Amédée could embark on a military career. He had sacrificed himself. Yes, he, the man in black. He had done everything. Now, if things developed as he wished, he might be able to turn over a new leaf. He would rid himself of Tardier's burdensome friendship and shameful activities. One thing he vowed – he would sell no more children, even if it meant abandoning the goal he and Tardier had set themselves – to train children in theft and to form a gang of ruthless criminals who would bring them a large income. Like little Raphaël, who was all set to become the new Cartouche of Paris.

The sight of the Catman suddenly pulling a face had torn him from his grandiose daydreams. 'What's the matter?'

'There's something I forgot to tell you.'

Even if everything had been all right, the Catman would not have been able to stop himself sowing doubt in his accomplice's mind, just for the pleasure of it. That was just the way he was.

'What is it?' Burdin had asked, growing sombre.

'The Mullet has slipped up again. He forgot to take off Jesus's ring. He noticed at the end of the trial, when the sentence was being pronounced.'

Burdin had immediately become annoyed. 'Ring? What ring?'

'A ring with a snake on it. I see you hadn't noticed it either. That's a good sign. It was just an oversight. I don't suppose it'll make any difference.'

'You don't suppose it'll make any difference? You idiot! Are you brain-dead or what? What if, during the funeral of the supposed Marius Pontmercy, someone notices this ring on his finger, what'll happen then? I'll tell you what'll happen. They'll realize the supposed Marius Pontmercy is not what he seems and an investigation will be ordered. Is that what you want?'

The Catman had remained speechless. 'We have to get it back,' he had said at last.

'Absolutely. And since that idiot Mullet made the mistake, let him fix it himself. And as quickly as possible!'

'You said it, not me,' the Catman had agreed, stooping a little more.

Needless to say, the two men's leave-taking had not been especially cordial.

Now, pacing up and down his room, Louis-Désiré thought again about his master, worrying that the marquis might lose his nerve. The sight of the floor, the camp bed, the two striped horsehair armchairs, depressed him. Unable to stand it any more, he went to find the marquis. Amédée was no longer in the little drawing room. He must have gone back to what he pretentiously called the games room on the first floor. Louis-Désiré climbed the stairs and found him lying on a sofa.

'I hope I'm not disturbing you, Monsieur?'

'What is it now?'

'I think you should go to see Baroness Pontmercy and tell her the sad news.'

'Do you suppose she doesn't know?'

Amédée's tone was petulant and ill-tempered. The time for confusion had passed. The game was over. Thanks to him, a man was dead, a man he had been weak enough to like and esteem, though he had not admitted it to himself. The people one likes often disappear before one has had time to tell them. Damned reticence! Amédée thought. And, what's more, my legendary indifference is letting me down. What's happening to me? I thought I was so different from everyone else! Did I love him, then?

'Yes, you're right,' he finally conceded to his steward. 'I shan't tell her anything, but at least I'll reveal to her what I've never been able to reveal to anyone.'

Louis-Désiré did not like these words – they smacked of repentance. 'Monsieur, I beg you, be strong.'

'Leave me alone, Louis-Désiré. I don't need your advice. First, I'm going to see Clémence, and then I'll offer my condolences to Baroness Pontmercy. I shan't be going out tonight. Make me a simple meal.'

'As you wish, Monsieur.'

Louis-Désiré withdrew again. He did not greatly appreciate his master's fallibility. He feared it would grow as time went on. Here was a problem he had never expected to encounter and which had fallen on him without warning. What was the use of all that education he had given the young fool?

Amédée went to see Clémence. The terrified young woman had not left her apartment since Marius's death. Her maid looked after her needs, but she barely touched the food prepared for her. Her silence was painful to behold. Suffering from an unquenchable thirst, she drank gallons and gallons of tea, constantly repeating that she was going to stay with her aunt in the country. Strangely, neither her anxious state nor her self-enforced fast had altered the freshness of her outward appearance. Her mouth remained firm and proudly drawn, like a rose that no blemish could spoil. The orgies and the tragedies had left no trace in her eyes. Despite their faraway look, they still expressed a gentle warmth. Her hands were soft, white and transparent – the hands of a woman who could melt hearts without ever taking them by surprise. Only her nails, which she had been chewing incessantly since 14 April, betrayed the state of anxiety and depression in which she found herself.

'What time did Marius leave?' Amédée asked her.

'Who's Marius?' replied Clémence, without even looking at Amédée. She was sitting in the armchair near the window, her eyes fixed on the street. 'My little boy?'

Distressed at her response, Amédée took Clémence's face between his hands. 'What about me, Clémence? Do you recognize me?'

'Of course I recognize you.'

'So tell me how Marius was when he left your apartment. Was he drunk, ill, worried, or what? Did someone come to fetch him?'

'Who's Marius?' she said again, with disarming sincerity. 'My little boy?'

'Marius was our friend, Clémence. My friend and your lover. He might even have become your husband.'

Clémence gripped Amédée's hands and pulled them away from her face. 'Do you know why I never married, Monsieur? Because I never wanted anyone to have any kind of hold over me. If I'd kept my child, my little boy, it would have been different.' She was smiling grotesquely.

Amédée recoiled in horror. 'What child, Clémence? What little boy?' He raised his two fists in a gesture of impotent imprecation. 'You've gone completely mad! How many times must I tell you? Your child, our child, is dead!'

'No,' retorted Clémence, her countenance a strange mixture of gracious serenity and terrible gravity. 'They took my child away from me the other morning. He was sleeping in my arms and some men came to fetch him.'

Amédée calmed down. 'All right, then, they took away your child. But who were these men? Where were they from?'

Clémence shook her head violently and bit her hand until it bled. 'They took away my child, they took away my child . . .'

Running out of arguments, and helpless before Clémence's attitude, which was as disturbing as it was incomprehensible, Amédée stood looking at her sadly. 'Since I learned to lie, I've ceased to believe anyone,' he murmured as he left, a gleam of bitterness in his eyes.

From the moment she had learned the terrible news, Cosette was incapable of uttering a word. Weeping would have been a relief, but something deep inside her pumped her dry of tears before she could shed them. The previous day, after the police captain who had come to inform her of Marius's fatal accident had left, Cosette had gone up to her bedroom and thrown herself on the bed fully clothed. She had felt crushed and desperate. She could not believe it. Madeleine, her faithful maid, had been unable to do anything to check her despair. But what can be done to check the despair of someone who has devoted her life to a single being and who loses him suddenly, without even being able to contemplate his beloved face one last time?

'Your husband's body is in the morgue,' the captain had said. 'But it would be better if you didn't see him, Baroness. His face is horribly mutilated.'

The morgue was on the south side of the Quai du Marché-Neuf, close to the Pont Saint-Michel. A carriage entrance led to a vestibule, from which a glass partition gave a view of a macabre exhibition hall. Other rooms served as washroom, autopsy room, depository, offices – and even lodgings, for the employees, yellowish functionaries whose hands, though red from constant washing, were forever impregnated with the smell of human entrails, lived on the premises.

'Believe me, Madame, I'm truly sorry,' the captain had added with a distinctly bureaucratic stiffness. 'Where will the religious ceremony take place?'

'In the church of Saint-Sulpice,' Cosette had replied in a choked voice.

'We'll arrange for the body to be taken there – though I hasten to add that the transfer will be at your expense. By the way, I've taken the liberty of bringing you this. I found it in the pocket of your husband's frock coat.'

And he had handed her the rock crystal.

Cosette had locked herself in her room and curled up on her bed, the stone in her hand. A magic stone, she had told Marius. Where was its magic now?

She did not close her eyes all night. The lamp went out when there was no more oil, but she was no more aware of the darkness than she had been aware of the light, nor was she aware of the sun when it rose in the morning. Grief had masked her eyes and through it she could see only Marius.

In the morning, on the verge of suffocation, she walked up and down the room, talking disjointedly, then entered what had once been Marius's room and placed the stone on top of the wardrobe. Looking in a little mirror, she imagined she saw Marius's face. She ran to the window and flung it open. Outside, near the little bench between the two statues, she imagined she saw him again. And in the winter garden with a bouquet of flowers in his hand. And again on the path along which he had walked happily that cursed evening of 13 April. She called his name several times and put one leg out of the window, as if to throw herself into the void.

'Madame! No!' Madeleine shouted sharply, just in time, from below, her hands clenched, not knowing what to do to alleviate her mistress's sufferings.

Cosette went back into the room and opened Marius's wardrobe and chest of drawers. She unfolded his shirts, then folded them again, smelled his waistcoats, buried her face in his frock coats. Nothing is more terrible than a glimpse into the intimacy of a lost loved one. The illusion that they are alive takes us by the throat. This overwhelming sensation leads us to the realization that we only truly become ourselves through the sum of our failures. And thus it is that, shaken by repugnance and uncertainty, we lose our taste for everything but death.

For Cosette, the universe had begun and ended with Marius. What was she to do without him? What she missed already, desperately, irreparably, was his presence. Not his spirit or his soul, but his body, his flesh. Life was that more than anything else – flesh. Everything else was merely metaphysical. Who would have dared to say to Cosette at the moment of her greatest sorrow that the body was a temporary envelope? Who could even have talked of faith, resurrection, the miracle of eternal life?

The wardrobe and chest of drawers were imbued with Marius's smell – a scent of lavender. The only words that crossed Cosette's lips now were blasphemies. Distress gave way to anger, only for distress to return all the more ferociously. How was she to deal with this catastrophe? How was she to find a way out of the depths of injustice and uncertainty? Her only thought was to die. I must find him again quickly wherever he is, she said to herself, and have done with this life, which strives so hard to plunge us into chaos and misfortune. She said so many things to herself. And so many things around her, so benign, so everyday, brought her back endlessly to the impasse of death.

Her eyes fell on her father's candlesticks, which stood on the mantelpiece, and the episodes of a life she thought she had put behind her came back to her now in a confused, disordered torrent, an endless parade of misery and despair.

'Marius, my love,' she whispered, feeling her childlike confidence dying within her.

The joyful confidence that had carried her through life was now denied her. Never again would she be able to see things without sorrow, without shame, without hesitation. Never again would she be able to sing to herself without remorse. She thought of the child she was carrying and she almost hated it. Then the questions returned. Where was Marius? Why had all the objects that were familiar to him not disappeared at the same time as him? Why was the earth still turning?

She looked at the furniture, the curtains and the carpet. She hated them. *They* were not weeping, *they* were not lamenting. She took the pitcher of Tournai porcelain, in which the sunflowers and immortelles seemed to be mocking her, and threw it against the wall. But the gesture gave her no respite from her pain. Her chest was burning. She was suffocating.

A little later still, sitting on her bed, her hair loose, her hands ice-cold, she let her gaze wander to the window. The sky was lit by streaks of grey light. Marius had never liked that kind of sky, with the sun hidden behind a thick veil. Her own Marius, her beloved, the light of her life . . .

'I'd accept everything if you came back to me . . .' she stammered.

She had already accepted everything – his hasty departures, his sudden changes of mood, his prolonged absences. Would he have been so beautiful if he had been more accessible? She would have preferred to live with the uncertainties of a chaotic life together than to be without him. Hadn't she detected his lies and pretended to ignore them? Well, now nothing more would happen. Marius was gone. But she loved him all the more now that she could no longer tell him that she loved him.

In the afternoon, she received visits from Louis de Vergne and Henri de la Roche-Dragon. Marius's aunt, Mademoiselle Gillenormand, also came, dressed all in black, her hands filled with crucifixes and rosaries, and through her tears talked of fate and redemption. Father Rillet and Monsieur Verjat came to offer their condolences, searching for words that should console but never do.

'To live truly, one must pass to the other side of despair,' declared Verjat gravely. 'I am at your disposal, Cosette. If you think it appropriate, you can come and see me whenever you wish.'

'The funeral will take place tomorrow,' whispered Father Rillet. 'In accordance with your wishes, the religious ceremony will be held in our church. Courage, my child.'

Courage was what Cosette needed to confront all these people, who adopted appropriate faces and recited their litanies with a stunned air. She held herself quite straight, her face hidden by a black veil. She was amiable and patient with her visitors, embarrassed at the thought of imposing her grief on others. From time to time she would claw the air with a clumsy gesture, in an effort not to curse this God with his good, his evil, his judgements and decrees, his pointless sacrifices. She had to restrain herself from running to the morgue and embracing one last time the dear body that had been snatched from her. She wanted to keep intact the memory of Marius's handsome face, his brilliant smile, his sometimes childish pride. God deserved to be banished for ever from the hearts of men for having allowed such an injustice to take place. One day their friend Frédéric, also now dead, had quoted to her a sentence of Pascal's: 'We can only know God well by knowing our own iniquities.' The sentence appalled her. What iniquities? What sin had she committed to deserve such a punishment?

Late in the afternoon, as Cosette was resting in her room, Madeleine announced Amédée d'Iguerande. It was an unpleasant surprise. With a degree of tact that was unusual in him, he was waiting downstairs at the gate for Cosette's permission to enter.

'Show him to my room,' said Cosette.

Madeleine was slightly offended. 'To your room?'

'Do as I say, Madeleine. I have my reasons.'

When Amédée appeared in the doorway, soberly dressed, hat in hand, devoid of his usual smile of self-satisfaction, Cosette was sitting on the bed. She was refusing to behave as ladies of good society were supposed to behave in such circumstances. She did not give a fig for the rules of decorum. With the others, she had bowed to protocol. With Amédée d'Iguerande, it was different. Was he at least stricken with remorse? He had to see what a disaster he had provoked, what a catastrophe.

'Stay where you are, Monsieur. Take your time. Have a good look at the room that once belonged to your friend, the man you murdered!'

Then Cosette saw what she supposed nobody else had witnessed – an Amédée d'Iguerande who was feverish, demoralized, silent, powerless, on the verge of tears. In leaving outside his coldness and indifference and in trying to drive away the pain that gripped him, he was, for once, sincere. But pain cannot be driven away as easily as that. The wounded man carries it with him always.

'I beg you, Madame,' he finally said, fidgeting with the brim of his hat, 'do not add remorse to my distress. I loved Marius like a brother.'

Cosette's face showed her despair and hatred. 'Like a brother whom you corrupted and whose wife you coveted?' she said in a hollow voice.

Amédée had never been so sincere in his life, but he did not know what to do to assure Cosette of his good faith. His change of heart surprised even himself. What had happened to the man who was indifferent to everything and who never allowed himself to feel anything that might break the ice in which he wrapped himself like armour? What had become of his pride, his sarcasm?

'I didn't realize it until now, but I swear to you I loved Marius like a brother,' he stammered, still in the doorway, horrified by Cosette's tone and feeling his legs give way beneath him. 'And the only thing I covet at the moment, Madame, even if I don't deserve it, is your forgiveness.'

Cosette gave a brief, harsh laugh. 'Once more you're indulging in your favourite pastime – lying. Have you no shame?'

Amédée would have liked to find the sparkling adjectives, the dazzling formulas, all the eloquence that, until now, had got him out of the most dangerous situations. But now irony had turned against him and an overwhelming feeling of helplessness was making him suffer a thousand deaths. Deep within him had been born the first seed of a fatal ulcer – guilt. He seemed to see in the room the friend he had sacrificed to his shameful schemes, pale and threatening, giving his hand to Cosette. And in his soul there was a moment's hesitation. He first recoiled in terror, then almost turned on his heels and fled from the place whose harmony he had broken. He had so often fled – fled the truth, fled his responsibilities, fled his inability to love or satisfy women. How could one love others when, all things considered, one does not love oneself? And the thought brought a dull, hitherto unknown throbbing into his chest.

'Allow me to leave you, Madame,' he said, with a heartfelt sigh.

As he left, his eyes fixed on Cosette, who was still sitting motionless on her bed with her head buried in her hands, he heard her weep. He paused. She was not weeping, she was sobbing, and her sobs were like an uninterrupted stream of poignant moans that shook her body with violent and uncontrollable spasms. She was shaking her head and twisting her arms in pain. Then she collapsed back on the bed, emitting groans that horrified Amédée.

'Cosette, no, I beg you . . .'

He went to her, knelt by the bed, and took her icy hands in his. She felt nothing. Madeleine, hearing her mistress's sobs, came rushing upstairs. She saw the marquis on his knees. In other circumstances, the situation would have appeared improper. But it was not. The marquis, as his ravaged face bore witness, was like a child comforting his mother. When he saw the maid, he stood up and put his hat back on. He searched in his pocket and handed Madeleine a visiting card.

'If there's anything at all I can do, don't hesitate to send for me, whatever the hour,' he whispered, barely concealing his desolation. He cast a final glance at Cosette, who was still lying on the bed. 'May heaven come to her aid.'

*

You have to be a fool to commit certain acts, and even more of a fool to enlist the help of individuals who will betray you at the earliest opportunity. The Mullet's reputation in this respect was beyond doubt. From Montreuil to Bercy by way of Charonne and Vincennes, everyone knew about his blunders, his brutality, his staggering clumsiness, his inability to listen and understand and, above all, his unfailing propensity to boast and display his superior knowledge, which is often the prerogative of weak-minded people. Confusion and amazement followed him everywhere. Not that the noisy disregard in which his intelligence was held ever touched him. On the contrary, he took a certain pride in it. He was never troubled by doubt.

That morning, as he stood in the corridor leading to the workshop and listened to the Catman calling him every name under the sun, the Mullet swallowed his rage. The old man's ingratitude revolted him. After all, he had killed a man for him. He was sure he would soon find an opportunity to get his revenge. In the meantime, he made amends.

'You'd better hurry up and get me back that ring,' said the Catman, in a tone that no longer had anything honeyed about it. 'How could you have forgotten something like that? Do you want to send us all to the scaffold?'

The Mullet immediately asked Horse Face to go with him to the morgue. He had not been able to contact Pegasus or Twenty-Two. Since Jesus's murder, both had been lying low in Saint-Antoine.

'I trust you, Horse Face. You have to come with me to the Quai du Marché-Neuf and help me distract the attention of the meat packers. You know why? I like you, so I'm going to tell you. That fellow Marius took Jesus's ring and kept it for himself. Now, when Jesus gets back from hard labour, he may be happy to get his ring back. Do you follow me?'

'So you trust me?' asked the boy, sarcastically.

The Mullet glared at him. For the occasion he had put on a clean jacket that made him look like a peasant in his Sunday best. 'Does it bother you, or what?' he replied, through clenched teeth.

'I'm surprised, that's all.'

'Well, don't be too surprised and do what I tell you. We'll see about payment later. If you play your cards right, I'll turn a blind eye when you resell catmeat. And I'll even give you a new shirt.'

At the morgue the Mullet presented himself as the principal witness to the tragic events that had cost Baron Pontmercy his life. He had been mandated by the family, he said, and had in his possession a document signed by the judicial authorities of the city of Paris. He explained that the dead man had to be presentable.

'He is,' they replied. 'He's been washed, his clothes have been cleaned, his face has been bandaged. All paid for by someone called the Marquis d'Iguerande.'

'Good,' said the Mullet, 'but I'd like to make sure.'

The morgue official adjusted his pince-nez hesitantly. He was a neat little man with lacklustre brown skin, surrounded by a cloud of disinfectant, and dressed in a black bum-freezer which made him look like a prison porter. 'I can't do that, Monsieur.'

'Don't you have any heart? I'll be forced to tell the family that you denied me access to the body. If they think the dead man looks horrible, you'll be held entirely responsible. Baron Pontmercy is not just anybody.' Reluctantly searching his pocket, he took out a few sous and gave them to the official.

'All right, but quickly, eh?' said the man, pocketing the money. 'Normally you should be accompanied by a police inspector.'

'I know,' lied the Mullet, 'but that's the way it is. In times of misfortune, one sometimes forgets to attend to the formalities. In any case, I have the official documents,' he added, brandishing several irrelevant sheets of paper. He assumed a winning expression. 'While I'm discharging this painful but nonetheless necessary duty, my young companion will stay with you. By the way, is the victim still wearing his gloves?'

'Monsieur, everything here is carefully noted and recorded,' replied the official stiffly, 'as the employees of the undertakers, Henri de Borniol, can confirm.' He pointed to a door near the large glass partition, where two employees were busy with a naked corpse on a wheeled trolley. 'Number fourteen!' he cried in a falsetto voice.

Number fourteen, like the date of the massacre, thought Horse Face, noting the stink in the air. He watched as the Mullet went through the glass partition, then reluctantly followed the official to the offices.

When the Mullet was shown Marius's corpse, he could not suppress a shudder. Under the bandages was the face of Jesus. And only I know it, he said to himself, thinking of the pressure he would one day be able to exert on the Catman as revenge. He dusted the sleeve of the corpse's frock coat, checked the creases of the trousers, and adjusted the cravat. 'He seems quite presentable,' he said to the two employees who had brought out the body. 'Can you leave me alone with him for a moment?'

They grunted. It was all the same to them.

No sooner had they turned their backs than the Mullet removed the glove from Jesus's left hand. There was the ring. He tried to slip it off, but it would not budge. Then he tried pulling, but again to no avail. He glanced to the side, stared for a long moment at the glass partition, and took a knife from his pocket. Leaning slightly on the table, he cut through the first phalanx of the finger, like a butcher cutting a tail from a bull. Then he stuffed the finger into his pocket and put the glove back on Jesus.

'See you in hell,' he murmured as he walked away.

People sometimes make disconcerting gestures. Cosette made one on the day of the funeral. They were about to nail down the lid of the coffin before the funeral ceremony. It was pouring with rain. In a moment of weakness she did what she had not dared to do these past few days. She went to the faceless corpse and seized the left hand of the man she took for Marius. She wanted to hold the cold, stiff hand in hers one last time, even though it was clad in a leather glove. As everyone knows, a fingertip is exceptionally sensitive. Thus, when Cosette tried to stroke the wedding ring on her husband's finger, all she felt through the flaccid envelope of leather was an empty space. With a start, she let go of the hand. A multitude of confused thoughts crowded into her mind. She staggered, so great had been the fright. Then she regained her composure. Why did Marius no longer have his ring finger? Had his attacker, not content with disfiguring him, also cut off his finger?

She looked around for Verjat, but her eyes met only those of Amédée d'Iguerande, who had still not recovered his grand manner and was staring numbly at the rain beating on the ground. Without advertising the fact, he had borne all the funeral expenses. As for his steward, he was absent.

Cosette moved away from the coffin. Leaning on Verjat's arm, she forgot what had happened to Marius. In the end, it did not matter. All that mattered was that he was dead.

As the bells of Saint-Sulpice echoed in the ears of the mourners like a warning from heaven, the cortège set off for Père-Lachaise. Cosette had been determined that Marius should be buried beside her father.

'The two people I loved most in the world,' she had told Father Rillet.

The mourners, who included Armand Carrel, Amédée d'Iguerande, Eugène Sue, Louis de Vergne and Verjat, all admired the young widow's courage and selflessness. Even those like Robert d'Androisy, who felt nothing, who were there just to see and be seen and who assumed the appropriate faces expected at this kind of ceremony, could not help but be impressed by Cosette. Paradoxes sometimes accentuate reality. Baroness Pontmercy's undimmed beauty made the terrible tragedy that had befallen her all the harder to bear. But she had not shed a tear. Her eyes were full of strength and dignity – the eyes of Jean Valjean.

As Father Rillet was delivering the funeral oration, Verjat, sitting on Cosette's right, took her hand in his, as one takes the hand of a child, then released it again immediately. She almost burst into tears. The gesture had recalled a memory. Eleven years earlier a man had reached out his hand to her as she was returning with water from the spring in the forest, near Chelles, on the outskirts of Montfermeil. It was a cold winter's night in 1823 and Cosette was eight years old. If she had suppressed this memory, it was perhaps because it shocked her social conscience, or because it forced her to rethink her ideas about things and men. Cosette was barefoot and had a black eye from a punch given to her by Madame Thénardier. The bucket was heavy and the man had seized the handle to lift it. Cosette had not forgotten the contact of that huge, powerful hand. It was not the kind of thing you forgot easily. She was angry with herself for having kept it hidden, for having put it away in a corner of her memory. And now, with his unexpected gesture, Verjat had reawakened the memory. Cosette's feelings were so strong that she could not move. This man, who looked like a night bird, and who seemed so hard and inflexible, recalled the stranger on that night in 1823. How could she fail to make the connection with her father, the incomparable Jean Valjean?

Verjat remained impassive. He sensed Cosette's embarrassment. Many thoughts were jostling in his head. He was a survivor who no longer believed in much, and his negative stance had encouraged in him an infinite melancholy. But there is a difference between melancholy and despair. Verjat had never lost his lucidity, a lucidity that made some people's self-love intolerable to him and other people's love for their fellow men admirable. He admired the courage and fortitude of this young woman, who was still not twenty. She was truly the daughter of Jean Valjean. In the everyday world, filled with idle chatter and the vain activity of most of his fellow creatures, Verjat felt that the antidote to mediocre convictions was irony. 'One should disdain confronting one's doubts,' he would often say. With Cosette, disdain was impossible.

When they reached the cemetery, Verjat opened his umbrella to protect Cosette. 'You're right to rebel, Cosette,' he said to her gravely. 'Rebellion is proof that you're still alive. Never change. And I know whereof I speak.'

Cosette thanked him and wrapped herself in the black shawl that suited her so well. It was neither the time nor the place for such judgements, but the dark colours she wore enhanced her beauty. She looked like a weeping madonna. Verjat, conscious of this, screened her. He protected her from the others, from their looks, their vulgarity. He felt as if he had been entrusted with a great mission. He had a debt to repay – a debt to Jean Valjean and a debt to Cosette. He had to learn to live again. He who had spent so much of his life hunting down criminals, sacrificing everything to the law, the state, justice, duty, avoiding the study of character, refusing to allow anyone any extenuating circumstances – for a policeman with feelings is no longer a policeman – now felt ready to show compassion and mercy, and even to analyse the workings of the human soul impartially and methodically. It had not taken him long to realize that Cosette had a sharp intelligence, a great deal of curiosity, an overflowing sentimentality, and sometimes a naive gullibility. For the moment, though, death over-shadowed everything.

When Verjat saw the tombstone of the man he had pursued relentlessly for years, his sad face lit up. Nobody seeing him could have said whether this light revealed the proud conviction of an executioner who still owed allegiance to a time of great turmoil, or that of a victim duped by the system in which he had believed and which had been his only reference point. But Verjat himself knew very well what he was feeling. Error, he murmured. Nothing but error. All men should come close to death at least once in their lives, and early enough to understand their error.

The coffin was lifted above a gaping hole, the bottom of which was like a greasy swamp, full of water and mud – Marius's last resting place. Cosette could not restrain her tears at the sight of the flowers thrown onto the coffin and the shovelfuls of earth that fell with a hollow thud. There had been two men in her life, her father and Marius, and the second had been taken away from her soon after the first. The recurrence revolted her and she was overwhelmed with a profound disgust for life. Yet she had to go on. But in the mind of this young woman, who had become old overnight, it was no longer a question of living. It was just a question of surviving. But for how long?

Victim of a narcotic which had plunged him into a state of apathy and uncontrollable numbness, Marius had, unwittingly and narrowly, escaped death. Between his arrest and his trial, he remained in this state for four days. The dose administered by the Mullet had proved almost fatal. When

Marius awoke the day after his imprisonment, he felt as though he had been sleeping for years. And when he saw where he was and the grey, foul-smelling, ill-fitting uniform he was wearing, he rubbed his eyes. What was he doing in this cell with these other poor devils grinning at him?

'You're in Bicêtre, my lad,' one said.

'What's Bicêtre?'

'Are you making fun of me or what?' retorted the prisoner, leaning his back against a wall dripping with filth. 'You're in prison, my lad. We're waiting for the chain.'

'The chain? What chain?'

'Are you doing this on purpose? Just listen.'

A terrible noise was coming from somewhere deep in the dungeons, a huge rolling and creaking, whose dull echo in these squalid surroundings was uniquely disturbing. In the big courtyard they were unloading the irons. There were voices, heated arguments, the heavy tread of the gate-keepers coming and going around the jail.

'But what am I doing here?' asked Marius, hammering on the door.

The man who had first spoken to him eyed him scornfully. His hair was grey, his body large and menacing, his hands disturbingly purple and stubby. The scar on his right cheek gave his face an alarming appearance. He looked like a strangler. 'Truth is, you've been sentenced to hard labour. Is that what you wanted to hear?'

Marius was seized with panic. 'Hard labour? But that's impossible! What for? What am I accused of? I'm innocent! Do you hear? Innocent!'

A burst of laughter greeted his words. There were innocents galore here. Marius hammered even harder on the door. A guard unlocked it. Behind him stood a number of armed soldiers, an officer and a man in civilian clothes who, to judge by the remarks of the prisoners, must be an inspector of prisons.

'Monsieur, I'm innocent,' said Marius.

'Get back!' bellowed the guard, brandishing a truncheon. But Marius pushed forward, trying desperately to collar the inspector, and the guard hit him in the small of his back.

'I'm innocent!' he screamed, bent double.

The inspector lowered his nose and gave him a sly look through his round glasses. 'Yes, I know,' he said in a soft voice, 'you're all innocent.'

Then he asked the others how they were being fed and if there was anything in particular that they wanted. Everyone replied with one voice that the food was dreadful and they wanted their freedom. The inspector then asked them if they had anything else to say to him. They shook their heads. What else could prisoners ask for except their freedom?

The inspector turned to the soldiers. 'When you've seen one prisoner,' he said with a smile, 'you've heard them all. It's always the same. They're innocent, they're badly fed, they're all victims of miscarriages of justice. Sometimes I wonder why they ask us to make these pointless rounds.'

Marius again advanced, unsteadily. 'Monsieur,' he said to the inspector, 'I repeat that I'm innocent.'

'Who is this rascal?' the inspector asked the officer, who was carrying a register under his arm.

'A lunatic, Inspector. Number 24. Name of Alexandre Tixier. Arrested for murder, given a quick trial, sentenced to twenty years.'

'What exactly are you innocent of?' the inspector asked Marius.

'But my name isn't Alexandre Tixier!'

If the inspector had said the name Jesus, which, being only a nickname, did not appear anywhere in the report, Marius might have had some glimmer of an explanation for what had happened. But the nickname was not mentioned and he leapt forward, hands together.

'Halt!'

Thinking that this Tixier was about to attack the inspector, the soldiers immediately raised their bayonets, but the inspector merely laughed. 'Once he's completely mad, Monsieur Tixier won't suffer any more. The climate in Toulon will do him good.'

Marius stepped back. So they thought he was insane. He had no idea why. His last vague memories were of Clémence's apartment, Clémence herself and drinking a glass of port. He certainly had no memory of murdering anyone. He launched into a moving appeal, expressing himself with a fervent eloquence that surprised even the soldiers and the officer.

The inspector listened to his speech to the end. At last, Marius thought, this man is showing some humanity.

But when he had finished, the inspector turned to the soldiers and smiled at them without any emotion. 'You see, gentlemen, this man recoiled at the sight of the bayonets. A madman does not recoil at anything. I can say that with some certainty, having made a number of interesting observations on the subject at Charenton.'

'Wouldn't he be better off in an asylum?' asked the officer.

'What on earth for?' retorted the inspector. He turned back to Marius. 'So what exactly do you want?'

'I want justice, Monsieur! I want my own name, my own clothes, my rights! I want a fair trial!'

This madman did not seem as mad as all that. To set his mind at rest, the inspector consulted the register himself. According to the report, Alexandre Tixier had one distinguishing characteristic, a strawberry mark under his left eye. The prisoner before him had such a mark in that very spot. The evidence was conclusive.

'You're right, Monsieur, I shall have to look into this,' said the inspector, at the same time winking conspiratorially at the soldiers, as if to say: let's humour him, he'll get tired of it in the end. After reassuring Marius again, he went out, had the door locked and advised the warrant officer on duty to keep an eye on Tixier.

'He's a lunatic. I don't think he's necessarily dangerous, but, as the report makes clear, he could be unpredictable.'

'Let's see how he is when he's in chains!' said the warrant officer at the top of his voice.

There was a great deal of activity in the prison courtyard. Although the prisoners were still in the cells, the doors were constantly opening and closing and it was almost time to put them in irons. It was about eleven in the morning and the sky was grey.

'Right, let's go and see the merchandise,' said a naval captain in a blue uniform, who was in charge of the chain. He was accompanied by a pale-faced lieutenant. When the cell door opened again, Marius's heart began to pound. Were they going to release him, admit their unfortunate mistake, offer their apologies even?

That didn't happen. The two officers were simply coming to check if among these outcasts from society there might not be some old acquaintances, in other words old lags or escaped convicts.

'I'm Marius Pontmercy.'

The captain lifted his eyes from the register and looked scornfully at the young man with the cadaverous complexion. 'And I'm the king,' he said sarcastically. He turned to the guards. 'Take this lot down!'

The convicts were taken to the courtyard and the prison doctor, a short man with a twitch and a pronounced squint, inspected them briefly, to make sure they were all in good enough shape to tolerate the hardships of the road.

Despite being extremely weak, Marius was beginning to seethe. His proximity to this scum revolted him. Where were his wife, his friends, his cashmere waistcoats and his pale pink trousers? He convinced himself that the nightmare would end soon. Bureaucracy being what it was – papers to check, to sign, to countersign, orders to give, release – he supposed it would all take time. Marius resigned himself to obeying. He would have to be patient.

'Get undressed!' yelled a voice – a voice that reeked of spite, rancour, too much tobacco and cheap wine. The prisoners took off their prison uniforms and put their own clothes back on, the clothes they had worn from the time of their arrest until they were sentenced.

Marius was given a pile of old clothes, which he rejected with a disdainful sweep of the hand. 'These aren't mine,' he said.

'Shut up and do as you're told!' said a guard. With a wicked smile, he unsheathed a long knife and began to slash Marius's clothes.

'But—'

'But what?' the guard cut in. 'With your coat in tatters, you won't be so much of a bohemian! Come on, at the double!' He caught Marius under the chin and stared at him. 'And what's more, I don't like villains with strawberry marks under their eyes. It's the mark of the devil!' He let go of Marius abruptly.

What strawberry mark? Marius wondered, but he did as he was told without protest. Within him, fits of rage alternated with moments of lethargy that made him want to weep. What the devil was he doing here? What slander had thrust him into this darkness? Could he find the strength to cry out, to rebel, to escape this monstrous machine, whose terrible progress could only be stopped by a miracle?

'Don't worry,' one of the other prisoners whispered. 'They only cut up your things as a precaution. In case we escape, they say. No chance!'

The preliminaries over, the prisoners were introduced to the warders – nasty-looking characters, each one surlier than the last. Most came from the Auvergne and, when not travelling with the chain gangs, worked as water carriers or coalmen. In the middle of these warders stood a large wooden crate full of irons, an anvil and some hammers.

'Like animals,' sighed an old man next to Marius, wearing only a smock and a pair of grey cloth trousers. 'They treat us like animals.'

'That's because you behaved like animals,' barked a guard.

Marius felt a succession of shivers go through his body. So they were going to put him in irons and make him part of a chain gang – like a beast! 'But I'm innocent!' he cried, with the energy of despair. Then, leaning his head to the side and assuming the ecstatic and emaciated look of an El Greco Christ, he put his hands together, turned his eyes heavenward, and prayed to the God whom everyone talked about and who manifested His presence so little.

In front of him, the warders had got down to work chaining the prisoners. It was even worse than he had feared. Of course he thought of Jean Valjean. Was he, too, to take the road of penitence, so that one day he might find redemption? But what redemption? And what sin had he committed from which he needed to be redeemed? I haven't even stolen a loaf of bread, he thought, shaking his head in despair.

'Your turn!'

They brought the convicts forward, sorted them into pairs according to height, and joined the pairs with a six-foot chain, which was immediately joined to a longer chain that was used to surround a group of twenty-six prisoners. Each of these twenty-six unfortunates was held to the chain by a triangular yoke of iron called a cravat, with a hinged button on one side which opened and closed, and a cold riveted nail on the other side.

When it was his turn, Marius was pushed to his knees, his head was forced to one side and the yoke was placed round his neck. He took good care not to move, for the smallest movement would mean that, instead of striking the anvil, the hammer blows would smash his skull. Like a dog, he said to himself as he stood up, clenching his fists with rage.

'Next!'

It took until about five in the afternoon to put all the men in irons.

'No more frolicking like a puppy,' said the old man who had previously approached Marius. 'No more buttercups and haystacks. Just chains on our wrists and shame on our faces. You're bound for Toulon. Hard work and not a penny to show for it. You're a convict now. As far as society's concerned, you're dead.'

Marius shook his head in disbelief. He couldn't understand what circumstances had led him there. Broken and demoralized, crushed and overwhelmed, he followed the herd. Wherever he turned, he met with cynical silence, crude sarcasm and monumental indifference. He was confronted with a walking abomination, with the torturers and the victims, the believers and the heretics, the pitiless and the pitiful, all blurred together by a Manichean power at once invisible and omnipresent. He felt an indescribable nausea. Had Jean Valjean felt what he was feeling now? The same feelings of revolt, injustice, blazing hatred? A titanic, meteoric, universal hatred. He did not know whom, or what, he hated, but he did know that with each new torment his hatred would grow, would swell and ripen until one day it exploded. Only someone who has known humiliation can feel such hatred – only someone who has known privation, insults, opprobrium, blows, the rotten taste of poverty. And this disparate and foul-smelling mob suddenly recalled to Marius that filth known as humanity, from which he had tried to escape and into which he had once more been plunged.

He could have done without the pernicious effects of this involuntary memory. Suddenly he saw again the room he'd had as a student, the grime, the excrement, the saltpetre on the walls, the Gorbeau tenement, the prying but evasive face of Thénardier, the cholera epidemic . . . The smells came back like a whirlwind, so similar were they. Viewed from a distance, poverty could almost be picturesque. It could even be a talking point. You could discuss it in fashionable salons and move your audience with your compassion and sense of injustice. If you were an intellectual you could toss fine words to one another, like tennis balls, and if you were a socialist, you could weep genuine tears. It was a good feeling, talking about those who were out in the cold, when your own feet were warm. Such demagoguery was nothing more than false pity, and merely helped to lull, deceive and exploit the working masses. And when it wasn't this that crushed the poor, then it was the constant game of musical chairs. This colourless period had seen an enormous number of formerly poor people become newly rich. And the only way all these vulgar turncoats could find self-esteem was by then becoming the chief destroyers of the cause they had once served. The world, thought Marius, was nothing more than a giant snake swallowing its own tail.

Once all the prisoners were in irons, the warders left. Only those convicts who had been given permission to receive visits from their families remained in the yard. On the verge of their departure for the land of infamy, Marius watched as these unfortunates who had been sentenced to light terms said their goodbyes to their loved ones. For one it was a mother, for another a wife, for a third a child. He spotted a boy who looked barely eighteen. Such was the unconcern that emanated from his person, it was hard to believe that he was a convict.

Marius turned to look at the entrance. A poor old woman, dressed in black, stood trembling uncertainly by the gate. An imperceptible shudder tightened Marius's face. The thought came to him that here was an opportunity he would never have, one that he had never had, for his mother had died when he was five. He watched as the old woman crept around the yard, as if ashamed to find herself there, and finally came to a halt by the young boy. A cry escaped her lips, and she pressed her arms against her heart. Then she clasped her boy to her breast and covered him with kisses, caresses, tears. It was as though she had not noticed the irons that gripped him, the rags he wore – or did not want to notice them. She had eyes only for him. Marius, standing among those who had no right to visitors – a clear indication of how severe his sentence was – felt compassion for her. Foreseeing that this innocent boy would return a hardened criminal, she gave her child a little medal of the Holy Virgin. It was the only thing of value she possessed. This was true poverty, in all its horror.

Marius turned away from the woman and the boy, overwhelmed by the thought of what he, too, could have had and did not have. He glanced at his companions in misfortune. In this dark corner, the most remote in the yard, they enjoyed the only freedom they still had by shouting crude jokes and making obscene gestures to provoke the laughter of their comrades.

'Where do we sleep?' Marius asked the old man.

'Did you imagine a bed and a little tart all to yourself?' said the old man, in a throaty voice. 'We get our shut-eye on the cobbles. You'll get a plate of soup and some wine, and tomorrow at six o'clock you'll hear, "Those leaving for Toulon, get on the coaches!" Then we'll pile into these supposed coaches and we'll set off. On the way out of Bicêtre, you'll see people watching our departure and they'll be very happy to see us go. It's a thirty-day journey. I know, I've already done it. If you want, you can walk. The ones who walk get extras. A ration of brandy in the morning and an extra half-litre of wine. In the coach, you have two pounds of bread a day, two ounces of cheese and half a litre of wine. And then after, a long time after, it'll be Toulon, my lad.'

And with that he put one hand on his heart and the other on his head, somewhat in the manner of Rouget de Lisle about to sing the Marseillaise, and started to declaim:

> *The chain gang is the place, my boy,*
> *It's beatings all the way.*
> *Don't think you'll get to see much joy,*
> *Just work the livelong day.*

Marius staggered under this new blow to his morale. This grotesquely jolly poet made him want to scream, but a dry lump in his throat prevented him.

Later, as night fell and he sat amid his drunken and noisy companions, degraded creatures who trampled under foot everything respected by the society that rejected them, he buried his face in his hands and wept silently. Certain now that he had been tricked and abandoned, and that his rights were from now on to be measured by the length of his chain, he was already thinking of escape. Hadn't the lieutenant of the chain gang told him he was in for twenty years? He was thinking again of revenge. On Amédée, Clémence, Jesus. On the whole of France. And what of Cosette, what had become of her? The thought of losing her for ever overcame him.

Suddenly, the old bard began to sing the song of the chain gang. And a hundred voices took up the chorus:

> *Nobody likes the chain,*
> *But it doesn't cause any pain.*

With a wink at Marius, the old man continued:

> *We wear caps instead of hats,*
> *Scarlet clothes with no cravats.*
> *We really have no cause to complain,*
> *They love us so much, they keep us on a chain . . .*

All evening Bicêtre echoed to the repeated chorus of this savage poetry. Then gradually silence fell, as each man sought the courage he would need the following day to begin a journey whose end was a place of disgrace and infamy.

Marius could find no rest. He kept thinking of Jean Valjean and the upright and generous man he had become after his hard labour. He himself did not possess such generosity of spirit. He had not even begun his sentence, but already he felt only a mixture of rancour, astonishment and injustice. What had happened during those long days he could not remember? Had he been drugged, knocked unconscious, bewitched? Had Clémence lured him into a trap? Or Amédée?

If ever he escaped, he would show no pity.

2

The journey lasted thirty days and, by the time it was over, Marius had a fairly good idea of what he would have to endure. Only someone who has lived and suffered in the middle of this herd, conspired with it, seen tears run and flesh bleed beneath the stick, can know quite how horrible, how dreadful, is the world of the prisoner. For Marius there were no longer culprits or victims, just one long walking lament, an endless Golgotha.

The old man whose acquaintance he had made in Bicêtre died of exhaustion when they reached Chalon. He had chosen to go on foot, with the sole aim of getting extra rations. Well, he'd had his ration.

Something else happened at Chalon. While the convicts were embarking on long barges to cross the Saône, one of their number – sentenced for disembowelling a young girl who had rejected him and hanging her body from the sails of a windmill – managed to saw through his yoke and throw himself in the river, where he sank straight to the bottom. Or did he merely feign drowning, resurface further up the river, and manage to escape? Nobody ever knew. The officer in charge of the chain gang, furious at his escape, brandished his sabre and threatened to slaughter anyone who claimed to have seen nothing. The occupants of the barge, including Marius, escaped with a beating.

'You have to understand,' a prisoner explained. 'Every time someone escapes, he loses three hundred francs.'

At Lyons the prisoners were searched. Hundreds of people had come from the town and the surrounding countryside to enjoy the spectacle.

The prisoners were given a thorough inspection. The warders, stained and unshaven in their grey-blue uniforms with red epaulettes and yellow bandoliers, were only too happy to use their truncheons at the slightest opportunity. Some of them had whips like those carried by coach drivers, which they cracked at regular intervals. While some examined the prisoners' clothes, others inspected their bodies, searching in their hair, their ears, their mouths – and in other places, too ... The humiliation was appalling, especially as the inspection took place amid the laughter and jeers of the public. Marius resigned himself to it without protest, though the thought of his body being reduced to a piece of meat filled him with shame. Big as he was, he made himself little. None of his companions on the chain, even the worst cut-throats, rebelled. Except one – the young boy whom Marius had seen with his mother.

'My crime doesn't warrant this!'

'Do you want a beating before you even get there?' screamed the officer in charge of the chain. 'On your knees!'

As the boy refused to obey, he was forced down onto all fours. A warder struck him on the neck and the small of his back, then violently pulled down his trousers and searched the most intimate part of his body with his truncheon. 'You wouldn't be hiding a file or a hairspring there, would you? You all hide them up your arses!' Finding nothing, he struck him again on the calves. 'You're lucky, my lad!'

After which, he passed to another prisoner, his truncheon under his arm and a mocking look in his eyes.

Sobbing, the boy pulled up his trousers with a feverish hand, while with the other hand he beat the air impotently, as if trying to erase what had happened. Marius took the hand in his. The boy tilted his head to one side and lifted his eyes. 'I'm innocent . . .' he stammered, trying to get back on his feet.

'So am I. What's your name?'

'Julien. Julien Leroy. Sentenced to five years' hard labour for stealing a loaf of bread.'

Marius's face clouded over. Thirty-eight years ago, Jean Valjean had been given the same sentence for the same theft. It was now 1834 and nothing had changed.

'I'm Marius. Sentenced to twenty years for a crime I didn't commit.'

Julien Leroy nodded, indicating his chains. 'I hope we'll be friends.'

'I hope so too.'

And each went back to his place.

After Lyons, they rested for two days under a blazing sun in Tarascon. But there was no end to this human tide covered in irons, nor to the constant noise of clanking chains. After Tarascon, the chain gang arrived in a small town a quarter of a league from Toulon.

'Castigneau!' bellowed a warrant officer.

As soon as they arrived, the future convicts were surrounded, jostled and harassed. Hundreds of men, women and children, aware of the custom, had come to offer them cakes, sausages or tobacco. Nothing was free. Those who had no money paid with a jersey or a hat. There were cries, cheers, oaths and insults. The hubbub was enough to make a deaf man hear again. For a brief moment, among all these wretches bartering tattered clothes for a couple of apples, Marius thought he saw someone he recognized – a man with curly hair like a troubadour's, whose powerful torso was reminiscent of a Hercules. But he soon lost sight of him and, besides, who could he possibly know among these murderers?

'What about you?' a prisoner asked him. 'Aren't you getting anything?'

Marius shrugged. 'I'm keeping my clothes.'

'Your clothes? In Toulon, they'll take them away from you anyway and give you a uniform.'

So Marius got rid of his rags in exchange for a pound of bread and a portion of pâté. He wolfed it all down on the spot. Then he waited for orders.

At one o'clock the prisoners arrived in the antechamber of the building next to the arsenal, the Palace as the convicts called it. It was close to the penal colony and was where the prisoners were cleaned up.

Marius watched as a group of men came to meet the chain gang. Among them were the commandant of the penal colony, a naval commander and a host of high-ranking employees.

They proceeded to the roll-call. When the name Alexandre Tixier was called out, Marius answered, however reluctantly. Soon he would demand an explanation from one of these men – and perhaps a settling of accounts.

Once roll-call was over, the warders took the yokes off the prisoners. A huge sigh of relief seemed to burst from each chest, but their joy was short-lived. Immediately the trusties arrived to rivet temporary rings on to the prisoners' legs. Then they were stripped of whatever clothing they still had left, so that they could bathe in the sea while their rags burned in the middle of a blazing furnace.

The warrant officers then checked that each man still wore the shackle that had been put on him when the big chain was taken off and another roll-call was taken. Marius passed his hand over his beard and his chest. What did he look like? It had taken him more than two weeks to recover from the effects of the narcotic, and he was still completely in the dark.

He felt refreshed after his bathe in the sea. The sun's rays felt good on his salty skin. He turned his gaze to the horizon and asked himself if all this was real. Would he ever get out of this nightmare? Would someone – the commandant of the penal colony, the naval officers – finally take the trouble to listen to him?

He inhaled a great breath of air and shook his head. It was all too clear that here the only people he could expect to listen were the prisoners.

'Get a move on!'

The warders shouted to the prisoners to take their places on a small boat. Once they were all aboard, it set sail for the penal colony. The crossing was short and, as they came alongside, Marius saw that the whole colony was glowing in the sunlight. So this was the penal colony – a port with its sailors, its ships, its quays, its bustle, its arsenal, its long white buildings, its pointed roofs, and there, in the distance, mountains that stood out against the horizon. Marius had never seen a port. He looked up and saw birds, like white down, making great circles in the azure sky. Their cries reverberated endlessly, and as they echoed they were transformed into laughter and chuckles.

Another laugh drew Marius's attention, a human one this time, immediately followed by the comment, 'There are at least four thousand slaves in there, comrade. And soon we'll be joining them.'

Marius did not even glance at the man who had spoken. Once again, he felt overcome. His mouth was thick with saliva. As he gazed at the quay, he thought he heard a nightingale singing in the elms. He was becoming delirious. He thought of Paris, the parties he had attended, Saint-Germain, his good friend Amédée d'Iguerande . . . Amédée would pay a hundredfold for what Marius had endured so far and would endure in a future he preferred not to think about. And Cosette? Could he at least write to her from here?

'Disembark!' cried the voice of a warder. 'And get a move on!'

The prisoners were lined up on the quay in front of the arsenal. Their deformities, their wounds, their distinguishing marks, in fact anything unusual that might appear anywhere on their bodies, were checked. On Marius, they found a strawberry mark under his left eye. Instinctively he raised a finger to the spot and felt a slight bulge. Not having had the opportunity to look at himself in a mirror since his arrest, he had no idea what his face looked like. Who had given him the mark? Clémence? Amédée? Rage overcame him and increased as he saw himself again in La Battut's coach on Shrove Tuesday, handing to Amédée the letter which gave him power over his property and – Cosette. Was that it, then? Had

Frédéric been telling the truth? Had Amédée got rid of the husband in order to get his hands on the wife and the capital?

You're not one of them, old chap.

La Battut's words echoed in his ears like a grim prophecy. Hatred burned his throat. If he was not proved right, if they would not reopen his case, then he would get out of here. Like Jean Valjean before him, he too would become a fugitive, a man on the run, banished from society. Strangely enough, the thought calmed him.

After being identified, each convict was given the uniform of the division to which he would belong. There were three divisions – the first for new prisoners, the second for ordinary prisoners, the third for recidivists and hard cases. Marius belonged to the third. His head was shaved and he was given a red smock and cap, a pair of yellow trousers, shoes and two shirts.

'I've got my eye on you!' barked a warder to Marius, prodding him with his rifle butt.

There was yet another roll-call, supervised by Raynaud, the colony's commandant. As each prisoner answered, he was given a tin badge with his number on it, which he had to wear on his cap at all times. Marius's number was 9430. By a coincidence of which he was unaware, the number had been Jean Valjean's.

'To the irons!' cried a voice.

While Marius was heading for the place where he was to be chained, someone called out his name. Had he been recognized, then? His face lit up with hope. He stood on tiptoe and leaned on his companions' shoulders. When he saw Julien's youthful face, he frowned.

'So you're all in red?' said Julien.

'As you can see.'

'I'm in the first division. Look, I have a yellow cap. In five years, it'll all be over.'

'Yes, in five years . . . See you soon, Julien.'

Just then he felt a sharp pain in the small of his back. He turned and recognized the warder who had already threatened him. 'Silence! Understood, prisoner 9430?'

Marius was no longer Marius, he was not even Alexandre Tixier, he was only prisoner 9430.

He entered a dark hall reeking so strongly of sweat and mildew he thought he would faint. There was no end to the nightmare. Chains rattled and faces grimaced out of the shadows. The floor was soiled with excrement. In their panic, the prisoners could not control their bowels. In the centre of the hall was a plank of wood about three metres long with anvils fixed to it.

By the time his turn arrived, Marius was trembling all over. The prisoner before him had had his leg broken and was screaming in agony.

'He moved,' said a convict holding a hammer, by way of excuse. 'He moved . . .'

'Take him to the hospital!' yelled a warrant officer. He turned to Marius. 'Your turn! Whatever else you do, make sure you don't move! You've seen what happens to those who try to be clever!'

Marius lay down flat on his stomach on the piece of wood, bending his knees. He raised his foot in the air so that one leg was at right angles to the other. A convict held it while the warder in charge fixed the shackle and rivet. The operation required a great deal of accuracy, as the trusty, bringing down the hammer with all his might, risked breaking the convict's leg if he missed.

When the blow fell, Marius clenched his teeth. Looking sideways, he saw the warrant officer was watching him, his arrogant features glowing with dumb complacency. Here was a man who would no more tolerate deviation from his duty than he would a crease in his uniform. As soon as the operation was over, his narrow brown forehead furrowed with triumph, his eyes blinked and his jaw tightened – the only expression of which his self-satisfied face was capable.

'Have you understood?' he asked, unshakeable in his certainty that he was the earthly incarnation of divine justice, light and truth.

'I've understood,' murmured Marius, who was sweating profusely.

'I've understood, Monsieur!' the brute corrected him, standing with his hands behind his back.

'I've understood, Monsieur,' repeated Marius submissively.

'Stay like that, it's not over yet!' bellowed the warrant officer, gesturing to those putting irons on the prisoners.

A wad of cloth was placed between the shackle and Marius's skin, to prevent chafing. Despite this precaution, very few convicts emerged from this trial without feeling pain from the combined weight of the shackle and the chain, which was four and a half pounds. Each prisoner was also fitted with a leather belt, to which was fixed an iron hook which kept the chain taut against the leg from the shackle to the hip.

'Prisoner 9430 with prisoner 9431!' barked the warrant officer.

Prisoner 9431 was the man Marius had noticed on the beach at

Castigneau, whose face had seemed familiar. Prudently, he stopped himself speaking to or even looking too closely at the man, who had broad shoulders, fiery eyes and a shaven head like him, and also wore a red smock and cap.

'And not a word!' cried the warrant officer.

A link was placed and their two chains were joined. The shackle was nothing special, but the chain was something else. Only when you had to share the weight of it with another convict did you realize. And what a convict! He might be a murderer, a rapist, a child-killer, a pervert with unspeakable passions.

At the thought of it, a shiver of anxiety went through Marius. At the same time, he was curious to get to know the man. Where the devil had he seen him before?

For two days Marius's partner did not say a word.

'What's your name?' Marius asked him several times, but he would not reply.

They were in a cell on the ground floor of a building near the warders' barracks, on the same quay as the naval hospital. Prisoner 9431 stayed close to the little shuttered window, staring into space. He consumed his ration of meat, soup and wine in silence. Marius concluded that he must be mute.

On the third day – the last rest day granted by the prison authorities to allow the prisoners to recover from their long and exhausting journey – Commandant Raynaud appeared, accompanied by a number of naval stewards, to talk to the new arrivals. In a harsh, high-pitched voice, he explained the rules, promising a reward to those whose conduct deserved consideration, and severe punishment to the others. 'That's the way things are,' he said. 'If you don't like it – tough!'

As he was about to go, Marius raised a finger. 'Commandant, may I be allowed to present you with my grievances?'

The commandant considered him with mocking interest. Raynaud had cold, inhuman, almost glassy eyes, surrounded by a large number of fine lines that looked as if they had been etched with a razor. His mouth, which sagged to the right, suggested authority, reason, the full conscious-ness of the law, the finality of judicial decisions. Commandant Raynaud loved order and would go to any lengths to protect it. No sooner did he glimpse defeat in a convict's eyes than a glint of victory would appear in his. In his frock coat, he was a fierce archangel, burning with the determination which had established him as an avenger of society's ills.

He was a servant of the absolute, which, in his hands, became a sword of redemption, crushing whatever seemed relative.

'What can I do for you, prisoner 9430?' he asked, reading Marius's number on his cap.

'I'm not the man you think I am, Commandant. My name is Marius Pontmercy and I don't know why they've given me the name Alexandre Tixier.'

Commandant Raynaud's face was suffused with an ironic and macabre radiance. 'You're not the man you are? So your number doesn't suit you, prisoner 9430? Well, let me tell you this. Virtue has but one vice, error. But here error is the vice of your so-called virtues. Anything else, prisoner 9430?'

'No, Commandant,' replied Marius, growing very pale.

'Perfect,' said Raynaud, signalling to a steward to approach, who showed him a thick register.

Nothing was more heartbreaking to Marius than the commandant's words. With his emphasis on probity and conviction, Raynaud was proof of what evil could be engendered by the desire to do what was considered good. Was there nothing, then, to be done? In the three days he had been carrying them, the irons had never felt so heavy. The commandant consulted the register. 'Did you practise a trade?' he asked, looking him up and down with his cold, piercing eyes.

Marius did not know what to say. It was then that his partner nudged him with his elbow and whispered in his ear. 'Tell him you were a carpenter.'

Marius, surprised to at last hear the man's voice, remained speechless. As the commandant was asking the steward to write a cross in the register against the number 9430, Marius finally made up his mind and replied, 'Carpenter, Commandant.'

The commandant lifted his pointed nose and again looked hard at Marius, though with a changed expression now. 'Not before time,' he said at last. 'Put down carpenter for 9430.'

Marius looked then at his partner, who was still turned away from him, his eyes fixed on the commandant. All at once he felt better.

'And you, prisoner 9431?' asked the commandant.

'Carpenter,' replied Marius's partner.

In the cell prisoner 9431 held out his hand to Marius. 'So who are you?' he asked, in a throaty voice. 'Jesus or Baron Pontmercy?'

Marius was at first taken aback, until at last he recognized the man standing before him. 'Perfect Love? The landlord of the Clan Destin?'

'Right first time. And you?'

The reason Perfect Love asked this question was because there was no ring on the young man's finger, certainly not a ring encrusted with an emerald-eyed snake. As all personal effects were confiscated, all heads were shaved and all uniforms looked much the same, it was easy to make a mistake. In any case, Perfect Love had been as little acquainted with Jesus as with Marius. A fight didn't make you an expert on faces – nor did a ring. Besides, here in the penal colony all faces looked alike.

'Marius Pontmercy,' replied Marius.

'I thought as much. But why the other name? What happened to you?'

'I have no idea. One fine morning I found myself at Bicêtre with a bad headache, no memory, a bunch of wretches as companions and a sentence of twenty years ahead of me.'

'What about your trial?'

'I don't remember it.'

'Were you drugged?'

'Rather heavily, I think.'

Perfect Love assumed a disenchanted expression. 'I also got twenty years. In a fit of rage, I killed my wife. You know – the one they called Gammy Leg. I escaped a life sentence by confessing my crime. As it was a crime of passion, I benefited from the jury's clemency.'

'That's what they told me, too, at Bicêtre,' said Marius, feeling the chain that linked him to Perfect Love. 'They decided I was simple-minded.'

'And you really don't remember your trial?'

'Not at all.'

'Let's face it, they speeded the process up a bit. With revolution in the air, they skimped on ordinary trials. A lot of people were sent down that week. Reprieves are always for the rich – but not for the simple-minded!' Perfect Love pointed at Marius and laughed. 'And who did this simple-minded man kill, to find himself in the clink?'

'I killed myself,' replied Marius, irritated by his laughter. For days he had not said a word, and now all he could do was laugh.

'Meaning?'

'Meaning that I'm accused of killing Marius Pontmercy on the same day that all the occupants of a building in the Rue Transnonnain got themselves legally massacred by the troops. That's justice for you. And my name is now Alexandre Tixier.'

'Never heard of him,' said Perfect Love, who had no idea of Jesus's real identity. He made a vague, dismissive gesture. His eyes were following the sun, which was quite low on the horizon. 'Over there is freedom,' he murmured. He turned back to Marius. 'You must have been tricked by the Mullet and the Catman,' he said in a louder voice.

Marius appeared surprised. 'I've never met them.'

'Not even at the Clan Destin?'

'Never.'

'They were there both the evenings you came. They must have known you because Jesus was a friend of theirs. So what's your explanation of why you're here? Are you sure you don't know who the Mullet is? A big red-headed man, a real backstabber if ever there was one.'

'Perhaps,' said Marius, thinking. 'Jesus, on the other hand, I can see very well. In fact, I almost came to blows with him. It was in a workshop. He was beating the children who worked there.'

Perfect Love shook his head. 'No, you're wrong there, my lad. The one who was always picking on the kids was the Mullet. Jesus used to take their side. There was a time when he was hanging around the Kitten. I should have broken his neck, but he was a good lad. Trust me, this whole thing was masterminded by the Catman and his friend, the man in black – a hunchback. They were in cahoots.'

'A hunchback?'

'Dresses like a notary and behaves like a rogue. Mind you, I'd recognize him by the way he walked, not by his face. He was always hiding, never showed himself by daylight.'

Marius felt unsteady on his feet and had to lean against the cell wall for support.

'What's the matter?' asked Perfect Love.

'Nothing . . .'

Everything was becoming increasingly confused in the young man's mind. All these names, these memories . . . And then the spark – the hunchback . . . Of course, he thought, Louis-Désiré. He helped his master to steal my name, my honour, my wife. The faithful Louis-Désiré . . . He moved cautiously, overcome with dizziness. 'And this Catman,' he asked in a muted voice, 'who is he?'

'The man who's in charge of everything. I'd wager my life he's already taken over the Clan Destin.'

'But what does he do?'

'I couldn't tell you exactly. He's got some kind of trade in children and catmeat and it's made him rich in just six months. You'd remember him if you'd seen him. A vile, smooth-tongued, lying, toadying creature, dirty as a comb and hard as bricks. A face like a weasel's and a neck like a vulture's. Spiteful little eyes, a horrible greyish beard, hooked nails. His dirty mug was his own doing, he can't blame his parents for it. If you give him your hand, you never know if he's going to give it back. He and the Mullet testified against me at my trial and never looked at me once. The jackal and the skinflint. Two bastards of the worst kind.'

Marius looked around him, at the camp bed – they were chained to it at night, attached to a long iron bar – then at the little table, and the tub overflowing with spinning materials. He looked again at Perfect Love. He felt a desire to rave, to say just anything, to throw himself at the cell wall and bang his head against it. There had to be a way out! He certainly wasn't going to spend twenty years in this hell hole for a crime he hadn't committed!

'One day, I'll get out of here,' he said in a resolute tone. 'I can't stay here.'

'Neither can I, my lad. But we don't get a choice.'

Two months passed. For Marius they felt like two centuries. Perfect Love and he had escaped certain tasks, such as cleaning out the port, transporting sludge, placing and removing ballast, unloading, piling and clearing wood for masts and for construction, transporting timber for shipbuilding. Had they gained much by the deal? In a sense, yes. When they saw some of their fellow prisoners handling the rough timber, they thanked heaven that they were not in their place.

Essentially, Toulon was one huge building site, the largest of its kind in France – and the most profitable. Of course, many of the convicts were kept busy with towing the vessels, or emptying and cleaning the docks. But there were also the other slaves of the state. Those who did not work as servants in the officers' houses were employed as quarrymen, stonemasons, brickmakers or furnace workers. In the morning they would set off, streaming out in a human tide like a pharaoh's slaves, singing as they went. By the time they came back in the evening, they could no longer keep on their feet. They had built warehouses on the Saint-Mandrier peninsula, drained the marshes of the Mourillon, constructed the Castigneau dock and consolidated the Vauban harbour basin. The work never stopped.

'Everything that gets built in Toulon and the surrounding area is our work,' said one of the convicts. 'And, to be honest, we prefer hard labour to being locked up. Here, at least, we can talk and laugh to our hearts' content. We work hard, but we see people. We're almost free workers.'

Marius and Perfect Love worked as pit sawyers in a workshop between the entry channel to the old harbour basin and the quay of the Grand-Rang. A pit sawyer's work consisted of sawing trunks of timber lengthways. It was exhausting. By the time evening came, Marius and Perfect Love could not feel their arms. They no longer even had the strength to think.

Since his arrival in the penal colony, Marius had written Cosette ten letters, but had not received a single reply. He no longer knew what to think. During the break, around midday, he would look at the vast building site, which stretched as far as the mountains. The heat was intense. From time to time a rooftop, the shiny edge of the naval hospital, the halyard of a brig or a frigate, would glitter in the sun. Layers of heat covered the port in an angular and burning undercurrent. Late in the afternoon the wind rattled the roofs, bringing a degree of coolness. In the distance, where freedom lay, the colours of the hills seemed to fuse into red and bronze lava. Murmurs and strange smells rose from the great woods. A kind of sickliness lay over everything.

Every morning at five the whistle blew, and it all started again. Hard labour. Sawing wood for twelve to thirteen hours a day. A break around midday, then back to work at one o'clock, to finish at eight o'clock in the evening. If he kept up this pace, Marius thought, he would soon be a force of nature.

'A strapping fellow like me!' Perfect Love would joke. 'You'll see, nobody will pick a quarrel with you any more.'

The hardest thing was sleeping. Marius could not get used to it. Perfect Love and he were not in the part of the Arsenal quay that ended in the Chaîne-Vieille, nor were they in the new prisoners' section, which was the colony's purgatory, while the section for hard cases was its hell. As its name indicated, this section, which was situated in the inner courtyard not far from the general store, on the ground floor below the commandant's offices, contained the most unruly elements in the colony and was a place to be avoided.

'At least it must be dry there,' Marius would say stubbornly.

'Perhaps, but that's where they beat you,' Perfect Love would reply. 'Are you still thinking of escaping?'

'What do you mean, still? I'm thinking of it, that's all.'

'Well, good luck, my lad. In all the sections there's a vestibule crawling with warders, who can see the prisoners' beds through the bars of the door. The warders are everywhere, armed to the teeth. At the least disturbance, at the slightest sign of revolt, they have orders to open fire. Did you know that?'

'I know.'

'So you're mad.'

'Nothing ventured, nothing gained. Besides, I've had enough of Number One.'

Marius and Perfect Love had been allocated to Prison Ship Number One. There were four thousand convicts in Toulon, housed in the three sections on dry land and four prison ships. Prison Ship Number One was horrible. Its sides were painted black and its portholes covered with iron bars, giving it a gloomy air. Every evil could be found there – promiscuity, filth, stench. No less than eight hundred convicts slept in the lopsided, worm-eaten old boat. Some vomited and relieved themselves on the spot. The smell, a mixture of urine and rotting wood, was suffocating and sickening. The constant damp left sticky patches everywhere. Needless to say, the arrival of bean soup aroused little enthusiasm. Some sold their ration for next to nothing as they found it was almost impossible to keep anything down. But if they didn't eat their daily ration of soup, their pound and a half of bread and their wine, they would end up wasting away. And if the guards caught a prisoner selling his ration, he got a beating.

Prison Ship Number One was moored near the section for hard cases. One day a prisoner named Papety was given fifty lashes for threatening to smash a warrant officer's head in. By the fortieth, he had stopped groaning and instead was spitting mouthfuls of blood. He was quickly taken to the hospital, where it was found that his stomach and lungs had been perforated in several places. He died during the night. In the autopsy, the doctors found the muscles of the back part of his torso, from the neck to the buttocks, had been reduced to a blackish pulp.

'The man who does the beatings is a real torturer,' an old convict had warned Marius and Perfect Love. 'His name's Le Bitteux. He does it for an extra ration of wine and a bonus of a few centimes.'

'You mean he's a prisoner?'

'Just like you or me, but he enjoys special treatment. He likes blood. You must have seen him around the general store or the workshops. He's tall, one-eyed and tremendously strong. I'll point him out to you next time.'

Access to the prison ship was aft down a broad wooden staircase. When you reached the last step, you had to bend to enter the mess, in which the warders' loaded rifles stood lined up on a rack by the ship's gunwale. On one side was the warrant officers' post, on the other the prisoners' lockers and kitchen.

'From there, Holy Smoke can see us all the time.'

Holy Smoke was the warrant officer who had put Marius in irons, a man of about fifty, scabby, ruddy-faced and slow-minded, with a uniform that was always stained.

'You've got it coming to you, 9430,' he would say to Marius. 'I tame the simple-minded. Holy smoke! One fart out of place and you're for it!'

Since he had first heard the oath was in vogue that year, he had been using it constantly, hence his nickname. Everyone hated him, including the other warders. But he had authority on his side, and in an administration authority is what counts.

'With me around, you'll know what it's like to be scared!' he would threaten whenever the convicts entered the ship's main hall after work. 'And at eight o'clock, as soon as I've blown my whistle, I don't want to hear a sound! The first to speak is for it!'

There were no beds on the prison ship. The men slept on the bare floor, attached to a long iron bar, which was bolted and weighted on both the port and the starboard sides. Lying there with their scarlet caps, they looked like a crew of massacred sailors, whose blood had reddened the deck.

Thus the days passed, monotonous and repetitive, beneath the blazing sun, surrounded by thick columns of flies that shimmered like ash dust. In the port, a large number of convicts worked on construction, some sawing wood, like Marius and Perfect Love, others carrying big pieces of timber on their shoulders, like Julien and his partner.

'How are you, my friend?' Marius called to Julien one day.

The boy lowered his head, his face stained with dried sweat and his smock torn by splinters of wood. He was being hurried on by his partner – a bald little man with a face like a corpse and a big nose, curved like an eagle's beak, with unusually wide nostrils – but he managed to give a surreptitious nod, to show Marius that he had heard him. A few days later Marius learned that Julien was being physically abused by his partner. He found out the details from another prisoner whose job was harnessing hand-trucks and wagons.

'That Bonnet's a dangerous character. His vices are not the kind you can mention. When he isn't thrashing your friend, he's getting all lovey-dovey with him. He's quite affectionate, in his way. To thank him, he even pinches his pack of cards, if you know what I mean.'

'His ration?'

'That's right.'

'And what's more, this Bonnet, who raped little boys in civilian life, is as friendly as can be with Le Bitteux.'

'The flogger?'

'That's right. So, you see, it's all a bit complicated.'

'Thanks, friend.'

Marius talked it over with Perfect Love. 'We have to do something.'

'What can we do?'

'Julien's only eighteen. He's just a child.'

'Be careful, Marius,' said Perfect Love anxiously. 'We could get into trouble with the warders. Especially Holy Smoke.'

During the next few days, Marius did not see Julien again. He had got used to the sights of the port. By now he could recognize the lifers, who pulled heavily laden carts in teams of six to eight men, like beasts of burden. And always there was the sound of chains. A thousand thoughts would jostle in Marius's head. Seeing these criminals in such a debased state, it seemed to him that the idea of making them better people was nothing but a pipe dream. As for himself, what had he done to deserve this punishment? He would turn his eyes away from this human tide, from these ants, these insects carrying great pieces of timber, sawing wood, coming and going between the workshops and the military buildings, and he would set to work with determination.

'You're tireless, you are,' Perfect Love said one day admiringly. 'But don't forget we're here for twenty years. No point in overdoing it.'

'I'm not overdoing it. I'm just telling myself we could get out of hard labour and into the workshops. You're a carpenter, aren't you? You even have a speciality, don't you?'

'Staircases.'

'Well, then, we have to tell Raynaud. I've heard the vice admiral is looking for someone to make him a staircase.'

'Are you sure?'

From that day forward, Perfect Love became tireless in his lectures. Marius soon knew all about risers, straight and equal stringboards, unequal and sloping stringboards, and so on. In Paris, in his workshop in Saint-Antoine, Perfect Love had begun a number of staircases, each with several banisters and landings with corners.

'Because of the Mullet and the Catman, I never finished them. But now I could knock them up in a trice. Not to mention equal and parallel banisters, and spiral stairs. You know, a staircase is a beautiful thing. It's as if you were climbing to heaven. When you assemble the stringboards, it's almost like a miracle. Hands can do incredible things. They're such obedient workers. When we've done our time, I'll show you.'

'You'll be sixty-five . . .'

'That doesn't matter, I'm strong. I'll hold out and I'll still be able to do lots of things when I leave here. As long as you have plans, you're alive.'

'You perhaps. Not me. I have no desire to rot here. What about the Kitten?'

Perfect Love clasped his hands together. 'I don't know what's become of her . . . When they arrested me, her face looked like a bowl of crushed cherries . . . By now she may be dead . . .' His hands beat the air helplessly and big tears rolled down his cheeks. 'We, the poor, we're despair personified. What do we have left when even futility has gone?'

In the evenings, lying on the floor of Prison Ship Number One, Marius occasionally thought about futility. He would pass through all the degrees of unhappiness common to prisoners, about which there was nothing futile. He even came to doubt his own innocence. Putting away his pride, which was merely an extension of hope, he would lose himself in prayer. But sometimes prayer is only a monotonous procession of sounds, which cannot relieve pain. And all at once he would refuse to ask God to forgive him his trespasses as he should have forgiven those who had trespassed against him, for he forgave nothing. Asceticism would give way to rage, and he would yell blasphemies that scared Perfect Love, and vow to inflict terrible tortures on the men who had condemned him to his fate. Even the thought of Jean Valjean could not calm him. He was young, passionate and fiercely attached to the idea of happiness. But now he felt death hovering about him. By convincing himself that the only peace was death, he began to make plans for suicide.

At first, he would throw away the food he was served. A few lashes dissuaded him from that. Everything was repugnant to him. Perfect Love would give him a little of his bread, force him to drink wine, and remind him of his vow at the beginning of his imprisonment. 'Don't you still want revenge? "One day, I'll get out of here." That's what you said, wasn't it?'

Despite his weakened state, Marius still had only one thought in his head – freedom. It was a thought that never left him, that ate away at him like a cancer.

Like the four thousand other convicts in Toulon, Marius had at first made every effort to appear timid and submissive, anxious to carry out his duties. He had felt crushed by what he saw as the staggeringly irrational behaviour of the warders and the brutality with which any resistance was suppressed. But he grew used to it. By the end of the first three months, he was feeling rebellious. At night, on the ship, he might surrender to despair, but by day he showed none of it. Whatever good intentions he had had at the beginning had gradually become transmuted into dark and daring plans. Perfect Love was getting worried. Marius's nature had changed profoundly.

One day, as they were busy sawing an oak trunk lengthways – though the bell had already sounded to announce the end of the day's work – Marius and Perfect Love saw Julien and Bonnet shuffling in their direction, carrying a load of planks.

'Look, there he is,' whispered Marius, breaking off from his work. 'Come a little closer, Perfect Love.'

'What are you going to do? Nothing foolish, I hope.'

'Don't argue. Move, damn it! I'm going to pay Bonnet back in his own coin.'

The biggest problem with wearing chains was getting about. And the danger, especially around the port itself, lay not in the duties, which never exceeded a man's strength, but in the awkwardness of your movements and the possibility of falling under your load, not to mention the warders' commands and the need to accommodate your actions to those of your partner.

Marius and Perfect Love placed themselves in Julien and Bonnet's path.

'What are you doing?' cried a warder.

'I've got cramp,' said Marius, kneeling.

The warder did not insist, for Julien and Bonnet, still approaching with planks piled on their shoulders, had plenty of room to pass.

Julien brushed against Marius.

'Everything all right?' asked Marius.

Julien did not reply. He was in a pitiful state, his face swollen and his body bent.

As Bonnet passed close to Marius, the latter, still kneeling, abruptly put out his leg. Bonnet stumbled and fell, dragging the unfortunate Julien down with him. The planks toppled with a dreadful crash.

Quick as lightning, Marius seized a plank and, taking care to pull on the chain that hobbled him, whirled it above his head and brought it down on Bonnet's face. Already on his knees as a result of his fall, Bonnet let out a horrible cry. There was a sound of broken bone.

'Guards!'

At the whistle, six soldiers came running. They overpowered Marius in an instant.

'Don't ever do it again!' Marius yelled at Bonnet, whose face was covered in blood. 'Ever!'

Holy Smoke could do nothing but note the damage. Bonnet had a smashed nose and Julien had broken his leg when he fell. The officer turned to Marius. 'You're for it!' he said.

Marius was to make Le Bitteux's acquaintance. He would happily have forgone the pleasure, but the rules were very clear. *Any prisoner who files through his irons or uses any means to escape, or who is found in possession of a disguise, or who steals a sum larger than five francs, or who gets drunk, or who plays games of chance, or who smokes in the port or its vicinity, or who sells or damages his uniform, or who writes without permission, or who is found in possession of a sum greater than ten francs, or who hits a fellow inmate, or who refuses to work, will be punished by flogging.*

Before undergoing his penalty, Marius was taken to see the commandant. Raynaud was sitting behind his desk, casting his rat's eyes over a pile of papers. He did not even look up when Marius entered.

'Is this what you wanted, prisoner 9430?' he asked, in a tone at once ironic and serious.

'My name is Marius Pontmercy, Monsieur.'

'That's as may be, 9430. But you haven't answered my question. Is this what you wanted?'

'I came to the aid of a young boy who was being ill-treated by his chain partner. Tell me, Commandant, why do you put petty thieves together with hardened criminals? To corrupt them too?'

Raynaud got to his feet stiffly. 'Perhaps you'd like to take my place, 9430? I'm sorry, I was forgetting – Marius Pontmercy! That's it, isn't it? You wouldn't by any chance be pulling my leg, 9430? Well, the lash will take you down a peg or two!' He re-read a section of Alexandre Tixier's file, and pointed to Marius's left cheek. 'What happened to your strawberry mark?'

'I've never had a strawberry mark, Commandant.'

'What are you talking about, 9430?'

'The truth, Commandant. I've never had a strawberry mark under my left eye, and my name has never been Alexandre Tixier. I repeat, my name is Marius Pontmercy and I'm the victim of a miscarriage of justice.'

Raynaud folded his arms and assumed a falsely pensive air. 'We really can't have vanishing strawberry marks, 9430. It's just not done. What a lot of trouble you are. You were asking me why we put petty thieves together with hardened criminals.' He made a peremptory sign to the warders surrounding Marius. 'Prisoner 9430,' he went on, in a cynical tone, 'you'll have the opportunity to meditate on this question when you meet Monsieur Le Bitteux. A convict is a convict, whatever his crime. The only reason he's here is because he deserves to be. Your punishment will be forty lashes.' He turned to Holy Smoke. 'Forty lashes for Bonnet, too. Such offences against morality must be dealt with severely. He should count himself lucky we're not going to tie him over a barrel. As for you, you should have been much more vigilant in protecting the morals of the colony. Didn't you notice anything?'

Holy Smoke, who usually ranted and raved, was all sweetness and light with the commandant. He was one of that race apart in whom servility, blindness and stupidity go hand in glove, and who never feel satisfied unless they can satisfy the hierarchy. They are said to be necessary. But the more there are, the more we need.

Marius was immediately led to the ground floor. He recognized the hall where he had been put in irons. Facing him, hands on hips, was the infamous Le Bitteux. He looked like a wild animal. It was said of him that he had never felt the need to arouse sympathy – it was enough for him to inspire fear. No sooner had he begun to apply the first lashes to his very first victim's naked body than his lungs had dilated, a bright glint had come into his one eye, and a look of immeasurable satisfaction had spread over his features. He had found his vocation. This was the man who was going to take care of Marius.

'Strip him,' he said calmly to the two trusties who were assisting him, snitches both. He turned to Marius and showed him a tarred rope. 'You'll see, 9430, no kid gloves with me.'

Two warders were also present, standing on either side of Holy Smoke. Both had bushy moustaches, rings in their ears, double-breasted blue uniforms and regulation cross-belts, and each was armed with a rifle and a sabre.

'Don't take your eyes off him,' said the warrant officer.

Marius was stripped of his smock and his trousers. At the sight of the young man's smooth torso and long, slender muscles, Le Bitteux clicked his tongue several times and a cruel and greedy smile twisted his scornful mouth. At his feet was an enormous block of wood, on which the prisoner was made to kneel.

'Come on,' Le Bitteux said to the two trusties. 'Hold this pretty boy for me – we're going to mess him up a bit.'

The curious thing about it was that Le Bitteux, who on these occasions represented the arm of justice, was himself a murderer. He had stabbed his father-in-law twenty-six times twenty years ago. Since then, Le Bitteux had been administering punishments carnivorously. He would get so excited at the sight of blood that at least two warders had to be with him to make sure he did not prolong the patient's torture beyond the limits fixed by the sentence.

'Give him a good flogging, he'll enjoy it!' cried Holy Smoke. 'Go to it, man!'

Le Bitteux lifted the bolt-rope and began to strike.

Throughout the time the punishment was being applied, no sound emerged from Marius's mouth. Even Le Bitteux was impressed, though that did not stop him beating Marius even harder after the thirtieth lash. The convicts holding Marius's arms and legs found it difficult to hide their admiration. Apart from a slightly greater tensing of the muscles during the last ten lashes, they had felt nothing.

When it was all over, they saw Marius had pierced the wooden block with his teeth.

'That's what I call a man,' Le Bitteux remarked to the officer.

Holy Smoke nodded evasively – to him it was all the same.

Marius's back was little more than one big open wound. Diluted vinegar was sprinkled on it, followed by a layer of salt, a mixture which apparently prevented permanent scarring. In any case, Marius lost consciousness. When he woke up he was on a stretcher, being taken to the naval hospital. There, in the courtyard, he spotted Bonnet, a dressing on his nose, chains on his wrists, flanked by two warders. It was his turn to be flogged.

Bonnet looked at Marius. 'You're dead,' he whispered.

*

Despite his links with Le Bitteux, Bonnet was not spared. He, too, was brought back on a stretcher. His hatred of Marius grew all the deeper.

Marius discovered that Perfect Love had been moved, and was now working in the carpentry workshop. It was rumoured that Commandant Raynaud had ordered the move to please Vice Admiral Jacob. Perfect Love was to build an open-work staircase in a rectangular well, which would give the vice admiral, who was a keen amateur astronomer, access to an observatory.

In the hospital Marius had a respite. Julien was his immediate neighbour. Of course, he was chained to his bed, but he could talk, rest, eat a little better – and even write. He had already written twenty letters to Cosette, but still had no reply. The only explanation he could find was that his mail was being sorted or diverted, or else spirited away. He was sure of it. And so his thoughts, vague and elusive though they were, assembled again on that wonderful chessboard, where it can take just one move to re-establish the superiority of the man you really are over the beast you were on your way to becoming. Despite his painful back, he was feeling better. Hope was returning.

The hospital's common ward was divided into three sections, and at one end there was a chapel, where Mass was celebrated every morning by the naval chaplain, a chubby but agile priest called Félicien. There the patients were able to receive from him the spiritual succour that consoled them in their illness. And apart from the benevolence of this priest, whom they all called the padre, Marius and the other patients were the objects of much attention. The doctors and surgeons made a fuss of them, the nuns even more so.

The most charming of the nuns was Sister Agnès. Her wimple barely veiled a beauty that a queen would have envied. She could be recognized by her smell, a fragrance of musk and thyme – as if she had crossed a paradise of sun and bracken, the patients said. Most of these worthy sisters were devout women who had obeyed an irresistible vocation. But some were poor creatures who had sought refuge and comfort at the foot of the altar, victims of life who had been given shelter in the convent as others were given shelter in hospital. Sister Agnès was one such case. Nobody knew her secret. But that she had one was certain.

'You should not treat your fellow man roughly,' Sister Agnès said one day to Marius, on discovering the reason for his flogging.

'I did it to help Julien,' retorted Marius, pointing to the bed where his young friend lay.

And as he said it, he thought he saw an embarrassed look in Sister Agnès's eyes, though he could not have said why. And that was not all. Whenever Sister Agnès looked towards Julien, her cheeks would flush slightly, as though she was breathless, and she would place her hand on her brow, which, pale at first, would redden, as if boiling hot.

Seeing her thus, Marius felt great pity. He wondered what mystery lay behind such humility and resignation. When Sister Agnès had finished with Julien, she would deal with Marius. She would cover his back with soothing cream, check his scabs, and keep an eye on the healing. She would often linger. She liked to be near Julien.

'Do you like Sister Agnès?' Marius asked Julien one evening.

'She is beauty, Marius . . . The beauty that saves us . . .'

Marius realized that Julien cared deeply for Sister Agnès – a feeling that uplifted the heart and purified the soul, a kind of sublime exaltation that took one far from earth and closer to God. It was love, a love all the more passionate because it had been born within these walls oozing with crime, but an impossible love, a love that was completely insane.

One day, while smearing Marius's back, Sister Agnès gave herself away. 'You know, my son, the work here isn't so hard. Some people build, some transport materials, others pilot the officers' boats or clean the streets of the arsenal and the town. When you come down to it, the work isn't really tiring. The expression "hard labour" is inaccurate. I've even heard prisoners say they preferred being in a penal colony like this to being locked up in prison. You're almost lucky. Anyone can get through, if they marshal their strength. Besides, five years is not so long.'

Five years was Julien's sentence.

'I'm here for twenty years, Sister,' replied Marius, with a regretful smile, 'so what you've been saying doesn't impress me. I'm sorry.'

Sister Agnès abruptly stopped massaging Marius's back, and dropped the flask of balm. She seemed extremely agitated. Marius, feeling embarrassed, bent and stretched out his hand to pick up the flask.

'Forgive me,' he said, handing the balm back to her. 'I love Julien like a brother. Sometimes, perhaps, I identify with him too much.'

Sister Agnès lowered her eyes, as if she had committed sacrilege. 'I, too, am fond of Julien.' She looked up again. 'But I think you've recovered from your wounds, Alexandre,' she continued sadly. 'You'll soon be able to get back to work.'

'My name isn't Alexandre, Sister.'

'Yes, I know. You lie like all the others. Julien told me your name was

Marius and you were innocent of the crime of which you'd been accused. But Julien is a true innocent. He's so young. I must protect him.'

And there and then, with her arms folded and her face rigid, she delivered an unusual sermon.

'Take an ordinary man leading an ordinary life, earning an honest wage with his wife and children by his side. Is there anything worthy of interest or comment in such a man? No, absolutely nothing. His existence is quite predictable. He will die as he has lived, calmly, modestly, without a care, leaving behind him less trace than a ship leaves on the waves of the ocean. The criminal is quite another matter. For him, life's conditions are reversed. His soul desires, covets, it is devoured by ambition, it quivers with passion. In him, the heart beats, the head burns, the blood boils. Life has made him promises and he wants it to keep them. If it doesn't, he'll sink. So he avenges himself on society and other men. He'll do anything to get what he wants. He'll lie, he'll cheat, he'll pretend. I've seen people like you who claimed to be innocent and used spurious arguments to gain a trust they didn't deserve. To claim that a dose of morality could convert such villains and bring them back to the straight and narrow would be false. Crime is their element. Their only joy comes from exaggerating those they've already committed, and their only consolation from committing more.'

Marius shook his head. How could Sister Agnès be so wrong about him? He turned his head and looked at Julien. The boy was shunning him, too. What had Sister Agnès told him? 'So, you believe that my path is strewn with curses and carpeted with other people's blood?'

Sister Agnès looked at him with a curious air, in which Marius thought he detected her shame at being suspected of having a liaison with Julien. He wanted to tell her that, in fact, he was pleased about it and would never do anything to undermine the complicity that seemed to unite them. Above all, he did not want to return to Prison Ship Number One. If divine help did not come to his aid, it was all over, and every effort he made would plunge him that little bit further into damnation. Destiny was showing him a gaping abyss, and at the bottom of this abyss there was nothing.

'Have you no pity, then?' he asked in a low voice, straightening himself on his pillow.

Sister Agnès, who had already put away the case of medications, raised her eyes to heaven. 'Yes, I have pity. It's my religious duty to have pity. I mean you no harm. I certainly shouldn't like to see you back in that terrible prison ship. But I warn you that your future conduct will determine what I decide. If any further punitive measures are taken against you, you'll have only yourself to blame.'

'I'm grateful to you, Sister.'

'I hope so, Alexandre. And I hope you'll stop exerting a bad influence over Julien.'

That night, while the warders dozed and snores shook the windows and iron bedsteads, Marius found it hard to get to sleep. On Prison Ship Number One, he had become accustomed to listening out for the rats which sniffed around the prisoners' feet under the covers. He would count them instead of counting sheep, until at last he fell asleep.

There were no rats here in the big ward. There was just the beginning and end of everything – and death silently prowling.

Hearing a slight rustling, he lifted his head. A frail figure was creeping along the line of metal beds. He buried his head in his pillow and closed his eyes, listening to the footsteps. A scent of musk and thyme reached his nostrils. He knew it was Sister Agnès.

'He's asleep,' whispered a voice.

In the dark, the slightest unaccustomed noise takes on a strange resonance. Marius could hear almost everything that Julien and Sister Agnès said.

'My love, you've come to find me again,' Sister Agnès was saying. 'We must do it.'

'Do you really think so?'

'It's the hand of God reaching out to us. Everything is logical. I took the veil when you left, now you've returned I shall give it up. Beauty is our universe, Alphonse.'

Why was Sister Agnès calling Julien Alphonse? Softly, Marius turned his head and opened his eyes. Julien and Sister Agnès were holding hands.

'When, my love?' said Sister Agnès.

'Tomorrow,' replied Julien hesitantly.

'No, better the day after tomorrow. Because of the other one.'

'All right.'

Sister Agnès kissed Julien on the lips, then crept hurriedly away along the aisle.

What was supposed to happen the day after tomorrow? Marius wondered. And who was the other one?

He was not to find out. The very next day he was taken back to the prison ship.

*

Marius found himself chained to a chicken thief named Victor, who had been given the nickname of Garlic Arse, because he smelled and was not very bright. Garlic Arse had a fat, flaccid, jaundiced face.

'What are you in for?' he asked Marius on the sawing site.

'I killed a man. And to tell you the truth, I want to kill again. It's like a wild urge that takes hold of me.'

Garlic Arse looked at Marius with a mixture of respect and fear. 'And when do you get these wild urges?'

'When people annoy me.'

Garlic Arse let out an ostentatious sigh of relief that made his big, flabby face quiver. 'Well, you don't have to worry about me. I'm not the annoying kind.'

'Good for you.'

'I'm only a poor thief, with five years to do.'

'Good for you,' repeated Marius, with a sombre expression, 'because if you look for me, you'll find me. And if you're stupid enough to inform on me, you'll end up with a knife in the ribs and no questions asked. Understood?'

'Understood,' replied Garlic Arse, convinced that he was dealing with a hard case and vowing to watch his step.

Crushed by circumstances as he was, gripped by a convulsive and worsening anguish, well aware that everyone betrayed everyone else, Marius still refused to let his bitterness get the better of him. He liked the idea of passing himself off as a hard man because it was one way to avoid being bothered by the others. Besides, thrashing Bonnet and getting flogged had given him a new prestige. That morning, when he arrived at Prison Ship Number One, tough characters like the Cutthroat, the Dodger and Slant Face had all given him friendly pats on the back.

'You're a good man, Tixier. Congratulations.'

He was even applauded. Nor, according to Holy Smoke, were the warders unaware that prisoner 9430 had not let out a single groan while the formidable Le Bitteux had flogged him. From now on nobody would dare to mock him, and that at least was an improvement.

That evening, though, Marius abandoned himself to bitter thoughts. He was back on the ship's damp floor, with the smell of mildew and the rats. His mind was like a mist, incapable of condensing around a single thought. Was he, too, going to become a wild beast, a killer clinging to his petty privileges and his meagre living space?

A deceptive impression of rest stirred his senses. Was this one of those immortal longings so beloved of the Romantics?

He laughed nervously. The ship lay around him like a sleeping octopus. Marius tossed and turned on the stinking floor, its mustiness impregnating his mouth, his hands and his clothes. Each time he moved, the chain – the damned chain! – clanked like that of the grim reaper.

He lifted his head slightly and let his eyes sweep across the bodies that lay like pieces of meat on a butcher's slab, covered with flies. He despised these bodies so close to him, so like his, not men but numbers, shaken by tremors, convulsions, groans. He supressed a desire to vomit. He could no longer swallow the beans they gave him to eat. Filthy beans, disgusting soup. Beside him, that fat pig Garlic Arse lay snoring like a bell ringer, slobbering, mumbling, lips all aquiver, his face like a gargoyle. This was the man who shared everything with him in an intimacy that he hated. What misery! What humiliation!

Suddenly, he thought of Perfect Love and wondered what had become of him. And then of Julien and Sister Agnès.

He became aware that his thoughts were going round in circles. Wasn't that just what the authorities wanted? Weren't Commandant Raynaud and his henchmen trying to destroy the slightest hint of resistance in the prisoners?

'I won't surrender,' vowed Marius, 'either to vice or to renunciation.' He tried to find strength in the memory of Jean Valjean, of all he had endured and all the beneficial energy he had been able to derive from spending so many long years in this world of dead men. Nineteen years! Would he be capable of spending nineteen years in this hell hole? How had Jean Valjean stood it?

A noise caught his attention. It was less a noise than a murmur, a groan – the sound of muscles relaxing, bellies slackening, jaws cracking. He knew it well, this horrible symphony, this minuet of the gut, which came and went between the walls of the hold. It was like a world of misery that hung in the air, like death in instalments. He had the curious impression that it was Jean Valjean who lay here, listening to it. And he felt almost strong.

The next day it was back to the routine. The whistle blowing, the bells chiming, rifles trained on red and white ghosts. For hours on end the foul-smelling chain gang stretched out in Indian file. The anthill of the damned. And then the work, the sawing, the cutting, the handling, the pieces of wood coming and going endlessly, the wretches covered in iron moving heavy burdens. It was another minuet, a minuet of chains, orchestrated by filth and brine and by an army of warders with ugly faces and mouths full of threats.

That morning Marius had bathed. He had even been able to shave. In the colony, you could shave twice a week and bathe in the sea only twice a month. The resulting smells can easily be imagined. The overheated atmosphere in a stinking hold that resembled a dungeon. The sour juices constantly saturating the prisoners' bodies. As they changed underwear only once a week, their shirts and trousers soon became as stiff as board and could have stood up by themselves. And the heat did not help. In the distance, towards the Pyrenees and the sea, the hills were so white it was as if there was no horizon. The only things to blacken this expanse of white were the flies, great swarms of them buzzing ceaselessly around the convicts as they worked.

Garlic Arse was not as skilful a worker as Perfect Love. He was fat and flabby, and always managed to slip or miss his cut.

'I'm getting tired,' he would say. 'It's my heart.'

Marius had noticed it the previous day. He would have to straighten the wood, look again for the right grain and reposition the blade.

At about two in the afternoon Garlic Arse paused from his work. The warder had his back turned and was smoking his pipe.

'Hey, Marius, have you heard?'

'Heard what?'

'About Julien and Sister Agnès.' Marius went pale and his threatening glare filled Garlic Arse with terror. 'Don't take it out on me, eh?' Garlic Arse's lips were quivering and he made a curious noise with his mouth, as if sipping from a plate of scalding hot soup.

'Go on.'

'Well, they found the bodies of Julien and Sister Agnès in the chapel. It seems the padre found them this morning. Dead like heroes of antiquity, he told the commandant and the officers. They opened their veins with a scalpel, sat down side by side and died just like that, hand in hand. Did you know him well?'

'A little.'

'According to the warder I buy tobacco from,' the big man continued, 'the sister and Julien left a kind of will. Nobody could make head or tail of it. The sister wrote that she'd been reunited with her lover, who drowned five years ago. Some say it's witchcraft. Do you believe in witchcraft?'

Marius was thinking of Julien and his mother at Bicêtre. She'll no longer clasp her little one to her heart, poor old woman. I suppose she'll die of grief, old age and poverty. In any case, nobody will even remember her and her boy. And all for a loaf of bread.

'Of course I believe in witchcraft,' replied Marius, looking Garlic Arse straight in the eye. 'In fact, I've made a pact with the devil. The more souls I give him, the more chance I have of becoming immortal.'

Garlic Arse gave a little cough. 'Well, shall we get back to work?'

'I was waiting for you.'

During the week that followed Marius hardly spoke to Garlic Arse or any of the other convicts. When he had heard the news of Julien's death, his head had begun to burn. He would curse poor, mad Sister Agnès. He would curse everybody. At the same time, paradoxically, he took care to keep his body fit, doing press-ups and other exercises. I hold my destiny in my hands, he would tell himself.

At the end of that week, Garlic Arse was rude to Holy Smoke.

'You smell of tobacco,' the officer remarked, pointing his finger at his face.

'That's none of your business,' retorted Garlic Arse.

'A week in solitary!' growled Holy Smoke. 'Have you forgotten the rule? I'll get rid of your taste for tobacco! Who's your supplier?'

'If anybody asked you a question like that, you'd say you didn't know.'

Marius could hardly believe what he was hearing.

Holy Smoke banged his fist on a plank. 'Another week!' He turned to the warders. 'Take the irons off this big slug and throw him in the hole. He ought to have a report as well! Holy smoke! If I find the jackass who cuts him a piece of tobacco, he'd better watch out.'

'You see, I can stand up to them too,' the fat man whispered to Marius, as they were separated. Surreptitiously, he slipped him a hairspring. 'Use this and you'll be able to make a run for it. It's all over for me. My heart, my poor Marius. I can feel it.'

How easy it is to misjudge people, thought Marius a week later when he learned that Garlic Arse had died in solitary after a heart attack. His body, like Julien's, was deposited in the naval lecture hall, to be used in anatomy lessons for surgical students. Bodies had to be useful for something.

Following this latest blow of fate, Marius was moved to the section for hard cases.

'Prisoner 9430 is a bad influence on the other prisoners,' Holy Smoke told Commandant Raynaud.

'Simple-minded he may be, but he's starting to get on my nerves,' said Raynaud. 'We're going to tame him.'

For the moment, Marius was delighted at the news, as it meant farewell to Prison Ship Number One and its stench.

'It's also to protect you from Bonnet,' a warder called Moreau told him. 'They don't want a murder on their hands. Bonnet's been telling everyone he's going to get you.'

'Just let him try.'

'Don't do anything stupid, 9430.'

The section for hard cases, which Marius already knew because it was where he had tasted the lash, was situated in the inner courtyard of the colony, not far from the general store. The general store was a vaulted hall lit through a high glass partition. It was there that the trusties worked, and it was the paradise of the colony because the trusties had privileges. Needless to say, Marius was hoping to get to this haven as soon as possible. The convicts who worked there made various fancy items, such as slippers, shopping bags made from cloth of aloes, mother-of-pearl napkin rings, pipes decorated with figurines, little wooden boats complete with sails, objects sculpted with improvised tools – sometimes a nail, sometimes a blunt knife – out of coconut shells, as well as straw boxes of different colours, little pieces of furniture, and baskets made from sheets of coloured paper rolled and stuck together. These objects were displayed in the windows and could be sold to visitors. The prisoners kept what they earned. It was a way for them to express themselves.

In the section for the hard cases, the outer windows had shutters, and when they were closed the cells were plunged into darkness. To the side of the entrance there was an iron gate through which the warders kept an eye on everything. Marius, like the others, was attached with a double chain to the long iron bar of the camp bed. He could walk only in the space prescribed by the length of the chain, which was no space at all. In addition, he had no partner, and it was forbidden to speak. But Marius did not complain. At least I have a bed, he would tell himself.

On Sunday mornings, a compulsory Mass was celebrated for everyone by Father Félicien. That Sunday, after the service, Marius was being taken back to his section by a warrant officer named Lestrade, who had a slight limp, when he suddenly saw a man walking rapidly towards them, his right hand folded over the sleeve of his smock as if to conceal something. A knife, thought Marius. The man was Bonnet.

'Watch out!' he screamed, attracting the officer's attention to the danger and in the process saving his own life.

Bonnet, foaming with rage, tried to strike the officer. Marius intervened, and despite his chains managed to parry the blows with his arm. As he was faster than Bonnet, he brought him down in the twinkling of an eye.

'Handcuffs for this madman!'

At the officer's call, the warders came running. They handcuffed Bonnet and took him to solitary.

Marius was dripping with blood. His forearm had been gashed by Bonnet's knife. Lestrade was bleeding too.

'I owe you my life,' he said to Marius, and immediately gave orders for every care to be lavished on him.

'No, it's I who must thank you,' replied Marius and bowed to him, judging that Lestrade might be a useful man to have on his side. 'It's only a scratch,' he added. 'And I'm delighted to have received this blow in your place.'

The officer gave Marius a dig with his elbow. 'I like lads of your calibre. You act like a soldier. A few years ago I served under Admiral Villeneuve, who was defeated at Trafalgar. As you can see from my leg, I still have a souvenir from the battle. But let me tell you something. I used to be a dab hand with a sabre. If you like, I can give you a few lessons. I know a few thrusts you might find useful when you get out of here. It'll be my way of paying my debt to you.' He put his finger in front of his mouth. 'But let's keep it a secret, shall we? It's better if nobody else knows.'

Bonnet was quickly dealt with. The rule was clear. *Any prisoner who strikes an officer of the law, or who kills his fellow prisoner, or who rebels or causes others to rebel, is to be punished by death.*

The special tribunal convened without further ado and the expected sentence was delivered swiftly. Bonnet would be executed in two days' time at noon.

At about three a.m. on the night before the execution, the warders' whistle echoed through the hard cases' section. A squad was picked to erect the guillotine and Marius was one of them.

He and his companions lined up in silence. None of the men exhibited any disgust at the task they had been assigned.

An hour later, by torchlight, the guillotine rose in the yard. A short distance away a man stood, following the final preparations. It was Le Bitteux. A solitary man, despised by everyone, living under constant threat from those he had either flogged already or might one day be called on to flog, he was smiling. He was looking at his sinister fiancée, the guillotine, outlined against the sky, and he was smiling. He was going to put a friend to death and he was smiling!

'With me, Bonnet won't suffer,' he boasted to an officer, loudly enough for the prisoners to hear him.

'The bastard!' one of the convicts whispered to Marius. 'We'll get him one of these days.'

The warders threw themselves on the convict and rained blows on his back.

'It'll be your turn soon, 2048,' said Le Bitteux. 'And when that day comes, I won't use a guillotine, I'll use a saw.' He turned to Marius, who was fixing a last nail to the floor with a knife. 'You, too, 9430.'

Marius raised his head and stared at the bloodthirsty cyclops who took pride in never turning down an opportunity to sate his contemptible appetites. He wanted to kill him.

When the boards were ready, Le Bitteux went to fetch the fatal knife, which he had spent most of the night carefully sharpening. The blade was adjusted and a bale of straw was brought to test the machine. Le Bitteux pressed a spring and the blade fell and cut the bale in two.

'Just how I like it,' he muttered. And bending his head twice, he mimed with his hand the movement of the blade on his neck, punctuating his gesture with a huge shout of laughter.

Day broke. The torches were put out and the prisoners were taken back to their section. Le Bitteux remained on the boards, huge and triumphant, casting an expert's gaze over everything.

Around ten a battalion of marines took up their places on one side of the vast yard. Cannons were brought in by a company of gunners. The scaffold raised its two red arms towards the sky. The triangle of steel cast sinister reflections. Everything was ready.

At noon the doors of the colony opened and the convicts rushed like a herd of wild beasts into the yard. Their places at the spectacle had been reserved. It was meant to teach them a lesson. There were even some inhabitants of Toulon present. After all, this was a celebration.

At a command from the warders, the convicts took their caps off and knelt. With one hand they lifted the links of their chains, while with the other they held their woollen caps. There was a drum roll. Marius, in the front row, watched as Bonnet arrived escorted by Holy Smoke and four soldiers. Behind them came a group of penitents from the town, their faces hidden by grey hoods, carrying a coffin. What astonished Marius was how calm Bonnet was. He did not even glance at his old companions.

As he was climbing the first steps of the scaffold, one of the executioner's assistants told him that Father Félicien wanted to speak to him. Bonnet grimaced. Father Félicien advanced nevertheless, holding his crucifix in front of him. Bonnet spat on the crucifix and kicked the priest. 'Get away from me! Leave me my courage!'

And with these words, he rushed at Le Bitteux, shouldered him aside and made desperate efforts to break his bonds. Le Bitteux and his assistants pushed the priest out of the way and surrounded Bonnet.

'Long live death!' Bonnet cried to the convicts. 'Rather the supreme punishment than slavery!'

A cry arose from the huge crowd. Marius could not help but feel admiration for Bonnet. Soldiers rushed to the foot of the scaffold and the cannons were pointed at the convicts. At the first sign of rebellion Commandant Raynaud would not hesitate to give the order to fire.

Taking advantage of the general amazement, Bonnet had made a dash for the scaffold. 'Long live death!' he yelled once more.

Breathless and wild-eyed, as if in a trance, he threw himself to his knees on the block next to the plank, to which he would be fastened with straps. Looking up, he gazed at the fatal blade.

'It'll be your turn next! They can't kill the dead!' he cried.

Then he stood up abruptly and placed himself on the block. Le Bitteux, almost terrified, tightened the straps.

Commandant Raynaud, irritated by the whole affair, made an impatient gesture and read out the death sentence as pronounced by the tribunal.

'Let the executioner do his duty,' he said finally.

Bonnet looked at the sky one last time, then the plank was lowered, the blade of the guillotine fell, swift as lightning, and it was all over.

Marius had followed the scene without blinking. It was the first time he'd witnessed an execution. How could anyone take pleasure in such a spectacle? To make things worse, when the blade fell, half his face was splattered with blood. He vomited immediately. Two of his neighbours did likewise. There was blood everywhere. The warders intervened at once, truncheons in hand. On the left another convict stretched out his hand, dipped it in the blood and lifted it to his mouth.

'Drink it! It'll give you guts!' he cried in a booming voice. 'Corpus Christi!'

'Sacrilege!' exclaimed the commandant and his stewards.

The blasphemer was apprehended and thrashed on the spot. Four warders rained blows on his head and shoulders. The marines waded into the crowd and began beating the convicts on the small of the back with rifles. There was a furious scramble as the prisoners tried to avoid the blows. The crowd heaved like a monstrous centipede.

'Back to the cells! At the double!'

Chains clanked as the convicts broke into a giddy, lurching run. Marius, spattered with blood and vomit, followed the general movement. One thing was certain: if you wanted to be proved right in this world, indignation wasn't enough. As he ran, he looked up and saw that the sky had not changed colour. A man had just died and it remained chalky white. Where was God? It seemed as if all this would never end. But he, Marius, would not follow Bonnet's example. He would fight. He would not spend twenty years in Toulon. That was impossible.

It took several weeks, though it seemed an eternity. The idea germinated in his mind when a warder brought him a large quantity of tow for spinning.

'You didn't think you were going to twiddle your thumbs, did you, 9430? Here's work – and hard work, too!'

Marius wasted no time. In his cell, chained by the foot, he managed to detach the crossbar from his camp bed. With it, he made a hole next to the window of his cell and proceeded to scratch away plaster from the wall until he was able to pull free several large stones. The work required time, care and, above all, great caution. Repeated blows on the wall could have aroused the attention of the warders. Fortunately, there was always a lot of noise in this part of the colony – the clanking of chains, the squealing of pulleys, the knocking of hammers. It was unlikely that the sentries on the quay would hear anything, and in fact they heard nothing. In any case, Marius had muffled the blows by tying his smock around the crossbar.

He put the stones and plaster under his bed and cleaned everything with his smock. Even though the hole was not very big, he had to be careful during visits and at mealtimes. Again, his smock did the trick.

And then, for ten days and ten nights, he attacked his chain with the hairspring that Garlic Arse had given him. As a file it was microscopic, and so was the work. He would not go right to the bottom of the chain, in order not to arouse the warders' suspicions. In a penal colony, the sound of chains was like a guarantee, a kind of signature tune.

The hole had to be concealed and Marius found an ingenious way to do this. He stuffed softened tow into the demolished section of the wall – not only tow but also mashed bread from his daily ration. Hunger gnawed at him, but he held out. And to hide the tow and the bread, he used dust from the plaster, making a filler out of the dust and his own urine. The illusion was perfect.

Helped by the darkness in his cell, he managed to hide his work from the eyes of the warders. They always entered from the outside, and the only window had a shutter over it. Whenever they came into the cell, they had the feeling they were in a cellar. It was impossible to see anything.

When he broke through the wall completely, Marius managed to recover the stones from the other side without anything falling on the quay. The moment of truth had arrived.

One evening he broke the last little piece of chain. He took off his trousers and hid the biggest stones in them. Then he put the tub – the only piece of furniture in his cell except for a camp bed and a little table – under his smock. He filled the smock's sleeves with plaster and dust, fixed his red cap on the tin can that was used to bring him his food, and placed two stones to represent two feet outside the trousers. Thus arranged, his clothes gave quite a realistic impression of a man sleeping with his back to the door. Sometimes the old tricks are the best.

As he surveyed his work, the thought of freedom intoxicated him. Heart pounding, he waited for nightfall. When the patrol went by, he hid to the left of the door. The orderlies noticed nothing amiss. The subterfuge had worked. Dressed in just underwear and a shirt, Marius heaved a sigh of relief. Fortunately, it had not occurred to the warders to enter the cell. A simple glance had been enough for them.

Bit by bit, Marius removed the bread and tow. When it was all out, he looked at the hole in disbelief. He touched his arms and wondered how he had managed to do it. A tremor of pleasure went through his body. He went closer. The hole seemed hardly big enough for a mouse. But I'll get through, he told himself, even if I have to tear all the skin from my body.

He heaved himself up to the hole and inserted his body, head first. After much painful effort, his hand and forearm hung outside the wall. Marius was suffocating. It was so narrow. A whiff of brackish air tickled his nostrils, and he thought it smelled wonderful. Then he went back to his crawling.

Finally he was able to slide his head outside and look around. There was nobody nearby, but his position was dangerous and barely possible to hold. On the one hand, he was afraid that a stone might fall and attract the attention of an orderly, on the other, he might fall head first and kill himself. He seemed to be about eight feet above the ground. But this was one of those occasions when it was better not to think too much. Marius felt a great surge of hope. He wanted to be finished with the colony and regain his freedom.

He had calculated well. He knew this part of the quay by heart and had studied every inch of it. Along the walls of the hospital, at intervals of about fourteen inches, wooden bars were sealed into the wall which were used for drying swabs.

The weather was fine. If anything, it was almost too mild. Earlier, when the warders had done their rounds, drunk as usual, Marius had heard them talking about a storm. The moon, like a placid ball, illuminated the quay. No, Marius told himself, a storm seemed unlikely. The light from the quay merged into the colour of the wall. He looked around again. There was nobody to be seen. He slid the front of his body forward and with a rapid and violent movement, like a gymnasium exercise, he seized the wooden bar with both hands and hung from it like a trapeze. He swung two or three times. Once he had regained his balance, he let go of the bar and dropped to the ground.

It was a perfect and almost silent landing. His physical training had paid dividends. For a while, he remained on all fours, his arms coiled like a monkey's, ready to leap. When he was sure that there was no sentry about, he crawled to the edge of the quay and stopped. The smell of sludge caught him by the throat. He gazed at the town, on the other side of the sound, its shops all lit up.

Still lying down, he looked at the boats around him. One of them was a single-masted tartan with a bowsprit, loaded with planks and beams. Gently, holding on to the tartan's mooring rope, he slid into the cool, black water. When he reached the vessel, he slid one of the planks out. He could already see himself in Toulon, finally free of this terrible nightmare, and on the way to Paris. Paris . . . His eyes misted over for a second. Better not to count your chickens before they hatch.

He climbed astride the plank and lay with his chin flat. Using his hands as paddles, he headed for the floating wooden beam that marked the boundary between the military port and the merchant port. He managed to pass beneath the beam on his plank and finally found himself in the middle of the port. From there, he went in the direction of the merchant ships moored at the end of the old harbour basin, where the sea seemed to be trapped. He took care not to be spotted by the military boats and veered towards a little building named the pile, which was in the middle of the water and served as lodgings for the man who guarded the vessels of the fleet.

By the time he reached the edge of the little enclave, puffing like a seal, he already felt exhausted and the dirty water had penetrated his throat. As he was about to hoist himself up, he noticed a guard pacing up and down the quay, smoking a pipe. Marius immediately dived under the plank. As he could barely swim, he clung to the piece of wood, his head under the water. He thought he was going to drown. Luckily, he managed to regain his breath, beating feebly with his feet as his grandfather Gillenormand had once taught him. And he prayed.

The time passed interminably, while he drifted noiselessly as far as the merchant quay. By the time he hoisted himself onto the edge, with the help of a chain, he was shivering all over. The skin on his palms was wrinkled like curdled milk. He could barely put one foot in front of the other. If only he had had a file to get rid of what was left of his chain!

On the quay he found a sheet used to patch the tartans' sails. It smelled of rotten fish. With the help of a mooring post, he managed to tear it in the middle and slide it over his head like a poncho. Then he tied a rope around his belly and set off, barefoot and hesitant, in no particular direction, keeping close to the walls.

He walked for a good hour, leaving the town and its lights behind him, suddenly becoming aware that he was in open country. All at once his blood froze. A cannon shot had rung out. They had already discovered his escape. He looked around him and leaned against a tree, gripped once more by a sense of discouragement. He did not know that he was near a village called La Valette. He knew nothing.

He sat down at the foot of the tree and dozed off for a short moment. As his throat was burning, he tore off a piece of moss and lifted it to his mouth. He licked it avidly, chewed part of it, and spat it out again in a horrible fit of coughing. Hunger gnawed at his stomach. Having used part of his bread ration as filler for the hole in the wall, he had hardly eaten in the past fortnight.

There was a crack of thunder, dry as the crack of a whip. The warders had been right after all. A storm was on its way. Marius got to his feet. He could no longer see a single star in the sky. Thunder, he thought, might be his salvation. Wouldn't the peasants confuse the cannon shot with claps of thunder?

The thunder continued, drowning out every other sound. At first, the rain was nothing but a fine, lukewarm curtain. Marius threw his head back and opened his mouth to let the rainwater in. He had to find shelter and clothes. Now the rain was starting to come down in sheets so heavy and so thick that the earth resounded dully. Marius broke into a headlong run. He kept going straight ahead, drunk with freedom, jumping over stones and bushes, imagining an enemy was chasing him.

'I'm free!' he screamed, as the rain redoubled in intensity. 'I'm free!'

He stumbled against a tree stump and fell flat on his face. The violence of the storm was already soaking the soil. The rain was soon falling in torrents and Marius felt the tepid stickiness of the earth on his face. He clung voluptuously to the clay and buried his face in an eiderdown of moss and rotted leaves. Then he got to his feet, let out a burst of laughter and started running again, leaping like a demon, waving his arms in the silvery glare of the lightning.

Suddenly he saw lights. A house. Fishing nets. He advanced cautiously. The thunder claps continued to echo like hammer blows on the anvil of the earth. It was an apocalyptic spectacle. Marius came to a halt. The wind whipped the tops of the cypresses and sycamore trees and slapped his face with rainwater. He felt alive again. He went on until he reached the front door of the house. Calmly, he scratched at the door.

An old man appeared in the doorway. Seeing Marius, he suppressed a gesture of terror.

'I'm lost,' said Marius, humbly. 'Bandits stripped me of my clothes and I got caught in the storm.'

The old man looked at Marius's shaven head, his bare feet, his face covered in mud and twigs. He nodded. 'Come in and take cover.'

Inside, the house consisted of a single room with whitewashed walls, lit by three candles and the glowing light of an open fire. It reeked of dried fish. In an armchair next to the fireplace, an old woman sat sewing. She wore a little white bonnet on her head and clogs on her feet. She was so short that her feet did not even touch the ground.

'Mother, give this poor fellow a bowl of soup,' said the old man.

The old woman immediately did as she was told. Marius sat down at the table. Sitting down, he caught his feet in his poncho, revealing the shackle and the chain link on his ankle.

'Pee! Pee!' roared a voice that made him jump.

At the other end of the room, a boy was sitting on a pile of wood, twiddling his fingers. He was clearly mentally retarded.

'Happy,' explained the old man, signalling to Marius not to pay attention. 'My son thinks you're happy.' He stole a knowing look at Marius's ankle. He had suspected as much. He thought he had heard the roar of a cannon earlier. In fifty years of miserable existence in this rats' hole, he still knew how to distinguish between the roar of a cannon and the roar of thunder.

At the end of the room, sitting on his pile of wood, the awkward lump was still twiddling his fingers and staring at the fire.

'Come here, son,' said the old man. He whispered something in his ear and slapped him on the back of his head.

'Any problem?' Marius asked anxiously.

'I asked him to fetch a piece of bacon from the shed,' the old man reassured him. 'For the long journey ahead of you, it won't come amiss. I'm only a poor fisherman, but I also dry meat. When I catch bream or weevers in my nets, I sometimes exchange them for beef or pork. We have to live. In the meantime, eat your soup. It's quite hot, and it'll be a change from your usual fare.'

'My usual fare?'

'Come on, don't try to be clever with me. I can see your head, I've seen your ankle. Don't be afraid. I help convicts. We unfortunate wretches have to look out for each other. Go on, eat.'

The old woman had placed a big bowl of onion soup before him. Marius did not need to be asked twice. Eagerly, he lowered his lips to the bowl and swallowed the soup down in no time at all. The old man did not stop talking. With his large white moustache and his big hands eaten into by salt, he seemed a decent sort. He told Marius how many fugitives he had saved and how he went about it. It was fascinating – and above all reassuring.

The old woman disappeared again and came back with a piece of cheese and goat's milk. For Marius, this was a feast. Outside, the rain had died down. Suddenly, a noise was heard.

'Here's my son,' said the old man.

The door opened with a crash, and a man wearing a top hat appeared, a pistol in his hand. Behind him, two gendarmes armed with carbines, and bringing up the rear, the simple-minded boy, rolling his eyes and sticking his tongue out. Marius looked incredulously at the old fisherman.

'Sorry, my boy. Fifty francs is not to be sneezed at.'

The man with the top hat was La Valette's police chief. He congratulated the old man. 'You've earned your fifty francs, old Marion. It's the fifth this year, isn't it?'

'The sixth, Monsieur.'

The police chief guffawed. 'Your house is like the last outpost of the colony! Strange, isn't it? Despite their shaved heads and the chains on their feet, these idiots always think they're going to escape us. Anyway, good for you. You have an eye for it.' He turned to Marius. 'How long were you in for?'

'Twenty years.'

'You'll get three more. That's the ration. Not to mention the fifty lashes that go with it. You see, my lad, nobody escapes from Toulon.' He turned to the gendarmes. 'Tie up this scum and take him away in the wagon.'

Marius wanted to scream, but no sound came from his chest. They put the cuffs on him and flung him in the wagon. In the distance, a cry could be clearly heard.

'Pee! Pee!'

3

There was little likelihood of Cosette receiving any of Marius's letters. For the past three months Louis-Désiré Burdin had been sending one of his henchmen to the Rue Plumet every morning to intercept her mail. The henchman would conscientiously sort the letters and bring back to the steward whatever he wanted. Louis-Désiré had, of course, guessed that Marius, sentenced to hard labour for a crime he had not committed, would immediately write copiously to his wife, but that his stubbornness would soon give way to discouragement. It was the same with all prisoners. When you were abandoned by everybody and incarcerated far from your loved ones, there came a moment when renunciation became stronger than any other sentiment. Marius had written to the prefect of the region and the minister of justice – nobody had replied. Louis-Désiré had known a number of convicts and he understood the way their minds worked. Time was on his side. For this reason, he kept exhorting his master to make use of the famous letter and appropriate Baron Pontmercy's property.

That morning he was more than usually insistent. Marius had been presumed dead for three months. It was time to act.

'And what about Cosette?' replied Amédée. 'Do you think I can just arrive at her house, wave the letter under her nose and tell her I'm the new owner? Have you no heart?'

With his usual mixture of dissimulation and evasion, Louis-Désiré tried to outwit his master by making him feel guilty. 'Of course I have a heart, Monsieur. But what about you? Do you think it's noble to leave the baroness languishing and postpone endlessly what must be done? When it comes down to it, that letter belongs to you and nobody else. It gives you authority. And you made a vow to your friend the baron – may his soul rest in peace – that you would take care of his affairs. So pay a visit to the baroness and show her your compassion, if not your affection.'

'I've been to the Rue Plumet twice, and twice she has refused to receive me.'

'You must insist. Send her flowers.'

'Her garden is full of flowers.'

Louis-Désiré made a gesture of exasperation. 'I no longer recognize you, Monsieur. You used to be so enterprising, but now you're reserved. Absence, even if it is motivated by reserve and tact, doesn't solve anything. Even your friends Louis de Vergne and Robert d'Androisy are complaining that they never see you. What has happened to that fine detachment of yours? You always said you would never fall in love, and so you refused to be loved. Now that you are in love, you still don't want to be loved. This inconsistency is harmful to everyone.'

'You mean you?'

'No, you, Monsieur. My future is behind me. I'm merely a humble and devoted servant who thinks only of his master's happiness. The rest is of no importance to me. And I won't hide it from you, I'm deeply distressed to see you in this state.'

'What do you want me to do?' retorted Amédée testily. 'I have a hot head and a cold heart.'

'You're mistaken, Monsieur. I think it's rather the contrary. With this change of temperature, which is so unusual in you, I think you've caught what amounts to a cold in the soul. So you've changed? All right. I can't say I'm very happy about it. The only way not to suffer is never to fall in love. But if you've changed, then accept this change fully. If you won't go so far as to declare your love to the baroness – since it is all too obvious that now is not the moment – then at least offer her your friendship and attention. Anyone who has been wounded needs a friend in these tragic circumstances. Be that friend.'

'You may be right. But leave me now. Monsieur de Vergne will be here soon.'

The steward withdrew with a heavy heart.

Amédée paced up and down. Though he agreed with most of what Louis-Désiré had said, nevertheless he had his own opinions on things. He had discovered that he was weak and this weakness revolted him. He had lost confidence in himself. Everything seemed to be deserting him. His conversation, once brilliant, had become as flat as the pavements of the Boulevard de Gand, where he loved to strut. Indeed, he no longer strutted, he strolled. Everybody's ideas seemed to criss-cross in his heart, with a touch more irony, a little affectation and a lot of bitterness. His overweening ambition was no more than a memory. Why had he let Marius be murdered?

He lit a cigar and poured himself a glass of rum. I loved Marius like a brother and didn't know it, he told himself as he sat down. Then he stood up again. He remembered those times that had vanished so suddenly and that now seemed endowed with an irresistible freshness and charm. He no longer even thought about his female conquests. Only Marius counted. He felt nostalgic for his smile – his innocent smile.

He poured another glass of rum. Louis would be here soon, but Louis irritated him. He found him too affectionate, too eager to please. As for Robert d'Androisy, the conceited fellow had exasperated Marius and now exasperated him. And Clémence had gone to the Poitou. Not that he had been able to find out anything from her. She wanted to rest. Let her rest – let her go to the devil, he said to himself, emptying his glass in one draught. His other friends were mere shadows, insignificant drinking companions, quick to take advantage and just as quick to disappear. La Battut had vanished. Eugène Sue was spending his time in Versailles working on a study of the sea. Of the reigning sibyls, Olympe had left for Bologna with Rossini, while Marie d'Agoult was living the perfect love with Liszt. The only ones left were the usual strumpets.

Amédée wondered what was to become of him. He was not alone. Uncertainty was everywhere in the summer of 1834. Lamartine had become a deputy, his politics a form of liberal and social Christianity. La Fayette had died. The Duc de Broglie had resigned from the government. Paris was enjoying itself less. The 21 June elections to the Chamber of Deputies had seen a bitter defeat for the Republican party. As for the literary world, the same names were still on everyone's lips – Dumas, Balzac and Musset.

The bell rang and Amédée went to open the door. Louis de Vergne entered and took off his top hat.

'A drink?' Amédée offered.

'You drink too much, my friend.'

'Take care of your own health, not mine,' retorted Amédée, pouring himself a third glassful.

Louis de Vergne talked about Dumas, who had recently fought a duel with a journalist called Maurice Alhoy, after which he had been reconciled with Victor Hugo, who was having a passionate affair with the actress Juliette Drouet. Amédée lifted his eyes to heaven. He did not give a fig for all this tittle-tattle. He swore to himself that soon he would take up absinthe and opium. As everything is permitted, I must try everything, he said to himself.

'Fat old Balzac is riddled with debt,' continued Louis. 'He's been telling everyone he's about to get down to a novel called *Old Goriot*. The book will be serialized in *La Revue de Paris* before the end of the year. All that coffee he drinks must help him to write as much as he does. He's like Falstaff – truly indefatigable.'

'Do you really think any of that interests me?'

Louis looked at Amédée despondently. He visited him at least twice a week to tell him the latest gossip, which delighted a minority who made up in malice for what they lacked in influence, but apparently he bored Amédée.

As Louis-Désiré had done earlier, he went on the offensive. 'You stay at home, overcome with grief, you never go out, you hide from your friends. What have we done to deserve this?'

'Nothing. That's just it. You do nothing. You're nobodies. We're all nobodies.'

'Are you still thinking about Marius?'

'I miss him.'

'Well, then, let me tell you that if our unfortunate friend were still with us, he would condemn your behaviour.'

'I can't let you say that.'

'Well, I let myself!' said Louis, raising his voice. 'Your silence towards his widow is unspeakable. What are you waiting for? Why don't you go and comfort her? You disappoint me, Amédée. We're nobodies, are we? Then you're the worst nobody of all. Detachment is one thing, cowardice is quite another.'

He picked up his hat and left, slamming the door on his way out.

Amédée burst out laughing and threw his glass at the door. Then he collapsed in his armchair and took his head in his hands. For a moment he thought of finishing the rum, then changed his mind. Very well, then, since everyone was pressing him to go and see Cosette, he would go. He would make a final attempt, even if it was only to talk about Marius.

Cosette no longer left the house. As she had stopped going to Saint-Sulpice, Monsieur Verjat and Father Rillet visited her at home, but she barely spoke to them. The same happened whenever Armand Carrel or Henri de la Roche-Dragon called. It was Madeleine who received them, Madeleine who played the mistress of the house. Cosette still carried on her charitable work, but purely in memory of her father. Nothing interested her any more, nothing mattered to her. Marius's death had been her death, too. She would lock herself in her room and not reply when she was spoken to. She had even become cantankerous.

This isolation worried Madeleine. The faithful maid no longer knew what to do to take her mistress's mind off things, and she would often panic at Cosette's unpredictable reactions. Cosette would spend most of her time arranging the drawers in her room, playing with satin ribbons or with the wire of her wedding bouquet. She would listen, in an attentive daze, to the wind shaking the leaves against the walls of the winter garden. She would search constantly for her rock crystal, losing it then finding it again. Some days she would talk feverishly, then, all at once, these sudden fits of elation would be followed by periods of inertia during which she sat without speaking or moving. She came and went between Marius's room and her own. Without any reason, and to Madeleine's great despair, she would begin to run in every direction. She would come back to Marius's room and sprinkle lavender water on her arms.

'Marius's scent!' she would cry joyously.

At other times Madeleine would hear her cursing the house.

'I hate it, I hate it!' she would cry convulsively.

Madeleine helped Cosette as best she could. But what to do against this unhappiness, when it has decided to set up home in your house and to revel there?

Cosette abhorred God's injustice. She would say it loud and clear. She would press her head against the walls to weep and she would curse the child she was expecting. Only the sight of her father's candlesticks seemed to calm her down, but it was short-lived. As Madeleine had told Verjat, Cosette had begun to express contradictory opinions. She would censure what she had earlier approved and approve what she had once censured.

'She doesn't even tend her garden any more, Monsieur Verjat. She envies turbulent lives, wild nights, every kind of excess.'

'Be patient,' Verjat replied. 'Let her work off her grief. It's the rare product of an inner conflict and an outer apathy. It's quite normal for a desperate person to idealize all that is despicable. And I know whereof I speak.'

So everyone waited patiently.

When summer came and the heat rose, Cosette remained glued to the window of her room. When she looked at the stone bench and the two statues, she always saw Marius standing there like a sentry on duty, with his sky-blue frock coat that he loved so much, his yellow gloves and his shiny waistcoat. She would let out a long sigh and fan herself with an old copy of *La Tribune* to calm herself. Her complexion was pale, and her hair had lost its sheen. On the verge of tears, she would descend to the kitchen and drink pure milk and cupfuls of black coffee.

One evening, after glancing at the garden bench, she was seized with a destructive frenzy. She went to the winter garden and seized a pickaxe.

'Madame, where are you going?' asked Madeleine.

'It's none of your business!'

And Cosette struck at the two statues in a wild fury, smashing them.

'Leave the pieces on the ground!' she yelled at Madeleine, her hair wild and the edges of her lips flecked with spittle.

Madeleine was careful not to disobey this order. Her mistress frightened her.

All Cosette's days were the same. In the morning she would lie in bed. At night she would stay up. Insomnia kept watch over her distress and prevented her from wasting away. She would ask Madeleine to go shopping for food and then barely touch it. She was quickly full and even more quickly sickened. Life was making her ill.

She spent her days moving from one memory to another. 'And now what am I going to do?' she would ask herself ceaselessly.

This mixture of bitterness and pessimism seemed to have no direction, but found expression in sudden mood shifts and nonsensical trains of thought. One day she had cut down all the flowers in the winter garden, then thrown stones at the windows, smashing the glass. Her laughter had echoed throughout the house.

She who had once been so careful and neat now spent hours on end wearing nothing but an old black dress, a waistcoat, woollen stockings and garden clogs. One morning she had shocked Madeleine by putting on a pair of trousers and a frock coat that had belonged to Marius.

'What of it, my dear Madeleine? What's the matter? Don't you know that George Sand also wears trousers and dresses like a man? She even smokes cigars.'

So she would smoke cigars and cough for hours.

On another occasion, while Madeleine was busy sewing in the kitchen, Cosette had startled her by suddenly appearing naked except for a pair of boots and with a cane in her hand. She broke a pitcher and a sugar bowl. 'I can't stand this house any more!' she cried and burst into tears.

It was a daily litany. But the more she repeated it, the more she shut herself away. She would sit on a chair and stare for hours at the ring Marius had given her to celebrate their wedding anniversary. In its setting of gold and coral, the diamond shimmered beautifully in the light. But the light, the true light, where was it?

That particular day Amédée was not sent away by Baroness Pontmercy. To his surprise, he was well received, though he saw no reason for self-congratulation in this. As the weather was mild, Cosette suggested that they have tea in front of the steps leading from the garden to the house. The previous day she had thrown Marius's ring into the garden. Today, however, she had made an effort with her appearance and was wearing a pink afternoon dress with a cape spread over her arms. You, she said to herself when she saw the marquis, you're going to pay a hundredfold for what you did. And she sat down next to him.

'Your roses are magnificent,' she said through gritted teeth, a glazed expression in her eyes.

Unlike Cosette, Amédée had not taken any care over his appearance. In his black suit with its ill-fitting waistcoat, and his burgundy cravat wrapped twice around his neck, he looked like any respectable young man from a good family. Before his arrival, he had sent Cosette twenty roses.

'Put the roses here on the table,' Cosette said to Madeleine. Madeleine did as she was told. Cosette smiled and, with a pair of shears, cut the stems off ten, and threw the roses into the garden. 'I cut half of them because there is only half of me left.'

The marquis did not flinch. Earlier, when he had seen Cosette on the steps, he had opened his arms as if to say: You are in my heart like a Madonna on a pedestal. Now he was paralysed. 'Your garden is really well tended,' he said, hesitantly.

'Do you think so? That's because you don't see anything, Marquis. Take a look at the statues near the little bench, look at the winter garden. No, don't bother. I think that's really what makes you unique – you don't see anything!' And she burst into forced laughter.

Amédée would do anything not to hear any more of Cosette's sarcastic remarks. 'You know, when things are beautiful and clear, one wonders if one day they were perhaps not—' He broke off abruptly, disconcerted by Cosette's scornful gaze. He cleared his throat. 'Listen, Cosette,' he said, deciding to come straight to the point, 'I understand you. You hate me and you have every reason to. But I simply wanted to see you to show you

my friendship and what it is that ties me for ever to Marius. That's all.'
With that, he made as if to stand.

'No, wait,' said Cosette, reaching out her hand. Amédée's last sentence
had surprised her, for she had thought that he was going to say her name
and not Marius's. 'Wait,' she repeated, less harshly. 'At least drink your
tea.'

She gestured wearily. Madeleine, whom she had asked to stay close by,
was busy in the garden. The earth around the bushes was russet like
tobacco powder. The leaves were still. Irises peeped out under the tangle
of trees. Wallflowers spread over the old walls, and pink snapdragons
yawned out of the cracks in the stones. There were daisies and buttercups
in the high grass. White butterflies fluttered between the trees.

Amédée looked rapidly around the garden, reflecting bitterly that he
had shattered its soul and its harmony. Seeing his eyes wander towards
the little bench, Cosette told him that that corner had been hers and
Marius's. 'But inanimate objects are not always faithful,' she added, with a
lump in her throat. 'When a place you love is linked to the memory of a
person, you suppose it will change when the person is no longer there.
You imagine that it will grow sad, too. Well, that's wrong. Places and
objects don't care about anything. They have no life. They're rather like
you – intolerably frivolous.'

Amédée turned to look at Cosette. He picked up his cup and drank a
little tea. He would not react to this latest gibe. 'I've changed,' he said.
'Perhaps you think I'm trying to mislead you or make you feel sorry for
me. Well, you're wrong. I've changed, whether you believe it or not.'

'One does not change as easily as that, Marquis. You talk of grief? You
don't know the meaning of the word. My life has lost all meaning. I don't
know what keeps me from ending it all.'

'You mustn't say that, Cosette. End it all? Why deprive yourself of the
pleasure of cocking a snook at life?'

'No, you haven't changed! You still talk of mockery. It's obvious you
don't know what true discouragement is.'

'Yes, I do. The loss of my friend Marius has disheartened me for
everything else. I no longer even have superficiality as a means of self-
defence.'

'That's because you're unfeeling and always have been.'

'I think, above all, that the collapse of one's hopes should remain a
private matter.'

Cosette looked attentively at Amédée. She hated him as much as ever, yet he struck her as being sincere now. She drank her tea and turned her head to the winter garden. Near the bushes she heard the sound of beating wings, then the unpleasant chatter of a magpie as it flew up and away.

'Life is a thief,' she said, following the magpie with her eyes as it perched on the big oak. 'Like that bird. At the moment, I don't want anything. My existence is a total failure.'

Amédée stood up, shaking his head. 'Trust my long and depressing experience – a man or woman who pursues an aim against his or her nature is always bound to fail.'

'Am I hearing this from *you*?' Cosette seemed disconcerted. What had become of the proud little dilettante, so sure of himself, his charm, his extravagant remarks, his wit which was not witty at all? 'Are you leaving, Marquis?' she found herself asking.

Amédée took up his hat and riding crop. 'Friendship shouldn't be a burden, Cosette. I mustn't take advantage of your time. Through my selfishness, my rudeness and my indifference, I have caused the death of your friend Frédéric Rivolier in a duel, and the death of Marius, for which I suppose I was partly responsible – though, as God is my witness, it was the last thing I wanted. My negligence is unforgivable. That, more than anything, is what I was anxious to tell you.'

Cosette made no comment. She walked with Amédée to the gate. There, before he left, she placed her hand on his arm. 'Please forgive me for what I said earlier. Despair is often blind.'

Amédée raised his hat to Cosette by way of farewell. 'It is I who was blind, Baroness,' he replied, in a strangled voice.

He put on his hat and mounted his horse.

'One day you may be welcome here,' said Cosette as he was about to go.

Cosette and Amédée saw each other every week. Amédée was still in love with her, but he gave no sign of it. To cheer her up, he would exaggerate a good humour he no longer possessed, and entertain her with anecdotes about the fashionable Parisian world that he was now neglecting. Sometimes he irritated Cosette, who loathed the smugness of that society, but she was readier now to forgive him for what she had once considered his dishonesty.

'And even a lack of intelligence,' she said.

Amédée agreed. He still sometimes felt cynical enough to allow himself to be insolent, and whenever he did Cosette would treat him mercilessly. She mistrusted this young rooster who was trying too hard to behave like a friend. He would give in immediately. She could easily imagine him in the role of whipping boy.

They were seen together in the Tivoli Gardens, on the terrace of Tortoni, in the salons of the Café de Paris. Cosette was learning to laugh again, and Amédée was learning to talk without constantly declaiming. She was gentle, attentive and friendly, while he was modest, discreet and generous. They had not, of course, forgotten their grief. But they no longer wallowed in soul-destroying despair. They avoided punishing others for being happier than they were

One evening he noticed that Cosette's belly was becoming rounder. Although he said nothing, it weighed on his mind.

In the days that followed, they strolled on the Boulevard de Gand, through the Palais-Royal and along the Champs-Elysées. Amédée talked wittily about the fashions of the age. He could be irresistible, especially when he mocked himself, and it was clear to Cosette that he was making commendable efforts to master his vanity. She told herself that this servant of reason was finally being moved by genuine feelings. She hated him a little less. Didn't he have a right to redemption too?

One day Amédée arrived in the Rue Plumet to find Cosette standing on the steps in conversation with a tall man. The man had dark eyes, a pinched mouth and a salt-and-pepper beard, and was dressed in a brown frock coat and a hat with a turned-down brim. Amédée had seen him before, at Marius's funeral. He gave off a smell of oranges and old prayer books. Amédée found himself impressed by this sharp-eyed man with greying hair.

Cosette introduced Monsieur Verjat to Amédée. Throughout the conversation, Verjat remained standing. He could sense that his gaze was upsetting the young man, and so deliberately did not take his eyes off him.

Cosette had to attend to something and left the two men alone.

'So you're d'Iguerande?' asked Verjat, with the hint of suspicion in his voice which often underlay his questions.

'The Marquis d'Iguerande,' corrected Amédée, with an embarrassed smile.

'Iguerande is the name of a village in Burgundy, Marquis.'

'I didn't know that.'

'Indeed?'

'Why do you say "indeed"?'

'No reason. So you were very close to Baron Pontmercy?'

'Like a brother, Monsieur.'

'Indeed?'

Amédée stiffened. 'Why do you keep saying "indeed"?'

'Did I say it again? I'm really sorry, Marquis. I'm no longer even aware of it. But tell me, what was the name of the tavern you and the baron most often frequented?'

'We went to several, Monsieur,' replied Amédée, surprised. 'What does it matter?'

'It doesn't matter at all.'

'What I can tell you is this – the man who killed poor Marius was present one evening in the tavern we made the mistake of frequenting. More of a cheap restaurant, by the way. One of those sinister dives where people go to mix with the riff-raff. I'm sorry I ever went there, believe you me. The place was called the Clan Destin and it was in the Rue Aubry-le-Boucher. To be perfectly frank, I never want to set foot in there again.'

'Do you remember the man?'

'Vaguely. If memory serves me correctly, he looked not unlike Marius. I imagine he was a mainstay of the establishment.'

Cosette returned, and there was no further mention of either the man or the Clan Destin. Verjat soon took his leave of Cosette and her guest.

'I must be on my way, Marquis,' he said to Amédée. 'But we shall meet again. And do you know why? Because everything that troubles us allows us to be ourselves!' He accompanied this cryptic remark with a laugh.

Ill at ease, Amédée noticed that when Verjat laughed, his nose wrinkled like a mastiff's. He gave Amédée the impression that he was getting ready to bite. Amédée made an effort to smile.

'He's a strange fellow, isn't he?' he said to Cosette, once Verjat had gone.

'Why do you say that?'

'He questioned me like a police inspector.'

'Monsieur Verjat in the police? You must be joking!'

The air of Paris was fresh with the scent of lime trees. Revolution was no longer on the agenda. Amédée and Cosette saw each other in the afternoons. One day Amédée invited Cosette to dinner. He was afraid he would meet with a refusal.

'At the Véfour,' he specified.

Cosette did not refuse.

Near the colonnades of the Palais-Royal they met Balzac, Thiers and

Musset. Amédée greeted them politely. For a brief moment, Cosette had the feeling she was with Marius, and instantly reproached herself. She thought about her melancholy, that never-ending feeling of regret.

The restaurant once frequented by Bonaparte and Murat had red velvet seats. Cosette and Amédée were seated not far from Sainte-Beuve and Lamartine, with whom the marquis exchanged innocuous remarks about the weather. Like them, they dined on duckling terrine and chicken Marengo. The food was delicious and the conversation witty.

'Paris is sick and its restaurants are full to bursting,' Amédée noted ironically. 'My dear Cosette, just look at the people around us. They could certainly inspire Monsieur Daumier. The thought of becoming like all these sullen people with their shiny faces could almost make me consider death with serenity.'

'Don't start again, Amédée. Aren't these people exactly the same as those you used to seek out?'

The women were all plump, and all wore their hair plastered down on the forehead, twisted at the nape of the neck, and dressed with tiaras and branches of jasmine and cornflowers. They all wore brightly coloured gowns, and pearl necklaces and diamonds shimmered on their bodices and glittered on their chests. The men peppered their conversation with words they did not always understand but from which they derived a certain pride. They scratched affectedly at the long side whiskers that hung over their turned-down collars, and wiped their lips on gold-embroidered hand-kerchiefs. The old ones were trying to look young, while the young were already old. With their rounded elbows and arrogant mouths, they exuded wealth and effrontery, an effrontery born of power and brutality. These people were tiresome, like the era they lived in.

'A world I'll never be a part of!' said Cosette to Amédée derisively. 'My poor friend, when I think that you were both its master of ceremonies and its performing monkey!'

'And oh, how I regret it,' murmured the marquis.

Arms folded, he watched Cosette, admiring the blue and saffron gleams in her eyes, and inhaling the scent of lemon and green tea that gave fragrance and lustre to her blonde hair. In a way, he thought, I'm damned because of this woman. I've betrayed my friends and abandoned my companions. What am I left with? Not even her affection. Just a certain degree of indulgence and a lot of contempt.

He watched her from anguished eyes, which slanted over his cheek-bones because of the blood beating under his white skin. His face, once so chubby, was gaunt. This practised society ladykiller was the victim of a little blonde. But pride prevented him from making the slightest move. Better to suffer a thousand deaths than to beg the least favour. He was condemned to admire her in silence and gradually sink deeper into despair.

When they had finished their meal Amédée got to his feet, but Cosette did not stand up immediately. She tilted her head to one side with an embarrassed air. Amédée saw the pearly tips of her white teeth between her lips.

'Wait a moment,' said Cosette. Amédée placed his hat on the table and sat down again. 'I have a confession to make, Marquis. But first of all, are you really my friend?'

'May my heart stop beating now if I'm not,' he replied, at once moved and intrigued. Revolted by a world that conspired against the most noble instincts and the purest sympathies, he thought for a moment that Cosette was going to tell him that they were two poor lost souls drawn together by fate, who might yet learn to love.

What Cosette, in fact, said was not quite what Amédée had been expecting, though to his ears there was a certain similarity. 'I can no longer bear to live in the house in the Rue Plumet,' she declared in a faltering voice. 'It reminds me constantly of Marius. But the worst of it is that every day I'm forced to confront the one thing I've been trying so hard to avoid and can't avoid any longer – the truth. The truth is the revenge of the dead on the living. I shall never see Marius again and that's it. It's not a bad dream, it's simply the truth. Having inherited a little of my father's strength, I don't want to imagine how far down I could go.'

'And what do you plan to do?' asked Amédée, with some trepidation.

'To move as soon as possible. I can't keep my despair alive much longer. The memory of that house in the Rue Plumet and the sweet sensations that it brought, made up of expectations and desires, are whirling in my head like grains of sand in a gale. Those grains of sand are my memories. My decision is irrevocable.'

'I understand,' said Amédée, thinking of Marius's letter. 'I'll take care of it. Do you have anything in mind?'

'I leave that to you. These past weeks you've proved to me what a dear friend you are.' She looked at him. The idea of taking revenge on Amédée had not left her. She would play with him as he had played with Marius.

The marquis's face lit up. He did not believe in justice, but his dread of the irreparable had just lessened slightly.

Once outside the restaurant, Cosette turned to him with a slightly ironic smile. 'I have another secret to tell you, Amédée,' she said. 'But not now.'

'So have I,' he replied.

He drove her home in his tilbury.

It would have been an exaggeration to say that Javert had changed radically since his failed suicide – which, far from being a failure, he now considered a success. A policeman remains a policeman. He needs to be on the lookout, to ferret, to investigate, to poke his nose where nobody else will. He was still tenacious and stubborn, even though his stubbornness was now directed against the ideas that he had abandoned. His convictions, whether justified or not, still required a certain degree of fanaticism. It was the business of his soul – almost its essence.

And his soul was anxious. He was wondering if Cosette might not be falling under the Marquis d'Iguerande's thumb. He thought him a pretentious young man, far too witty and far too elegant. As for me, he told himself, I've never been elegant or witty. I've been fighting a crusade against the uncertainties of a world in decline. Now this declining world makes me feel uncertain. How could I be elegant and witty in such circumstances?

So, in order to be less uncertain, he decided to investigate the Clan Destin and the origins of the little marquis. He would go about it rigorously, for he was a rational man. It was enough to see him arrange his books, dust his familiar objects, fold his linen, polish his shoes with egg, brush his hat, eat his soup, or even peel his orange, to be convinced of that. He was fanatical about detail.

It was this Verjat who went one evening to the Rue Aubry-le-Boucher, disguised as a man of the people.

When he reached the end of the street, he took a black band from his pocket, removed his cap and tied the band around his head so that it covered one eye and made him look like a pirate. Then he put his cap back on and went looking for the sign of the Clan Destin. He could not find it. A number of fine carriages – a cabriolet, two tilburys, and even a pretty phaeton with black wheels – were parked at the corner of the Rue Saint-Martin and the Rue Aubry-le-Boucher. Further on, towards the Rue Saint-Denis, elegant couples strolled in the pale light of the street lamps. The summer weather was mild enough for walking. The alleys almost inspired confidence. There was a feeling of safety.

Verjat appeared pensive. He was remembering this same district two years earlier. The riots in Saint-Antoine . . . The barricade in the Rue de la Chanvrerie . . . Enjolras condemning him, Inspector Javert, to death for being a spy . . . And then Jean Valjean intervening, pistol in hand, claiming the honour of executing Javert himself . . . Jean Valjean had drawn a knife from his fob . . .

'A knife!' Javert had cried. 'You're right. That's more your style . . .'

Jean Valjean had cut the martingale that Javert had about his neck, the ropes he had on his wrists, then, stooping, the cord that bound his feet . . .

'You're free, Javert.'

And Jean Valjean had discharged the pistol in the air . . .

Verjat took a deep breath. That had been the start of everything – the start of his doubts. Jean Valjean, who could have taken his revenge, had let him escape. He had even deceived the insurgents and the Republicans into thinking he had executed him. Why? Verjat had never known. But doubt had intruded into his world, depriving him of his old certainties. He had nothing left but impressions – and gratitude.

He walked the length of the Rue Aubry-le-Boucher. There was no sign of the Clan Destin. As he came back in the opposite direction, his attention was caught by a flowery sign swinging from a wrought-iron bracket, on which figured the name the Chat-Malin. It was an inn and clearly one with a hand-picked clientele.

Verjat approached one of the windows and glanced in. The interior was rustic in style, with polished hexagonal floor tiles, a wooden counter, a dresser with flasks like those in a pharmacy and two sideboards framing a fireplace in which the fire had not been lit. People were dining at farmhouse tables lit by candles. The whitewashed walls were covered with agricultural implements. The waitresses appeared charming. Verjat was surprised. This place was nothing like the dive described by the Marquis d'Iguerande. He needed to be sure.

He opened the door of the inn and entered. His nose caught immediately the smell of shallots boiled in red wine. The room was full. No cut-throats or disreputable individuals here. Everything smelled clean and new.

'Does Monsieur want anything?'

Verjat had not seen the man approach him. He was tall and thin, wearing an impeccably cut black suit, and it was clear from his behaviour that he was the manager, perhaps even the owner.

'Do you have a table?'

Seeing Verjat's eye-patch and smock, he gave a caustic chuckle. 'We're full, my friend.'

Verjat liked neither his tone nor his critical stare. The man had an emaciated face and a pointed chin. His leaden features were shameless. There was something both penetrating and nonchalant about his gaze. His eyes held the smugness of a man whose daily needs were satisfied, but they also had a satanic gleam.

'Has there been a change of owner?' asked Verjat, noting in passing that this serpent-faced man wore his hair long and gathered back in an old-fashioned bow.

'Indeed there has,' replied the other, in an icy tone. 'And I regret to have to inform you that we no longer welcome persons of your class in this establishment.'

'So this inn is no longer the Clan Destin?'

The man assumed a superior air. 'Didn't you read the sign outside? You don't see very well with your one eye, my friend. This is the Chat-Malin.'

'And who's the owner?'

'You're very curious,' replied the man, with a grimace. 'Come on, my friend, go back to where you came from, or I'll have to call my people.' And he gestured to him to leave.

In front of the kitchen stood a big red-headed man in a gilded waistcoat and a kitchen boy armed with a club. Verjat did not resist and was walked to the door with the civility appropriate to what this place had become. 'This is an inn for respectable people,' the manager said, as he opened the door. 'So take a running jump, one-eye.'

'I'm sorry, Monsieur,' muttered Verjat. 'I must have made a mistake. I won't come back.'

Once outside, he vowed to return to the Chat-Malin as soon as possible.

He appeared at the restaurant two days later dressed in his smartest clothes – a black frock coat and a sky-blue cravat. He was greeted respectfully and shown to a table. He ordered stuffed mushrooms, rabbit chasseur and a carafe of Burgundy. The manager was extremely affable. While not going so far as to engage the new customer in conversation, he nevertheless detailed the specialities of the menu with the mastery of a true chef. 'We have a scientific cuisine. I myself have been a scientist and cooking owes a lot to chemistry. Quite simply, I have the nose for it.'

Verjat found the meal very satisfactory. When he had finished, he congratulated the very man who had shown him the door two days earlier. 'I shall return. Your scientific food is excellent. May I know your name, so that I can recommend this place to my friends?'

The man approached Verjat, intrigued by his smell, a musty smell reminiscent of oranges and old prayer books, not unlike that of the one-eyed man the other night. It must be a coincidence, he thought. He bowed. 'My name is Gérard, Monsieur,' he said, softening his gaze. 'Just like the artist who painted Marshal Murat, and just like the marshal of France who has been appointed prime minister.'

Verjat paid the bill and stood up. 'Well, Monsieur Gérard, you'll see me again at the Chat-Malin.'

The man pouted with satisfaction. His mouth drooped slightly to the right, indicating a corrupt and mendacious character. 'All our customers become regulars,' he replied, swelling with pride and with a glint in his eye – a glint made the more disturbing by the fact that his general manner was indolent and easy-going, as if he was anxious not to reveal the terrible prejudices he must have about people and events. 'And whom have I had the honour of welcoming this evening?' he asked, as he walked Verjat to the door.

'Monsieur Moreau,' lied Verjat.

'Well, I hope to see you soon, Monsieur Moreau.'

Verjat nodded and went out, not unhappy to have borrowed that name, as Jean Valjean had borrowed the name Madeleine at Montreuil-sur-Mer. Wasn't he following in his footsteps?

Verjat dined at the Chat-Malin almost every night. He always ate the same thing and never felt tempted to risk another dish. Gérard was always very polite to him, though the centre parting that cleaved Monsieur Moreau's greying hair made him smile. He had become a regular. When he arrived – always at the same time – the red-headed man in the gilded waistcoat he had seen that first night would welcome him with a 'Good evening', and when he left – also at the same time – he would bid him 'Goodnight'. Those were the only words he spoke. Verjat wondered what his role was.

'He's responsible for service and security,' explained Gérard. 'The district has a bad reputation, Monsieur Moreau, but you've seen the kind of clientele we attract. I must assure these people of a modicum of security. You never know. For instance, only the other evening I had to refuse admission to one of the bandits who abound in this district. A one-eyed man. A one-eyed man who smelled of oranges, Monsieur Moreau. Rather like you. Amusing, isn't it?'

'Oh, so you noticed?' replied Verjat, untroubled. 'Monsieur Gérard, allow me to say that you really do have a nose. You could have made a fortune in the perfume business.'

'I have thought of it, Monsieur Moreau.'

Gérard was reassured and Verjat was warned.

The red-headed man was known as Tricot. He grew more and more interested in Verjat and a sort of friendship sprang up between them. Their conversations, cursory at first, limited to the proprieties and the smooth running of the service, soon grew more extensive. They often chatted about money and those who had it. It was a subject that fascinated Tricot. Verjat noticed how obtuse he was in his judgements and how limited in his intelligence. But he was talkative, and as Verjat wanted to find out more about how the Clan Destin had been miraculously transformed into the Chat-Malin, he flattered Tricot, now complimenting him on the way the service was organized, now complimenting him on the quality of the clientele – and always coming back to the subject of money.

'I was the one who chose the waitresses,' Tricot would reply. 'As for the customers, they were the ones who chose me. I make the rich cough up.'

To hear him, he was responsible for everything. Needless to say, Gérard did not look kindly on the complicity that had sprung up between these two ill-matched individuals. But what could he do about it?

After a month Verjat had a reserved place and his own napkin. His table stood at the foot of a stepladder laden with sheaves of hay, dried flowers and ears of corn, all arranged very artistically. This stepladder had once led to the sleeping quarters of the Clan Destin, which were now bricked up. It was at the far end of the room, sheltered from indiscreet glances.

Every evening Tricot would sit down at Verjat's table and have a liqueur. He could not have explained why, but he was fascinated by this austere man, who was different from him in every way. He appreciated the rare moments of relaxation he spent chatting with him. As for Verjat, he was openly pursuing his charm offensive, even telling Tricot that he would make an excellent manager and that he possessed human qualities that Gérard, though not entirely lacking in them, was far from equalling.

'Do you think so?'

'If I didn't think so, I wouldn't say so.'

Tricot's infatuation with Verjat was such that he insisted on serving him in person, even though he knew nothing of his present or past activities. On this point, the two men were on an equal footing. They knew practically nothing about each other. The only difference was that Verjat impressed Tricot, while the opposite was not the case.

One evening, when the restaurant was full, Tricot came to Verjat's table earlier than usual. The candle flames threw long reflections on the silvery, bell-shaped lids of the dishes. The faceted crystals glittered palely, covered in pink steam. It was an atmosphere suitable for confidences. Sufficient time having passed to give a perspective to memories, Verjat judged that the moment had come to ask Tricot a few questions.

'You're stealing work from the charming Proserpine,' he joked when Tricot brought him his rabbit chasseur.

Proserpine was one of the waitresses. There were three waitresses in all – like Macbeth's witches. They wore red dresses with white kerchiefs knotted around their heads. Slightly languid in manner, although efficient and diligent, they had the peculiarity of not being very talkative, with the exception of Proserpine, a redhead with a long pointed nose, whose green eyes and swooping décolletage troubled more than one of the gentlemen who frequented the Chat-Malin.

'I'm not stealing anything,' replied Tricot, with the falsely wheedling air of the truly sullen. 'That kind of girl has no difficulty in supplementing her salary.'

'Do you mean to tell me that charming girl is a strumpet?' asked Verjat, inviting Tricot to sit down.

'I'll say! A real whore. It was Gérard who picked her. If it was just up to me, I'd sort it all out.'

'Oh!' said Verjat, keeping a close watch on his interlocutor. 'It's quite simply an inheritance from the previous establishment.'

'Did you know the Clan Destin?'

'A little,' lied Verjat.

Tricot banged on the table with his fist, and glanced to right and left. 'I kept telling myself your face was familiar,' he said in a low voice. 'So you knew the great days?'

'Somewhat sombre days.'

Tricot put his elbows on the table and brought his face closer to Verjat's. 'You came here?' he asked, with a conspiratorial air.

'Yes, but you mustn't tell anyone. I'm respectable now. Butter wouldn't melt in my mouth.'

'And what did you steal?'

'Rocks.'

'Diamonds? Bloody hell! And are you still at it?'

'Indirectly. Look at this.' Verjat took his eye-patch out of his pocket and covered his face with a rapid and precise gesture.

'The one-eyed man the other night? That was you?'

'That's right,' replied Verjat. It was clear that in revealing himself to be part of the same brotherhood of schemers and villains, he had immediately won Tricot's trust. 'But these days I only work occasionally. I'm getting a bit long in the tooth for all that.'

'I was never involved in anything too big,' said Tricot. 'I never found myself having to steal things or bump anyone off to make ends meet.'

As Tricot was too stupid to be a good liar, Verjat deduced that all that he was claiming not to have done – that is, rob and kill – he had done. His antipathy was all the stronger. 'So you don't have any dirty linen?'

Tricot guffawed. 'My only problem is having enough linen. Let's just say I'm like you – I have a good front and I make other people graft for me.'

'In other words, you're a pimp?'

'Like you said, I know a thing or two. The rozzer who throws me in the clink hasn't been born yet. I have standing, believe me. But talking of diamonds, here's something that'll interest you. It so happens that my associate – an old rogue by the way, as tight-fisted as they come – has found a curious way to keep his stones safe. One of the kids I work with told me.'

'You have children working for you?'

Tricot frowned. 'Why? Do you have anything against it?'

Verjat bit his lip. 'Good heavens, no! Anyway, what does it matter what I think? You're not obliged to tell me everything. But I'll have you know I consider you a friend.'

'And me you,' said Tricot, immediately relaxing and proud to have a friend.

'Tell me a bit of your story,' said Verjat. 'I'm sure it must be fascinating.'

With idiots of Tricot's kind, it is enough to make them feel confident and not argue with them too much, and they become inexhaustible. Like the alcoholic, the rogue seeks accomplices. Such was the case with Tricot. He needed to shine.

'Well, the old man loaded the stones in a hunting rifle and shot them into the wall. A layer of whitewash on top, and the work was done. Out of sight, out of mind.'

'Extraordinary,' said Verjat. 'But a taste for the extraordinary is sometimes a characteristic of mediocrity.'

'Why do you say that?' asked Tricot, taking his elbows off the table.

'I didn't say it, it was Diderot.'

'Diderot? Who's he?'

'The man who said it. And this same Diderot could help you to find a way to get hold of those stones.'

'No, no, don't even think about it.'

'Yes, of course we should. He's not very clever, this associate of yours. If he were, you wouldn't even know about the stones.'

'You're right. I hadn't thought of that. We have to study the problem.'

'I quite agree.'

Suddenly, as Verjat glanced towards the counter, his gaze froze. A man dressed in a caped coat and a fur hat was talking to Gérard. Verjat never forgot a face. And the face he saw, with its wrinkled and hollowed brow, its beak-like nose and its bright, prying eyes, a face full of cowardice and dissimulation, was Thénardier's, a man he had once arrested. He could still see him in the Gorbeau tenement on the Boulevard de l'Hôpital, with his six accomplices. Just as he had been about to get his hands on him, Thénardier had resisted. He had even pulled out a pistol and fired at him. The shot had missed. Police officers armed with clubs and truncheons had burst in and tied up the bandits, and the whole lot of them – Thénardier at their head – had been put inside. That was the day that Javert, without knowing it, had narrowly missed Jean Valjean, who had been a prisoner of Jondrette, alias Thénardier, and had escaped through a skylight. The rope ladder was still shaking when Javert had approached. He remembered the words he had spoken.

'Damn! That must have been the best of them.'

He had taken the whole gang to La Force. At that time the prison of La Force had been in the Rue Culture-Sainte-Catherine, now the Rue de Sévigné. Thénardier was later to escape from it with the help of his son, Gavroche.

Verjat stared at Thénardier for a long time. What a small world this is, he thought, unmoved. Gérard pointed in his direction, and he lowered his head. He was sure Thénardier was looking at him. He reflected. He thought about Marius and Cosette, and about all the things that had taken place in the Clan Destin and had been swept under the carpet. Thénardier must have been in on it. Verjat was certain he had a lead. He was barely listening to Tricot. When he looked up again, Thénardier had disappeared.

'You were saying?' he asked Tricot.

'I was saying we could be a great team, you and me. By the way, you can call me the Mullet, if you like.'

'All right, Mullet. It's a deal. Let's drink to our association.'

The two men lifted their glasses and drank them down in one go.

'What if we fail?' asked the Mullet in a low voice.

'Elegance, my dear Mullet, sometimes consists in disguising one's victories as defeats.'

'You're amazing! Look, I have to go now. They need me at the counter. I can see Gérard getting impatient. The other evening, he told me off for spending too much time with you. If only he knew! When shall we meet again?'

'Perhaps tomorrow,' replied Verjat, who wanted to keep an aura of mystery around himself.

'Anyway you know where to find me.'

'I know,' muttered Verjat, his death's-head face a picture of approval and satisfaction.

When Amédée told his steward that Baroness Pontmercy had asked him to sell the Rue Plumet house for her and find other accommodation, Louis-Désiré smiled satisfiedly. The thought that Amédée had finally made use of the letter took root in his mind.

'I congratulate the marquis on his powers of persuasion. And, if the marquis will allow me, it will be a pleasure for me to help him in his search to find a fitting place for the baroness.'

'And myself,' added Amédée.

The steward stared at him in surprise. 'I beg your pardon, Monsieur?'

'I intend to put our wretched mansion in the Rue de la Cerisaie on the market as well as the house in the Rue Plumet, my dear Louis-Désiré.'

'Does that mean the marquis intends to wed the baroness?'

'Steady on, my friend. There's absolutely no question of my suggesting anything of the sort to Cosette and, besides, she'd never consent. She's become a close friend. Need I remind you that it's only a few months since Marius died and that I must maintain a certain reserve?'

The steward immediately thought of the letter. The damned fool still hadn't used it. He'd been too much of a gentleman. 'I don't doubt it,' he replied, squirming. 'But what is this about?'

'I haven't yet told Cosette about the letter Marius gave me,' said Amédée, looking murderous. 'To tell the truth, I find the idea repellent. I've even thought of destroying it.'

Louis-Désiré's nostrils dilated. 'Cast such a thought from your mind, Monsieur,' he said immediately, at once insistent and exasperated. 'To destroy that letter would be tantamount to destroying the baroness. Do you secretly want to see her decline and neglect what she cannot do herself? All these money problems are deadly dull for a young woman. A woman is made to spend money, not to manage it. To add this burden to the already painful one of her husband's death would be criminal.'

'You may be right,' admitted Amédée, although he was irritated by his steward's advice, finding it almost too good. Feigning a profound sadness, he touched Louis-Désiré's hump lightly. 'I hope this will bring me luck.'

'I hope so, too,' said the steward through gritted teeth.

Amédée walked around the ground floor, where the satins and the laces no longer had the sheen they had once had. He turned and raised his hands to heaven. 'I shan't miss anything here!' he cried, without knowing what Louis-Désiré was getting at, thinking naively that he was quite simply attached to the walls and his habits.

No, he would not miss the time he had spent in this mansion. There was nothing really mansion-like about it. He would not miss the little library that led to the smoking room, the gaming room where the Erard piano had pride of place, the piano he never used and which Liszt himself, one evening, had not deigned to touch with his august hands. Nor would he miss his room, so old-fashioned in its arrangement and decoration, with its mirrors and its gilding and its big, dusty bed, which he had shared only with strumpets – with the possible exception of Clémence.

'No, no regrets!' he cried, thinking that Cosette would surely hate this confined place, which for him was synonymous with a time gone by. 'The devil take habits and conformity, my dear Louis-Désiré!'

Amédée thought again of Clémence. He did not miss her either, but in bidding farewell to this house he felt as though he was bidding farewell to the only thing that still attached him to her. Poor Clémence. He had given her neither a name nor a fortune. He had never been able to satisfy her. He had even forced her into Marius's arms. Yet she was the only woman who had truly loved him. And what had he done? He had spurned her. And the child? He had never really worried about it. He had let Louis-Désiré take care of it. Louis-Désiré always took care of things.

All things considered, he said to himself, Clémence had charm. And that slight melancholy caused by the inevitable disappointments of life made her all the more lovable. If we had had that child, we might not be in this position now.

At the sight of his steward's face, as blank as marble, he felt angry. He's always taken himself for my father, he ruminated. He's the cause of all my failures. He's always hoped that I would be the way he wanted me to be. I hate him.

And yet, a moment earlier, he had been pleased with Louis-Désiré's wise advice. But who had taken care of Clémence's stillborn child, who had organized the evenings at the Clan Destin, who had managed this house, who had seen to so many other things? Wasn't Louis-Désiré behind it all?

He raised his hands over his steward's head, as if about to place a terrible curse on him. 'I don't want you involved any more in my personal affairs, do you understand? I'm not a child any more! If my father were still alive, he'd be only too pleased to tell you himself! I curse the day he was killed at the Battle of Essling!'

Louis-Désiré lowered his head respectfully, but his pride was terribly wounded. It was all Cosette's fault. He was seething with rage. He would deal with the silly girl soon. She would be got rid of, just as her conceited husband had been. He took two steps back and considered his master with a curious look. Amédée's countenance was still arrogant, his agitation incessant, and his manner of mocking everything irrepressible. But the hunter had become his own victim. The strong man had become the weak. It was a transformation that made Louis-Désiré indignant. Cosette must be made to pay for it – and the sooner the better.

Affairs moved very quickly. The house in the Rue Plumet was sold to a banker from the Chaussée-d'Antin, who lived in it for two months before letting it out. The mansion in the Rue de la Cerisaie fell into the hands of a well-to-do shopkeeper from the Rue des Deux-Portes. In that period of political uncertainty – in which two thousand Republicans had been arrested, four thousand witnesses were to be heard, and the file on April's abortive insurrection contained two thousand documents – there was a general feeling of indecision and inertia. In order to keep going and compensate for this monotony, the rich bought houses for no other reason than for the sheer pleasure of buying. They not only bought, they speculated and resold. The poor, as usual, paid for all this chaos and bad management. Quite simply, incompetence and short-sightedness triumphed, a short-sightedness as vast as the desert in Algeria to which people attached so much importance. There were hundreds more sharks and usurers than there had been, even under the Restoration, when the number of arrogant little tyrants whose dealings could only be called shameless had risen enormously.

As for Louis-Philippe, the king of a bourgeoisie cut off from the people, the king of the financial dynasties – the Schneiders, the Wendels, the Periers, the Rothschilds – he limited himself to lambasting the Republican ideal.

He was, in fact, quite a likeable man, this monarch supported by the duettists Thiers and Guizot. But so bourgeois with his cone-shaped cotton bonnet and his obscene plans for redeveloping Paris . . . Everyone felt the same. Obviously not the grand bourgeoisie which had replaced the old aristocracy, but the petty bourgeoisie, the class which included tradesmen and the liberal professions, the hot-tempered class whose taxes were not high enough for it to be part of the electorate, let alone the electable, the class that was a political force in search of a role, the phalanx of the Republicans, the descendants of those who had guillotined Guizot's father.

'This sinister protestant is haunted by the horror of disorder,' wrote *La Tribune*. 'Together he and Louis-Philippe make for certain boredom.'

Economic prosperity, however, had returned. With three hundred and twenty deputies supporting the government and fewer than a hundred in opposition, the autumn of 1834 would smell of dead leaves, ministerial instability and the victory of capitalist society. It could not have been more different from the Empire. This was the triumph of mediocrity.

As one might suspect, Amédée – unlike his steward, who speculated a lot, and in the least brilliant circles – was completely untouched by the surrounding inertia, to which he continued to display a fierce indifference. He was a libertarian who hated the left as much as the right. The aristocracy disappointed him, the bourgeoisie disgusted him, the common people left him indifferent. He hated Soult, that illustrious sword who was nothing but an illustrious scabbard, de Broglie, that pomaded old duffer whose mind moved at a no more exalted level than his silk stockings, and Cavaignac, that Fouquier-Tinville in miniature who dreamed of cutting off heads. He hated even more the thought of talking about them. He hated everything.

He found an old mansion in the Rue Saint-Fiacre, with balustrades and mullioned windows. Neither very sumptuous nor very pretty, the house at least had the merit of not being too expensive and of being located not far from the Opéra and Saint-Denis. When he told Cosette about the purchase, her first reaction was indifference, her second was to reject it outright. This was understandable enough, since what the marquis was proposing was no more or less than that she live under the same roof as him, though he hastened to add that the three levels, joined by a wide stone staircase, were quite independent.

'Each in his own home,' explained Amédée. 'You on the second floor, me on the first. Or the contrary if you wish. And the top floor for my steward and your maid.'

After a few days' hesitation, Cosette agreed. The purchase was concluded, the notarized deeds recorded. She did not even inform her friends. At the same time, she asked Amédée to sell the furniture bought by Marius, the rosewood chest of drawers and the Louis XIII chairs as well as the backgammon table and the Louis XV wall clock. She kept only what she had inherited from her father: the Coromandel lacquer chest, the Aubusson tapestries, the canopied bed and, of course, the two candlesticks. Amédée asked his steward to take care of the sale. Thanks to his contacts among the merchants of Saint-Antoine, he made a substantial profit on the transaction.

In the house in the Rue Plumet, or more precisely in the garden, the little bench remained in place and the fragments of the two statues were left where they had fallen. On the day she left, Cosette did not give them a second glance. Seeing her face in a mirror, she was surprised that it was so smooth. She took down the mirror and threw it to the floor angrily. Never had her eyes been bigger, bluer or deeper. Madeleine could not fail to notice and held Amédée's influence responsible.

'Never say that again!' Cosette threatened.

It might even have been thought that something more subtle was transforming her. Nothing was further from the truth. Her features belied the torment she felt at this break from her past. That was why she had broken the mirror in a rage. It had irritated her to see her face looking so pure.

In abandoning the Rue Plumet, only one thing warmed her heart – the prospect of having a child. After first hating it, as if the foetus had been responsible for Marius's death, she now longed for it. If it was a girl, she would call her Fantine – if it was a boy, Jean.

In her apartment in the Rue Saint-Fiacre, Cosette placed her father's candlesticks on the black marble mantelpiece, the dominant element in the drawing room with its sombre mouldings. Settling into her bedroom, she thought of Marius, of his clothes which had been given to the Daughters of Charity in the Rue du Bac, of his personal possessions sold to the highest bidder. That was what death was like. The disappearance of everything. The one thing she had kept was the rock crystal. She had no taste for relics.

During the first few days, Amédée was tactful enough not to come to the second floor. He was afraid of exposing himself to Cosette's reprimands, her melancholy, her rancour. The move had taken place in haste. One day, despite everything, he took his courage in both hands and presented himself at the Baroness Pontmercy's with Marius's letter. 'This is the secret I wanted to tell you about,' he said hesitantly, his heart in his boots as he handed the letter to Cosette.

She was busy sewing cushions for her bedroom. Amédée noticed her white nails, almond-shaped and polished like ivory. At the sight of her long pale hands, which moved like obedient workwomen, he winced slightly. So everything about this woman is perfect, he thought. He had lost all hope of ever kissing those beautiful hands, those slender fingers smelling of lemon and green tea.

He trembled as Cosette boldly skimmed the letter and her face fell and her eyes gradually filled with shock and sadness. She handed it back to Amédée. Then, taking up her work again as if nothing had happened, she pricked her finger, gave a little cry, and lifted her finger to her mouth to suck it. This vision troubled Amédée so much that he felt weak at the knees. He stood there with the letter in his hand, unable to utter a word.

'So I'm at your mercy?' asked Cosette, without even looking at him.

'Don't think like that!' he cried. 'This letter's yours if you want it. I have all the notary's papers concerning the sale of your house – they're yours too. Didn't you ask me to take charge of the sale? I did that while you still knew nothing of this letter.'

'That's true,' admitted Cosette, lifting her head proudly. 'But your secret's not very pleasant to hear. Or rather to read,' she corrected herself, looking at the letter, which Amédée still held in his hand.

'In any case, as you've seen, this letter will be invalid after two years. I'd like to point out to you that it was I who insisted that Marius append that rider to the letter.'

'Was he so desperate, then?'

'Yes, because he loved you too much, Cosette.'

'I don't believe you.'

'And yet it's the truth,' lied Amédée, folding the letter and putting it back in its envelope. 'But sometimes one is afraid of not living up to a great love. One blames one's fate the better to reconcile oneself to it. He loved you to distraction, Cosette.'

'How solemn you are,' she said, amused at his embarrassment. 'Are you sure you aren't talking about yourself?'

'Absolutely not. Marius thought you were granting your favours to Frédéric Rivolier.'

'Frédéric wasn't my lover, if that's what you want to know!' retorted Cosette, glaring at Amédée. 'He was a friend!'

Amédée blushed slightly. The story had always bothered him, and not even killing Frédéric in a duel had brought him rest. Now, realizing how stupid his jealousy had been, he was stricken with remorse. He hated himself for having offended Marius, then Cosette. Now, in insisting on Marius's love for Cosette, he was deliberately wounding himself as if to punish himself for his mistake.

Cosette threw him a devilish smile and stuck her needle in a ball of silk. Despite her friendly feelings towards Amédée, she would continue to treat him roughly as he had treated everybody roughly. She was even discovering gifts as an actress. 'Keep the letter,' she said, feigning resignation. 'You'll make better use of it than I. You have my trust, Amédée.'

The marquis made a slight bow. 'I'm honoured, Cosette. But never say again that you're at my mercy. A victim is someone who sees everything the wrong way round, like the devil. Let's not be victims. We've both known the joy of living. Now that Marius is dead, let's not transform it into the joy of dying. We're not enemies, Cosette. At any rate, as far as I'm concerned, we are no longer enemies.'

Cosette stood up and went to the window, which looked out onto a dark courtyard. On the ground floor a stable led to a paved courtyard with a simple little fountain and a tree, an elm, surrounded by geraniums.

'It's rather sad here,' she said, scratching the window.

She was in profile. Her belly had become rounder, he had noticed.

'All places are sad for lonely souls,' murmured Amédée. 'We need to take our minds off things. Allow me to invite you out to dinner this evening.'

She moved back from the window and brushed against him. She assumed a despondent expression. 'Perhaps you're right – we need to take our minds off things.'

4

The Catman visited the Chat-Malin twice a week, though he never lingered. He would stay just long enough to check the accounts, talk to Gérard and give the Mullet his orders.

One evening he was approached by a man with curly, pomaded hair, a neat waist, a woman's hips, a flower in his buttonhole and a club sticking out of his pocket. The Catman was standing at the counter when the man called out to him. The Catman pretended not to recognize him, but the man caught him by the collar.

'What's the matter?' he whispered in his ear. 'Don't you recognize me? It's Lacenaire. Don't play games with me or I'll tear your guts out. I'm just out of prison and I don't have a lot of time. Where's Jesus?'

The Catman feigned surprise. 'Didn't you know? He's in Toulon. They sent him away for twenty years.'

Lacenaire stiffened. After his recent failures with Vigouroux, the owner of the Bon Sens, and Scribe, the author of *Bertrand et Raton*, which had spelled the death blow to his literary ambitions, this was the last straw. He let go of the Catman. 'Damn it,' he said. 'I need to recoup my losses.'

'Well, I'm in debt,' replied the Catman, with a fatalistic gesture. 'But I've got a better idea. Come this way.' Under Gérard's suspicious gaze, he led Lacenaire to the kitchen door and ordered him a lemonade. 'It's as easy as pie. You just have to deal with bank messengers. You draw a false draft on a fictitious person who's renting an apartment, and when the bank messenger appears, you bump him off and pocket the loot with no risk of getting nabbed. I've heard the Pillet-Will and Rougement de Lowenberg banks are in funds. For you, it'll be a walkover.'

Lacenaire nodded silently, his handkerchief in his hand, as if enjoying a bitter pleasure of which he considered himself the advocate. He drank his lemonade and threw the glass to the ground. A waitress ran to pick up the pieces – he did not even glance at her.

'Sounds fine. We'll look into it. But I give you two months. Let's meet at the Ogre de Barbarie in the Rue aux Fers. Five o'clock sharp. Don't force me to come and get you here. And in the meantime you'll have to offer me something else. Something solid.'

'You can trust me,' mewed the Catman, walking him to the door.

He had gained time. But Lacenaire had become an obstacle, and in two months he would have to get rid of this obstacle once and for all.

It was seven o'clock in the Café de Paris, and people scented with vanilla and bay were gently idling their lives away in inconsequential conversation. Their subjects were horsemen, puce silk coats, the Prince de Wagram's carriages and horses, the race meetings at the Champ-de-Mars, the Jockey Club, Lord Seymour's wardrobe, an evening at the Tivoli where Lord Bury had won a twenty-thousand-franc chicken at clay pigeon shooting, the presence of the king's three young sons at the Chantilly racecourse, and the Renaissance-style palace Monsieur de Rothschild had built for himself in the Rue Lafitte.

From where Cosette and Amédée sat in the middle of the room, they could see and hear everything. Some fashionable women were wearing damask scarves, poults-de-soie scattered with little bouquets, bodices gathered at the waist, and white muslin skirts that swung, bell-like, as they walked. Others covered their shoulders with black silk mantlets decorated with lace, which showed off their waists and necks. These women were mostly young, but they hid their faces under hats covered with ribbons, long feathers and ears of corn. The men were dressed in the French style, with gold buttons, which were then the height of fashion. They wore either black tailcoats moulded over their hips, or tea-green or apple-green frock coats. This was insignificance in evening dress.

At one table sat Eugène Sue and Balzac, at another Alexandre Dumas and Victor Hugo. Amédée greeted Eugène Sue, who was drinking a lot of punch, and pointed out to Cosette the author of *Hernani*, who was listening as Dumas told him about his debts, his mistresses and his new play. A little further away, Monsieur Véron and Monsieur Romieu could be seen commenting on the latest performances at the Opéra.

'It's all positively derisory,' said Amédée. Setting foot back in his once preferred territory, he was rediscovering his old linguistic mannerisms.

'Positively – are you sure?' asked Cosette ironically.

'I'm incorrigible!' cried Amédée, as excited as a young girl. He forced himself to calm down. 'Marius and I often used to come here for an orangeade or a smoked tea after our exercise at the fencing school, which is just near here. Did you know that being admitted to the Café de Paris makes you a certified Parisian?'

'No, I didn't know. I'm positively stunned, Marquis.'

'You're making fun of me, Cosette.'

'Do you think so?'

Amédée smiled. He loved to be teased by Cosette. But Cosette did not care about that. All she wanted was to see the places that Marius had frequented and charm Amédée with her apparent gaiety. Amédée, for his part, had to do what he had always despised and pretend – pretend to be happy, pretend to be completely satisfied with life, pretend to share a true complicity with another human being.

He ordered a sweet white wine from the Pau region and two foies gras garnished with truffles, followed by red rock partridges, birds lauded, he explained, by Cyrano de Bergerac, Nostradamus and Grimod de la Reynière, who believed that they should only be tasted on one's knees.

'You should have been a chef,' Cosette joked.

Lifting his nose and his eyebrows with a mixture of superiority and vanity, Amédée explained the best way to cook partridge. He had been given the recipe by Lord Seymour's mother, the Marchioness of Hertford, a miserly and cantankerous old hag who owned the Café de Paris and had decided it should close at ten o'clock every night.

Amédée's description of how the rock partridges were roasted in butter, stuffed with foie gras, truffles and cognac, then soaked in two spoonfuls of fresh cream and a half-glass of madeira, did not greatly interest Cosette. She heard him out because she was polite, but she barely listened, for even her politeness had limits.

At the end of the meal Amédée was still droning on, like a constant trickle of water. He had no idea how to deal with Cosette. Her face looked quarrelsome. The opulence disgusted her, her fellow diners' declamatory language tried her patience and their theatrical poses exasperated her.

She would have liked to slap Amédée, and spit in the faces of these conceited people who turned their backs on the poor. And to think that Marius had wasted his time in such a vacuous place!

She almost got up and left, but Amédée's imploring expression dissuaded her. Poor boy! Never had she had so much esteem for herself and so much contempt for him and his like. This little world dismayed her.

'This afternoon,' she said suddenly, cutting him off in mid-sentence, 'you told me your secret. Now it's my turn to tell you mine.'

She smiled ambiguously. A deadly numbness pinned Amédée to his chair. Forestalling Cosette, he silenced her with a gesture and took a thick envelope from his pocket. 'You may think me coarse, but I wanted things to be settled. It's all in thousand-franc notes. The proceeds from the sale of the Rue Plumet and its furniture.'

'I don't think this is the best moment.'

'I know. But I don't feel that you trust me entirely.'

'You're mistaken,' replied Cosette, taking the envelope. 'I trust you so much that I was anxious to tell you I'm pregnant. I'm carrying Marius's child.'

Amédée turned pale. His lips trembled and his eyes looked into a future that seemed to him entirely empty. He had, of course, noticed that Cosette had been getting rounder, but he had refused to face the truth.

'I'm very pleased,' he managed to utter. 'And when are you expecting this happy event?'

'Towards the end of September.'

'Well, we must make sure that you get the best treatment. If you have no objection, I request the honour of being godfather to Marius's child.'

'Granted,' said Cosette, amused at his embarrassment.

Amédée was hiding his true feelings. The news merely added to his sense of failure and exacerbated his wounded pride. He stood up, paid the bill and came back for Cosette. Then he walked quickly to the door, without saying goodbye to anyone. Pale and trembling, he put on his hat and suggested to Cosette that they go to the Café Turc. 'It's in the Boulevard du Temple. With my tilbury, we can get there in no time at all.'

'I know it,' said Cosette. 'I went there with Marius.'

Once there, they sat down near a kiosk. The Café Turc had become Amédée's headquarters. Cosette marvelled at the eastern decor, the fezzes and hookahs hanging round the walls. Delacroix felt quite at home here, among the bowers and arbours, said Amédée ironically. An orchestra was playing quadrilles. Amédée, having drunk three rums, now became voluble and started denouncing his country, which never stopped beating its breast, with its ideas that fed on renunciation and compromise, and its people, who only ever said what they were expected to say and took care never to say anything that drew attention to themselves.

'I shall nurse my solitude by making myself obnoxious,' he announced.

'It's already done,' Cosette joked.

He tried to take her hand.

'Oh, no!' she cried, recoiling violently.

Amédée was mortified. All he had wanted to do was kiss Cosette's hand and thank her for coming with him. He embarked on an explanation of his past behaviour, and began to apologize vaguely, being unable to invent anything better.

'Solitude has become my torturer, Cosette . . .'

And her solitude, what did he think of that?

He turned away and ordered another rum. Two men passed their table and congratulated him warmly. They were Louis de Vergne and Robert d'Androisy. Two grisettes were with them, loud and simpering, their shoulders covered with mantlets fastened with gothic medallions.

'So he's come back to life!' exclaimed Louis, cordially enough for Amédée not to be offended.

'And it looks as if he's making up for lost time,' added Robert, with a glance at Cosette bawdy enough for Amédée to take umbrage. It should be said in his defence that Cosette, in a spirit of provocation, had given him an intent, almost seductive look. Sowing discord among the people who had corrupted Marius delighted her.

'I beg your pardon?' growled Amédée. He had not forgotten Marius's hostility towards Robert d'Androisy. This time the insensitive fool had been insufferably rude. In Cosette's presence, Amédée felt as though he himself were Marius. 'I beg your pardon?' he repeated, staring at his former companion in vice.

'Robert was joking,' said Louis at once, trying to calm the situation.

But Amédée did not take it that way. 'Robert doesn't joke because Robert doesn't know what joking is.' With that, he stood up and slapped d'Androisy with the full force of his arm. 'Eight o'clock tomorrow morning in the Bois de Boulogne, Monsieur. I leave the choice of weapons to you.'

D'Androisy stood there, stunned, holding his cheek. He was no firebrand, but it was difficult to withdraw in the presence of so many witnesses. Cosette made as if to intervene, but Amédée stopped her imperiously. 'This gentleman has insulted your honour. I shall therefore defend that honour.'

It seemed to Cosette that she had gone too far. She knew only too well what disasters duels could bring. Quietly she begged Amédée to draw back from this folly.

'Certainly not, my dear.'

Robert d'Androisy, instead of apologizing, treated it all with an irony that made the encounter unavoidable. He had not wanted to insult anyone. He had merely been playing. But some games rebound on those who start them. 'In fighting for that honour, you will no doubt be fighting for the thing you lack most!' he exclaimed, hammering out his words.

'Get out of my sight, you swine!' cried Amédée, beside himself with rage, and he pointed towards the exit. 'It would take too long to list all the things you lack! In any case, where I'm going to send you, you won't need any of them!'

He turned his back on his old friends and sat down noisily. Louis and Robert immediately left, sheepish and dumbfounded, followed by the two grisettes, still simpering.

There followed a long silence, during which Amédée drank another two glasses of rum.

'What are you trying to prove, Amédée?' Cosette asked at last. 'That there's a good chance I'll lose another friend?'

'I'm not your friend. You despise me and you've proved it to me again. In any case, whatever happens to me, you'll still have your child to console you. There's no more to be said.'

They returned to the Rue Saint-Fiacre and their respective apartments without saying any more apart from the usual pleasantries.

The following day, at the agreed hour, the two adversaries met on the field. Louis again tried to mediate, but to no avail. Amédée's seconds were his steward and Eugène Sue, who would be able to exercise his talents as a surgeon if the need arose. Robert d'Androisy's seconds were Louis de Vergne and a penpusher on *La Quotidienne*. It was all being kept in the family. Deprived of the opportunity to make mincemeat of each other in battle, these idlers were finding another outlet for their heroic longings.

Placed thirty paces apart, the duellists had to fire when Louis de Vergne's handkerchief touched the ground. For the moment Louis was holding it in his outstretched hand. Robert and Amédée took aim and cocked their guns.

'My friend!' cried Robert d'Androisy, his legs unsteady.

'I have no more friends!' retorted Amédée.

The signal had not even been given when Robert fired. His bullet lodged in Amédée's left shoulder. Amédée fell to the ground on his side. Louis-Désiré rushed to him, moaning like an old woman. 'You're wounded, Marquis, you're wounded . . .'

Amédée pushed him away, somewhat roughly. Eugène Sue, who was already bending to examine his wound, received the same treatment. 'The fight isn't over!' protested Amédée, getting to his feet. 'What's more, Monsieur d'Androisy fired before the signal. That's typical of his cowardice.'

In a broken voice, Louis de Vergne confirmed that the duel had to continue. Sweating and trembling, Robert d'Androisy could barely stand upright. 'You're just like your friend Marius,' he stammered at Amédée, 'You're mad . . .'

Unsteady on his feet, his shoulder smashed, his face pale, Amédée took aim at his adversary and fired. His bullet hit Robert in the centre of the forehead, killing him outright. Robert fell with his arms in a cross.

'Marius is avenged,' murmured Amédée, collapsing in Eugène's arms.

'God be praised,' muttered Louis-Désiré in his corner, his face drained of colour. Thinking that the marquis's last hour had come, he had thought his own had come, too. As for Louis de Vergne, he no longer knew where his allegiance lay. It was as though he had lost two friends.

Amédée was taken back to the Rue Saint-Fiacre, where Eugène extracted the bullet from his shoulder and bandaged him up.

When the marquis opened his eyes again, Cosette was leaning over him. 'So, are you happy now? Let me watch over you.'

Amédée suddenly felt overjoyed. At the same time, he feared Cosette's changes of mind. She had never spared him. 'I'm thirsty,' he whispered.

'Would you like a glass of water?'

'No, an orange.'

Cosette asked Madeleine to fetch an orange. Suddenly, because of the orange, she thought of Verjat. She had not been in touch with him for a very long time. She remained lost in astonishment, conscious only of the blood beating in her arteries. What an ungrateful woman I am, she thought. Even if I avenge myself on Amédée and all his friends who stole Marius from me, this is no kind of example to set myself. What will Monsieur Verjat think of my indifference?

*

Verjat had thought nothing of it, for the good reason that he was too busy trying to cement his friendship with the Mullet – and succeeding beyond all expectation. The Mullet had invited him to visit the workshop.

'You'll see – there, I'm the boss.'

Verjat made the acquaintance of the Pointer, Madame Fouillet, Horse Face, Raphaël and the other children. The sight of these sickly and emaciated creatures revolted him, but he made no comment. Although his scepticism had inured him to the most repugnant and degenerate behaviour, he found the Mullet's spiteful vanity even more unbearable than usual, no less than his false arrogance. Verjat had tracked down and punished many men like him – cut-throats, rapists, murderers fearing neither God nor man – and he despised them all. Some of them, he had once believed, did not even deserve to live. At present, he believed nothing. Instinct had taken the place of his reason and nothing surprised him any more.

'Look around you, Moreau,' said the Mullet. 'One day all this will be mine. And I'm counting on you to get me there. We can share the spoils.'

When they left the workshop, the Mullet showed him the staircase that led to the Catman's lair.

'The Catman?' asked Verjat, feigning ignorance. 'Is that the old man I saw the other day at the Chat-Malin?'

'Did you see him?'

'He rushed in and out.'

'He's always rushing in and out. I hate him. The Catman, they call him – Tardier's his real name.'

Verjat suppressed a smile. Thénardier had clearly spent his life changing his name.

'It's up there, on the top floor.'

Verjat began climbing the stairs. The Mullet followed him, groaning, more than a little nervous.

When they reached the door, Verjat bent to examine the lock. He slid some wire into the hole, then looked up with an air of satisfaction. 'That's good,' he whispered. Raising his eyebrows and curling his lower lip, he looked at the Mullet with a terrible, almost ghostly expression.

'All . . . all right,' stammered the redhead, lowering his eyes in the attitude of a serf before his lord and master.

They went back downstairs.

'They must be worth a packet,' said the Mullet, once they were out in the street. 'Horse Face told me.'

'Is that the boy with the big jaw?'

'That's right. The Catman made the mistake of trusting him. Now I've got him eating out of my hand. We share a lot of little secrets.'

'Oh, yes?'

'Right now, the old man's a bit worried. And the reason he's worried is connected with the secrets I'm talking about. He had a right-hand man nicknamed Jesus, who kicked the bucket. And it was no accident – you can take my word for that. Two months ago Jesus's friend comes to ask the old man what had happened. This friend's name is Lacenaire. A real scorpion.'

'Well, well.'

'Why do you say, "Well, well"?'

'No reason ... When the wolves eat each other, we must take advantage.'

'My opinion exactly,' said the Mullet with a broad smile.

The two men separated at the corner of the Rue Saint-Martin, after agreeing to meet again the same evening at the Chat-Malin.

Late that afternoon, while he was talking to Father Rillet in the sacristy of Saint-Sulpice, Verjat saw Cosette behind the altar. He left the good father and walked towards her.

'Well, Cosette,' he said, in a falsely offended tone, 'where on earth have you been?'

Cosette looked guilty. 'You must think me very ungrateful, Monsieur Verjat. I've moved from the Rue Plumet to the Rue Saint-Fiacre and I didn't even let you know.'

'No, I don't hold it against you. I, too, have had many matters to deal with.'

They left the church and walked round the square. On the other side of the street a man in a smock stood watching them. Verjat spotted him immediately. He pulled Cosette towards the fountain and asked her to sit down on the stone edge. Surprised, Cosette complied. As the couple were now out of sight, the man ran to the fountain, where he found himself face to face with Verjat.

'Looking for something?' Verjat asked with a threatening air, taking him by the arm and drawing him away. Cosette remained seated on the stone edge.

'I must have made a mistake ...'

'I hope you did,' said Verjat, letting go of him. 'Now push off, and don't let me see you again.'

The man did not need to be asked twice. Verjat's savage expression had terrified him. He walked away, with his head down and his hands in his pockets.

Verjat returned to Cosette.

'Who was that?' she asked.

'A mistake.'

A mistake he supposed was due to either the Mullet or Gérard. The plot was thickening. He took Cosette by the hand and walked with her as far as the Rue Servandoni. She talked about her new home, but he barely listened to her. His mind was elsewhere.

Cosette did not explain that she had moved into the same mansion as Amédée, nor did she mention the duel or the marquis's wound. Verjat did not see fit to explain that he was investigating in Marius's old haunts. For the first time they were hiding things from each other.

They ate oranges at the entrance of the Rue Garancière, and parted in the square in front of the church, promising to meet again very soon. Verjat had to prepare for dinner, Cosette to return to Amédée's bedside.

'You aren't hiding anything from me, are you, Monsieur Verjat?'

'No, Cosette. And you?'

'No, Monsieur Verjat.'

The Catman sat in a tavern in the Rue Saint-Denis, drinking a lemonade. He was worried about the Mullet. He suspected that his sidekick, whose stupidity knew no bounds, was waiting for the first opportunity to betray him and appropriate what belonged to him. The Mullet knew too much. Not only had he killed Jesus and recovered his ring, he had also started asking indiscreet questions about the way that he, Tardier, his boss, had transformed the Clan Destin into the Chat-Malin and sold the premises in the Rue Greneta. He seemed to be showing altogether too great an interest in this twofold operation, the profits from which Tardier, with the help of a fence named Chardon, had changed immediately into diamonds. And what was he to think of the Mullet's attempts to force the children to work even faster than before, simply to be able to claim a larger commission for himself?

The Catman finished his lemonade, paid, stood up and left. He had begun to notice that the workshop accounts were unreliable, that certain items were missing. The Mullet again. It always came back to the Mullet. Not only was the man a nuisance, but he was becoming greedier with every passing day. The Catman was starting to think seriously about getting rid of him.

As he walked, he thought also of Horse Face. It had not been a good idea to ask for his help in hiding the diamonds in the wall, although it had been a useful test of his loyalty. What if the young fool had already put the Mullet in the picture? And what if he and the Mullet were plotting behind his back?

He walked for a while through the warren of dark alleyways, waving his cane and talking to himself. It was then that he stumbled on a brawl between three men. Two of them were short and fat. The third, dressed in grey and wearing an otter-skin cap, was tall and spidery, with a roman nose, cauliflower ears, a grey scar across his forehead, and an empty, almost expressionless look in his eyes. He looked like a dangerous character. The Catman hid behind a shutter and watched.

With a brief movement of the hand, the man in the otter-skin cap gestured at the other two. They were both armed with knives.

It all happened incredibly fast. There were two whistles, a gurgling noise, then the sound of bodies falling. The man in the otter-skin cap was the only one left standing, a pruning knife gleaming in his hand. One of the others was already dead, the second was on his knees, shaking, blood pouring from his throat. The tall man stood watching his victim, a half-smile on his lips. The sight of his suffering seemed to make his mouth water. He lifted the pruning knife to his lips, licked it, then, quick as lightning, planted the point of it in the wretched fellow's skull. The victim reared up, fell back on his side and lay motionless. The man in the otter-skin cap removed his pruning knife. A black, bubbling jet squirted from the skull.

The Catman swallowed his saliva. That's the man I need, he thought. He emerged from his hiding place. 'Hey, friend!'

The man in the otter-skin cap turned his gaze to the old man. With a defiant gesture, his legs well apart, he passed his pruning knife from one hand to the other. 'Are you looking for me?' he asked in a harsh voice.

'Softly now, friend. I like your style. What would you say to earning some money – a lot of money?'

'It depends what I have to do.'

'Protect me.' The Catman took out two gold coins and threw them to the other man, who caught them in mid-air.

'You interest me,' the man said, putting away his knife. His voice seemed to emerge from the shadows. 'They call me the Wolf,' he went on, aware of the Catman's admiring gaze. 'Just like a wolf I wander, I prowl. And just like a wolf I always get my prey.'

'I think we're going to get on just fine, Wolf. My name's Tardier, but they also call me the Catman. As a matter of fact, I have two or three losers who'd be ideal prey for you.'

The Catman gave the Wolf a room in the building which housed the workshop. The room was small, dark and filthy, but the Wolf did not complain – he was indifferent to comfort. The effect he made when the Catman introduced him in the workshop was terrifying – on the Mullet above all. The Catman was sure things were going to change.

'The Wolf is here to check the work and keep an eye on you,' he announced without further ado. 'I've had the feeling lately that there's been some slacking. And slacking is something the Wolf doesn't like. Isn't that so?'

'Absolutely,' said the Wolf in a lugubrious voice, turning his gaze towards the Mullet. It was a glassy, abstracted gaze, which made his hooked nose, his scar, his big bony hands, his black clothes – in short, his whole person – seem all the more disturbing. The Mullet could not help shivering. This bird of ill omen made him think of a phantom – a ghost.

The Catman patted the Mullet on the shoulder. He explained to him that the Wolf was the right man for the job and that he would train the boys to be first-class cut-throats.

'Any complaints?'

'No, no . . .' spluttered the Mullet. 'It's an excellent idea . . .'

There was silence in the workshop. The boys did not dare look at the Wolf. They were starting to feel nostalgic for the days of the Mullet.

The schemes of the various men cancelled each other out. Each one was waiting expectantly to see what the others would do. The Mullet was wary of complaining to the Catman – and even warier of complaining to the Wolf. He was too proud to deal with what he disliked.

For the moment, what most worried the Catman was his appointment with Lacenaire. The two months had gone by and there was no escape.

He arrived at the Ogre de Barbarie and sat down at the back of the room. The place was filled with beggars and murderers. Next to him two drunkards were arguing over a toothless old woman. A smell of sewers from the surrounding houses' cesspools mingled with the stench of food and alcohol. The area was the quintessence of filth.

Lacenaire came at five o'clock sharp, accompanied by a stocky man with a pug nose, dressed in a brown smock and wearing a wide cap on his head. The man's name was Avril and he was curiously considerate towards Lacenaire. Lacenaire himself was impeccably dressed. With his lanky body, his elegant cuffs and black silk cravat, he looked extremely aristocratic. He sat down facing the Catman, and Avril sat down beside him. Lacenaire placed his hat on his knees. 'I was just saying to Avril that lying is the strong man's weapon. What do you think, Catman?'

'I don't think anything,' replied the Catman, noticing that Avril had his hand on his friend's thigh.

'I'm not surprised. I wonder what you did with Jesus. You'd better pray I don't discover anything compromising about you. Because if I do . . .' He opened his frock coat to reveal the handle of a stiletto shining at his belt. 'As for the bank messengers, we didn't wait for you. But we were sold down the river. It wouldn't have been you who spilled the beans, would it?'

'Could be,' said Avril with a pronounced working-class accent. 'With that ugly beak of his, he looks like a snitch.' Grinning all over his face, he took hold of the Catman's nose and twisted it slowly from left to right. 'We're strapped, Catman,' he said, letting go abruptly.

'Completely broke,' said Lacenaire, offering the Catman his handkerchief.

'Thank you,' whined the Catman, refusing the handkerchief. 'You upset me, Lacenaire. Because I've been thinking about you – and not in the way you imagine. I've got something for you that's right up your street. A money-grubber of the worst kind, a fence, rolling in cash, a thorn in everyone's side. A whining character by the name of Chardon. Do you know him?'

'I'll say!' exclaimed Lacenaire. 'Who doesn't know Chardon? I met the old queer in Bicêtre in 1830.'

'All the better,' said the Catman, rubbing his nose with a contrite expression. 'Just imagine, Chardon's expecting a grant from the queen to found a hospital for men. Ten thousand francs, no less. Apart from that, his workroom's full of silver, valuable paintings, even precious stones.'

'Is he still living with his old mother?'

'That's right. In the Passage du Cheval-Rouge.'

'We'd have to do it about mid-December. What do you think, Avril?'

'The old are more frail when the weather's cold,' said Avril, tickling the Catman's chin.

The Catman agreed servilely. Then, as delicately as he could, he mentioned the possibility of using a third man on the job. Naturally, he had the Mullet in mind.

'It's kind of you, old-timer,' retorted Avril insolently, 'but we work alone.'

The Catman's face showed that the blow had struck home. Clearly, he couldn't expect anything from these two. 'And how will I know you've succeeded?' he asked.

Lacenaire stood up, as did Avril. He leaned over the Catman and hit his face with his handkerchief. 'You won't know a thing, you old creep. We'll contact you if we feel like it. As far as I'm concerned, you don't deserve to live or to think. What I seek is the intoxication of the summits, the dilettantism of fate, the inevitability of fame. Do you understand that, you hopeless loser? Your calculations are as alien to me as your way of dressing, drinking, speaking. You're a pig, Catman. And pigs get bled.'

When Louis-Désiré Burdin had heard from Madeleine that Cosette was about to give birth to a child, it had seemed to him that all his fine dreams were doomed to go up in smoke. He raged – above all against his master, who, once he had recovered from his wound, had started to feel terribly sorry for himself. What had happened to the arrogant and cynical Casanova of not so long ago?

When he knew for certain that Cosette was pregnant and would give birth very soon, Amédée shut himself away at home. He refused to follow Louis-Désiré's advice, and dismissed Louis de Vergne. Then, when he ventured out again, it was to visit seedy taverns, brothels, the low dives in the Boulevard du Temple. He was resuming his old ways, without his old pride and with a new dose of regret.

When Cosette found out, she was unmoved. In fact, Amédée's decline delighted her, just as she had secretly savoured the pleasure of seeing him wounded, diminished, defenceless. His pain made hers more bearable. Increasingly she had come to feel a supreme indifference towards things, people, tastes, the future and even herself. There was nothing feigned about her indifference, in which her affectations, her selfishness, her nightmares and her quest for the absurd drifted without cohesion. In fact, she cared now about one thing and one thing only – her child.

Amédée was all too well aware of this. Cosette's coldness drove him to despair. He consoled himself in the company of Louis, his faithful – perhaps too faithful – friend, who had never stopped loving him and seeking him out. They went out together and drank until their thirst was quenched. Never did the name of Robert d'Androisy pass their lips. Amédée would yell like a ruffian, choose the ugliest girls, get into brawls.

One evening, he told Louis that lies – the lies in which he had wallowed, literally feeding on them – were an illusion, a murky illusion that merely served to reveal to us what we most lacked. 'Cosette will never be mine. And now I have nothing left but the truth, my poor Louis.'

To which Louis de Vergne, still in love with his friend and desperate to rescue him from a self-imposed purgatory, replied that a lie sometimes explained what was going on in the soul better than truth.

'So let's continue to lie!' exclaimed Amédée. 'Isn't that the best way to explain ourselves?'

Cosette gave birth to a beautiful baby boy weighing six pounds, who was immediately christened Jean. Amédée, who had almost been hoping that the child would be stillborn, stayed in his apartment. He had made sure that a doctor and midwife were called, and had filled Cosette's bedroom with flowers. It was a respite from his debauchery – but not from his sorrow. He could not restrain his tears. Everything was in league against him.

In the meantime, Louis-Désiré was fretting. Cold and calculating as he was, his cynicism accentuated by his physical deformity, untouched by any scruple, firmly believing that loyalty and honesty were inimical to success – even he almost gave in to discouragement. So he decided to act. There was no more time to lose.

The day after the birth of Jean Pontmercy, he paid a call on the Catman.

'You're mad, I told you never to come here!' exploded the Catman, rushing to the stairwell and checking constantly to make sure that nobody had seen or followed Burdin. He even descended one floor, then a second. He turned his head in every direction, muttering that everything had to remain hidden. The only things that had value and truth in his eyes were those that were deeply concealed, hence the strength of the vilest sentiments. He only felt safe in the street, lost in the crowd, anonymous, for there, starting with identity and social status, everything melted away and became unimportant. A crowd is like a uniform, he would say.

The other things that mattered were his diamonds.

Burdin had sat down at the only table and was waiting for his return. The disorder in the Catman's garret horrified him. It was grey and dirty, with a low, sloping ceiling. All kinds of objects were heaped one on top of the other. The furniture was old and barely stood up. The table was surrounded by three twisted chairs and a number of little esparto doormats. The thick, colourless waxed tablecloth was covered with dust, spotted with the oil from an old Argand lamp, and strewn with hardened scraps of food that were enough to take away your appetite for ever. There were no paintings or prints on the walls, nothing but that fine white coating, which stood out against the rest.

Burdin looked down. On the floor there was a strange mixture of twisted tiles and carbonized wood. On a pedestal table he saw a kind of trick box, with many drawers which slotted together. Also on the table was a stuffed cat. He grimaced. In every corner of the room there were cardboard boxes, crates, and rotten and broken packets, containing things that were even more rotten and broken. He pinched his nose. The place stank like a poorhouse.

'I'm sorry,' he said, when the Catman returned and closed the door behind him.

'You should be! You're doing the exact opposite of what we had agreed.'

'Sorry, but this is urgent. This Cosette Pontmercy is causing me too many problems.'

The Catman looked at him searchingly. 'Look here, Burdin!' he said, beating on the table with his fist. 'We can't get rid of everybody. Just calm down! Keep a level head, old chap. Abstinence! Abstinence, believe me, confers infinite power.'

'Abstinence? That's a laugh coming from you, Thénardier! What about your workshop, the Chat-Malin, your plans to expand, the wealth you must be hiding in your lair?'

The Catman's face fell. The size of the obstacle he would have to overcome if his schemes were to succeed was written in the curve of his mouth. 'All right,' he went on in a softer tone. 'What do you suggest we do? Murder the baroness?'

In criminal circles, it is always a good tactic to make someone else say what you have been thinking yourself.

'We don't have to go that far,' replied Burdin, feigning indignation, 'but my master is squandering what little money we've managed to gain because that chatterbox not only rejects him but has also just given birth to a brat.'

'The convict's kid?'

'That's right. If you can find a solution, I'll ask Gérard to leave the Chat-Malin. You'll be in sole charge and I'll let you keep my share of the profits. I'll even dig into my savings to help you buy another tavern in the location of your choice.'

A drop of saliva formed at the corner of the Catman's lips. 'You interest me, my friend. The brat's no problem. A little dive into the Seine, and that'll be the end of it. The lark's another matter entirely.'

'What do you mean?' said Burdin, with an expression of disgust.

'I've got Lacenaire on my back – the fellow who gave me Jesus. I have to get rid of him. And I don't suppose you're going to do it for me.'

Irritated, Burdin stood up and paced about the room. 'And this Cosette sees other men,' he muttered. 'Gérard told me she was seen at Saint-Sulpice with a queer customer. A man named Moreau . . .'

He stopped near the trick box and passed his hand over it. A drawer opened and a gold ring, a snake with emerald eyes, appeared. 'Jesus's ring?' he asked, pointing an accusing forefinger at it.

'I couldn't help myself, I like relics,' conceded the Catman. 'It's quite valuable. I should offer it to a fence.'

Burdin, his jaw clenched, walked to the door. Thanks to his avarice, this old crook Thénardier was not even capable of taking the most elementary precautions. 'So, not before the end of the year?'

'The beginning of next year would be better still,' the Catman corrected him, standing up in his turn and bringing Burdin his hat obsequiously in a gesture of solicitude.

Burdin took it and opened the door. 'Well, the ball's in your court,' he said curtly. He glanced at the stairwell and crept out.

'You're right,' muttered the Catman, closing his trick box. 'The ball's in my court.'

At the beginning of December the Catman informed Sergeant Carignol that something was brewing in the vicinity of the Porte Saint-Martin. 'The Impasse du Cheval-Rouge, to be exact. We know all about it at the workshop. Be ready to come on the evening of the thirteenth.'

Unfortunately, Carignol misunderstood and thought that he had to come to the workshop first.

The Catman went to see Chardon and advised him to be on his guard around the 13th. He had had wind of an attack. The fence thanked him, but assured him that he was afraid of nobody. 'I have nothing to steal. Except my virtue! But what about you? Don't forget you owe me money.'

The Catman looked scornfully at the fat, effeminate, slobbery-lipped creature. No sooner said than done, you big slug, he muttered under his breath.

He left with a light heart. The number thirteen will bring me luck, he told himself, sure it would be the end of Lacenaire and Chardon – with that bastard Avril as an added bonus.

The weeks passed. The Catman was restless. He took the Wolf with him whenever he had to go out, even for short distances. As a result, the Wolf had less time to supervise the workshop and keep an eye on whatever the Mullet was up to. One day the Catman was on the Ile de la Cité looking for new premises – to extend his field of operations, as he put it. He stopped in front of a decrepit facade in the Rue des Ursins.

'You see,' he said to the Wolf, 'you never knew the Clan Destin, but I can tell you this – I miss that tavern. At least there was life, there was movement, all the shady goings-on that we like. Now everything is smooth and polished. High society is boring. I must confess that I'm in two minds.'

'You want to buy another restaurant?'

'Well, that may be going a bit far! I don't have the means, I've never had the means. But I'm getting into debt. And a man who doesn't pay his debts gets rich.'

The two men entered the building.

Meanwhile, the Mullet was waiting for Verjat outside the Chat-Malin. He had left Horse Face and the Pointer in charge of the workshop. The weather was gloomy.

Verjat arrived wearing a smock and an eye-patch. The two men walked on opposite sides of the street as far as the Rue de la Verrerie and joined up in the Rue Saint-Martin.

'I've checked,' said the Mullet in a low voice. 'The Catman is on the Cité. The coast's clear. We can unlock the door and just help ourselves.'

Over his shoulder, Verjat was carrying a sack containing his hat and his frock coat. You could never be too careful. 'I warn you,' he said, 'if anything happens, I don't use a knife. My only weapon is my picklock.'

'That's the way I understood it. The only reason I've got a knife is to scrape at the wall. I steal the rocks and that's it. We've got just one hour to do the work and then we clear off.'

'And what if the Catman asks you where you were?'

'I'll tell him I went to the Chat-Malin earlier than planned. In fact, I've asked Horse Face to fetch me from there at seven. For the rest, I'll sort it out with Gérard.'

As they walked, Verjat told the Mullet that he mistrusted Gérard. When they came within sight of the workshop, the Mullet stopped by the little carriage entrance and looked intently down both sides of the street. 'You have the gift of second sight,' he said in a low voice. 'Gérard runs a whorehouse. They say he even holds black Masses.'

'Black Masses?'

'Proserpine told me. You know, the pretty red-haired waitress who took your fancy. One night she tried to blindfold me and take me to see their dirty work. I refused. No chance! It ends in an orgy with a lot of rich people. Gérard used to be a doctor, but the only thing he's kept from all that is the bad side – magic potions and fiendish ointments.' The Mullet opened the door and put his finger to his lips. 'Right, from now on, no more blunders. Have you got your lamp?'

'I have.'

'Let's go then.'

When they reached the Catman's floor, the Mullet stopped. He had just heard footsteps downstairs. The veins in his forehead throbbing, he took out his knife and leaned over the stair rail to look down. His blood froze when he saw a cocked hat. It was Carignol.

'What's that bent rozzer doing here?' he whispered, clutching his knife.

But the sergeant left his men outside and did not come upstairs. To the Mullet's surprise, he walked towards the workshop. Was this another trick of the Catman's? What was he up to this time?

The Mullet turned to Verjat. The latter's imperturbable expression impressed him. 'You're not even shaking.'

'Why should I be shaking?' He took out his picklock and set to work. The door was opened in no time at all. Verjat lit his oil lamp and the two men entered the room.

'It's even more disgusting than I imagined,' murmured the Mullet.

He hurried to the wall indicated by Horse Face and began to dig feverishly.

Verjat inspected the premises. He turned over objects and put them back in their place immediately. There were no compromising documents to be seen. In any case, in the middle of so much senseless disorder, it would be like looking for a needle in a haystack. Swinging his lamp, he saw the trick box, which Tardier had moved from the pedestal table and put under a stack of cardboard boxes. Verjat ran his hand over the surface. A drawer opened and the ring appeared. Verjat seized it. Meanwhile, the Mullet, digging at the plaster with frantic, jerky movements, had just come across a stone himself, set in its white cradle like a glass eye.

'Look,' said the Mullet, taking it out of its plaster casket with the point of his knife, and holding it between his thumb and forefinger in order to hold it up to the light of the lamp. 'Our fortune is assured.'

'Keep it for yourself,' said Verjat icily. 'But what's this?'

The Mullet screwed up his eyes to look at the ring. 'That? That's nothing – just a ring that used to belong to Jesus, a thug who's no longer with us. He's rotting in hell right now.' In his greed, he was losing all sense of caution.

'It's an emerald, though,' said Verjat, affecting a certain indifference.

'Well, it's yours if you want it.' The Mullet looked at his watch. 'We have to get a move on, we've only got half an hour left. Nose around a bit more, I'm sure the old villain must have some bangles or some loose change stashed away. He doesn't trust banks.'

The Mullet was sweating like an ox. In the darkness, by the light of his lamp, with his crimson face and his bulging eyes, he looked like a blacksmith. He was hopping from one foot to the other, as if a sudden hysteria had seized him. Verjat shook his head and put the ring in his pocket. He had just made a major breakthrough in his investigation.

The boys were working. For once, there was nobody in the workshop to order them about. The Mullet and the Wolf were both away. There was only the Pointer's fierce eye to watch them, but although the horrible old cripple still raised his finger from time to time, there was something derisory about it. He was so used to informing that it had become a tic, an instant reflex. Not that he appeared to derive any pleasure from it. His remaining faculties seemed only to serve his sense of resentment, which had survived the disintegration of his memory. He was taking revenge for what he was.

The old man, with his wrinkled face, his flat skull and his flabby, speckled skin, was a vegetable, who had to be fed like a circus animal, rewarded for his services with chicken stock and a beaten egg yolk or a hunk of bread. He was nothing but vermin. He did not speak, did not blink, did not move. It was a moot point whether he still had any thoughts in his head. Twice a week the Mullet picked some of the boys to wash him. Although there was a pot fixed under his chair, it was always a punishment. They had to clean the excrement off the old dodderer, whose body was covered in scabs, bedsores and pustules. If the boys happened to pinch him, he would jump with a squelching noise. But he was feared, as whatever does not move is always feared – like a crocodile, a creature of the swamps.

With the Mullet and the Wolf absent, the boys were not very busy. Raphaël was dozing over his work, and Horse Face was whistling as he stroked his comb with its sharp wooden teeth. The others worked on without glancing at the Pointer. The Mullet had forgotten to place lamps at strategic points, so everybody was more or less in the dark. Mother Fouillet was arranging the food and scouring her pans. The Pointer was barely visible, huddled like a bundle of linen, occasionally making the chair creak when he pointed his forefinger or moved his legs. Only his shadow could be seen, which was worse.

'Are you sleeping, kid?' Horse Face asked Raphaël.

No reply. The little fair-haired boy knew the ropes. It was not uncommon for him to give the impression of working while snatching a few moments of sleep. In fact, all of the boys were familiar with this pretence. In general, the system worked. When night fell, it was necessary to get very close to them to see if they were shirking. As they worked in rotating teams – those who went hunting for cats and those who stayed behind – some would keep watch. To give the alarm, someone would cough or clear his throat. They organized themselves as best they could. The most important thing was to avoid a beating.

Horse Face glanced sideways at Raphaël – he was sleeping. He did not try to wake him. A few minutes earlier, Carignol had been in. He had wandered around the workshop like a sleepwalker, and then, all at once, had struck himself on the forehead.

'Bloody hell, I should have gone to the Impasse du Cheval-Rouge!'

And he had left. Horse Face had no idea what was going on. But that was the moment when he decided to act, especially as Mother Fouillet had gone out with her pans.

Accustomed to the darkness, he looked around the workshop. This time of day was always a slack period. After the soup, to help them put their hearts into their work, the boys had drunk wine mixed with brandy and eaten a few crumbs of bread. As a result, they were dozing. Some were sleeping openly. Horse Face was pleased. He bent and picked up a little mallet that was used to unblock the looms. Wedging the comb between his teeth, he walked stealthily to the Pointer's chair. A ray of light threw a whitish sliver on the old man's slippers. Horse Face stopped. It was perfect.

He took up position behind the Pointer, removed the comb from his teeth and raised it above the old man's head. Softly, he rose to his full height and stared at the skull with disgust. It was grey and speckled, and covered with spots and wrinkles. The Pointer must have felt a presence, for twice he raised his forefinger, as if he were beating time.

'I'm going to play you another kind of music,' whispered Horse Face, raising the mallet. 'For all the blood and all the money you've cost us, I'm going to smash your skull. Promises are made to be kept.'

With all his strength, he brought the mallet down. The comb sank into the skull as if into a rotting cake. Something spurted, making a soft, viscous sound. Horse Face struck again, then again, until the teeth of the comb disappeared altogether. The old man was shaking in his chair. He was trembling, jerking, stretching in agony. He was like a one-man earthquake.

Horse Face knelt behind the armchair and wiped his blood-spattered face with an old cloth. Then he waited. The old bastard had to give up the ghost eventually, didn't he? Not a bit of it. His forefinger was pointing even more, coming and going, bending like a hook, scratching the air. Luckily, he could not cry out or stand up. But he was squealing like a rat caught in a trap.

Horse Face peered round the side of the chair, first at the door, then around the workshop. Nothing stirred. But he had to finish it. The old man was in his death throes.

Horse Face stood up and stuck his mouth to the Pointer's ear. 'You're going to croak, you old sneak. I'm going to give you a nice little centre parting.'

And with an abrupt gesture, he pulled the comb out of the old man's skull. The Pointer's whole body gave a terrible jerk. The legs of the chair lifted and came down again with a crash, though even that was not enough to wake the boys. Out of the corner of his eye, Horse Face checked that Mother Fouillet had not come back. Then he stretched out his hand, seized a sack full of cats' heads, plunged the old man's head inside, tied a string around his neck and pulled it tight to strangle him. Then he dealt him three more blows with the mallet. There was a loud noise, as of something cracking – whether it was the Pointer's head or the cats' heads, he did not know.

It didn't matter. Horse Face caught his breath. He wiped the comb and the mallet, then returned to his place. There, in the corner, he saw Mother Fouillet rummaging about in her scrap iron.

Wonderful, he told himself. He turned to Raphaël. 'Are you sleeping, kid?'

The child shook himself like a little dog. 'No, Horse Face, I'm working.'

'OK, kid. Carry on.'

At that very moment, Lacenaire and Avril were attacking Chardon with files. It was a bloodbath. Leaving Avril to finish him off with a cleaver, Lacenaire went into the next room, where Mother Chardon was dozing in her bed. She was as deaf as a post and had heard nothing. Lacenaire seized her by the hair, hit her several times in the face, then tipped the mattress over her and smothered her. No sound emerged from her old carcass. She went quickly. And what was it all for? A pitiful haul of five hundred francs, some silver and a pink waistcoat.

'Let's clear off,' said Avril, throwing a sack over his shoulder.

The two men left the Passage du Cheval-Rouge. In the murky light of the Rue Saint-Antoine, they stopped to debate their next move. Avril wanted to go to the Chat-Malin and settle accounts with the Catman. 'He must have warned the fence. You saw, there was almost nothing there. Maybe he squealed on us to the rozzers, too!'

Lacenaire was in two minds. But vengeance was certainly on the cards. He should never have trusted the old scandalmonger. 'You're right, we should finish him off. We don't know his address, but we'll work the manager of the Chat-Malin over with a knife and soon find out. Did you keep the cleaver?'

'No, but I've got my knife. That can cast quite a spell, too, believe me.'

They had not gone far before they ran into a group of gendarmes, headed by Carignol, who was walking with chest thrown out and epaulettes held high. The fool was exulting in his victory, like Lannes at the Battle of Marengo.

'What did I tell you?' exclaimed Avril, stopping dead. 'Who do you think that lot are after? We've been had good and proper.'

The two men turned back, plunged into an alley, and did not stop running until they reached the Porte Saint-Martin.

'Any ideas?' asked Avril, out of breath.

'Seeing the state we're in, we'd be well advised to go and pay a visit to the Turkish baths. Look at us, we're covered in blood. We've got to get cleaned up. After that, you can go and sell the silver. I'll wait for you at the Epi-Scié.'

'What about the Catman?'

'To hell with him. The rozzers'll nab him in the end.'

When the Catman got back to the Rue Aubry-le-Boucher, he sent the Wolf to the workshop and went up to his room. At that hour the Mullet should have been at the Chat-Malin. Discipline was necessary.

When he reached the door, the Catman slipped the key in the lock and turned. Nothing indicated that there had been a break-in. Verjat had locked the door perfectly. But when the old man lit his lamp, he felt his stomach heave. The wall had been hacked at with a knife.

His first thought was of the Mullet, and then of Horse Face. The youth must have blabbed. Holding his lamp up against the wall, he felt every crevice with a feverish hand. He had hidden a small fortune in there – six little diamonds. To judge by the three holes and the chalky craters surrounding them, only three had been taken, but that was three too many. A terrible emptiness overcame him, an obscure feeling that everything was collapsing around him. It was as if his heart had been torn from his breast. He slumped on a chair. His face looked like a fish head, expressing nothing but determination and silent madness. He was brooding on revenge. He took off his hat, put it back on, grasped his cane and again pointed his lamp at the wall. He almost choked. Tears pricked his eyes.

'My diamonds,' he whispered, crushed.

Then, abruptly, and with unsuspected energy, he leapt to his feet, rushed to the door, slammed it behind him and ran down the stairs to the workshop, quite unaware of what awaited him there.

'Those two are dead,' he muttered, thinking of the Mullet and Horse Face.

When the Mullet and Verjat had finished their work, they went to the Chat-Malin. From the bundle over his shoulders, Verjat had put his hat and frock coat back on. Once again he was Monsieur Moreau. Outside the restaurant the Mullet had an unpleasant surprise, for who should he meet but Twenty-Two, the albino who had helped him to kill Jesus?

'How's it going?' asked Twenty-Two, gazing intently at the bourgeois who was with the Mullet.

'Fine.'

That was the end of the conversation.

'Who was that?' asked Verjat.

'The man who killed Jesus,' replied the Mullet. 'The one whose ring you took.'

'Well, well.'

The Mullet looked at Verjat with a superior air. Not only had he just pocketed three diamonds, but in addition he was exculpating himself from a murder on the cheap. And he thought his plan was unstoppable. Hadn't he asked Horse Face to meet him at the Chat-Malin at seven? 'The perfect alibi,' he assured Verjat. 'In order not to arouse any suspicions, stay and eat here tonight. We'll meet again tomorrow at the usual time.'

He drank a glass of burgundy and exchanged a few words with Gérard, who was looking at Verjat curiously. For a bourgeois, thought Gérard, this Monsieur Moreau had behaved rather brusquely towards the spy he had sent to tail him.

Horse Face was punctual. Hardly had he entered the tavern than he headed straight for the table where Verjat and the Mullet were sitting. With unaccustomed humility, he took off his cap and lowered his head with a distressed air.

'Well, Horse Face, I don't recognize you any more!' said the Mullet, in a swaggering tone. 'What's the matter?'

The youth had also been planning, but they couldn't fail to make connections.

'It's . . . It's the Pointer,' he stammered. 'Nobody knows exactly what happened . . . It was dark . . . Mother Fouillet was cleaning her pans . . . And then Carignol came by . . . I have to confess, we were all dozing off a bit by then . . . Anyway, when we got back to work, we saw the Pointer on his chair . . . He'd kicked the bucket.'

'Dead?' The Mullet stifled an oath, caught Horse Face by the collar and waved his fist at him. 'If I find out it was you—!' he said, in a choked voice.

Verjat caught his hand and twisted it slightly. The Mullet let go of the youth and glared at Verjat. From his vantage point near the counter, Gérard had watched the whole scene.

'What are you looking at?' cried the Mullet in a rage. 'Do you want to remember my face?' Then he stood up, tipping over his chair. All the customers were staring at him. 'I'm going,' he muttered.

With barely a glance at Verjat, he hurried out. Verjat cut short his dinner. To Gérard, who asked him what was happening, he simply replied that something unfortunate had taken place. Because of the theft, it was better not to say any more. Then he picked up his bundle and went out with Horse Face.

'Are you a friend of the Mullet's?' the youth asked, with a defiant expression in his eyes.

'An acquaintance, my boy. Let's just say I'm doing him a service.' He put his hand in his pocket and took out Jesus's ring. 'You see this ring? The Mullet's asked me to sell it to the highest bidder.'

Horse Face thrust out his big jaw in surprise. He drew Verjat beneath a street lamp and asked him to show him the ring again. 'But that's Jesus's ring!'

'Jesus? Who's he?'

'The one who protected us from the Mullet. They say he was sent down for twenty years.'

'And he left his ring behind?'

'He wouldn't do that.'

'So it was stolen from him?'

'That's hard to believe.'

'Why?' insisted Verjat.

'Because he was a man, Jesus. A real man. Whenever that pain in the neck, the Mullet, tried to pick a quarrel with us, Jesus would give him a hiding like you've never seen. Nobody would have dared to pinch his ring. I'm beginning to think someone did him in. Unless it was Old Nick himself.'

Verjat started walking again, one hand behind his back, the other carrying the bundle, his cane wedged under his forearm. 'The devil doesn't exist, my boy. He was invented to make us believe that God existed. It's a question of circumstance.'

The youth looked oddly at Verjat, who, with his solemn voice and heavy gestures, for some reason inspired confidence in him. 'Well, I think the devil could well be the Catman and the hunchback!' he retorted vehemently.

'The hunchback?' asked Verjat, surprised. The Mullet had also mentioned a hunchback.

'I saw the two of them together, the morning of the massacre in the

Rue Transnonnain,' Horse Face continued. 'They seemed really interested in the bodies of Jesus and the smart man who gave Raphaël his coat.'

'His coat?'

Horse Face frowned. 'That's what I said. But then the Mullet grabbed it for himself.'

'And what was this smart man's name?'

'Marius. He looked a hell of a lot like Jesus. One day they almost came to blows. What's more, the Mullet and me went to the morgue to get something back.'

'What was it?'

'The Mullet never told me.'

'Perhaps it was this?' asked Verjat, showing him the ring.

'But it was this Marius in the morgue, not Jesus!' protested Horse Face.

'What if they lied to you?'

The youth stopped in his turn and stared intently at Verjat. This fellow was making him all confused.

Verjat nodded. 'You know, if I were you, I wouldn't trust the Mullet.'

'I don't trust him!' protested Horse Face. 'And anyway, I don't even know you! What's the point of all these questions?'

Verjat calmed him with a gesture. Two things intrigued him. One was this visit to the morgue. The other was the presence of the Catman and the hunchback in the Rue Transnonnain, on the very spot where Marius's body had been found and the supposed Jesus had been arrested in a cataleptic state.

'Calm down,' he said to Horse Face. 'I'm not your enemy. Let's just share what we know.' He put down his bundle and scratched his cheek with the knob of his cane. 'What you're telling me is all very well, but can you prove any of it?'

'I'm not lying!' said Horse Face. 'Look, there was a journalist there. A man who was drawing. He even sketched the scene in his notebook. His name was Daumier. I know, because he told me.'

Verjat picked up his bundle again and tapped the youth lightly with his cane. One day in May his attention had been caught by an outstanding series of plates in a collection called *Monthly Lithographical Association*. The publisher was a man named Philipon, who also owned *La Caricature* and had spent several months in Sainte-Pélagie prison. One of the drawings, by Daumier, had been called *The Rue Transnonnain*, and had caused a great stir. Verjat had been struck by its terrible realism. A pot-bellied man lay against a bed, his nightshirt barely covering the top of his short legs. The power of those legs had not saved him from the bayonet thrust that had dispatched him. Beneath him lay a little dead child, blood pouring from his head. The tragic immodesty of the half-naked corpse, the honesty of the slaughtered man, had impressed many, on the right as well as on the left, in the same way as Delacroix's painting *Liberty Leading the People* had a few years earlier.

'Thank you,' said Verjat, giving Horse Face a coin. 'Be careful now. Go straight back to the workshop.'

When Horse Face entered the workshop, the Catman threw him a black look, drew him aside and asked him if he had told anyone their little secret. Horse Face asked which one. The old man's face became sly and sharp. 'You know perfectly well what I'm talking about!'

'The wall? I haven't said a word, Catman. Cross my heart and hope to die. But, you know, Carignol came by the workshop. He even hung around for quite a while. In the end I didn't pay any attention to him.'

The Catman turned away and wiped his nose on his fingers. 'Look at the Mullet,' he said, in a voice heavy with innuendo. 'When he saw his father, he vomited over the cats' heads. I don't supposed you saw what happened there either?'

'We were all having a bit of shut-eye.'

'This is all very strange to me, Horse Face. The place is swarming with rozzers, the Pointer gets bumped off, and everyone's having a bit of shut-eye. Do you really expect me to swallow that?'

'If I'd done anything wrong, I wouldn't have come back this evening, would I?' said Horse Face with a swagger.

The Catman shook his head silently. 'A point in your favour, Horse Face. But watch out. If the Mullet found out you killed his father . . .'

Horse Face looked up and eyed the Catman brazenly. 'Actually, the Mullet slipped out for a while to go to the Chat-Malin.'

The Catman's eyes lit up. 'When was this?'

'Earlier than usual.'

'Very good, Horse Face. I see I can count on you.' The Catman had said nothing about what had happened in his room, but he was sure that Horse Face was lying.

'And when I got to the Chat-Malin,' Horse Face added hesitantly, 'the Mullet was talking to someone else, an old geezer who was a bit shady-looking.'

The Catman smiled wickedly. The youth's confusion made him think that he was ready to squeal on anybody to save his own skin. The Catman called to the Wolf. 'Go and see what's going on in the neighbourhood. I'd like to know what our friend the sergeant is up to.'

An hour later, when the Mullet was still looking furiously at Horse Face, the Wolf returned with the latest news.

'Mullet,' said the Catman, 'deal with the Pointer. Get Horse Face to help you,' he added with a sardonic smile. 'Chuck him in the Seine, he'll feed the fishes.'

As soon as Horse Face and the Mullet had left, the Catman turned to the Wolf, who had just been to the Chat-Malin, where Gérard had confirmed that the Mullet had arrived late that afternoon, though he could not be specific about the hour. He had gleaned another piece of information from a concierge in the Rue Saint-Martin – Chardon and his mother had been robbed and murdered by persons unknown.

The Catman heaved a sigh of relief. Here was a piece of good news to wipe out all the bad. He was rid of Lacenaire and Avril for the moment. The Mullet and Horse Face would be next. Their fate would be sealed early in the New Year. With the purchase of new premises on the Ile de la Cité, Burdin's support and the Wolf's no-nonsense approach, his immediate environment was about to be cleaned up – radically cleaned up.

In the days that followed, Verjat did not change his routine. He continued to dine at the Chat-Malin as if nothing had happened. It was important to avoid arousing suspicion, even if it did mean throwing himself into the lions' den. But gradually he spaced out his visits. It seemed advisable, given how distant and nervous the Mullet had become. There was good reason for the Mullet's nervousness – Tardier had set the Wolf to keep an eye on him. Verjat knew this. One day he had the impression that he himself was being followed again to Saint-Sulpice. Now he visited the restaurant only once a week.

One morning he went to see the publisher Philipon. The Aubert lithographic publishing house was located in the Passage Véro-Dodat. When Verjat opened the door of the shop, he was met by a balding, pot-bellied man wearing little round glasses, who looked like a notary.

'Monsieur Philipon?'

'No, I'm his associate. Who's asking for him?'

The man had a head like a tortoise. Verjat replied that he was interested in Daumier. It was then that a restless little man made his appearance. He was in his shirtsleeves, with a red cravat and a lansquenet's cap. In his ink-stained hands he was carrying a roll of paper.

'I'm looking for Monsieur Daumier.'

'And I'm Philipon! So you're looking for that bruiser Daumier, are you? The dauber with the goatee?'

Verjat raised his eyes to heaven. He tried to keep his distance from cranks like this, who could not stop moving or talking, and who always answered questions with other questions.

'Are you planning to steal him from me?' Philipon went on. 'The Republic cannot be stolen, monsieur!' He unrolled the paper and laid the sheets on a cutting table, smoothing them with a flick of his hand. 'What are these, Monsieur?' he asked in a jubilant tone.

'Pears?'

'Yes, pears! I've discovered, my dear Monsieur, that the king's face, which is broad in the jowls, narrow in the forehead and topped with a curly quiff, is exactly the same shape as a pear. Can't you see what a perfect basis for caricature that is – the fact that our monarch resembles a fruit which is the symbol of stupidity?'

'Surely you'll lay yourself open to prosecution?'

'Prosecute an artist for drawing a fruit?' said Philipon, opening his arms. 'Anyway, what of it? It would only make the judges look ridiculous, my dear Monsieur!'

Verjat was getting impatient. 'What about Monsieur Daumier?'

'Monsieur Daumier?'

'I'm an admirer of his work and I'd like to meet him.'

'To steal him from me?'

'Monsieur, you're talking nonsense. I repeat that I'd like to meet Monsieur Daumier to tell him how much I admire him. Is that clear enough?'

Philipon looked questioningly at him. The stranger seemed to be honest.

'I thought you were a policeman,' he admitted, as he rolled up his papers.

Verjat laughed nervously.

'Monsieur Daumier lives at Twelve Quai de l'Hôtel-de-Ville,' said Philipon. 'Tell him I'm ready and waiting for him. The pear, Monsieur!'

An hour later Verjat was at the house that Daumier shared with his parents. The artist had a pointed nose and a disdainful mouth. He greeted Verjat coolly. 'I don't usually receive anyone here.'

'It was Monsieur Philipon who sent me. He even has a project for you.'

Verjat introduced himself as Moreau. He set about flattering the artist with all the necessary fervour, tempered with the reserve befitting a man of quality. Won over by this older admirer, Daumier agreed to show him his studio. He even became very talkative. Everything fascinated and outraged him. Putting aside his drawings, he showed Verjat a series of terracotta figurines – nothing but big heads on little bodies.

'Look, here are Guizot and Bailliot,' he commented with a giggle, quite proud of himself. 'The boring and the smug! After my lithograph on the kingdom of bedlam, which earned me six months in prison, I'm on the attack again! The glory of the July Revolution! I've done forty-five in all. Philipon has to display them in his window!'

'I see,' said Verjat, who could see nothing and was waiting for the young man to show him his book of drawings. 'How extraordinary. But my preference is for drawing. I have heard that it is a discipline – an art, I should say – in which you excel. Moreover, Monsieur Philipon asked me to remind you that he was waiting for the pear from you.'

'The pear?' Daumier burst out laughing. In his grey smock and pink-spotted cravat, he looked like a mischievous child. He went and rummaged in a vast sideboard, then came back with a box of drawings. 'Feast your eyes, Monsieur!' he exclaimed, with all the self-assurance of youth.

He placed the box on a trestle table, undid the string and opened the lid. Verjat approached. Greedily, he leafed through the prints and skimmed through the sketches. There were drawings and watercolours satirizing Louis-Philippe, the police, the clerical party, power, order, morality – everything that had once been the backbone of Verjat's life. At last he came across what interested him.

'Now these are remarkable,' he said, in a tone that would have convinced anybody that he knew what he was talking about.

Daumier was full of himself. Verjat studied the file more closely. There were sketches and portraits, there was movement, there were soldiers, onlookers, victims. And there was the Catman, instantly recognizable thanks to his catskin hat, and next to him a man in black. They were both grinning, with an air at once self-absorbed and exultant. The man in black, thought Verjat, must be the hunchback that the Mullet and Horse Face told me about. But why had these two villains been at the scene of the tragedy?

'Well, well,' he said, noting a detail that attracted his attention. There was a man lying across a cart, his face smashed in and his hand hanging down. Verjat placed his finger on the hand and turned to Daumier. 'Was there really a ring?'

'Yes, indeed,' said Daumier. 'In fact, I was much struck by it. It was quite showy!'

'Indeed,' said Verjat, 'very showy. Even a little too much so.'

The man with the battered face had to be Jesus. They had wanted to pass him off as Marius. As for the ring, the murderers must have forgotten to take it off Jesus's finger. That was why Thénardier had sent the Mullet and Horse Face to retrieve it from the morgue.

Verjat thanked Daumier for his welcome and promised that he would be back very soon to show his work to other admirers.

'This is not a museum, Monsieur,' joked Daumier, with an artist's pride.

'It certainly isn't,' admitted Verjat. 'Unlike a museum, it's absolutely alive. Quite a revelation, in fact!'

And he went away, as delighted as such an austere man could be.

5

Thanks to Perfect Love, with whom he had been working for Vice Admiral Jacob since September, Marius had learned all about tracing, hatching, mitre cutting, planing, rasping, drilling, notching, chiselling mortises, sanding, nailing, pasting, screwing and assembling. Carpentry held no more secrets for him. Even his sawing had improved, with his newly acquired knowledge of triangular notches. The rebel had calmed down. Indeed, he had calmed down to such an extent that his irons had been removed and he had been allocated to the trusties' section. This was a paradise compared with Prison Ship Number One, a paradise to which convicts were usually only admitted after some time. Everything depended on their good behaviour – and their submissiveness.

'The vice admiral interceded on your behalf,' Perfect Love had told Marius. 'I told him you were indispensable. He's so determined to have his staircase built that he's up for anything.'

Marius had a little tow mattress and a cover. He was no longer joined to another convict, and wore only a simple chain on one leg. At night all the chains were joined together and locked into a long iron bar, which was sealed, at intervals, to the planks of the camp beds with lead pegs. Marius was not complaining. Not only had he escaped the authority of Holy Smoke and his drunken warders, but he also found himself next to Perfect Love.

'That way I can keep an eye on you,' the big man would joke. 'It's good here, isn't it?'

Every Sunday, the bean soup was replaced by a ration of beef and green vegetables. Luxury, indeed. In addition, the company was different. The prisoners here were artisans for the most part – cooks, locksmiths, carpenters, wigmakers, letter writers – a welcome change from the usual gallows birds. But they were not the only inmates. A space in this section was reserved for incurable prisoners whose natural disabilities made work impossible – dwarfs, men with one arm, blind men, hunchbacks, legless cripples. The man on Marius's left, for example, was lame. He was a man in his sixties from Sète nicknamed Tripod. In civilian life, he had been a locksmith in Marseilles – a locksmith whose habit of unlocking doors had turned into a vice. He had been sent down for fifteen years, to which had been added another five for reoffending, and then three more for attempting to escape. He worked in the general store, which was a lucrative job.

'Don't trust that character,' Perfect Love would say to him. 'He reminds me of the Catman. Always scheming. The most important thing is our well-being. Don't forget you got another three years for your escape attempt.'

'I haven't forgotten.'

Working together in the carpentry workshop, the two men talked a lot. Perfect Love was very pleased with Marius's good intentions – or rather, with what he took to be Marius's good intentions, for the young man had not abandoned his escape plans and was, in fact, planning to escape with Tripod. But he was waiting for the right moment. He was taking notes, learning from others' mistakes. Only the other day, for instance, a cannon had been fired to announce that a prisoner had escaped. As usual, he had been recaptured the very next day. The prisoner's name was Piquignot. He had been serving twenty years for killing his mistress's husband with a hammer, and had two fading letters on his shoulder which had been branded there in 1830, two years before the scandalous practice had been abolished. To escape, the best that Piquignot had come up with was to disguise himself as a priest. Not that this was a bad idea in itself. In fact, by passing himself off as the colony's chaplain, he had succeeded in getting through all the doors without being apprehended. The sentries had noticed nothing, and even the gatekeeper hadn't stopped him. But, as Marius well knew, the danger did not lie there.

The danger lay outside. Marius had not forgotten the fisherman and his idiot son. In Toulon, the cannon shots were a signal that it was open season on convicts. The peasants would leave their work, arm themselves with sticks and rifles and set off in search of the fugitive, their eagerness fired by the lure of the reward.

'Fifty francs if they catch him in town, a hundred if it's outside,' Tripod had explained.

In short, the peasants' zeal was roused as soon as the cannon thundered. To march to the sound of the cannon found its full meaning here. The good peasant was transformed into a wild beast. It was a true manhunt, pitiless and relentless. What could the escaped convict hope for? He was like a cornered stag, an animal fit only for slaughter, a victim to be immolated on the altar of the god of money. He had nothing to hope for. No pity, no mercy. His shaven face, his close-cropped hair, his swarthy complexion – none of that could fool a peasant's trained eye. From the moment he escaped his fate was sealed.

That was what had happened to Piquignot. He had put his trust in a peasant, a decent-looking man with laughing eyes, who had shown him to a hiding place. Before long Piquignot had found himself surrounded by ten peasants armed with pitchforks and cudgels led by the peasant he had trusted, who was even more vehement and acrimonious than his companions. Piquignot had received a memorable thrashing. When he had returned to the colony, escorted by a corporal and a warder, he was thought to be dead. Nevertheless, they had put him in solitary. The next day he had appeared before the court martial and had been sentenced to three more years and fifty blows with the stick – though they had waited a few days to carry out the beating, to give him time to recover from the previous thrashing. This was considered favourable treatment.

Marius thought long and hard about the aftermath of this failed escape. A few months earlier, he had had the same misadventure. The next time he would make sure all the odds were on his side.

'When you're outside,' Tripod warned, 'there are the police, the soldiers and the peasants. But there are also the two Erzbet brothers.'

'Who are the Erzbet brothers?'

'Gypsies of Hungarian origin. Bounty hunters.'

Marius shook his head indifferently. It was March – he was planning to escape in April. Failure was out of the question, with or without the Erzbet brothers.

Marius and Perfect Love enjoyed special treatment. Working directly under the authority of Vice Admiral Jacob – an amiable and dreamy old man with a passion for astronomy, who was waiting impatiently for his staircase to be ready – they each had a cupboard to store their tools in. These consisted of gimlets, rasps, hammers, mallets, braces, glues, nails, screws, screwdrivers, marking gauges, chisels, tracing points, folding rules, set squares, bevels, compasses, sanding wedges, saws and several kinds of plane. But Marius, without telling Perfect Love, had made what was known as a plan. This was a cylindrical case, some fifteen to twenty centimetres long, and made of ivory or metal, which contained all you needed after your escape. To conceal it, the prisoner would insert it in the most intimate part of his anatomy. Sometimes the warders would purge a convict suspected of hiding a plan. They would isolate him in a cell, with his hands tied behind his back, and beat and humiliate him. Marius recalled one convict who had sawed through his irons with a hairspring that had been brought to him in a loaf of bread. He, too, had a plan. He escaped and was recaptured two days later.

'You see,' Perfect Love would say. 'None of that's of any use. They all get caught again. Is that what you want?'

'You're right,' Marius would reply, certain now that Perfect Love would not be coming with him.

'Don't we have a good life here?' Perfect Love would argue. 'Doesn't Raynaud treat us like kings?'

'Yes, of course,' Marius would admit. 'You're my friend and we have nothing to complain about. But I can't get Cosette out of my head. It's like an obsession. Don't you ever think about the Kitten?'

Whenever Marius mentioned the Kitten, Perfect Love would clam up. He would stop working and reply only in monosyllables. He would sit on the floor and pass his hand over his brow. He would feel dizzy, his legs would seem too weak to support him, his head too heavy to hold up. As the warder who supervised them kept out of the workshop, it was easy to stay like this for quite a while. One day Perfect Love at last replied to Marius's question.

'The Kitten?' he said, controlling his rage. 'I'll never see her again. As for our friendship, it'll be over the day you leave the colony.'

'You're wrong,' said Marius indignantly. 'You may be strong, but you don't have an ounce of common sense!'

Their voices became raised and the two men almost came to blows. They stood facing each other, ready to attack. Then they shook their heads and fell into each other's arms.

'We're like two fingers of the same hand,' said Marius. His right hand rose and struck Perfect Love's hand. They remained clasped in each other's arms for some time.

Then Perfect Love broke away. 'You're rich, Marius. You'll always be rich. I'm just a poor wretch. Here in the colony, or out in the world, it makes no difference. I'm still a prisoner of poverty. Everyone in his place, that's what I say. Do you remember the first time you came to the Clan Destin? That sums it all up. When we see how you lot live, the one thing we want is to take your places. When you see how we live, the one thing you want is to pretend to take our places. It's just a game for you. You enjoy mixing with the riffraff, but you know you'll go back to your comforts, your servants and your fine houses. The rich have nothing to do with the poor. They amuse themselves at our expense and pretend they're just like us. But poverty isn't a spectacle. It's an illness, an illness that takes you over and makes you feel even guiltier than you were. No, all we have left is humility. Do you want me to tell you about that? Well, humility is what poor people have instead of vanity. So you must leave us alone. Because you and your like, if you try and take what we have just for the hell of it, to be clever, to drag it in the dirt, then our humility will turn against you. And then there'll be a revolution, a bloodbath – even worse than '89. Is that what you want? What we feel is hate. What you feel is contempt. Hate, Marius, is stronger than contempt. Stronger and nobler.'

Marius did not answer, he merely placed his hand on Perfect Love's shoulder. Then he resumed work, leaving Perfect Love sitting on the floor, his head plunged in his hands. And as he sawed and planed, he thought again of La Battut's words: *'You're not one of them, my friend.'*

His eyes grew sombre. If he didn't belong among the well-to-do, nor with people like Perfect Love, where did he belong? Perfect Love had talked about hate. Didn't he, too, feel hate – didn't he feel it in the very depths of his being? Of course, he had managed to master it, to tame it. But it still smouldered inside him like a wild animal. And even if Jean Valjean's example urged him to devote himself to good and not wear himself out in futile rage, he still dreamed of vengeance and apocalypse. Convinced that he had been the innocent victim of a terrible conspiracy, he wanted nothing more than to escape from the colony and settle his accounts. So he really didn't care what Perfect Love said. They were both in the same boat. It was no use wasting your anger in pointless acrimony.

He looked at Perfect Love and then began to polish a step. This year in the colony had enriched him. Physically he felt strong – morally even stronger. He knew now that nothing was sadder than a life without risks, nor any defect greater than the kind of avarice that made you reluctant to give of yourself. The old indecisive Marius no longer existed. He had emerged victorious from the toughest stresses and strains, what he lacked in muscular strength he made up for in will and energy, and his pallor had given way to primary colours. A new Marius had been born. There were people who would learn that to their cost.

He helped Perfect Love to his feet. 'I suppose you're right,' he said, seeing his face light up. 'But I'm like you – I don't know how to feel contempt.'

'You're not upset with me?'

'Why should I be? You're my friend and you'll always be my friend.'

And their hands joined again, like two hands clasped in prayer.

The materials Marius was planning to use for his escape were very simple. For six months he had been shaving his pubic hair. He had stuck it together with blackened tow to make himself a moustache and side whiskers. In the workshop he had managed to steal a piece of mirror, a saw-file and four one-franc coins, which he had tied together with white thread. Outside, it was vital to look normal, and to have a little money and some clothes.

For the clothes, Marius had got hold of a sailor's shirt and a town jacket belonging to Warrant Officer Lestrade, whose life he had saved. Marius did not need too many objects. Another example of a failed escape attempt dissuaded him from burdening himself with too much equipment, which could prove fatal. A prisoner called Carline had secreted inside himself a plan so huge that he had difficulty walking. In the plan was a fringed cover, a case of beaten iron, an iron tube, a screw of tempered iron, a nut, a spanner, a wick with a gimlet shaft, a prismatic file, a piece of grease and a molten-steel saw. One day Carline fainted. He had perforated his intestines and he died in atrocious pain. Dr Chadoutaud, opening Carline's internal organs during the autopsy, was speechless. The other convicts were no less terrified.

'Stuff something like that up your arse and it'll kill you,' Tripod told Marius. 'I've got a better idea. Something that'll really do the trick.'

'What is it?'

'You'll find out one day,' retorted the old man.

He was said to be as rich as Croesus. In the general store, he traded with the visitors and was allowed to keep for himself the money he made from his sculpted coconut pipes, his straw boxes and his aloe-cloth bags.

'The old man's as crafty as a monkey,' Perfect Love would say. 'He must earn at least twenty francs a month. Where does he stash it all?'

Only Tripod knew.

One night, Marius saw him twisting on his bed, convulsed with pain, his teeth clenched, his eyes rolled back so that only the whites showed.

'Shall I call the warders?'

'Absolutely not,' muttered Tripod. 'If they take me to hospital, Dr Chadoutaud will put me under observation and I won't be able to escape. You won't squeal on me, will you?'

'I hope you're joking.'

'I know I can trust you. So listen carefully. If we manage to get out and anything happens to me, I want you to promise me something.'

'What?'

'That you'll get my loot.'

'How?'

'I'll tell you when the time's right.'

'Who says we're going to escape together?' asked Marius.

'We need each other, friend. I have a map of Toulon and a sea chart, and I can navigate. Have you forgotten?'

'No.'

'So don't forget what I've just asked you either. I'm counting on you to defend me. Are you still learning to use the sword and sabre with Lestrade?'

'Yes.'

Warrant Officer Lestrade had grown fond of Marius, not only because Marius had saved his life but because he reminded him of his son, who had been killed at the siege of Trocadero in 1823.

'Lift your guard!' Lestrade would constantly say to Marius when they crossed swords.

The lessons were held in a rope warehouse behind the carpentry workshop. Perfect Love kept a lookout while he worked.

And so Marius would lift his guard, lunge and touch at almost every thrust. He had learned more in three months with this ex-officer of the Empire than in six months at Lord Seymour's fencing school.

'What I'm teaching you is war fencing. You don't have to put on airs when you fight. You fight to kill.'

Before the lesson he would warn Marius not to make too much noise. 'If they catch us, that wet blanket Raynaud will be happy to get rid of me. And it'll be forty lashes and back to Prison Ship Number One for you.'

Lestrade was a man of medium height with greying hair and a moustache shaped like a gendarme's hat. Despite the wound he had received at Trafalgar, which made him drag his foot, he had taken part in the last campaigns of the Napoleonic wars. Waterloo was his claim to fame. Not that he had profited from it in any way. On the contrary, he had been thrown out of the marines regiment that he had loved so much. For eight years he had devoted himself to the career of his only son, who had become a lieutenant in the Jura hussars in 1822. How proud and happy he had been to see his beloved son wearing a hussar's white cockade! What bearing, what presence the boy had had! But happiness is not for the humble. At the end of the French expedition led by the Duc d'Angoulême to restore King Ferdinand VII to the throne of Spain, Lieutenant Lestrade had been killed at Cadiz. Old Lestrade never recovered. One day he requested an interview with Marshal Oudinot, the Duc de Reggio. The ex-sergeant who had fought at Waterloo, raised now to the rank of warrant officer, wanted to join the service again. The army was his only family – his only recourse.

'The only thing I can offer you is Brest or Toulon,' the marshal replied. 'Given your infirmity, you will understand that I can't send you to Greece or Madagascar.'

'I'm not a prison warder, Monsieur.'

'Take it or leave it, my friend.'

Lestrade had taken it. He found the job of jailer repugnant, but it was that or nothing. Toulon reminded him of his son in his beautiful blue and red uniform, and of the marines. He could dream of the open sea, of cormorants. He never showed a trace of self-pity.

When they had started their fencing lessons, Marius had mentioned that his father had also fought at Waterloo. 'He was a cavalry officer. A colonel and a baron of the Empire.'

Lestrade smoothed his thick moustache with a pensive air. 'I never came across a Colonel Tixier.'

'You can't know the names of three hundred thousand men,' Marius replied with a smile. 'In any case, my name's not Tixier. My real name is Pontmercy. Prisoner 9430 isn't Alexandre Tixier but Marius Pontmercy.'

Lestrade scratched his ear. Pontmercy, Pontmercy – the name was vaguely familiar. A man named Pontmercy had been wounded by a horse guard and found lying lifeless on the battlefield. The stretcher bearers had thought he was dead. 'I'm telling you this, but don't forget it was twenty years ago . . .' His memory often played tricks with him. But he recalled a sergeant wandering in the area who had boasted of saving a colonel's life.

'Thénardier?'

'That's right, Thénardier!' exclaimed Lestrade in astonishment. 'How the devil do you know his name?'

'He was the man who saved my father.'

Lestrade bristled. 'At the risk of disappointing you, my boy – if your name is truly Pontmercy as you claim – this Thénardier didn't save your father. I found that out later when I was repatriated with the wounded. Thénardier was a scavenger. He thought your father was dead, and was trying to rob him when your father regained consciousness. That's how a vulture became a hero.'

'You don't really surprise me,' said Marius, remembering the evasive face of the man who had come to see him in Paris to expose Jean Valjean and demand money. 'It fits better with the idea I already had of the wretch. In fact, it's quite good news.'

'Why? Are you in prison because of him?'

'Not at all. I was the victim of a miscarriage of justice. Don't laugh, I know all prisoners say that. But in my case, sadly, it's true. As for the man of whom we were speaking, and with whom I have the misfortune to be acquainted, I imagine he's somewhere in the Americas by now – a slave trader, perhaps, or a pirate or smuggler. Though it takes a certain degree of courage to be a pirate or a smuggler, and he was a coward. What you've just told me confirms that.'

And both men took their guard.

The fencing lessons seemed like lessons in life. The two men would engage, attack and stamp their feet. The blades would ring out brightly. Then the men would break and circle like dancers. They cut and thrust vigorously. After an attack and a backhand, Marius touched Lestrade on the shoulder. A thrust to one side, a simultaneous sidestep and retreat, and again he touched, this time the head. He saluted Lestrade and bowed. He knew by now how to fight with a sabre and Lestrade had even taught him some secret thrusts.

'You're almost invulnerable,' Lestrade said, recovering his breath. 'But remember – these thrusts are to be used only as a last resort.'

Marius raised an eyebrow. He quickly made a *coup fourré*, and his blade whistled in the air. He did not dare contradict the old soldier, but deep down he wondered if there was any point to all this. Who needed fencing in an age when lying and cheating were considered good form? Was there still a place for honour and loyalty in the France of Louis-Philippe and his moneyed cronies?

Marius could not forgive himself for having been born too late. In Paris, when Louis de Vergne had talked to him about his friend Henri Beyle, who had been a dragoons officer in the imperial armies, his imagination had been fired and he had longed to meet the man who had written *Scarlet and Black* under the name Stendhal. It had been the wrong moment. Stendhal had left for Italy, making part of the journey with Musset and George Sand, and the meeting had never taken place.

Marius told himself that many young people must be thinking the same as him. Condemned to boredom and inactivity by the rulers of this world, assailed on every side by pedants, many of them found themselves with only two choices – conformity or debauchery – rather like Amédée and Robert d'Androisy. Those two Marius was keeping for himself. He would beat them in a clean fight.

'Don't get ideas in your head,' warned Lestrade. 'No man can escape divine justice. Everything would be absurd and unfair if there wasn't a God above us. With all the bad things I've been through, I've chosen to do good.'

He lifted his sabre and, after a feint and a pause, attacked, stamping his heel. Marius retreated. He parried and covered himself. Lestrade's hand was still heavy. His thrusts made the blades ring out.

'Missed!' cried Marius. 'But since you're talking of God, in my opinion, his absence from this earth makes him more a model of indifference than a model of love. The only thing he knows how to do is punish. My God is the God of Voltaire and Babeuf! As for the other God, the one with the flowing beard who houses his friends in the bellies of whales, asks a father to kill his son, dies with his arms on a cross and a smirk on his face and then comes back to life three days later to rise to heaven – you can keep him! If there were miracles once upon a time, why are there no miracles today? Why should there be two different weights and two different measures?'

Lestrade's sabre point whistled in Marius's ears. He retreated again and climbed onto a sack. 'What energy, Lestrade! But you won't stop me!'

They came together in a *corps à corps*. Marius pushed Lestrade off. 'Two weights and two measures!' he went on. 'For centuries we've suffered from the villainous and Jesuitical manipulation of the clergy. To hell with hypocrites! Why not? Why not be Caligula and St John of the Cross at the same time, Attila and St Vincent de Paul, Gilles de Rais and Joan of Arc, Sardanapalus and Aristotle? Don't they all, the good and the bad, the judges and the victims, die the same way, without hope of reward or fear of punishment?'

'Who the hell knows, prisoner 9430?'

Marius lost his temper. 'Don't call me prisoner 9430! Or Alexandre Tixier! My name is Marius!'

This time, it was Lestrade who gained the upper hand. He attacked *en flèche* and carried his thrust. The tip of his sabre came to rest on Marius's throat. 'As you wish, Marius,' he said, smiling.

In a fit of pique, Marius handed his weapon to Lestrade and paced up and down.

'Never lose your temper,' said the officer, putting the weapons away. 'Everything will be settled at the Last Judgement.'

Marius shrugged. The Last Judgement! Why couldn't the Last Judgement come right now? Get the apocalypse over with, get the end of the world over with, so that everyone could meet again, all those who had been separated and torn apart! He couldn't wait to embrace the father he had loved so badly, the mother he had barely known, his Cosette whom he missed so much. But he knew history. You didn't need to have studied Hegel or Fourier. You only had to think about it, think about all that had happened since the beginning of the world. What was the Last Judgement waiting for? Why didn't it come now to grant our wishes and put an end to the constant round of birth and death? What would it be like? Did all the bodies come back to life intact, as the priests promised? Marius's parents, his grandfather Gillenormand, Cosette's adoptive father, all together? With all the martyred, the beheaded, the drawn and quartered, the burned, the disfigured? With all the murdered children, the stillborn babies, the premature, the disabled, the torturers, the victims? Adam and Eve, the people of the Stone Age, the Greeks, the Gauls, the Romans, the armies of all the empires and all the civilizations? Centuries and centuries of men? All in the same sack? Billions upon billions? In the air, in the heavens, in paradise? Where, then?

For a year Marius had been turning these questions over and over in his mind, and he had found no answer except nothingness. He had even reached the point of hating certain places because they reminded him of the dead. Jean Valjean, Monsieur Gillenormand, Courfeyrac, Enjolras, Gavroche, Eponine, Frédéric Rivolier ... You should always hate places, he told himself, just as you should hate God. Places are like the empty sockets of eyes that have seen too much. The ideal would be to see nothing, to remember nothing, to be like a stone or a rock, motionless and immovable, exposed to the onslaught of the wind and the age-old sea.

'That's where you're wrong,' said Lestrade.

Marius fixed a sombre gaze on him. 'Why? Because you think you'll see them again, all your dead? Your mutilated comrades in arms? Your son who was killed at Trocadero?'

Lestrade crouched down and hid the sabres in a large sack. Then he stood up and began hopping on the spot, moving his arms to the rhythm of an imaginary dance. 'But I'm alive!' he cried. 'And all these dead are in my heart, Marius. You reason, but life still surprises me.'

During the following three months the discussions between Marius and Lestrade were not so lively. The two men would begin with fencing, then the officer would put away the sabres, light his pipe and sit down on a tangle of rope. He would invite Marius to join him, staring at him with eyes blazing beneath his thick brows. Marius would wait for the signal. Lestrade would lead the debate.

They often talked about the marines, about justice, about everyday life. The two men would talk like this for a good half-hour. Four o'clock was the time for the daily distribution of sea biscuits and after this Marius would rejoin Perfect Love to finish working on the staircase.

'You're too passive,' Marius would sometimes reproach Lestrade.

'And you're too hot-headed.'

The two men had nevertheless come to agree on one thing – hate was a dead end and the expense of energy that it required was pointless.

As Marius worked with a plane or chisel, he would think over his conversations with Lestrade, which were his daily cleansing. Poverty was the great subject and he saw it now in a different light. Thanks to Lestrade, he could study it and dissect it. He felt at one with it. It was no longer a question of revolutionary fashion.

At least Toulon will have been of some use, he told himself.

Seeing the poverty of these people of the abyss, he saw his own. Hearing their yells of rage, he heard his own. In probing their wounds, he probed his own. In understanding their bitter pain, their despair, he understood his own. It was not a romantic pose, not the petty suffering of a consumptive scribbler, but something lived. Iron and blood. He was finally learning to know himself.

'It's strange, you talk of Toulon as if it was in the past,' remarked Lestrade.

'Really?'

One day, after a particularly lively fencing lesson, Lestrade looked hard at him. 'I think there's still an idea that's nagging at you.'

'Oh yes?'

'Yes.'

'And what is it?' said Marius, looking embarrassed.

'Escape.'

'Nothing could be further from my mind.'

'Look me in the eye and repeat what you just said.'

Marius, who had been about to hand Lestrade his sabre, stood still for a moment, his weapon in his hand. Then his whole body relaxed. He took his guard and gave Lestrade a defiant look. 'Nothing could be closer to my mind.' And with a gesture he had repeated a hundred times, he threw the sabre into the air, caught it by its tip, and handed it to his master.

'I suspected as much,' said Lestrade, taking the sabre. 'One of my jackets is missing and I know it's you who took it. Keep it. I haven't forgotten what you told me about the plot of which you were the victim. Nor have I forgotten that you've sworn to take your revenge. I understand you, Marius, and I like you. But if the soldiers shoot at you, there's nothing I'll be able to do.'

Marius took a step forward. 'I like you, too. But if you'd been the victim of a miscarriage of justice, what would you do in my place?'

'The same as you, I suppose. If you succeed, you may obtain reparation for what you've suffered. I hope so with all my heart. But, of course, I haven't been the victim of a miscarriage of justice. It's my life that's been a miscarriage.' The old soldier approached Marius and clasped him to his heart. 'You remind me of my son, Marius.' A tear ran down his cheek. 'And when is it planned for?' He immediately shook his head nervously. 'No, don't tell me. I know you – if you're recaptured, you'll start imagining all sorts of things. And in a way, I'd like you to be recaptured. So let's leave it at that.'

Marius did not insist. 'Tomorrow at the same time?' he asked, opening the door leading to the workshop.

'Of course,' said the old soldier sadly.

And he hobbled out of the warehouse, in his crumpled uniform, his shoulders sagging. For the first time, Marius thought, he looked like an old man.

The vice admiral's staircase was finished somewhat earlier than predicted. As Marius had been planning to escape on St Philippe's day, this was a setback.

'Now that I'm no longer in the workshop, I wonder how we're going to manage it,' he said to Tripod.

'It doesn't have to be a particular day,' replied the cripple. 'We'll find another date. It's up to us to deal with it.'

Marius was furious. Since escapes were signalled by the firing of the cannon, his reasoning had been that on St Philippe's day, when a twenty-one-gun salute was fired in honour of King Louis-Philippe, nobody would pay any attention.

'What about going through the general store?' he suggested.

'Too risky. There's always a platoon of soldiers armed to the teeth.'

Perfect Love lay on his bed, pretending to have heard nothing, an appalled expression on his face. He had caught only snatches of the conversation, but the word escape had struck his ears, and that had been enough. Between seven-thirty and eight, when the signal for lights out was given, the Saint-François hall was like a tavern. The convicts ate and drank, while the warders walked up and down the aisles.

All at once, a whistle blew, and silence fell. Commandant Raynaud, dressed in his little black suit, entered the hall down the central aisle. Hands behind his back, he launched into a short speech. The authorities needed some twenty artisans in the Saint-Mandrier building yards for two weeks.

Marius and Perfect Love were picked as a matter of course. Tripod was also included for his expertise as a locksmith, as were seventeen other careful workers who were commendable in every respect. Weren't they supposed to be trusties?

It was a mistake to trust anybody – especially a convict. The very next day Marius was able to get a closer look at the men with whom he was going to share long hours of work and a few moments of intimacy. Their sniggers and sidelong glances were not promising, nor was the way their grins stood out in their pale, amorphous faces. There were two particularly fearsome characters among them, made no less fearsome by their constant bowing and scraping to the warders and officers. The first was a man with a lisp, named Sartier. He had a smooth skull, gummy lashes and little eyes that gleamed with a hard and metallic brightness. The colour of his skin was greenish and his squashed nose resembled that of a lizard. A former tax collector, sentenced to twenty years for bigamy and forgery, he had already been in Toulon for ten years and had ended up in the old lags' section because of his good behaviour. He hated Tripod because Tripod worked in the general store and earned a lot of money. He could not bear the fact that a man in Tripod's condition was allocated a paid job while he himself, with all his past experience as an official, was employed here for counting and did not get a sou.

Sartier liked to appear reckless, though he had neither the character nor the physique for it, to impress the man in the next bed with whom he had teamed up, a huge bear of a man, white as a larva, with a twisted mouth like the Mullet's. To his neighbour, Sartier seemed a learned man and good friend, who talked in glowing terms about his past as a tax collector and gave him some of his soup and wine. That was all Lemoine, whose nickname was Runny Nose, needed to hero-worship the ex-functionary.

Lemoine had been given this unflattering name because of his nostrils, which were two enormous holes, like a bull's. His grey eyes gleamed ferociously and his big flat head looked as though it was buried between his two broad shoulders. He was hardly more than five feet tall, but his powerful bow legs and his long, muscular arms hinted at his uncommon strength. A carpenter by trade, Runny Nose had been sentenced to fifteen years for crushing his mother's head between his hands. He had always pleaded not guilty, explaining that he had simply wanted to massage his mother's skull after she had complained – or so he said – of a buzzing in her head. He had his lawyer to thank for escaping the scaffold, for the lawyer had lodged an appeal and won. But Lemoine was not the kind to thank anyone for anything.

Marius did not trust either of these rogues. After a year in the colony he knew how unpredictable and cruel, how ungrateful and resentful, men could be, caught as they were in the web of their hidden vices and their desperate attempts to adapt to prison life. Nor was he unaware, despite Lestrade's advice, that tolerance sometimes engendered more ill will than intolerance.

The work at Saint-Mandrier was not too hard and consisted of renovating a warehouse belonging to the naval administration. Saint-Mandrier was a mountainous and wooded peninsula, some four leagues in circumference, which was joined to the mainland by a narrow isthmus called Les Sablettes. To get there, it was necessary to take two boats and pass Fort Bregaillon, some distance from La Seyne-sur-Mer.

The first week passed without incident. It was the end of April and a scented breeze blew gently. In the evening, when the convicts left, the peninsula was fragrant with mimosa and the harbour was suffused with a soft purple glow. Gradually, pink shade fell over the landscape. Marius, motionless in the middle of his comrades and the warders, scanned the distant valleys for the last rays of light, imagining, though he could not see them, the fleecy umbrella pines on the slopes of the hills. It was a beautiful region, even though he would have appreciated it more under other circumstances.

Spring was coming. The day was filled with the scents of pepper and lavender. The hills were carpeted with thistles and cornflowers, around which birds swarmed. The sea, now green, now turquoise, played hide-and-seek with the hills. Above them rose purple mountain spurs covered with boxwood.

'I hope we get there,' Tripod would say to Marius. 'I can already smell the sweet scent of the leaves mixed with the smell of the crops. Freedom, Alexandre!'

For Tripod, Marius was either Alexandre Tixier or prisoner 9430. The young man had not told him his real identity. Only Perfect Love and Lestrade knew that.

On the evening of 27 April Perfect Love overheard another conversation between Marius and Tripod, and an anxious look crept over his usually cheerful face. He did not breathe a word to Marius. But the following morning, with an officer's authorization, he went back to the carpentry workshop. Marius wondered what he was going to do there.

At Saint-Mandrier everything continued as normal. They fixed a double door, changed striking plates and bolts, and replaced a number of joists. There was enough for everybody to do and even Sartier and Runny Nose worked hard.

A group of Alsatian workers joined the convicts late in the morning, led by a foreman called the boss and Holy Smoke.

'What's he doing here?' muttered Marius.

'He's in charge of discipline,' replied Sartier.

During the lunch hour the warders took a siesta in the sun and the boats were unsupervised. It was tomorrow or never.

The previous evening, when Perfect Love had overheard the conversation between Marius and Tripod, Tripod had said that he knew something about navigation. A native of Sète, he was familiar with the winds and the currents. 'For the twenty-ninth I'm hoping for a nice little mistral.'

'You're not the only one,' Marius had replied.

The gods granted the men's wish. On 29 April a violent wind blew from the north-west towards the sea. That morning, when they left for the yard at Saint-Mandrier, Marius was wearing Lestrade's jacket beneath his smock. Being less supervised than the prisoners doing hard labour in the colony, he had not had to conceal his plan in the most intimate part of his anatomy, but had tied it around his thigh. Tripod had hidden his in his stick.

After disembarking at Saint-Mandrier, everyone set to work. Marius and Perfect Love were finishing the door to the warehouse.

'Will you give me a little of your bread?' asked Marius.

'Only if you're good,' replied Perfect Love with a smile.

Marius looked at the friend he was preparing to leave. He felt pity, and a sense of guilt he hardly dared admit. If it had not been for Perfect Love, always so confident and so generous, handing him a lifeline in the form of carpentry and intervening on his behalf with Commandant Raynaud and Vice Admiral Jacob, Marius would be rotting in solitary or among the hard cases. But there it was – Perfect Love would have no truck with the idea of escape. It would have meant facing reality and he had no desire to do that. He wanted a complete break with all he had suffered in the past. For him, the colony was a refuge. They had taken him into care and he was happy. Some people are like that. Although the Kitten, the Mullet and Tardier had all deceived him, he had no thoughts of revenge. Quick-tempered as he was, he bore no grudge. He no longer expected anything of life. Any other man would have called it resignation. He called it tranquillity.

Marius knew Perfect Love and had not tried to change his mind.

'All escape attempts are doomed to failure,' Perfect Love had often said, before Marius had even broached the subject.

Marius could not help feeling sad. In leaving Perfect Love and Lestrade, he was leaving his only two friends in the colony. The bonds of true friendship are formed in poverty and adversity, he would say to himself, not in the most conspicuous or popular places. Now he had to break these bonds. It was both terribly simple and terribly hard.

Towards midday they took a break. The warehouse was finished. The boss congratulated the convicts, the Alsatians and even Holy Smoke. They all ate their bread and drank their wine – except for Perfect Love, who sat next to Marius, looking pensively out to sea.

'Aren't you eating?' asked Marius.

'Not for the moment.'

Marius's plan was to wait for half an hour, until the warders were taking their siesta, leave the yard, give Holy Smoke the slip, stave in the hull of one of the two boats and steal the other one, which was fully rigged. All that was needed was to hoist the sail and take advantage of the wind. Marius and Tripod had it all planned. The only thing they had not planned was the unpredictable.

What happened was this. When work resumed, ten of the convicts, three of the warders and all the Alsatian workers were inside the warehouse. The warrant officer was standing near one of the boats, unsteady on his feet and drowsy, and a warder lay on the beach snoring. About ten of the convicts were not inside the warehouse, including Tripod, Perfect Love and Marius, not forgetting Sartier and Runny Nose. Sartier, who was respected by the others, closed the door of the warehouse.

'Let's see if it works,' he lisped.

The lock worked so well that he bolted the double door and did not open it. Then he turned to the other nine convicts. 'Those of you who choose terra firma, it's that way, towards Les Sablettes. Those who choose the sea, follow me.'

Three of the convicts made a dash towards the woods and the mountains, just as they were, without clothes or provisions, with the fleeting certainty that they could get through and succeed where their predecessors had always failed. The prospect of being free, for a prisoner, is an unending addiction, disorganized, impulsive and instinctive – a question of run first, ask questions later.

'I don't rate their chances,' said Sartier, following the fugitives with his eyes. 'They'll be caught by this evening.'

He was right. That very evening, during a search organized by the marines and the peasants, the three convicts were recaptured. The unfortunates had hidden themselves in the bushes, under heaps of dry branches. They reckoned without the thoroughness of the soldiers, who struck the trunks of the trees and the undergrowth with their bayonets as they passed. At about six in the evening, a cry of pain was heard, then a second, then a third. The three unlucky men, doubly unlucky because they had only short sentences, were each given a beating and three extra years.

But let us return to Sartier. While the boss and the warders were beginning to drum on the closed door, he signalled to the other six to follow him. Drawing near the two boats, they found the warrant officer sitting facing the sea, a pipe in his hand. The warder was still sleeping.

'Your turn, Runny Nose.'

The giant swooped on the warder and strangled him in a second.

'Oh no, not this!' Perfect Love protested, putting down his bread and raising his hands to heaven. 'We'll get the guillotine for this!'

'Shut up!' replied Sartier, glaring at him. 'He had a rifle, we had to knock him out.'

'He didn't knock him out, he killed him!'

'I said shut up!'

Sartier seized the warder's rifle and aimed it at Holy Smoke. Emerging abruptly from his lethargy, the officer rose unsteadily to his feet, taking some time to realize what was happening.

'But . . . But . . .' he stammered, raising his hand.

'That's right,' said Sartier, keeping his rifle trained on him. 'Give my friend your weapon and don't you dare shout.'

The officer was so drunk that he had difficulty taking his sabre out of its scabbard. His feet got tangled and he fell on his backside. Laughing, Runny Nose caught the sabre. 'Ugh!' he exclaimed, holding his nose. 'He's shat himself, the filthy bastard!' He twisted Holy Smoke's arm and slid the sabre under his neck, as if about to cut his throat.

'No!' cried Tripod, rushing at them with his arms raised.

The giant simply held out the sabre, and Tripod was impaled on the weapon.

'We told you we'd get you,' said Sartier, barely concealing his sudden nervousness.

At the same moment, before Runny Nose could see the attack coming, Marius and Perfect Love rushed him, tore the sabre from his hands and threw him to the ground. As Runny Nose lay on his stomach, Perfect Love dug his knee into his back, and with lightning speed seized him under the chin and twisted his neck until it broke. Runny Nose's head flopped lifeless onto the sand.

'Are you a witness?' Perfect Love asked the officer.

'Absolutely,' stuttered Holy Smoke. 'The naval authorities will take your intervention into account, 9430 and 9431—'

'Forget about that!' bellowed Sartier, who felt alone and defenceless and was starting to panic. 'Get back!'

Meanwhile, Perfect Love had taken off the warder's uniform jacket and tied it around his belly, under his smock. Marius, the sabre in his hand, was bending over Tripod and helping him to bandage his wound. The old man was moaning softly. He had been run through just above the heart.

'We'll get you out of here,' whispered Marius. 'You're bleeding a lot, but it's superficial.'

He raised his eyes and considered Sartier with hostility. Thanks to this imbecile, they were heading for disaster. The thought of ending up on the scaffold made him falter. He would never see Cosette again, or his house in the Rue Plumet. Like Bonnet, they were going to cut his head off, drain his blood. 'Do you want to kill us all? Is that it?'

Sartier evaded the question. With his rifle point, he gestured to one of the two boats. 'You and your stupid friends, get in that boat and get out of my sight!' He turned abruptly and hit Holy Smoke with the butt of his rifle. The officer collapsed on his side without a groan.

Marius and Perfect Love dragged Tripod to the boat indicated by Sartier and climbed in without protest. Perfect Love, in passing, picked up his bread and the warder's shako. Marius laid Tripod in the bows of the boat and seized the oars. He winked at the old man. What he had just seen proved that it was the right boat. The mainsail lay rolled on its side under the rowlocks.

'Let's pull hard!' cried Marius.

The boat moved quickly away from the shore.

'See you in hell!' shouted Sartier, pushing the two remaining convicts into the second boat. 'They make a fine bait, that lot. The warders and the marines are going to be on them like flies. Let them go. We've got plenty of time. We'll push along the coast as far as Cape Sisié and then go ashore.'

Once on the open sea, Perfect Love spotted a naval frigate on the starboard side. He stopped rowing, untied the uniform jacket he had taken from the warder, and held it out to Marius. 'Put that on, quick.'

Marius put on the jacket and rammed the shako on his head. Tripod had dealt with the rest, managing to kneel and put the rigging in place. 'It's at least force four,' he murmured. 'Hoist the sail, my friends.'

Marius and Perfect Love obeyed. The sail immediately swelled and Tripod took the tiller, his eye fixed on the frigate, which was getting nearer. Perfect Love seized his bread.

'Do you think this is the right time to eat?' asked Marius.

'That depends on your appetite,' said Perfect Love ironically. He broke the bread in two, lengthways, and opened it as though he was about to make himself a huge sandwich. Beaming, he removed a telescope he had stolen from Vice Admiral Jacob, a little cap and a sailor's blouse. He took off his smock and threw it in the sea.

'So you were planning to escape after all!' shouted Marius.

'Tie your collar and try to look like a sailor instead of talking nonsense,' said Perfect Love, disguising himself. 'They'll see us over there, on the frigate.'

'Well, they won't be the only ones,' replied Marius, seizing the telescope.

He looked first towards the frigate, then back towards the Saint-Mandrier peninsula. Sartier's boat looked frail as it rode the swelling waves. The wind was getting up and the sky was clouding over.

'We're doing well,' said Tripod, trying to put on a brave face, though he was doubled up in pain as he clung to the tiller. 'If we continue at this speed, we'll reach Porquerolles soon. There, we'll have to think about going ashore . . . When I was in Marseilles, I fished in that area . . . All the way up to Le Lavandou . . . If we could come ashore near Cavalaire, that'd be ideal . . . After that, we can vanish into the Maures massif and we've done it . . . Don't forget, I have a map . . .' The old man's delivery was more and more broken. His face grinned, ghostlike, through the sea spray.

'Are you all right, Tripod?'

'I have to be . . .'

Marius and Perfect Love exchanged a sombre look.

'To think the two of you wanted to escape without me!' said Perfect Love. 'Do you think I didn't know why you were so secretive? All that whispering, and looking like plotters, and imagining old Perfect Love was too thick to understand what you were planning! So much for the fine friendship you kept banging on about, Marius!'

'But I was sure—' Marius stopped short. Through the telescope he could now see the faces of the officers on the rear deck of the frigate. The three-master was cleaving through the waves in their direction. At first, he thought he was dreaming. One of the officers was observing him, too, through a telescope. And this officer was none other than Lestrade! What was he doing there?

Marius took off his shako and waved it, still keeping his eye stuck to the glass. Now he could see distinctly his valiant fencing master's furrowed face. Lestrade made a gesture with his hand and turned to the other officers. Apparently, the alarm had still not been given. Lestrade took off his hat in turn and waved it at Marius, as if to say: Good luck, son.

The frigate veered slightly to the side and headed for the tip of Saint-Mandrier – in the direction of Sartier's boat.

Marius lowered his telescope and put his shako back on. Just then, there was a tremendous gust of wind, and he lost his balance and had to catch himself on the mast. He smiled sadly and his eyes met those of Tripod.

'We're going to run into a squall,' warned the latter.

Marius did not care. He was thinking of Lestrade and his kindly smile. The warrant officer had just saved his life. They were quits. The way was clear. But for how long?

By the early hours of the morning, in driving rain, Marius and his companions were close to Cavalaire. Just as they were sailing into a hidden rocky inlet, they heard the cannon fire twenty-one times. It was a muffled, distant, almost joyful sound, like a salute to their new-found freedom.

'You see,' Perfect Love said to Marius. 'You finally got your St Philippe's day.'

But Tripod had tried his strength to the limit in handling the boat, and his condition was worse. The sabre must have perforated his lung after all, for he was spitting blood. Marius and Perfect Love carried him to a little wood. Then they retraced their steps, waded waist-high into the water, took the sabre and their belongings from the boat, pierced the hull, hauled on the sail and pushed the boat out to sea. As the wind had not fallen, the boat moved off rapidly. They stood watching it for a brief moment, then went back to Tripod. Perfect Love loaded him on his shoulders and they set off in the direction of the Maures massif.

'We'll take turns carrying him,' said Marius, consulting Tripod's military map.

Thanks to the map, they were able to avoid villages. They had long since finished Perfect Love's bread, and hunger gnawed at their stomachs. Towards midday they halted. The silence was extraordinary. They had crossed woods of oaks and small pines. The rain had not made their progress any easier. The stony ground was shiny and slippery and the trees were perfectly still. What surprised them, and also worried them, was the absence of birds. They had stopped near a winding clear stream, edged with pebbles and long grass.

'We mustn't give up,' said Marius to Tripod.

The old man had lost a lot of blood and life was gently ebbing from his body. He could hardly see the bone-coloured hills above the woods.

Towards evening the rain stopped and the sun even put in a timid appearance. Suddenly, at the top of a little path, Perfect Love, who was carrying Tripod, sneezed violently. The jolt reopened Tripod's wound and he started to scream. It was horrible. Perfect Love laid him on the ground. Powerless to help, Marius and Perfect Love listened to him, their hearts pounding.

'I can't believe a wound like that can cause so much suffering,' said Perfect Love.

'What could it be, then?' asked Marius.

Tripod crawled along the ground, tearing out handfuls of saplings and beating his head against the trunk of a cork oak. With his feet, he dug into the soil of the path, as if he wanted to get under the ground. Marius turned the old man over and noticed with horror that his stomach was stained with blood. But the most terrible thing of all was the screams. Marius had never imagined that such harsh sounds could come from a human throat. Tripod was gasping, choking, spitting blood. He tore his smock with his nails and snatched Marius's hand.

'I really got it bad . . .' he murmured. 'Don't forget my plan, there, in my stick . . . Watch out for the gypsies, or they'll get you . . . We talked about them back in Toulon . . . The Erzbets, two Hungarian brothers . . . They specialize in capturing escaped convicts . . . They're cruel and bloodthirsty . . .'

And there came another wave of sighs, groans and desperate cries. There were huge shadows beneath Tripod's hollow eyes. He could no longer see anything. Perfect Love wiped his sweat-drenched face, but he was delirious and rambling.

'It's over, I'll never again be able to pick locks . . .'

Suddenly his hand tensed on Marius's forearm. He wanted to whisper something in his ear. Marius bent to listen, then recoiled. 'But . . . but that's horrible,' he stammered. 'I can't—'

'Swear!' cried Tripod, twisting Marius's hand in a last burst of strength. 'I swear . . .'

A final thick spurt of blood came from Tripod's mouth and he died.

'What did he say?' asked Perfect Love.

'Something abominable.'

'What?'

Marius whispered in his ear.

'And you swore?' said Perfect Love, growing pale.

'Unfortunately, yes.'

In Tripod's plan, Marius found a blade. He thought carefully about what he would have to do. He felt enormous disgust. But he had sworn. He took Tripod's corpse by the feet, dragged it over to an almond tree and stripped it. He looked at Tripod's naked body, and a bitter taste filled his mouth. How ugly death was, how commonplace and insignificant! His hand trembled as he picked up the blade. He closed his eyes, placed the instrument on Tripod's navel and pushed with all his strength. As he punctured the skin, he heard a soft, cavernous noise. He retched and a jet of bile came out of his mouth. But he had sworn, so he pushed the blade and opened the belly as far as the sternum . . .

Perfect Love preferred not to watch. He stood looking up at the sky, which was tinged with a satin sheen by the setting sun. He was missing his quiet life. What about the gypsies that Tripod had talked about? Were they already on their heels? He suppressed a gesture of despair. He was not a narcissist, he did not even know the word, but he had a fierce instinct for self-preservation. Why had he embarked on this adventure? He would have been happier back in the colony, polishing wood and caressing dovetails in his workshop, amid the smells of freshly planed cherry wood. But he must banish all such thoughts from his mind. What was done was done. Besides, the sight of these tall oaks sparkling in the sun fascinated him. He had never seen anything like it.

He turned, and saw Marius standing there, his face as pale as a corpse, his arms red with blood up to the elbows. As he watched, Marius leaned against a tree and began to vomit copiously. He had cut Tripod's skin, removed the intestines, plunged his hand into the still warm and steaming entrails, and found fifty sous, red with rust, and ten gold coins. How had Tripod been able to bear all this metal in his guts for so long?

'Well, clearly, he couldn't bear it any more,' said Perfect Love, placing his hand on Marius's shoulder. 'He gave us a terrible gift. And you kept your word.'

'And what of his soul?' asked Marius, wiping his mouth with the back of his hand.

'It's already in heaven,' said Perfect Love.

'Do you believe in heaven?'

'Like everyone else.'

The two men buried their companion by a clump of blue thistles. Instead of a cross, they planted his stick in the soft clay.

After quenching their thirst at a spring of clear, ice-cold water and gathering wild watercress, they went on their way towards Collobrières. When night fell, they found a small cave where they could rest and dry themselves. There, they made an inventory of their possessions. In the cylindrical tube they had taken from Tripod's stick they found a cigarette lighter, some tow and a little flask of alcohol, which allowed them to light a fire and burn their prison clothes. Out of the warder's uniform and leather belt, they made themselves moccasins. Marius, who was wearing Lestrade's jacket, a velvet jacket with big brass buttons, detached the tube fixed to his leg and took out the shirt, the piece of mirror, the false moustache, the wig, the side whiskers, four one-franc coins and the saw-file. They crushed some broad beans on a hollow stone and mixed them with water. Then they added the watercress and heated it. It was not so much a soup, more a herbal tea, but at least it was hot. They also ate some parsley roots. Later, with the saw-file, they filed through their irons – the ignominious irons that had not left them for a year.

First there was a white dawn. Then a purple sun, filling the landscape with sparkling light. Birds were crying in a crevice of the cliff. Marius stood at the entrance to the cave, bare-chested, his eyes half closed, and took deep breaths of the cool air. He spread his arms and moved his fingers, the better to feel the caress of the wind on his body. He was filled with the hope of rebirth. He passed his hands over the marks the irons had left on his calves. He remained open-mouthed, his head upright, his pupils fixed. And then the sun again attracted his attention. It was so low that it seemed to touch the tops of the trees, even engulfing the razor-sharp tips of the pines.

Perfect Love now appeared, with a curious look on his face. 'I feel like a new man,' he declared, stretching lazily.

Indeed, Marius and he no longer looked the same. The tow had worked miracles, and with birdlime as glue, sticking was guaranteed.

'You were really inspired, taking that piece of mirror,' said Perfect Love. 'There's no doubt about it, you've got brains!' He burst out laughing. 'My lessons finally bore fruit!'

Marius shook his head, also laughing. He had side whiskers, a moustache and hair. He, too, felt like a new man. Yet he had not slept a wink all night. He had been assailed by nightmares, nightmares in which he had returned to Paris only to find that Cosette did not recognize him and denounced him to the police, who had sent him back to Toulon.

He stifled a yawn. 'We won't go round the next village,' he said decisively. 'We need provisions. Dressed like this, and with Tripod's money in our pockets, we can buy whatever we like.'

For breakfast, he suggested berries and dandelion roots. Perfect Love grimaced and spat on the ground. 'My teeth are like bayonets! And I don't want to go back to the colony!'

'You don't want to go back?' said Marius in mock surprise. 'I thought you wanted to stay there . . . I can tell you, I don't want to go back either. But we have to eat. We have a lot of walking to do.'

And the two men set off again.

There was no lack of water, and Marius and Perfect Love drank plenty. They needed it as they climbed hillocks covered with chestnut trees, descended into grey coombs where their steps raised flakes of ash, followed winding little valleys between walls of brilliant chalk, walked along white-hot escarpments, scaled hillsides in the cool shade, and skirted the edges of olive groves and fields of lavender, from which a fierce heat rose.

Late in the afternoon they stopped by a little pond.

'If the map is right, we're only a few leagues from a village called Besse,' said Marius.

'We'd have done better to follow the coast,' grumbled Perfect Love. 'I'm hungry.'

'And get ourselves caught? Certainly not. I'm hungry, too.' As he said these words, Marius noticed what looked like a length of thick rope unrolling lazily in the sun, studded with shiny scales. 'Look.'

'What?'

'A snake.'

'What of it?'

Marius advanced on tiptoe and unsheathed his sabre. When he was close to the reptile, he struck it a backhanded blow with the hilt. So great was his desire not to miss that he did. Stunned, the animal slithered under a stone. But Marius dived and caught it by the tail.

'It's cold!' he cried, standing up and running to a tree. He whirled the snake and smashed its head against the trunk.

Perfect Love, taken aback, had watched the scene without moving. He had an insurmountable revulsion for snakes. 'What do you plan to do with that thing?' he asked, as Marius walked towards him with the snake over his shoulder.

'Skin it and eat it.'

Perfect Love almost lost his tow wig. 'But it's the devil, Marius! It crawls!'

'In 1832, on the barricades, I met a fellow from the Jura who'd eaten snake. According to him, a grass snake tastes like an eel.'

Two hours later, as night was falling and they could distinguish a few flickering lights on the plain, the two men found a new shelter for the night.

It was a half-ruined cottage, of which part of one wall was buried in the ground. As they approached, a flock of crows emerged from it and enveloped them in a rustling of wings. They pushed open the door and entered. There, they were attacked by a huge dog, which almost knocked them over. The dog turned away and began to growl.

Perfect Love saw then what the animal was after. The corpse of a sheep lay on the floor, squashed like a big white cheese, guts bursting from its belly. Locked in the cottage, the dog must have been fighting over it with the crows. Marius took out his sabre.

'No,' said Perfect Love. With the tip of his foot, he pushed the carcass towards the dog, who gave a squeal, wagged its tail, seized the carcass in its mouth and dragged it outside.

'A lost sheep,' joked Marius.

'Don't make fun of religion, Marius. There's a God for everyone, even animals.'

Marius shrugged. Then, gathering a few stones into a circle, he improvised a grill from the branches of a green tree and lit a fire. He took the blade, made an incision in the snake's neck, peeled it like a dab and cut it into sections to make brochettes. Then he asked Perfect Love to go and gather rosemary and thyme. His resourcefulness surprised even himself. In Paris, he had read Daniel Defoe and Fenimore Cooper. Perhaps he, too, was turning out to be a cross between Robinson Crusoe and a Mohican. The thought made him smile. But what drove him was hunger.

The snake's flesh was dull, white and stringy, but the smell of grilled meat drew Perfect Love like a magnet. To make it more attractive, Marius had flambéed the meat with Tripod's brandy.

'Without the skin, cut into little pieces, garnished with rosemary and thyme, and especially with alcohol, it's almost edible,' said Perfect Love grudgingly.

'Look, we have a new companion,' said Marius. The dog stood in the doorway, its tail down and its tongue hanging.

He separated one of the brochettes and threw the animal a few chunks of meat. The two men exchanged a knowing smile. Tomorrow would be another day.

Late in the morning Marius and Perfect Love reached the outskirts of the village. The dog was still with them. The two men looked at each other and broke into smiles. They were back in civilization – and perhaps in trouble.

They bought bread at the baker's shop, salt and dried bacon at the grocer's, and two belts and some flasks at the saddler's. Nobody said a word to them. Nobody accosted them or asked where they were from. Everyone was used to wandering shepherds, fierce men who lived in the mountains, imitated bird calls and were involved in shady dealings.

Towards midday they set off again, careful about the way they walked, for the way convicts walked – rather stiffly and heavily, as if hindered by chains – often gave them away. As they left the village, they saw clouds gathering on the horizon. They were used by now to the fact that the days were hot and the nights ice-cold. A thick cloud as red as a beetroot was hovering over them.

'A bad omen,' muttered Perfect Love.

'What are you talking about?' said Marius, irritated. 'We have provisions, weapons, and even a dog. What more could we want?'

'We shouldn't stay on this road,' Perfect Love insisted.

It was not so much a road, more a rough path bordered with cypress trees. Marius would have none of it. He insisted there was nothing to fear. Some time later, as they neared Brignoles, they came across two horsemen. One seemed as tall and thin as the other was short and fat. They looked like Don Quixote and Sancho Panza, a resemblance accentuated by the fact that they had a mule with them. Perfect Love passed them without lifting his head. In the underworld, you didn't look at people, especially if they seemed suspicious in any way. As for Marius, he could not stop himself from staring at them. And what he read in their eyes made him uneasy, though he could not have said why.

A few minutes later Marius and Perfect Love turned round. There was no trace of the horsemen. Walking faster now, they passed through a little village, then a hamlet, then a town. The sunlight was sometimes so intense it blinded them. They had eaten half a loaf of bread and four slices of bacon each. Before them, the hills rose like pyramids. The fields stretched as far as the eye could see.

They did not even stop to drink. In their new flasks, the water tasted of leather.

'We should have put vinegar inside,' said Perfect Love, stroking the dog, who was now their constant companion.

'We have to keep up this pace,' replied Marius.

'What pace?'

'Eight to ten leagues a day.'

'We won't hold out. I don't know about you, but I wasn't on the retreat from Russia.'

Marius raised his eyes. This morning, choosing a spot at random on Tripod's map, his forefinger had fallen on Mont Ventoux. Before getting back to Paris, he would have to stay hidden for at least two months. He needed time to look human again, and to plan his actions carefully. He had therefore made the decision to get to that corner of the Vaucluse as quickly as possible.

'Where are we going?' asked Perfect Love.

'North.'

'That's vague, that is. I'm exhausted. Why don't we take our time? Of course, you're young. The colony even made you stronger and tougher than you were before. But I'm old. You're making a mistake, treating me like this.'

'You're the one who's making a mistake,' Marius replied uncompromisingly. 'And like most people when they make a mistake, you think you're in the right. You're behaving as I used to behave. One step forward, one step back. First you say we shouldn't go through any villages, then you want to go through all of them and stop in them. You love to contradict yourself. We're escaped convicts. If they capture us, we get three more years. And special treatment, too. Solitary, double chain, getting put with the hard cases. Just to satisfy Raynaud. Is that what you want?'

Perfect Love muttered under his breath and sank his head between his shoulders. Marius talked too well for him. He did not always understand what he was saying.

They came to a wood on a gentle slope. As Perfect Love's feet were bleeding, they decided to stop there.

'All right, we'll camp here,' conceded Marius regretfully. 'But I don't think there's enough shelter. Let's go into that clearing, behind that tree trunk.'

Perfect Love collapsed onto a nest of moss. 'Look at this – we need different shoes!'

'Make a fire behind the trunk. I'll go and have a look around.'

The dog followed Marius, wagging its tail. Perfect Love took off his imitation moccasins and rubbed his painful feet, finding a little relief.

Marius was away for a good two hours. The city man was adapting well to life in the country, perhaps because of his escapades with his grandfather Gillenormand. In any event, he was efficient. Spotting nests in the trees, he collected a dozen eggs. A little further on, as he was filling his empty flask in a fast-moving stream, he surprised some thirty big crayfish feasting on the corpse of a jay. Luring them with his fingers, he caught about twenty. With the eggs, the bacon and the crayfish we'll have a banquet, he told himself with good humour, retracing his steps.

As he passed under a canopy of green bristling with almond barbs and brownish creepers, he recalled his dinner at Hardy's and his evening at the Café Turc with Cosette. What had become of her? Was she seeing that false friend Amédée? Had she given herself to him? And was Louis-Désiré really in league with the Mullet and the Catman, as Perfect Love claimed?

It will all be settled in Paris, thought Marius, who, however often he repeated it to himself, would never be as magnanimous as Jean Valjean. He stole a loaf of bread. But they tried to steal my life. And I know who the guilty men are.

Once justice had been done, he would take Cosette to the Americas. Little Raphaël would go too, and Perfect Love, if he wished. As he was turning these thoughts over, pleased to be nurturing major plans, he heard a horse whinny, followed by an oath in an unknown language. He stopped. The dog growled.

'Hush,' whispered Marius, stroking the animal.

He was not far from the clearing. He went down on all fours and crawled along the ground through the dry grass. A gleam of light caught his attention – the fire lit by Perfect Love.

When he reached the edge of the clearing, his blood froze. The two horsemen they had passed on the road late that morning were there. Their horses and the mule were grazing some distance away. Despite the fading light, he could see their features. They were not very young – perhaps forty or forty-five. The taller of the two had black, shoulder-length hair and a face riddled with smallpox scars. His gestures were slow and precise. He was holding a sabre in the embers. Marius felt angry with Perfect Love. If only he had lit the fire behind the tree.

Perfect Love was sitting against the trunk, his hands tied in front of him, white mucus running from his nostrils. He had his tongue between his teeth and his face had turned blue. The second horseman, who was ruddy-faced and stout, was whipping his face at regular intervals with a switch.

'So, you don't know where your accomplice is? Or you don't want to tell us?' He turned to the tall, thin man. 'My dear Laszlo, this convict doesn't seem to be very talkative. But he doesn't know the Erzbet brothers. We know how to loosen tongues.'

Perfect Love was not even looking at them. Marius noted that they were dressed in a most eccentric manner, in jackets of skin, grenadier's gaiters, leather belts and fur caps, and that their belts bristled with sabres, cutlasses and pistols. So these were the Erzbet brothers, the Hungarian gypsies Tripod had talked about.

'I think you're right, Vlad,' said the tall, thin man, looking around. 'We're going to tell our friend a little story. I think he'll be much more talkative after he hears it!' He burst into fierce laughter and brandished the sabre, its blade almost entirely red hot from the fire. Then he took a few steps, swaying his hips, and pointed at the mule. 'This animal is just an old hack,' he said in a soft, wheedling voice. 'So I'm going to kill it. We'll open its belly and take out its organs. Then we'll undress you, convict, stuff you in the hot, stinking belly, put back the mule's organs and sew the whole lot up.' He smiled. 'I don't like the French. At Waterloo we cut them in pieces. And you know where your head will be, little Frenchman? Up the mule's arse! In the shit! You'll slowly choke to death in shit!'

He rushed at Perfect Love and told his brother to pull his arms out horizontally. Then he turned his back and nonchalantly twirled his sabre. 'Are you right-handed or left-handed?'

'Right-handed . . .' stammered Perfect Love.

'So you don't need your left hand!'

And he cut it off, leaving Perfect Love staring incredulously at the stump of his left hand, from which blood was gushing.

With that, the short, fat man took hold of Perfect Love's arm and plunged his stump into the fire. There came a sinister crackling sound and a smell like burning pork. The scream that burst from Perfect Love's chest must have made all the animals in the wood flee. Except the dog, which threw itself with a snarl at the short, fat man before Marius could stop it.

The attack was so quick and so sudden that the Hungarian did not have time to seize his carbine. The dog's fangs sank into his thigh. Now Marius threw himself out of his hiding place and rushed at the tall, thin man, yelling like a demon. 'So you were at Waterloo, were you?' he screamed, turning around the man. 'Well, commend your soul to God, you're going back there!'

The sabre is not like the foil. To use it with skill requires a warrior's qualities. It cuts, it severs, it tears. It is a noble weapon that despises sudden and uncontrolled movements. Thanks to Warrant Officer Lestrade, Marius had attained that nobility. His adversary realized immediately that he was not dealing with an amateur. Although he fought in *tierce* guard, he did not parry the attacks well. Marius's thrusts were forceful and precise. The Hungarian retreated, looking around for his horse as he did so.

All at once, a heart-rending cry was heard. The short, fat man had just cut the dog's throat. But Perfect Love, finding reserves of strength, threw himself on the Hungarian and stabbed him with his own knife.

That redoubled Marius's ardour. He brought his sabre down on the other Hungarian's right shoulder. Erzbet dropped his weapon and fell to one knee.

'Not mocking now, are you?' said Marius, placing the tip of his sabre on his throat. 'Don't you know you must never mock a drowning man if you haven't crossed the river yet? You're going to die, Hungarian.'

Erzbet was kneeling and hugging his arm, which hung almost severed from the shoulder. His eyes had lost their expression of overwhelming vanity and contempt. His lips and nostrils were quivering.

'Little Frenchman, did you say?' resumed Marius. 'Well, little Hungarian, did you know my father was killed at Waterloo? Maybe it was you who killed him.'

Erzbet shook his head, terrified. The man is mad, he thought. Meanwhile, Perfect Love was cutting himself a bandage from the dead man's shirt. He wrapped his stump and took the dog in his arms. 'They killed him . . .' he murmured, with a sob in his voice.

'You told my friend a beautiful story,' said Marius to the Hungarian. 'Thanks to you, he no longer has a left hand. People like you are a disgrace. I was sentenced to hard labour by mistake. I spent a year with the people of the abyss. Before, I'd never have done what I'm going to do now. In a way, I believed that God's reign on earth was near. Do you understand?'

'If you let me live, I'll plead in your favour . . .' stammered Erzbet.

'In my favour?' cried Marius jubilantly. 'For two years people have been pleading in my favour and where has it got me? And yet I've never coveted other people's goods, which is more than can be said of you – or of people in general. I've become a wild beast, Hungarian. As soon as a man learns to speak, he learns to lie. And you're lying!'

'No,' said the Hungarian, with an imploring air, his pockmarked face crumbling. In a panic, he made an attempt to throw Marius off balance and take his weapon away from him.

But Marius gave him a kick and gashed his wrist. 'You're going to die like a Greek hero!' he hissed. 'I used to move in exalted circles, where people were nostalgic for Greek tragedy. Well, you certainly look the part!' He ran to the mule.

'No!' screamed Perfect Love. 'Leave him!'

But Marius would not listen. The young dandy who had haunted Lord Seymour's fencing school was well and truly dead. He slid beneath the mule and plunged his sabre into its flanks, until only the hilt was visible. The poor beast reared, ran a few steps and fell on its side. A demonic light distorted Marius's features. He saw his task through and disembowelled the still living mule. Then, red with blood from head to foot, he came back for Erzbet and dragged him to the mule by his hair.

'Don't do it!' Perfect Love cried again.

'We're leaving no witnesses!' roared Marius.

He pushed the Hungarian into the mule's belly, stuffing his head towards the anus. Despite the foul stench, he took a strip of material and set about binding the animal's belly up again. Erzbet struggled like a demon. With a rage bordering on insanity, Marius hit him in the stomach, on the head, on his wound. All at once, a shot rang out. Perfect Love had seized a pistol and blown Erzbet's brains out. Marius fell to the ground, and lay face down, sobbing and cursing.

'My God!' he cried. 'Why have you forsaken me?'

6

That morning the Catman was walking along the Rue Saint-Denis with the Wolf. He had just learned that Lacenaire, after visiting Dijon, Beaune and Geneva, had been arrested in Lyons for trying to pass a false bill of exchange under the assumed name of Jacob Levy.

'Everybody knows everything in the underworld,' said the Wolf. 'We slander each other, we squeal, we hand each other over. Letters? Who needs letters when we've got mouths?'

'How right you are, brother! No honour among thieves, which is just as it should be. Lacenaire always thought he was too clever by half. Where have they put him?'

'In Dijon prison.' According to one of the Wolf's informants, Lacenaire, while waiting to be transferred to Paris, was spending his time writing verses. 'Listen to this,' said the Wolf, taking a paper from his pocket. 'It's called "The Thief" or "Petition".' And in a harsh, false-sounding voice, he intoned:

> Sire, I beg you, hear my plea:
> I've just returned from hard labour.
> You're the king, a poor thief me,
> Please treat me like a neighbour.
> My heart is hard, my soul is vile,
> Good people faint at sight of me,
> I cheat and steal and kill with a smile –
> A policeman is what I should be!

By the end of the fourth verse, in which the thief, having been successively a policeman, a prefect and a minister, now tried to take the place of the king, the Catman was shrugging. Having prided himself in the past on having some literary knowledge, especially during his days in

322

the Sergent-de-Waterloo at Montfermeil, when he had loved to quote Voltaire and St Augustine, he thought the text mediocre.

Regardless, the Wolf continued his story. When he had appeared before the judge, Lacenaire had claimed crimes that made the offences of which he was accused – petty thievery and swindling – pale in comparison. The astonished judge had sent him back for further investigation. 'And you know what happened then, Catman? He spilled the beans – confessed to murdering the Chardons!'

'I always knew the toff had a screw loose,' declared the Catman, with a satisfied expression. 'People who can't stop talking end up at the abbey of the Monte-à-Regret. Real suicides of the guillotine!' He stopped. 'Right, you go to the workshop. I'm off to the Marmousets, on the Ile de la Cité.'

Early that year, the Catman, who will henceforth be referred to by his real name, Thénardier, had bought a property on the Ile de la Cité, hoping to turn it into one of those shady taverns he loved so much. It was in the Rue des Ursins, near the Rue des Marmousets, just beside Notre-Dame. Thénardier had a particular fondness for such insalubrious premises, where all sorts of shameful activities went on in the shadow of the Cross, as if under divine protection. He loved this maze of dark streets where only a murky light penetrated, this leprous district where prostitutes and lowlifes had set up shop, where plaintive cries rose from the cobblestones or seeped through half-open doors. The atmosphere of the Chat-Malin did not suit him, he missed the days of the Clan Destin and only felt happy when wading through mire. Slander and intrigue were his predilections, not display and opulence. He could not stand extravagant spendthrifts and was not only mean on his own behalf, but also on behalf of other people. The idea of squandering money disgusted him. And he had an answer for everything.

Wealth? A mystery. Idealism? Useless. Pleasure? An obscene word. Pity? How horrible. Glory? A mere puff of smoke. What mattered to him was intrigue. It triumphed over all the values he despised. He was like a dog that always returned to its own vomit. It gave him an indescribable sense of joy, a fierce, deformed, mysterious sense of joy, to see these people of the lower depths twisted, weakened, emaciated and buried beneath the weight of their misery. He cherished their unchanging suffering and destitution, their pathetic and continuous wailing. Everything that stole the bread of the future, the soup of the weak or the rags of the poor, was for him suffused with glamour.

'The poor should raise a statue to me for all the harm I could have done them and didn't,' he liked to repeat, with a good-natured air.

But the poor ignored him, for he had never risen above his own mediocrity. Unlike most popular heroes, he dreamed of robbing the poor to give to the rich. The noblest of man's impulses, self-sacrifice, was unknown to him. The zest in his life came from solitude and avarice. Everything, even sex, was in his brain. Even Satan could not have become his friend, for the one thing he dreaded was having to share, whether his companion was real or supernatural. And what man deserves the name of man if he does not share?

It was a question Thénardier did not ask himself, had never asked himself. No sooner had he recovered from the theft of his diamonds than he had extracted the remaining stones and hidden them in a safe place. He suspected everyone – Horse Face and the Mullet in particular, but also Carignol. Had he not had so much cautious duplicity in him, he might have run screaming in all directions in search of his money.

But to admit his unhappiness would have been tantamount to admitting he had possessions, for a miser has to appear poor in other people's eyes. A miser owns nothing, is always the victim of others – even if in reality he is his own victim. His vice is suffering. He lives to tremble.

So Thénardier trembled. He saw crooks and profiteers everywhere. In order to be prepared for every eventuality, he had engaged the services of Pegasus and Twenty-Two, the two scoundrels who had helped the Mullet to kill Jesus, solely to stir up ill-feeling between the Mullet and his accomplices. And in order to avoid losing any more money, which would once again have broken his heart, he made the two cut-throats the managers of his new restaurant.

'In the Deux-Marmousets, you'll be the bosses. But be careful! Notre Dame is watching over you. From hell to heaven is but a small step, it has to be said. I get the profits, and whatever you make from your little dealings you can keep for yourselves. As for the everyday arrangements, we'll sort them out as we go.'

Thénardier had agreed to meet Burdin on the Ile de la Cité in front of his new tavern. When he had last seen him, the hunchback had seemed to be desperate, profoundly upset by what was happening in the Rue Saint-Fiacre. The Catman was perfectly well aware of the agonies his accomplice was going through, although, being the man he was, he was not moved by them. On the contrary, he was waiting eagerly for Burdin to ask him for a service, which would allow him once again to take over the reins. He was a man who took pleasure in being in control, in exerting a constant but invisible magnetism, without anyone being aware of it.

He had spotted Burdin in the grey light of dawn. Usually, as if to signify his own importance, the steward arrived late. This morning he was early.

Thénardier stopped at the corner of the Rue Chanoinesse, leaned on his cane and whistled a tune, savouring the moment. Workers were wandering in the streets like floating shadows. Gaunt and emaciated as they were, they still found the strength to put one foot in front of the other. There was something deathlike about their resignation. Thénardier cursed inwardly, wishing them all back in the limbo whence they had come. Shaking from head to foot with nervous laughter, he stepped forward and revealed himself to his 'dear' Burdin.

'Here already, old chap?' he said, pointing with his cane at his new acquisition.

'I don't give a damn about your business,' retorted the hunchback irritably. 'You promised me—'

'Are you talking about Cosette and the brat?' the Catman cut in, with an unexpected smile that made his face look younger.

'Of course.'

'It can't be done just like that, with one wave of a magic wand. What are you offering me in exchange?'

Burdin looked at him questioningly. 'Sole ownership of the Chat-Malin.'

'That's not enough, Burdin. What about Marius's property? This time we're talking about getting rid of a woman and a child. Children are more your speciality. The woman I'll take care of – but there's no question of doing away with her.'

'Who asked you to do away with her?'

Thénardier cleared his throat and laughed at the same time. 'I know you, Burdin. I do the dirty work, and you end up with the spoils. You don't want to get your hands dirty and I understand that. But if the fate of little Cosette worries you so much, why not take care of her yourself? I'll tell you why. Because there's a nice little pile of money at the end of the day!'

The two men were walking towards Notre-Dame without looking at each other. Burdin stifled an expression of disgust as his accomplice bent his body in an exaggerated manner and spat profusely. He cursed this revolting old man for always having creamy flecks of saliva sticking to the corners of his lips or spurting from his mouth as if he had just stuffed his belly. He found him repulsive. Strange, the aversion that repulsive people have for other repulsive people. And yet Thénardier did not eat or drink. He was not known to have any vice, any disease. This Jansenist of villainy was quite simply repulsive. Burdin regretted having given him a helping hand in Saint-Malo. He should have left him to rot in his own filth. He was too greedy, and too much of a nuisance.

Instead of reacting indignantly, though, he agreed. 'You're right, Thénardier, there'll be something in it for you. Something big. But what can we do? At the moment, we're all on red-hot coals.'

'How should we proceed?'

'I'll let you be the judge of that. Things have to be arranged by July.'

'What about the child?'

'I'll take care of it. As for Cosette, I don't know why, but I can easily imagine her in your new establishment.'

'That's an idea,' replied the old man, stealing a suspicious glance at the people gathered in front of the cathedral. 'In fact, I was looking for someone to deal with the food.'

He looked up at the sky. With the dawn, a brisk wind had arisen and fast-moving clouds fell across the sun like the curtain in a theatre. Thus obscured, Notre-Dame appeared heavier, more solemn, rising above the sea of tiled roofs on the Ile de la Cité and the Ile Saint-Louis. At times, the sun broke through and warmed the tiles, bringing out their varied colours. Some were russet, others golden, while some had turned green. Most were Romanesque in style, arched, round and wavy, but some were of the German style, flat and rectangular.

The two men crossed the square, their heads down. Burdin, although flexible enough to modify his original plan, could not resist the temptation to cut his accomplice down to size. 'Men,' he said, 'are rather like the tiles of these houses. Some are straight and some are crooked.'

Thénardier nodded with a good-natured air. 'But those who are straight can become crooked and those who are crooked can become straight, my dear Burdin.' He sniggered, thinking of the steward's hump. Then his smile turned to a frown. 'And besides, where do you see any men who are straight? You're ambitious and so am I. Your ambition is huge, mine is reasonable. In fact, ambition is the one thing we have in common. Only the more it consumes us, the more we have to keep it secret, old chap.'

The hunchback's sombre face filled with mockery. 'The one thing we have in common? That's going a bit far, Thénardier! I'll tell you the one thing we have in common. We both have blood on our hands.' He spread out his hands, displaying the palms.

Thénardier stopped, horrified. 'Don't talk so loudly, Burdin. Around here, the walls have ears.'

'When?' asked Burdin imperiously.

Thénardier was irritated by Burdin's superior tone – after all, in a way, he had him at his mercy. 'I don't want to hurry things,' he replied. 'And since you're so impatient, I'll have you know that I'm worried. My place was ransacked.'

'Was anything stolen?'

'Jesus's ring has disappeared. I'm sure the Mullet was mixed up in the crime.'

Burdin stifled a desire to burst out laughing, hearing this last word. 'Get rid of him, then. I'll have a word with Gérard, if you like. He's bound to have some arsenic in his reserves.'

Thénardier grimaced. He wanted to keep Gérard out of his affairs. He was an employee, full stop. 'Not for the moment. I still need the Mullet. It's his accomplice who worries me. A tall man who always keeps his hat pulled down over his eyes. He could be a snout or a rozzer.'

'What are you talking about? You're crediting your Mullet with a little too much intelligence,' said Burdin, glancing at his pocket watch. 'He's too stupid to be the accomplice of an informer or a policeman.'

'Well, anyway, you've been warned,' insisted Thénardier. 'If you see this man, try to make him harmless. I have no desire to get sent down for twenty years.'

Burdin hailed a fiacre. 'That's your job, Thénardier,' he said, with a disdainful curl of the lips. 'We'll meet again in a month.'

'In a month,' said the old man, nodding his head several times and bowing.

After Burdin had got into the fiacre, Thénardier retraced his steps. He held his nose as he passed a tavern that stank of quiche and hare pâté. In the Rue des Ursins, a crowd had gathered. Two men were fighting, surrounded by screaming women who were encouraging them to make mincemeat of each other.

'Bleed him!' cried a big portress with a gaudy headscarf.

'Break his neck!' retorted another, younger woman, whose jet-black hair gleamed in the sun.

A circle had formed around the two fighters. Bets were already being placed. At times the noise of this hideous crowd grew to a tumult of boos and cheers, at others it subsided into silence, from which emerged now the voice of the shrew, now that of the dark young woman. Thénardier went closer. Through a half-open window, he noticed a parrot tied to its perch and two children kicking each other as they fought over a crust of bread. 'God, how I love this place,' he said to himself. 'It's so human.' Then, fixing his gaze on the shrew and the dark young woman, he first shivered, then sniggered. These two sluts reminded him of Gammy Leg and the Kitten. One was dead, the other was as good as dead. An irrepressible fit of giggling took hold of him. Soon, it would be Cosette's turn.

'Your good daddy Thénardier is preparing a royal future for you, my little Cosette,' he murmured. 'It'll be like in Montfermeil, when you were eight. I'm going to make you dance, my lark. The sergeant of Waterloo will keep his appointment.'

And after a final glance at the two men rolling on the ground, he set off for Saint-Denis – on foot, because a fiacre would have been too expensive.

Verjat was sitting facing Cosette, his arms folded. The first thing he had done when he arrived had been to lean over little Jean's cradle, a wicker cradle decorated with blue silk ribbons, which was placed near a window looking out onto the inner courtyard.

'The very image of his father,' he muttered, remembering the young man to whom he had given two pistols to raise the alarm when Thénardier, alias Jondrette, was plotting in the Gorbeau tenement.

It was the first time Verjat had been to Cosette's new address. As their meetings in Saint-Sulpice and the Luxembourg Gardens had become less frequent, it was he who had made the move. He found the place a little sad, and Cosette no less sad.

He had brought a basket full of oranges and barley sugar and Cosette had kissed him on both cheeks to thank him.

'You shouldn't have, Monsieur Verjat. I've missed you so much.'

'And I've missed you, Cosette.'

He told her nothing about what he had been doing. He had been continuing slowly with his investigations, confident of success, with the aggressiveness for which he had been known in the past. He might have failed in his suicide, but he felt that he had succeeded in his conversion. A strange bitterness made him think that he had escaped from sorrow. But this escape, while giving him the opportunity to make amends for his mistakes, or at least to repay his debts, was turning out to be something in which he needed to invest a great deal of effort. This latecomer to doubt and questioning now found in his past failings a present virtue. He would throw light on the Pontmercy affair. Javert had sworn to do so and Javert always kept his word.

'And is Monsieur d'Iguerande well?'

Cosette shook her head sadly. 'I hardly ever see him these days,' she replied. 'I've been told he's resumed his old ways.'

'What else?'

Cosette was sometimes disconcerted by the abrupt manner in which Verjat asked questions, in the curt tone of a man used to being obeyed. 'He drinks a lot,' replied Cosette, unable to conceal her mixed feelings about Amédée's decline. 'I think he's unhappy.'

'Because he's in love with you?'

Cosette recoiled. 'I can't give him what he wants – not that he has ever dared to ask. And he *has* become a dear friend. But I'm torn about what to do for the best. I haven't forgotten anything, Monsieur Verjat. I haven't forgotten that he has some responsibility for Marius's death. And, in a way, it gives me a strange satisfaction to see him like this. When I met him on the stairs the other day he was quite charming. He asked quite naturally about Jean's health and tactfully about my own. Then, as we parted, he whispered, "Nothing equals the ecstasy of surrender."'

Verjat looked at Cosette with absent-minded benevolence. 'Many soldiers think the same,' he replied humorously.

'He was a soldier, in fact. He served in Algeria.'

'Not for long, I think. Don't let yourself be moved by his distress. I don't doubt the sincerity of Monsieur d'Iguerande's feelings, but you're dealing with a man who's unable to satisfy his whim, that's all. You feel embarrassed yet overjoyed at the sight of his degradation. Well, that may be a rather excessive reaction, but it's genuine, nevertheless. You must protect yourself, Cosette. And I know whereof I speak.'

Cosette smiled. Verjat's linguistic mannerism amused her.

'It's not in my power to bring you happiness,' he went on, 'but I can offer you consolation. Will you deign to accept it from a friend?'

'I may try to hide it, but even though my son is a constant joy to me, I am very unhappy, Monsieur Verjat. I dream of righting this injustice by any means possible. But does one suffer less by making others suffer?'

'Are you referring to the marquis?' asked Verjat.

'To him and to others.'

'If Monsieur d'Iguerande has a noble heart, he must understand that every man, however frivolous or depraved, owes a debt to life. Living by your side he could not become resigned to your sorrow. His powerlessness would make him full of hatred. He's still quite young, isn't he?'

'His heart is that of a man who has prematurely aged.'

Verjat lifted his eyes to heaven. 'To each his burden! I have mine, you have yours. Monsieur d'Iguerande lacks modesty. And that is something one can only gain through moments of great weariness and exhaustion – which amounts to saying that a man with Monsieur d'Iguerande's energy is never modest. Struggle will make him strong. Adversity eventually changes into good fortune. You're the perfect example of that, Cosette, and I know that you will succeed in rebuilding a future.'

Cosette shook her head wearily. 'You have too much confidence in me, Monsieur Verjat.'

'Because you have precedents.'

'What do you mean?'

'Your father.'

'Unfortunately, he's no longer here. The other day, in a moment of sadness, I thought of him and it did me good. If he were still alive, I worked out that he'd be sixty-eight.'

'And Javert fifty-six.'

Cosette gave a start. 'Javert? Why do you say that name?'

'He was a friend of your father's,' said Verjat, who had been thinking aloud. 'He was the same age as me.'

'But why do you always compare yourself to my father when I mention him?'

'I've already told you – I knew him well.'

Cosette gave a slightly malicious smile, and wagged her finger at him like a schoolteacher. 'I'm not satisfied with your answer.'

'One day you'll know,' said Verjat conclusively. 'But as far as Monsieur d'Iguerande is concerned, promise me one thing – that you won't fall victim to your own kindness and compassion.'

'I promise, Monsieur Verjat, but don't worry too much about me. You don't know me – I can defend myself.'

Verjat crossed his legs, smoothed the grey hair at his temples, and contemplated his big hands. He seemed reassured, but Amédée d'Iguerande was like all men. Just when his shame at his own failure threatened to overwhelm him, he might suddenly be carried away by a rush of pride and do something to harm Cosette. Verjat did not want her to run that risk, especially as he was almost sure that the man buried in Père-Lachaise as Baron Pontmercy was not Marius. But he did not want to raise Cosette's hopes falsely. 'By the way,' he asked, abruptly changing the subject again, 'was Baron Pontmercy in the habit of wearing jewellery?'

Cosette stared at him wide-eyed. So much had been broken inside and around her that she no longer had a taste for flirtatious nonsense. She stroked her wedding ring with her thumbnail. Verjat's question seemed out of place. 'Not to my knowledge,' she said at last, offended.

'Please don't be angry,' Verjat said quickly, uncrossing his legs and standing up. With his hands spread in front of him, he gestured to Cosette to wait. Carefully, he slipped his hand into a pocket in his frock coat. Looking hard at Cosette, he abruptly took out the gold ring with the figure of the emerald-eyed snake. 'Do you recognize this?'

'Certainly not,' said Cosette, lifting her head proudly. This ring, she thought, might have belonged to a woman Marius had been seeing, perhaps that insolent dark-haired creature they had met one evening at the Café Turc, whom he had seemed to know only too well. In trying to unravel matters that were none of his business, Verjat was merely reawakening her grief. 'Why are you so cruel? I'm beginning to believe Amédée. You behave like a police inspector—'

'Is that what he said?' Verjat slowly turned his head in his worn black cravat. Putting the ring away, he opened his arms and walked towards Cosette. 'My child,' he caught himself saying, 'what are you thinking?'

Cosette rose in turn and, fighting back her tears, took shelter in her protector's arms. Her face was pale, her eyes reddened by the insomnia caused by all these ills and nightmares, as well as by little Jean, who woke her three times a night. 'How can I live when there is nothing more to believe in?' she cried with a distraught air.

In the past, Verjat had been responsible for a thousand torments. He had often considered his victims with no more emotion than satisfaction at a duty accomplished. Now, he felt powerless. 'You will live, you must,' he whispered in Cosette's ear, inhaling with delight her scent of lemon and green tea. He held her for a brief moment in his arms, afraid that he might have hurt her. 'Trust me, Cosette.'

'That won't bring Marius back.'

'I know,' replied Verjat, with the perfect composure with which resigned souls cover themselves, like a shield. 'By the way,' he added, taking his cane and hat, 'is there anything you need?'

'Madeleine and Louis-Désiré take very good care of me.'

'Louis-Désiré?'

'Monsieur d'Iguerande's steward.'

'In that case, Cosette, you're in good hands. That takes a weight off my shoulders, for I'm going to be away for some time.'

Cosette walked to the cradle and placed her hand on the wicker. 'So,' she stammered, 'not content with hurting me, you're going to abandon me.'

'I'll be back within two months at the latest.'

It was March now and Verjat hoped to be back by the end of May. But he might be away for longer, depending on the information he obtained.

Cosette saw him to the door. She tilted her head to one side and held out her hand. 'Farewell,' she breathed.

'Farewell, Cosette.'

On the stairs, he passed a man dressed all in black, who was holding himself in such a way that it was impossible to suspect the infirmity from which he suffered. The hump, which in any case was not very large, would certainly have caught Verjat's attention. Conversely, Burdin found himself unwittingly in the presence of the man described by Thénardier, the same Moreau who had links with the Mullet and who threatened their plans. The two men nodded politely to each other. This was not one of those times when chance arranges matters well.

One evening at the Café Turc, where they had been drinking rum and absinthe, Amédée and Louis struck up a conversation with a red-headed woman wearing a wine-coloured mask and a dress that gave a glimpse of the raspberry tips of her breasts. She was laughing loudly and repeatedly announcing her adoration of Lucifer. Around one in the morning she offered to take the two men somewhere unusual. They accepted and staggered drunkenly out. They took a fiacre and, as part of the game, consented to be blindfolded.

The woman, whose name was Proserpine, took them to a brothel in the Rue Colbert known as the Diable-Blanc. It was a house frequented by a very select clientele. Proserpine led Louis and Amédée across a large room filled with men talking, drinking champagne and smoking cigars. A pungent odour of musk and bodies hung in the air. At the far end of the room was a staircase, which they descended cautiously. When they reached the foot, their blindfolds were removed and they were given grotesque masks to put on.

They entered a red and black crypt where some fifty men and women, all masked, stood around. The room was lit by torches on the walls. Four girls dressed in short skirts and high boots were lighting candles. There were benches, purple cushions and scarlet rugs. In the middle of the crypt, large glass globes stood on copper pedestals. Between two Corinthian columns was an altar on which lay a young girl, naked. Behind her an individual dressed in a black robe embossed with an inverted red cross and a ruby and bronze mask adorned with black horns was brandishing a chalice. This was a black Mass.

Louis wanted to leave, but Amédée insisted they stay. The grand master intoned incantations. The young girl was in a trance. Long flames trembled on the columns and the draperies that covered the walls.

The last words of the grand master were greeted with grunts and gesticulations. A fever of depravity ran through the assembly.

Amédée and Louis sat down. Encouraged by Proserpine, Amédée drank three glasses of rum.

Some time later, a couple – a one-eyed nymphet called Nina and a dark-complexioned man named Giuseppe – took their seats beside them.

Proserpine, now wearing a garland of acanthus leaves, played the go-between. They all got drunk together and were soon yelling insanely.

Alarmed by this turn of events, Louis stood up and gestured to Amédée to follow him, but he refused.

'Don't you want to have fun with us?' Giuseppe asked. He had fiery eyes, a hairy chest and a southern accent. 'Nobody refuses Giuseppe Fieschi!' he cried, slapping Nina's knee.

Louis recoiled. 'What about Cosette?' he whispered to Amédée.

'Be quiet!' bellowed Amédée, rising to his full height and pointing at his friend. 'Go away!'

Louis shook his head. As he made for the back of the crypt, he looked towards the altar. The grand master had been watching. For a brief moment he removed his mask, revealing grey hair tied with a bow and a gaze at once piercing and nonchalant. It was Gérard, the manager of what had once been the Clan Destin.

He replaced his mask and gave orders to two negroes who were assisting him, who ran and seized Louis. Nightmare creatures swarmed around Louis, leaping like young goats. Women spat at him and yelled obscenities. He hardly struggled. The negroes blindfolded him and whirled him round and round like a top. Amédée and Giuseppe were roaring with laughter. Finally Louis was dragged upstairs and thrown out.

'And not a word about what you saw here, or you're a dead man!' they called after him.

Once in the street, he swore to return and have his revenge. Then he thought again of Amédée. He wondered into what depths his friend was plunging – his poor friend who, no doubt conscious of his shortcomings, was beginning to confuse fear and boredom.

The trial of the insurgents of April 1834 was about to begin. The Duc de Broglie was now prime minister. Despite the opposition's efforts to hamper or intimidate the Chamber of Peers, the Chamber had managed to complete its investigation in time for the extensive trial. The public was apprehensive and the newspapers made no attempt to hide their anxiety. The accused were a singular collection, including Cavaignac, Raspail, Ledru-Rollin, Auguste Comte, Armand Carrel, Armand Barbès and Auguste Blanqui.

In short, it was the Republican party that was on trial.

Everyone had heard of Barbès and Blanqui. Even Verjat, thanks to Father Rillet, who did not hold them in high esteem. 'They want to redistribute everything, Monsieur Verjat! The property of the Church as well! Isn't that absurd?'

'It certainly is, Father.'

'You're not just saying that to please me, I hope?'

'Why should I do that?'

'Because I know you hold progressive ideas on such matters. Your students have told me. Well, I say that abolishing wealth is not the same as redistributing it.'

'Who says the contrary?'

'Why, you, Monsieur Verjat!'

'I simply advanced the proposition that by eliminating poverty, one would put an end to the exploitation of the weak by the strong. Isn't that a Christian sentiment?'

'Indeed it is, my friend. I've never been in favour of one group enjoying what's denied to another group. But aren't there limits we need to respect? You're surely not going to tell me that you have any sympathy for Jacobins like Barbès and Blanqui?'

'I have sympathy for everything that aims to democratize property without abolishing it,' replied Verjat, 'and antipathy for wheeler-dealers and sectarians, for Monsieur Thiers and Monsieur de Broglie, and for the others who advocate excessive sharing while flouting competition. My preference at the moment is for the equitable. I admit it may be utopian, but that doesn't mean one can't dream of free compulsory education for all children, an intellectual France that wouldn't be cut off from the artisan France, or a political world anxious to reconcile what remains of the old world with all that's come out of the revolutionary ideal. Yes, I now have sympathy for what used to inspire antipathy in me. Wouldn't it be a better world, Father, if every citizen had access to property?'

Verjat had uttered this last sentence with great care, like a foreigner who, expressing himself in a language that is not his own, pays great attention to his verbal constructions.

Father Rillet's benign face lit up. 'Does that mean you're no longer an anarchist?' he said, reinforcing his smile with a friendly pat on Verjat's back. He drew him out of the presbytery and they walked together to the church. 'Would you like me to tell you what I think about free access to property?' he went on. 'Well, it's obvious that Monsieur Thiers astonishes the masses with his promises and his verbal liberalism. And then he astounds them even more with his contradictions, his thirst for power, his repressive orders and his broken promises. It's obvious that the monarchy is stuck in a rut, and that the financiers and speculators encouraged by Guizot and de Broglie are continuing to plunder with impunity. It's obvious, finally, that I'm against poverty and in favour of everyone's happiness. But was Our Lord Jesus Christ rich? Did he own property?'

Verjat smiled in his turn, stopped, and raised his hands to heaven. 'Jesus Christ was Jesus Christ, Father!'

By now the two men were in the chancel of Saint-Sulpice. There were a few worshippers who had been unable to resist following their conversation. Some seemed amazed. Among them was the man whom Verjat had already chased away from Cosette's presence. He rose now with a laugh, made the sign of the cross and shook his head, as if to say: There's really nothing to fear from this old Bible-thumper.

The man's name was Grandet. A former boilermaker, police informer and pickpocket, he was now spying for Gérard and Burdin. They'd asked him to keep an eye on Monsieur Moreau and see what he got up to in his daily life, and he'd done as he was told, which was fine by him. He'd tell Gérard what he'd found – though, to be frank, what he'd found wasn't very much. It was obvious the man was a drivelling old fool, and a religious fanatic to boot. He left the church.

'Well, it's as I thought,' Father Rillet resumed. 'You've been won over by the revolutionary ideas of these people they call socialists. Your students were right.'

Verjat's face lit up. 'My students? They don't know who I am or what I think. And what about you, Father? Can I rely on you to keep all this under your hat?' He paused, then went on in a darker tone. 'Talking of my students, I must tell you that I intend to be away for a while, so I shan't be able to give them the few classes I still owe them. To be perfectly honest with you, Baroness Pontmercy needs my services. And I, in turn, may need yours.'

'You know you can count on me, my son. Nothing revolutionary, I hope?'

'Perhaps worse,' replied Verjat, 'and I know whereof I speak.'

Verjat was a meticulous man. A ring was in his possession and he wanted to be absolutely certain that it belonged to the dead man they had tried to pass off as Marius.

One evening, for the first time in a while, he went to the Chat-Malin. Gérard gave him a look at once mistrustful and mocking. According to his informant, who had followed him to Saint-Sulpice, this Moreau was nothing but a quiet, mediocre and sanctimonious bourgeois.

'Sit down, my dear Monsieur Moreau! What would you say to fritters in white sauce to start and coffee religieuses to finish?' He gave an insolent chuckle.

Verjat nodded, sat down and proceeded to ignore him.

As for the Mullet, he seemed extremely distant. He felt afraid and this feeling, in a man accustomed to inspiring fear in others, made him at once timid and boastful, panicky and conceited. At a certain point in the evening, with Gérard's blessing, he came and sat down at Verjat's table. The two men drank a glass of burgundy, and talked of this and that.

'Could you tell me something about Jesus?' asked Verjat suddenly.

The Mullet gave a start and almost left the table. This man really did scare him. 'He used to work with us . . .' he replied finally in an unsteady voice. 'He got twenty years for murder . . . Why do you ask?'

What made his panic all the greater was the fact that Moreau had Jesus's ring and it was too late to get it back. Unless . . . No, this Moreau was too dangerous. With his bourgeois clothes and his skull-like face, he must have contacts all over the place.

'Why, Moreau?' he asked again, raising his voice.

'Calm down, Mullet. I ask because I don't want any problems. A lot of people are prowling around. I wouldn't like your Catman to find out that we had paid him a little social call. What do you think?' He, too, had raised his voice.

The Mullet shook his head from side to side. 'Sshh, not so loud, Moreau . . .' he whispered, putting his forefinger on his mouth. 'The Catman is mixed up in all sorts of shady business . . . Right here, for instance, in the old Clan Destin that you knew, there was a murder—'

'A murder?'

'The woman in charge of the cooking . . . Her name was Gammy Leg . . . Her husband strangled her in a fit of rage . . . He got twenty years, too . . . He had a mistress, the Kitten, who was the cause of the whole thing . . . They say she's in the Salpêtrière hospital . . .'

'The Kitten? Well, well.'

'Why do you say, "Well, well"?'

'No reason. The Kitten, you say?'

'Her real name was Clotilde Lepetit . . .' said the Mullet, becoming increasingly nervous.

Suspecting that the Mullet would never admit that the ring belonged to a man he had killed, Verjat rose to leave, much to the other's relief. The Mullet hoped for only one thing – that Verjat would never set foot in here again.

'What about the diamonds?' asked Verjat all at once, with a sardonic air, leaning on the table with his hands.

'I never let them out of my sight . . . They're still in my pocket . . .'

'That's not wise, Mullet. You're going to get into trouble. Shall we meet again tomorrow?'

'If you like . . .'

No sooner had Verjat left than the Mullet ran to Gérard and said that he really didn't trust him. Now that he knew Moreau better, he suspected him of being in the pay of the police. 'A snitch, a rozzer in plain clothes, who knows?'

'Do you really think so?' asked Gérard, passing a bony hand over his brow. 'I thought he was your friend.'

'I've seen him lurking round the workshop . . . He even asked me some really strange questions about the Catman . . . I trusted him at first . . . But he's too nosy.'

'According to my information, this Moreau's just a civilian who gives
lessons and attends Mass.'

'Don't go by that, damn it!' stammered the Mullet, growing pale and
shaking all over. He was completely out of his depth.

'Is he coming back tomorrow?' asked Gérard, struck by the Mullet's
discomfort.

'So he said . . .'

Verjat did return the following day, but he did not enter the Chat-
Malin. Unrecognizable in his disguise, with his big black beard and his
top hat, he pressed his face up against the tavern window. Seeing Gérard
and the Mullet in the company of a third man, a menacing character
dressed all in grey who was none other than the Wolf, he gave the faintest
of smiles. He had not been mistaken. The Mullet was a real crook. He
left, vowing never to set foot in the tavern again. But the Mullet would
live to regret it.

The sun was shining brightly when Verjat presented himself at the
entrance of the Salpêtrière, in the Boulevard de l'Hôpital. He had visited
it once before, as a young and inexperienced policeman, and had heard
unspeakable things. The women who were considered to be incurably mad
were kept chained in squalid underground dungeons full of water and rats,
living like animals in the middle of their own excrement. Their food and
straw were passed to them through the bars. Even the rake used to gather
the straw for their litters was pushed through these bars. These wretched
women, poor for the most part, were placed in several categories – the
insane, the disabled, the able-bodied, the old and the young. Today these
categories still existed, although the place had changed. Since the architect
Viel de Saint-Maur had constructed four new buildings, surrounding a
square courtyard shaded by beautiful chestnut trees and with a fountain in
the middle, conditions had improved. There were four thousand inmates.

'I'd prefer the penal colony!' cried a sick woman, who was on her way
to see the doctor escorted by two nuns. 'At least you're not locked up!'

Verjat nodded in agreement. The woman was not completely wrong.
Life was less terrible in the penal colonies than in prison. In Brest, Toulon
and Rochefort you could breathe, whereas in prison you slowly suffocated.

Verjat approached a nun and a guard. 'Would it be possible to see
Mademoiselle Clotilde Lepetit?' he asked authoritatively.

Even though he was not dressed like a policeman, there was something

338

imposing about him. They did not ask him who he was or why he wanted to see Clotilde Lepetit, and he was taken at once to her room.

'Are you a policeman?' the nun asked him finally, when they reached the door.

'Indeed I am,' lied Verjat. 'Is it so obvious?'

'Perhaps because of your eyes, my son.'

'The past can change, but not the eyes, Sister.'

'Don't rush her,' said the nun, with a vague, almost regretful gesture. 'Mademoiselle Lepetit has had a terrible shock. She doesn't talk much. When you see her face, you'll understand.'

The young woman was sitting on her bed, with her back to the door. A pale light filtered through the barred window. Moans could be heard from the ward. When she smelled the odour of oranges and old prayer books, Clotilde Lepetit knew there was a stranger in the room. She turned her head three-quarters of the way to the right. Her profile was smooth, silky, almost beautiful. Her hair was tied with a red ribbon. She was wearing a shawl on her shoulders and a grey cotton nightdress.

'Don't come any closer,' she said.

'I'm not moving.'

'What do you want?'

The Kitten's tone was weary but calm. Verjat noticed a rosary in her right hand and a reliquary on her bedside table. 'I want to talk to you and to show you something,' he replied.

He held out his hand and showed her Jesus's ring. She looked at it out of the corner of her eye, without moving her head.

'So?' she said.

'So I'd like to know who it belongs to.'

'To a henchman of the man who caused my misfortune. His name was Jesus. One evening, he even tried to seduce me. Do you think he'd do the same now?'

She turned completely. What Verjat saw made his blood freeze, although in his many years as a policeman he had seen everything, every kind of horror. The left side of Clotilde Lepetit's face was nothing but a crater, a mass of cavities, bulges and blisters where the withered flesh had healed. Where there had been raw, ulcerous wounds, there was now only rough, weeping skin. The eye, the cheek and the eyelid were no more than memories. Part of the upper lip had been eaten away by the acid, so that it looked like a harelip, beneath which three teeth showed. Above it, the nostril, also eaten away, quivered obscenely, its wing resembling the bubbling surface of a compote.

Verjat took a deep breath. 'Justice will be done,' he said in a low voice, putting the ring back in his pocket.

'Oh, you believe in justice, do you? Who's going to give me back my face? You? The Catman? Or someone else?'

'Are you accusing the Catman?'

The woman had resumed her previous position. With stiff, clumsy movements, she took a little pot from the table and applied a thick yellow cream to her face. Only when she had placed a gauze compress over the wound did she finally answer Verjat's question.

'Death would be too gentle a torture for the Catman. When I was lying on the floor of the Clan Destin, half unconscious, I heard him talking. First to Gammy Leg, then to Perfect Love. I realized then that he'd planned the whole thing. Is Perfect Love doing hard labour?'

'Yes.'

'You see. And I'm sure the Catman is the new owner of the Clan Destin.'

'Yes, he is.'

The Kitten smiled bitterly. 'Not that you'd see his name anywhere. He's too cunning for that.' She made a weary gesture. 'But I no longer care about all that. My mind is elsewhere. That's it.'

Verjat stood watching for a moment as the woman kissed her rosary. Her soul, once stiff with pride, had found repose in Christian humility. He walked to the door. 'One day,' he said, 'I may need your testimony. An innocent man was sentenced to hard labour. His name is Marius Pontmercy.'

'The young baron who tried to whisper sweet nothings in my ear?' said the Kitten. 'Yes, I remember him . . . The Catman wanted to fleece him. The first night he came to the Clan Destin, he and Perfect Love got into a fight over me . . . How far away it all seems.'

'I'll get you out of here,' said Verjat resolutely.

The Kitten waved her hand, then dropped it weakly. 'Is that pity or compassion? Either way, it won't change anything, Monsieur. But thanks all the same.'

Verjat did not like to leave anything to chance. He had so often in the past locked people up without irrefutable proof of their guilt that he wanted to be certain of what he suspected. The testimony of Horse Face, the Mullet and the Kitten was not enough for him. He therefore asked Father Rillet for permission to exhume Baron Pontmercy's body.

'But for what reason?' objected the priest.

'For the reason that Baron Pontmercy's body is not his.'

'Are you sure of what you're saying?'

'Almost.'

'I don't like that "almost".'

Verjat insisted.

'The things you make me do, Monsieur Verjat.'

'It's perfectly logical, Father. If the corpse they buried is not Baron Pontmercy's, it means that Baron Pontmercy was sentenced to hard labour and is serving twenty years at this very moment.'

Verjat summarized the situation for Father Rillet – the origin of the ring according to the witnesses, its strange journey, and how it had come into his possession.

'All right, my friend, let's try. I know the district official. Like me, he's a friend of the prefect. He'll give me an exhumation permit without any problem. What about Cosette?'

'If you see her, don't breathe a word about this business. I want it to be a surprise. And, if I'm wrong, I want to save her a cruel disappointment. That would be a fatal blow to her. We have to keep this unofficial. If I get the result I want, I'm going to Toulon.'

'But without the baroness's agreement, I won't get permission to exhume.'

'Plead a higher necessity. Nothing must hinder the search for justice.'

'That's a good one!'

'I know the law, Father.'

'You should have been a policeman, my son.'

A week later the authorization was on Father Rillet's desk and the exhumation went ahead the very next day. To be on the safe side, Verjat had provided himself with a fake document stipulating that Cosette had given her agreement, but he did not need it. Thanks to his good relations with Prefect of Police Gisquet, Father Rillet had done all that was required.

A police officer and a pathologist examined the body. The smell was appalling.

'The glove,' said the priest to the pathologist, covering his nose with a handkerchief. 'Take his glove off.'

The corpse was indeed missing a finger – the ring finger of the left hand, to be precise.

'This finger appears to have been severed with a knife,' observed the pathologist.

The priest turned to Verjat, and they exchanged a conspiratorial look.

'Is that all?' asked the pathologist.

'That's all,' the priest confirmed.

Verjat was jubilant. Everything was starting to fall into place – the presence of Thénardier and the hunchback at the scene of the crime, the ring, which had been removed after the event to prevent discovery of the deception, the Mullet's agitation whenever he talked about Jesus.

'Are you satisfied?' Father Rillet asked Verjat once they had returned to Saint-Sulpice.

'I have reason to be, Father. But there's one thing that bothers me.'

'What's that?'

'The role of the Marquis d'Iguerande in all this. I was sure for a time that he was behind this plot, but if he was, surely he would have seized the baron's property by now, especially as he has a letter signed by Marius authorizing him to do so? But he hasn't. There's the rub.'

'Isn't the severed finger sufficient proof?'

'In my eyes, yes, but not in the eyes of the law. This preposterous story of severed fingers and rings doesn't prove anything. It wouldn't hold up before the public prosecutor, or any magistrate, for that matter. That's why I'm going to Paray-le-Monial on the way to Toulon.'

A veil of incomprehension dropped in front of Father Rillet's eyes. 'Paray-le-Monial?'

'There's a village called Iguerande a few leagues from Paray-le-Monial. To the best of my knowledge, there hasn't been a marquis there since the Middle Ages. Not that I deserve any credit for knowing that. Thanks to you, I spent quite a lot of time in the region.' He paused. 'One more thing, Father. When I get to Toulon, I'm going to introduce myself to the commandant of the penal colony under the name of Rillet. Do you see any problem with that?'

'By all the saints, you're worse than Vidocq! Who exactly was it I fished out of the Seine on June 7th 1832?'

'Me, Father.'

'And who are you?'

'Don't you know?'

Father Rillet went slightly red.

Verjat took his hand. 'I'll answer for you,' he said cryptically. 'An angel of hell who's become, thanks to your good offices, an angel of heaven.'

The Brionnais is a region in the south of Burgundy, a place of rest and meditation amid the tumult of the Christian world.

Cut through by the traffic of the Loire, and rich in Italian and eastern influences, although it lies in the benevolent shadow of Cluny, the Brionnais boasts some twenty churches with storeyed capitals and sculpted tympanums. Verjat knew them all. From Iguerande to Anzy-le-Duc by way of Saint-Julien-de-Jonzy and Semur-en-Brionnais, he had admired and visited them all. He had pondered long and hard there, seeking in the stone what men search for and rarely find – faith. These churches had contributed to the transformation of his character. In them, he had learned doubt, humility, compassion. Only God had been absent.

'It'll be different one day,' Father Rillet had said to him, lending him a cassock, a hat and a cloak. 'In the meantime, I have a letter of recommendation from Marshal Oudinot in person. He did me this service before he took up his command in Algeria. It'll get you into the colony. And with my identity, what's more! Now, God speed to Paray!'

A lot of people in Paray-le-Monial knew Verjat. He had lived in the general hospital, spending most of his time meditating on the fate of Marguerite-Marie Alacoque, a holy woman born in 1647 on the outskirts of Paray who had sacrificed her life to Christ. He'd had long discussions with Sister Angélique, mother superior of the Convent of the Visitation, and with Father Hippolyte, superior of the little Jesuit house in Paray-le-Monial, whom Father Rillet had recommended. He had often been seen pacing up and down the low-lying paths, where he would stop, hold his hands in front of his face as a frame, like a surveyor or a painter, and contemplate the landscape. Although he had never been to Flanders or Tuscany, the countryside had reminded him of paintings by the Flemish and Sienese primitives. He had loved its miniature valleys, the Lilliputian woods, the paths bordered by hedgerows, from which it was possible to see the mountains of the Beaujolais and the Massif Central, all these details in the landscape that echoed the details of the churches – the altars of greenery, the gaps in the hedges that were like windows opening onto the clear blue sky. The architectural delicacy of the stones emerging from the shadows had fascinated him. In the Brionnais, he had discovered the art of living and the splendour of humility. It had been like a hand outstretched towards the sacred.

'I could have almost believed that God is in each of us,' he had told Father Rillet to tease him.

Father Rillet had lifted his eyes to heaven. His protégé's dark humour no longer touched him.

In short, from Montceau-l'Etoile to Varenne-l'Arconce, from Perrecy-les-Forges to Marcigny, Verjat had never tired of looking at finely carved tympanums, lintels with airy arabesques, barrel vaults. He had discovered the unaccustomed joy of being able to walk between curtains of foliage and mountains of brambles, to sit down on the edge of a field or on a village bench and savour his new-found calm. In this way, he had discovered Iguerande.

It was Father Hippolyte who put him in contact with Monsieur Corneloup, the mayor of Iguerande. They met first in Paray, on the edge of the Bourbince, near the basilica built on the model of Cluny. Verjat had no difficulty in persuading the mayor to grant his request. He could consult the parish registers the very next day.

'But I can tell you this,' said the mayor. 'To the best of my knowledge, there is no Marquis d'Iguerande.'

Verjat almost gave up at that point. There might be several villages named Iguerande in France, in which case he would have to return to Paris and consult the national register. But Monsieur Corneloup's offer was so sincere that he could not refuse, even though he himself was far from sure what exactly he was looking for.

He worked for three days. He went through the parish registers with a fine-tooth comb, examined birth and death certificates, turned the names over in all directions – but all in vain.

On the third day, Monsieur Corneloup asked him if he was satisfied with his researches.

'I can't find anything, Mayor.'

'Do you at least have a first name?'

'Amédée.'

'When was he born?'

Verjat thought of Marius. He replied 1809, 1810. There was no such first name corresponding to these dates.

'There are a lot of Burdins in the register,' he remarked.

'It's a very common name in Saône-et-Loire,' replied Monsieur Corneloup.

All at once, going through the interminable list of Burdins, a first name caught Verjat's eye. 'This does say Louis-Désiré, doesn't it?'

The mayor confirmed it. But he had never heard of the man, who had been born in 1778. 'If he's still alive, he's never been back to Iguerande. Perhaps he was lost in the Napoleonic campaigns.'

'Perhaps,' said Verjat, growing pale.

Verjat had not forgotten the name Louis-Désiré, which Cosette had mentioned, and now he had found a connection between that name and the name Iguerande. Was it a coincidence? If so, it was one more. For a brief moment, Verjat thought of returning to Paris. Cosette might be in danger. But then he reasoned with himself. What danger could there be? Madeleine and Louis-Désiré were taking good care of her.

He therefore made no change to his itinerary. Having been in the Brionnais for almost ten days now, he would leave for Toulon the next day. Before his departure, he invited Monsieur Corneloup and Father Hippolyte to dinner. The red-faced, apoplectic mayor was a hearty eater, with a particular fondness for snails, crayfish cooked in a *court-bouillon* and meat from the Charolais. When Verjat mentioned that he was going to Toulon, the mayor told him that there was a stagecoach from Lyons that went there. 'If you're in a hurry, I think there's also a mail coach. Where it takes sixty hours by stagecoach to cover the ninety leagues from Lyons to Toulon, it'll take you thirty-two hours by mail coach.'

After the *île flottante*, Verjat thanked the mayor for his help and his valuable information. 'May I ask you another favour?' he said.

'Whatever you wish.'

'Could you make a few enquiries for me about this Louis-Désiré Burdin? I'll call on you again on my way back from Toulon.'

'I can't guarantee anything, Monsieur. But I'll try. Who knows? There may still be some old people alive who remember him.'

Three days later, Verjat was in Lyons. He set off for Toulon one morning at nine o'clock. It was a pleasant day and the movement of the coach filled his spirit with gaiety and a sense of adventure. By the time evening came, it was quite another story.

A night in a mail coach was no picnic, as Verjat learned to his cost. The other passengers jabbered on and never took their eyes off him, ate when they shouldn't, didn't eat when they should. It was impossible to get any sleep. A baby screamed for much of the night in its mother's arms and the horses' bells, the lighted lanterns that kept swaying from side to side, the road with its bumps and potholes, only exacerbated the horrors of the journey. In addition, there was the rolling and pitching. It was as if he was no longer in a coach but in a whirlwind, a cyclone on four wheels. Every bump in the road caused the axles to jolt. Every pebble became a rock, and his head was like an anvil being repeatedly struck in Vulcan's forge, an echoing abyss.

Verjat slept little. There is nothing quite like the dreams of a restless sleep. He slept and didn't sleep, he was at one and the same time in the real world and a world of fantasy. Verjat dreamed about Cosette, Amédée d'Iguerande, and even the man he had passed on the stairs in Cosette's building. The dreams kept recurring, burning themselves into his brain. It was like experiencing a night of fever.

Verjat arrived at the end of the second day, worn out and aching all over. His head was full of bells, his body seemed to vibrate by itself. The sea air revived him. As it was too late to go to the penal colony, he looked for an inn for the night. He found one called the Auberge du Siège, not far from the church of Sainte-Marie-Majeure. Its walls were covered with murals depicting the heroic way the young Bonaparte had repulsed the English in 1793. The menu was Mediterranean. Not being a great eater, Verjat contented himself with a dozen Bouzigues oysters and a plate of tomatoes and raw onions. He allowed himself a pinch of snuff and a glass of Syrah wine, which made his head spin. He wiped the back of his hand on the cloth and ordered a lime tea. Then, still in his tight brown frock coat, he fell asleep under the dumbfounded eyes of the innkeeper, an inexhaustibly loquacious fellow with lavender-blue eyes, who could not decide if this solemn and austere man had more of the policeman or the clergyman about him. Verjat did not have a forthcoming personality. His eyes were hidden beneath his brow, his brow was hidden beneath his hat, and his chin was hidden in his cravat. The only things that could be seen were his big hands, which were broad and horny, made to seize and apprehend.

When Verjat, who had paid for his meal in advance and booked his room for a second night in the name of Rillet, appeared early next morning, clean-shaven and with his head down, the innkeeper had his answer. The cassock, the long black cloak, the little hat, the prayer book, the green scapular with its bleeding red heart, left no more room for doubt. He nodded at the innkeeper, who returned his greeting.

'Did you sleep well, Father?'

'Like an angel,' replied Verjat in an icy tone, his eye fixed on the innkeeper, who coughed nervously. Verjat drank a glass of milk and ate a sugared brioche. He did not even sit down. Once again, he trained an inquisitorial eye on the innkeeper. 'What is the best way to get to the penal colony?'

The innkeeper bowed his head in submission – the clergyman had impressed him deeply – and told him the shortest route.

'Thank you, my son. There's nothing like a good morning walk to stretch the legs.'

And after having looked the innkeeper up and down again he left with his cane.

Armed with Father Rillet's papers and Marshal Oudinot's letter of recommendation, Verjat presented himself at the first guard post of the penal colony. An orderly accompanied him to the quarters of Vice Admiral Jacob. Each time he saw the red uniforms of the convicts working near the port and the warehouses or heard the noises of chains, he gave a start. In 1803 he had been a warder in Toulon. It was here that he had first met Jean Valjean, a man endowed with Herculean strength, a pruner by trade, who had been sentenced to five years for stealing a loaf of bread. Driven by hate and resentment, Jean Valjean had tried several times to escape. In all, he had spent a total of nineteen years in the colony.

'Hate allows one to survive,' whispered Verjat, shaking his head, 'but I've survived too long.'

Everything was becoming confused in his mind – his childhood, his convict father, his mother living in poverty in Toulon. He hated poverty. This confusion perhaps explained why he had been so inflexible towards the poor – first towards Fantine, Cosette's mother, then towards Valjean himself. I didn't deserve to live, he thought. As he walked, he shook his head again. He bumped into a convict and almost apologized. He recalled Jean Valjean's number. 24601. And when he had arrested Jean Valjean under the name of Madeleine, then mayor of Montreuil-sur-Mer, the ex-convict had again been sentenced to hard labour – hard labour for life. Verjat hid his eyes. That was in July 1823. Jean Valjean then bore the number 9430. He had not stayed long in Toulon. Four months later, after saving the life of a sailor on the *Orion*, a warship that had dropped anchor near the arsenal, he had taken advantage of the opportunity to escape. He was believed drowned. Verjat remembered it very well. Under his real name, Javert, he had returned to Toulon at the beginning of 1824, trying to find out more about the disappearance.

'The vice admiral is away, Father!'

The orderly's words shook Verjat from his daydreams. He clicked his heels and shook his head. Vice Admiral Jacob was not there. It was perhaps just as well. The vice admiral had been so pleased with the work of Perfect Love and Marius that the news of their escape had upset him deeply. Although Verjat could not know, it would not have been opportune to talk to him about Marius.

A naval lieutenant led Verjat to see the rear admiral, who did not even ask him what had brought him here. Oudinot's name was enough. 'The Duc de Reggio is a great man! You know him, then?'

'I have that honour.'

'How I envy you!' This fervent bureaucrat, very much a stickler for principles, gave Verjat a permit to move freely around the colony. 'Private Derpriel and Lieutenant Tarot will accompany you!' he barked. 'And if you need any further information, you can go and see Commandant Raynaud.'

Thus it was that the soldiers escorted Verjat to Commandant Raynaud's office.

Sitting behind his desk, the commandant gave the priest an icy welcome. He gestured to a chair facing him.

'May I know the object of your visit, Father? Are you studying the spiritual life of the convicts? I can reassure you immediately. Mass is compulsory once a week and these rogues of mine say their prayers every night before going to bed.'

'You're asking the questions and answering them, my son,' said Verjat, rubbing his hands slowly. 'No, I'm here on a rather more distressing mission. It concerns the sentencing of an innocent man to a term of imprisonment he did not deserve.'

The commandant laughed derisively. Behind him was a mahogany bookcase whose shelves were loaded with a miscellany of objects. Verjat's gaze lingered on a sextant, convict's irons, a naval sabre, a pair of Louis XV pistols, books on naval history, a capstan knot and two caps with their badges and numbers.

'Father,' said Raynaud, 'I don't believe in miscarriages of justice, if that's what you mean. There are no innocent men, there are only the guilty. A servant of the state cannot and must not make a mistake. As for a judge, he is never wrong.'

As he uttered this categorical statement, the man opposite him was staring at a cap that bore the number 9430. Verjat turned white. Why had they kept Jean Valjean's number?

The commandant, hands joined over his protruding belly, turned slightly to see what had caught his interlocutor's attention. 'I see you're looking at those caps, Father. They aren't trophies. I've put them there to remind me of my shame. Since I came here – and that's already ten years ago – there have only been two successful escapes. These caps bear witness to them.'

Verjat made a rapid calculation. It could not be Jean Valjean's cap. 'Commandant,' he resumed, consulting a paper he had taken from his pocket, 'I'm here to talk to you about a man named . . . Alexandre Tixier.'

The commandant gave a start.

'What have I said?' asked Verjat.

'Carry on, Father.'

'I have good reason to believe that the man sentenced under the name of Alexandre Tixier is not Alexandre Tixier, but—'

'Marius Pontmercy,' interrupted the commandant.

'How do you know?' Verjat stammered.

'Because this Tixier has consistently proclaimed his innocence and claimed the name of Marius Pontmercy, even though no such name has ever appeared on the registers. But I've made enquiries. Baron Pontmercy is dead and buried. Prisoner 9430 is the worst kind of riffraff, Father. When he arrived in Toulon, he had a strawberry mark under his left eye. Later, he no longer had it.'

Verjat stiffened again. Had the commandant really said prisoner 9430? His eye once again fell on the displayed cap. 'You mean—'

'That your innocent man has escaped? Exactly, Father. On St Philippe's day. Nearly a month ago today. Now an innocent man who escapes is no longer an innocent man. Even less so when there's a death involved.'

Verjat's face fell. 'A death?'

'A warder killed and an officer manhandled. The officer tried to exonerate Tixier and his accomplice. But that doesn't wash with me. Of the six who originally escaped, we recaptured three. They were executed immediately. I don't believe in half-measures.'

'But who was the murderer?'

'According to the officer, a man named Sartier. But that's of no importance. Your innocent is on the run. And, believe you me, we'll get him. When I go hunting for someone, I don't let go of my prey. Is there anything else you need to know?'

'No, Commandant. It's you who are right.'

Faced with Raynaud's cold determination, Verjat had surrendered. This man reminded him of what he had once been – an unscrupulous predator.

Pleased to have had the last word, Raynaud now became more amenable and generous towards the clergyman, who at least did not shelter behind remorse or the certainty that he knew the truth. He suggested a tour of the colony. 'You'll see for yourself the good treatment our inmates receive. You'll be able to tell them at the ministry in Paris that Toulon takes care of its prisoners.' He called a warrant officer, a man who limped, and with a twisted smile wished Verjat a pleasant visit. 'And since you know the Duc de Reggio, don't forget to tell him what you've seen. Toulon isn't hell, Father!' And he burst into sardonic laughter.

With a downcast air, Verjat left with the officer to visit the arsenal and the workshops. As they departed from the section reserved for hard cases, the officer introduced himself.

'Warrant Officer Lestrade at your service, Father.'

The next day Verjat set off for Lyons once more. Thanks to Lestrade, he now had confirmation of what he had been thinking. Alexandre Tixier was indeed Marius Pontmercy. And the good Lestrade refuted the commandant's account of the escape. According to him, Marius was in no way responsible for the warder's death.

'I know because I was on the boat that intercepted Sartier and his accomplices. Sartier accused Marius to save his skin. Unfortunately for him, his friends said that he and Runny Nose were the murderers. They were all guillotined.'

'You call him Marius. Does that mean he confided in you?' Verjat had asked.

'He saved my life, Father. We became friends. I gave him fencing lessons and to me he was almost like a son. What you're doing confirms what I thought about him.'

'Did you help him escape?'

'When I saw him on that launch with Perfect Love – a good man, by the way – I hesitated for one second. And that was that. It was a stormy day. We saw each other through our respective telescopes and he waved to me. I told the officer it was a naval launch with an officer on board. And Marius was able to sail out to sea. That was the last I saw of him. You see, I didn't help him escape. I just let it happen.'

'God will reward you, my son.'

At the guard post, when Verjat was on his way out of the colony, Lestrade had looked him up and down and asked him if he had always been a priest.

'Why do you ask me that, my son?'

'When I took up my post in Toulon at the end of the Spanish war, after the siege of Trocadero, which cost my son his life, I remember seeing a police inspector who'd come all the way to Toulon to investigate the disappearance of a convict – a convict who'd risked his own life to save a sailor. His name escapes me. But I've never forgotten the name of the inspector. It was Javert. He interrogated all the warders, including me. I remember his piercing eyes, his buttoned-up collar and his big cane. I'd never met a man so cold and meticulous. Apart from Commandant Raynaud, of course. And strangely enough – and I beg your pardon in advance – something about you, the way you act, the way you smile, I don't know what it is, reminds me of Inspector Javert.'

Verjat had already passed the guard post when he turned to Lestrade. 'Everyone has a right to redemption, my son,' he had replied, in a kind of half-confession. Then he had waved his cane with a resigned air. 'The most troubling thing is that the serial number of the man who disappeared in 1823 was the same as that of Marius Pontmercy!'

'But—'

'Goodbye, Officer Lestrade.'

So much wasted time. That was what Verjat was thinking when he arrived back in Paray-le-Monial. These repeated journeys had exhausted him. He decided to stay there for a week, both to wait for Monsieur Corneloup, who had been away for two days on a trip to Roanne, and to reflect on his next step. Once in Paris, he would inform Cosette. Following that, with the help of Father Rillet, he would go and plead Marius's cause and present his new evidence. Of course, as he knew only too well, none of it was proof. A ring, a strawberry mark and a few testimonies were not enough to quash the verdict. No, what he needed was the presence of Marius himself. He had to give himself up. Now it seemed obvious that Marius would return to Paris eventually. When he did, Verjat was confident he could persuade him. Afterwards, he would need only to summon the Mullet and Thénardier. In the meantime, he decided he would contact the Mullet as soon as possible to worm some more information out of him – even if it meant using strong-arm tactics.

For now, though, he rested. He thought of Marius. Knowing the psychology of convicts in general, and escaped convicts in particular, he suspected that Marius and Perfect Love would lie low for a while. They wouldn't show their faces for at least two months – the time it would take for them to start looking human again. So Verjat had time and the certainty of that restored his serenity.

One evening he saw Monsieur Corneloup again, glowing like a candle. He had come with good news. 'I have found someone who knew your Louis-Désiré Burdin. An old infantry soldier who lives in Marcigny.'

'When can we see him?'

'Whenever you want. Tomorrow, if you like.'

Verjat was punctual. The meeting took place in a little house with a bread oven on the outskirts of Marcigny, near the Loire. A woman with a bonnet and a single tooth greeted Verjat and Monsieur Corneloup. They had to drink a glass of hooch.

'That's something the Prussians will never have, for God's sake!' said the man they had come to visit. His name was Germain Lagoutte. He was sitting in a rocking chair, a cover over his legs, in a dark room that smelled of soot and sausage. He had a grey moustache, a red nose, eyes as cloudy as cream and a blue forage cap on his head. A Legion of Honour badge was pinned to his leather waistcoat, and he had a pipe in his mouth. 'Corporal of the third line at Wagram!' he said emphatically, brandishing the pipe.

He had been in General Morland's division, which had decided the outcome of the battle by taking the tower and the plateau of Neusiedel in 1809. For Corporal Lagoutte, the Napoleonic epic had finished in Austria. Like Major Daumesnil, commanding the cavalry regiment of the Imperial Guard, he had been hit in the leg by a cannon ball. The limb had had to be amputated.

'I was sent to Lobau, an island on the Danube. There were a lot of wounded from Essling, a battle before Wagram. Masséna was in command. My God, what an island! Like Babel or Cèdre-Rouge. It was chaos! A real city with lighted streets, industry, canals, workshops, casinos, taverns, prostitutes, bakeries where they made bread with Hungarian flour, thousands of oxen parked in the middle of the island. We ate well there, I can tell you! There were hundreds and hundreds of wounded. Operated on in a rush in makeshift billets. That's where they cut off my confounded leg. Mind you, it was only holding on by a little piece of bone and a few threads of ligament. Well, that's where I met Burdin.'

'What was he doing there?' asked Verjat.

'He was a nurse. He worked for a surgeon named Gérard. I haven't forgotten that name because there was a general with the same name. A marshal now, if you please! As for Burdin, I haven't forgotten him either. And I'll tell you why – because Burdin and Lagoutte are both names from round here! From the same part of the country, for God's sake!'

Verjat suddenly broke out in a cold sweat. Wasn't Gérard the name of the grim individual who managed the Chat-Malin, the former Clan Destin? 'And how did you meet Burdin?' he asked in a changed voice.

'In the military hospital. He was dealing with the seriously wounded. He operated with Dr Gérard. And I'll tell you something – in their hands, the dying didn't last long, and I don't think it was just coincidence! If you ask me, they finished them off themselves. And I'm pretty sure they robbed them too. There was an investigation, but nothing was ever proved. They must have made a fortune, those two crooks. Everything was fair game to them. Under the cover of humanity, they resold beef to the Tyrolean patriots, to the Austrian wounded, to a whole load of cripples and mutilated people. They even organized a mobile brothel. The girls were all Bavarian. There was one of them who was always with Burdin. A blonde girl, always painted up. A real little mischief-maker, that one! She had it off with every gunner in the billet! Burdin pocketed the money. He'd knocked her up ages before. Afterwards, I never saw Gérard or Burdin again.'

'Do you have any idea what became of them?'

'No. I was repatriated. But later, after Wagram and a few other little skirmishes, one of General Manulaz's hussars, who also had his leg amputated, told me that the surgeon and his henchman had knocked around the battlefield. From there to robbing the dead and wounded isn't such a big step . . . We'll never know. At Wagram, there were at least fifty thousand killed or wounded. That makes a lot of watches, rings, coins and valuables, if you see what I mean. Can you imagine the haul? Scavengers were usually shot, of course. But those two bastards were supposed to be helping the sick, for God's sake. They had a perfect cover.'

'And what about the girl?' asked Verjat.

'What girl?'

Verjat was getting impatient. 'The Bavarian girl, damn it!'

'I heard she kicked the bucket. But maybe she stayed with Burdin in Austria. And maybe they've even got a kid and are rolling in money now. Who knows?'

Verjat turned to Monsieur Corneloup with an expression in which there was a touch of anxiety. 'Thank you, Mayor. The information this good soldier has provided has been very valuable.' Then, as they were taking their leave of Corporal Germain Lagoutte, Verjat leaned over him. 'By the way, was there anything unusual about this Burdin?'

'Like what?'

'I don't know. Was he short, tall, fat, thin, whatever?'

'You know, I didn't see much of him. He was pretty elusive. And he was always wearing this big greatcoat. The whores certainly liked his company. With Gérard and him, they had some real orgies, I can tell you! It was rumoured he was hung like a mule, that Burdin! And you know what they said in the infirmary?' Old Lagoutte looked as though he was about to tell a dirty joke. He raised his two hands and placed them in a ball behind his back. 'Well, they said he was hiding a hump here, for God's sake! Funny, eh?'

'Yes, indeed,' murmured Verjat through gritted teeth.

As soon as he got back to Paris, Verjat set things in motion quickly. He went to the Chat Malin, but did not go inside. When the Mullet arrived at the usual hour, he practically set upon him. The Mullet jumped back, trembling all over. 'What are you doing here?'

Knowing how greedy – and how stupid – he was, Verjat tried to lure him with fine promises. And fine promises, for the Mullet, meant money. 'A tidy packet, if you see what I mean.'

'The profit from my rocks?'

'That's right. We'll talk again.' And he slipped quickly away.

Of course, he would not risk going into the tavern. He had no wish to see Gérard. Corporal Lagoutte's revelations and the Mullet's confidences about the demonic activities of the man with the ponytail coincided. But he would deal with Gérard later.

Disguised as a cut-throat, with a torn frock coat, a cap worn at an angle and the patch over his eye, he lay in wait near a street lamp. Late that night, when he saw the Mullet coming out of the Chat-Malin, he jumped on him again.

'Are you still here?' stammered the Mullet incredulously.

Guessing that the idiot must have already told Gérard, Verjat decided to take a gamble. 'I know who the hunchback is,' he said, dragging the Mullet by the arm. 'Don't turn round. His name's Burdin, he's Amédée d'Iguerande's steward. In case you didn't know, he and the Catman are planning to make you carry the can for this nasty business you're involved in. If you want to bring them down, you must promise to go along with me.'

'What do you mean?' said the Mullet, his stammer getting worse. 'I haven't done anything!'

'You still have the diamonds, don't you?'

'They're in my pocket.'

'That's risky. Imagine if the Catman found out.'

'What?'

'You know too much. Burdin and the Catman are greedy. Once they get their hands on the property of the man who was sent to the penal colony, they'll settle their account with you. On the other hand, if you come with me, you'll get away with it. And your fortune will be made.'

'Come with you to do what?'

'To meet the Marquis d'Iguerande and tell him what you know.'

The Mullet walked along in a daze. His brain – or what passed for his brain – refused to function. He hesitated, afraid to make a decision. But, in the end, he agreed.

'We'll meet in a week,' said Verjat. 'Eight o'clock in the Rue Montmartre, near the Uzès mansion.'

'Agreed.'

Verjat turned off to the right and vanished into the darkness.

The Mullet stopped and looked around him. Verjat had stopped a little further along and was watching him. The redhead turned on his heels and went back to the Chat-Malin. Verjat followed him at a distance. As soon as he saw him talking to Gérard, gesticulating dramatically, he left.

Verjat was reading the newspaper in the presbytery. The trial of the Republicans was in full swing and the painter Gros had drowned himself in the Seine. The latter event shook the ex-policeman, for obvious reasons. 'At least he succeeded,' he said with a grimace.

'What are you muttering, my son?'

Verjat looked up at Father Rillet and considered him for a moment. He had told him the results of his investigations, though not in full, for he always liked to keep an escape route for himself.

'I had a visit from a police sergeant last week,' said the priest. 'He was looking for you. He knows you live in the Rue Garancière. Thank God he doesn't know your name. He mentioned someone called Monsieur Moreau. What have you got yourself mixed up in, my son?'

Verjat bit his lip. He immediately thought of Carignol, the corrupt policeman the Mullet had told him about. And if the police knew where he lived, that meant that he had been followed – he, the former Inspector Javert. Who was it? Thénardier's henchmen? The man he had chased away when he was with Cosette near the Saint-Sulpice fountain? He was furious. I must be getting old, he told himself. At the same time, these moves confirmed what he had been thinking. He had not been wrong. He had to act quickly. This time Cosette was in real danger.

Verjat hesitated. He thought of going to the Rue Saint-Fiacre to tell Cosette that Marius was still alive. But if he was being watched, he had to be careful. He therefore decided to move out of the Rue Garancière, which he did the same afternoon, disguised as a priest. After that, he asked Father Rillet for hospitality. Although he could not let him stay in the presbytery, Father Rillet installed him in a secret room next to the sacristy. Access was through a cupboard, the back of which could be opened with a pulley. 'This hiding place has been here since the Revolution, my son. One of my predecessors escaped the guillotine by using it.'

When night fell, Verjat informed the priest that he was going out.

'In disguise again?'

'Certainly, Father.'

'Be careful, I beg you. Since the exhumation at Père-Lachaise, I've been fearing the worst. For my part, you can trust me. I'll do whatever is necessary. The truth must out. If need be, I'll go to Prefect of Police Gisquet himself.'

'Don't do anything for the moment, Father. I'll have a better idea of things by tonight.'

Verjat was sure of what he was doing. He had made an appointment with the Mullet in a week's time, but he would beat everyone to it. He would go tonight to see Amédée and Cosette. Two birds with one stone, he told himself. And then the nightmare could end.

Thénardier had not been idle either. Thanks to the Mullet's information, he had had Verjat followed by Gérard's man, Grandet. Then he had informed Carignol. The sergeant had seen Verjat going into the house in the Rue Garancière and into the church of Saint-Sulpice.

'This Moreau looks like a respectable bourgeois,' the sergeant reported to Thénardier. 'The only problem is that there's no record of anyone called Moreau living there.'

'A respectable bourgeois who talks a bit too much,' mewed Thénardier. 'He's trying to blackmail us.'

He wondered if the Mullet wasn't trying to lead him down a false trail. He discussed it with Gérard, who told him that the Mullet had an appointment with Moreau. 'He told me himself,' Gérard assured him. 'If he was betraying us, he wouldn't do that. It's in a week's time.'

'We'll keep the appointment,' said Thénardier. 'Thanks for the information. But I'm going to see what Burdin has to say about the rest.'

Thénardier and Burdin met, as usual, at the dyer's in the Rue du Jour.

'Well?' asked Burdin.

'I'm almost certain the Mullet and this Moreau have been sticking their noses into our business. A little too closely,' he added, thinking of his diamonds. 'This time, we're going to get rid of them. All the awkward witnesses in one go. The Mullet will take care of Horse Face and the Wolf will deal with the Mullet and Moreau. And that's not all.' He told Burdin that it was time to go on the offensive – time to make use of Gérard's miracle potions. 'I'm talking about the kid and Mademoiselle Cosette.'

'Together?'

'No, we'll separate them. Twenty-Two and Pegasus will be only too pleased to fetch Sleeping Beauty.'

Burdin chuckled. 'I'll take care of the child. I know the ideal destination for a little bastard like that. Do you have someone in mind?'

'The Wolf seems to me just right for the job.'

'And when's all this going to happen?'

Thénardier smiled a trifle regretfully. Having just learned that Moreau had been boasting to the Mullet that he knew all about Jesus and Baron Pontmercy, he did not want to take any risks. 'He threatened to tell the marquis everything.'

'Everything about what?'

'Everything about us. In my opinion, this Moreau is planning to blackmail us. So let's do it tomorrow. Make sure the marquis and Cosette's maid are out of the way. Leave the door open so our friends can get to work. An hour later, let's say about nine, the Wolf will come for the child.'

And the day Thénardier was talking about was precisely the day chosen by Verjat to visit Cosette.

In his priest's disguise, Verjat set out. He made sure that he took his cane. You never knew. He also wore a black hat and a big cloak to make himself unrecognizable.

At about nine he was walking along the Rue Saint-Fiacre. A carriage was parked at the corner of the Rue des Jeûneurs. There had been a shower and the cobblestones were still slippery with rain. A heavy, opaque fog lay over the surrounding roofs. It might have been London rather than Paris. The thick, whitish smoke escaping from the chimneys in the Rue Montmartre was dispersed by the swirling wind.

Verjat looked at the carriage suspiciously. He hugged the walls until he reached Cosette's building. Then he opened the door without making too much noise. It was dark and damp. All at once, he thought he heard weeping. He stopped in his tracks. The weeping seemed to be coming closer. He retreated quietly to the entrance. Thinking of the carriage outside, he preferred to hide there in a recess, behind a potted plant. He saw a man in a cap pass by with a baby in his arms. The man had a face out of a nightmare, a crooked face with a big hooked nose.

As the man was about to pull the door to, Verjat gripped his cane, ready to leap. Then he thought better of it. He risked hitting the baby – and he knew that the baby was Cosette's.

The man disappeared into the street and Verjat held out his cane to stop the door from closing. He left the cane jammed in the door and rushed up to Cosette's apartment. The unfolding drama seemed to have given him the energy of a twenty-year-old. The door to the apartment was ajar. Verjat entered. It was empty. No sign of Cosette or of Madeleine. Breathlessly, almost tripping over his cassock, he ran back down as quickly as he had come up. He opened the carriage entrance and recovered his cane. The most urgent thing right now was to follow the man and, if need be, to overpower him.

By the time he was outside, the carriage was moving off. He ran after it and, just as the coachman cracked his whip, managed to hoist himself onto the rear mudguard.

The journey lasted an eternity. At that time the Châtelet district was an extraordinary tangle of alleyways, dead-end streets and passages with colourful names. The carriage shook as it swung to the right and swerved to the left. Hunched flat against the rear and clinging on for dear life, Verjat recognized the Rue des Mauvaises-Paroles and the Rue de la Vieille Lanterne. The Pont-Neuf. The Left Bank. Several times, when the carriage jolted over the bumps in the road, Verjat almost lost his grip. But he held on. Time went by then, finally, the carriage stopped. Verjat jumped off and rolled on the ground. He immediately picked himself up and hid behind a tree. From there, he kept an eye on the carriage. The man got out with the child in his arms. The carriage turned and went to park at the other end of the street.

A shiver went down Verjat's spine. He knew Paris like the back of his hand. This was the Rue d'Enfer. And in the Rue d'Enfer there was an orphanage, in whose wall was an ingenious device, a kind of wooden cupboard in which a child could be placed and which could then be turned. Many a wretched woman had gone there with a heavy heart to abandon her child. The system had originated in Italy and had been put into widespread use by Napoleonic decree. It allowed children to be abandoned in secret, and reduced the incidence of infanticide, though it also deprived the abandoned children of any civil status, as it was practically impossible ever to track down their parents.

Verjat decided to intervene. Once the child had been put down and the cupboard turned, it was too late. Someone would pick him up inside the orphanage and that would be the end of it – unless Verjat rang the bell and announced himself, but that would involve him in an enormous amount of red tape.

Verjat crept up close behind the man, who stopped in front of the device, opened the cupboard, placed the child inside. He was about to set the turning system in motion when he glanced behind him and gave a start. There, two paces away, stood a priest.

'It isn't wise, Father, to be out at such an hour,' the man said in an unsteady voice, at the same time clutching the handle of his knife.

In this murky yellow light, it was difficult to see.

'I didn't want to frighten you,' said Verjat softly. 'Just to inform you that your friend the Mullet is in possession of diamonds that don't belong to him.'

The Wolf did not understand immediately. Taking advantage of the element of surprise, Verjat attacked. His cane came down with a dry sound on the Wolf's wrist, and then immediately, in a lightning movement, hit him on his chin. He collapsed without a moan. With his foot, Verjat lifted the man's jacket and saw a shiny curved blade. A curious weapon, he thought.

It was then that a cry rang out. 'Hey, Wolf, everything all right?'

It was the coachman. Verjat seized the child, wrapped it in his cloak, and ran away in the opposite direction from the carriage.

As he ran, the door of the orphanage opened and a nun appeared. When she saw the Wolf on the ground, she clasped her hands together. 'My God!' she cried.

The Wolf rubbed his chin and got unsteadily to his feet. 'Sister,' he said, pointing to the figure running in the distance, 'that man stole a child. He was going to get rid of it. When I tried to stop him, he knocked me out. I may need to call you as a witness.'

'Of course, my son. Wouldn't you like to rest?'

'No, my carriage is waiting for me. Until we meet again, Sister.'

And he walked with long strides to the carriage, furious at having been tricked, and dreading the thought of telling the Catman the bad news.